JOHNNY WORTHEN

OF CIVILIZED, SAVED AND SAVAGES

Coronam Book Two

This is a FLAME TREE PRESS book

FLAME TREE PRESS
6 Melbray Mews, London, SW6 3NS, UK
flametreepress.com

US sales, distribution and warehouse:
Simon & Schuster
simonandschuster.biz

UK distribution and warehouse:
Marston Book Services Ltd
marston.co.uk

Publisher's Note: This is a work of fiction. Names, characters, places, and incidents are a product of the author's imagination. Locales and public names are sometimes used for atmospheric purposes. Any resemblance to actual people, living or dead, or to businesses, companies, events, institutions, or locales is completely coincidental.

Thanks to the Flame Tree Press team.

The cover is created by Flame Tree Studio with
thanks to Nik Keevil and Shutterstock.com.
The font families used are Avenir and Bembo.

Flame Tree Press is an imprint of Flame Tree Publishing Ltd
flametreepublishing.com

A copy of the CIP data for this book is available from the British Library and the Library of Congress.

HB ISBN: 978-1-78758-796-0
PB ISBN: 978-1-78758-795-3
ebook ISBN: 978-1-78758-797-7

Printed and bound in Great Britain by Clays Ltd, Elcograf S.p.A.

JOHNNY WORTHEN

OF CIVILIZED, SAVED AND SAVAGES

Coronam Book Two

FLAME TREE PRESS
London & New York

For
Dorothy Diane

The Coronam System
Tirgwenin
Kanluran Cloud
The Gap
Dajjal
Silangan
Enskari
Ravan
Lavland
Maaraw
Hyrax
Temple
Claremond
Legend
Civilized Worlds
Enskari
Lavland
Hyrax
Claremond
Temple
Savage Worlds
Maaraw
Silangan
Dead Worlds
Dajjal
Ravan
Unclaimed World
Tirgwenin

PART ONE
AFTERMATH

'No one is going to give you the education you
need to overthrow them. Nobody is going to teach
you your true history, teach you your true heroes,
if they know that that knowledge will help set you free.'
Assata Shakur

CHAPTER ONE

Yes, of course there's a chance this is a doomed endeavor. But what choice do we have? We're doomed here for certain. A slim chance at Coronam is better than no chance on Earth.
Jareth, Interview
September 15, 2338, Auckland

10, Sixth-Month, 938 NE – Pemioc, Tirgwenin

Millie sat apart at the Feast of the Fortnight, distant from the Enskarans, who huddled across the courtyard, separate from the Tirgwenians, who'd fed them for two weeks.

A smell of rich food – spicy stew, pepper, and mint – filled the air alongside the sweet smokes of fruitwood. Millie thought how her father would have loved this. He'd been a woodworker, a carpenter by trade, and had always saved his trimmings and brought them home for the family hearth. He could identify any of Enskari's wood by its smoke. Millie had learned to differentiate fruit trees from hardwoods and knew the wood burning now was alien but sweet, the source of a wild cherry perhaps, a starch apple or pear, a life-giving food and a fuel for the feast. Her father would have loved this.

She could appreciate the woodsmoke since the food smells no longer made her swoon. She, like the rest of her refugees, was no longer starving. She thought of them that way, as her refugees. She was responsible for them, the sixteen souls who'd followed her here after fleeing Rodawnoc.

They'd been a sight. Rags and bones. Bloody feet from shoeless marching, eyes wild with fear. A group of hungry exiles. Helpless and lost. They'd come to Pemioc starving, surrendering themselves to one enemy in the hopes of defeating another. A hope for mercy where none was to be expected. Each and all gripped with a madness that had led them to believe the unbelievable, to follow the rantings of a child, giving their lives to her in famished faith like Old Testament pilgrims. To her, Millicent Dagney, the obnoxious sixteen-year-old girl who they'd known from her infancy. She'd felt wholly unworthy of that trust but wore it nonetheless because she alone had known the way.

She had led them, and they had come, though none, she knew, understood what it was that led her. They knew only the necessity of it, the strange truth of it, told in Millie's uncanny knowledge of the road and the places she should not know. They saw in her a prophet or a devil and didn't care which if survival was on offer.

She had gambled on the Tirgwenians having discernment above that demonstrated by her own people. Pemioc had no reason to take them in, and every reason to hate them. Her own worlders had murdered hundreds of them, burned their villages, destroyed their hives. Lahgassi, the leader of Pemioc, had lost her arm, breast, husband, and daughter to Enskaran barbarity. Millie knew the horror and loss she had endured as if it had been her own. It mirrored her sufferings in quality if not quantity. Millie's mother had died in a latrine en route to this planet, her father pierced with arrows on arrival. Her friends starved and beaten. Her people cruelly used, humiliated, and finally eaten. They'd come with such promise to start again, thinking they'd build a higher civilization, only to fall into savagery.

But it was more than abstract sympathy Millie shared with Lahgassi. That she knew the terrible details that had preceded her own doomed colony was a testament to the weird connecting power of the bees. As she knew the way to Pemioc, despite having never been there before, so she knew Hasin's crimes as if she herself had been there. It was memory, and she saw the terrible things through the eyes of the killers, felt the fear of the survivors, and the pain of the dead and dying. She'd seen the ruined body of Lahgassi's daughter, Krikhuia, crucified before the very fort Millie had called home for nearly a year, and she'd wept for the waste and horror of it.

The bees had done something to her, connected her to something. The bees would come to her and show her things she needed to know. Not everything, but some things. Necessary things and ideas, but not everything. She'd plumbed their depths as she might, and found the way to Pemioc and hoped for an innate goodness in a people who might forgive children their parents' sins and be merciful.

It was no certainty. Only a chance. But there was no other. They were weak and beaten and forlorn. Exiles from a group of exiles, begging at the gates of the people who had most cause to despise them.

And miracle – the gates had opened.

Surrounded by soldiers, arrow-nocked bows, and poisoned spears at the ready, they were herded inside the gate to an open space, over swept brown cobblestones, and made to stop. Behind them was the wall ten meters high, manned turrets and soldiers. Before them, a gathering crowd of natives, yellow-gold and twinkling in the daylight, double-lidded eyes upon them. Some watched with interest, others curiosity, and a few with unmistakable malice.

Millie recognized Lahgassi, tall, crippled, and scarred, moving through the throng. She stepped forward and greeted them in the Tirgwenian way. "Pax," she said coldly, her eyes dark, her expression flat. The air thick with tension.

Millie walked forward to meet her. She took just a single step, moved just a pace away from her people, closer but still far from the natives. It put her alone, set her apart, and placed her in the in-between.

Millie raised her chin and spoke. "And to thee," she said, her voice breaking, weak and parched. "Pax to thee, Lahgassi of Pemioc."

The Tirgwenian leader raised an eyebrow at hearing her name, but no more change than that came over her blank hard features. "Enskarans," she said in clear common tongue, "what do you want?"

"Life," Millie whispered.

Lahgassi's skin sparkled in the sunbeams, reflective and warm, golden-hued and beautiful. She wore a simple robe over one shoulder, tawny and open over half her torso – the mutilated side. Her face, neck, and chest were tattooed with lines of some unknown design – unique, man-made, and beautiful. Millie was weak, exhausted, famished, thirsty as the others, and still she awed at the beauty of the crippled leader. The Gauss musket that had disfigured her had left a map of scars across her body, a spreading bloom cicatrix like lightning from her missing breast, collected at the ends in new tattoos that spoke of survival and endurance, a nobility born of pain and loss.

Lahgassi's face was hard, her back straight, her eyes piercing as she scanned the refugees before her. She blinked in the summer sunshine, her inner eyelids flashing pale an instant before her others. She surveyed them, and Millie saw her jaw clench and release several times in the silence of her stare.

After a moment she gestured to a man with a spear and said something Millie didn't understand. The man approached one of the refugees, Richard Tomkins, and Millie knew why. He carried a Gauss musket over his shoulder, the only one they had.

"Ge mi den," the soldier said to Tomkins.

Tomkins's hand tightened on the weapon. His face was gaunt and skeletal, but defiant. He jutted his chin forward and looked into the man's face, as if daring him to try to take it from him.

The soldier waited.

"Richard," said Millie. "Mr. Tomkins, you should give up the gun. We've no use of it now."

"For protection," he said, his voice quavering. "It might be the only thing keeping us alive."

The others huddled closer together.

"Nay," Millie said. "Do not resist, Mr. Tomkins – any of you. We must be open to the hope we may have."

"We'll lose all control," Tomkins said. "It's the only thing between us and them."

"Aye," said Millie, "and that is why you must discard it. It is a barrier. It is an illusion. It is nothing."

"It is a symbol."

"Aye, the wrong one."

Tomkins shook his head. "Miss Dagney, I trusted you up to here, but I'll not –"

"You will," Millie insisted, a strength in her voice that surprised even her. "We give it up."

"It's not even charged."

"I should have had you toss it in the river before, but I feared Aguirre," said Millie, remembering the mad leader of their colony, and wondering for a moment where he was now. "We'll not need it here. It's useless."

"Then why do they want it?"

"For the same reason I want you to give it to them."

"What? You give me riddles? Damn you."

Through their entire debate none of the soldiers moved or readied weapons beyond what they had when it started. Like the soldier waiting for Tomkins to hand him the gun, they waited patiently, dispassionately, and observed. The same could not be said of the growing crowd.

"It is hard," said Tomkins.

"Aye," said Millie. "Aye. And that is the why. Do you not see the change? Do you not see the rebirth of this moment? Give it up, give it all up."

Slowly, hesitantly, Tomkins took the gun off his shoulder and passed it to the waiting soldier. The Tirgwenian took it like it was nothing important and walked away.

The refugees watched him go, watched their only weapon, the height of their technology, their best advantage over this planet, disappear down a path behind a row of wooden huts.

After a moment of settling and weight, Ms. Pierce, who had suffered as much as anyone in their trials here, stepped forward and fumbled in her bag. She produced a brooch and offered it to a Tirgwenian woman who held a suckling baby in her arms. Millie knew the brooch, had seen it. It was a cameo of a noble ancestor. A prized possession passed for generations.

The woman with the baby balked at the gift, but seeing the earnestness in Ms. Pierce's face, took it from her trembling fingers. Only when the token was gone and her hand was light for the loss, bare and open, did Ms. Pierce retreat back to the knot of people, her back straighter, her face brighter than Millie had seen it in weeks.

Mr. Hemmington took coins from his pocket and offered them besides, stretching them out on his palm for someone to take.

From the torn pack she carried, the Widow Lawrence took out her book of scripture, tattered, ripped, and water-stained, and placed it on the ground as if giving it to the stones. She moved with a solemn finality that bespoke a funeral. "There are new gods here," she said.

"Aye," said Millie.

The townsfolk whispered among themselves and their murmurs blended with the droning of nearby bees.

Looking past their faces, Millie found the place where the hives were kept. She remembered them burning, recalled the sweet smell of their destruction years past, honey and wax feeding the fire of their senseless ruin. There was no evidence of that now, only an echo in her mind, a memory she should not possess.

The town itself was similarly restored. The razed buildings rebuilt, the dead buried and mourned. A couple of houses were gone. Millie remembered what they'd looked like and saw now open places of sunlight where the wreckage had been, a garden set in their places. There was little physical remembrance of Hasin's massacre, and yet Millie felt it like a chilling breeze.

No one moved to take their other gifts, to pick up the dead book or gather the coins, but whispers spread around them.

After a minute or two, three perhaps, Mr. Hemmington upturned his hand and dropped the money into the dust. The Widow Lawrence removed herself a little from the group and sat upon a bench beside the path, straight-backed and strong.

The murmurs quieted and Millie could hear the bees in her head and wondered if it was in her ears as well. One fluttered around Lahgassi as she furrowed her brow and stared at Millie. It flitted from the Tirgwenian and then circled Millie. She felt its arrival like vertigo and stumbled to keep her feet.

The leader's expression hadn't shifted with the offerings. She was tense but otherwise unreadable. She ground her teeth and considered. The village, like the off-worlders whose lives she held in her hands, waited for her to speak.

After a long while, bees zooming in and out, Lahgassi shook her head as if dissatisfied with herself. "You'll be held in a barracks until we decide." She turned and marched away, saying three words to a guard before disappearing into the crowd.

The soldiers stepped forward and shepherded the Enskarans to a long, empty house.

Mille knew the building. Hasin had quartered there. His men had slept there, been fed with the best meal they'd had in a year, and repaid the kindness with blood.

"What happens now, Ms. Millie?" It was John Tydway. A quiet man by nature. His shirt was torn where he'd been whipped at Rodawnoc. Millie never knew why he'd been punished. Perhaps he didn't either.

"We rest," she said. "We adapt. We survive."

Five Tirgwenians brought food within the hour. It was warm broth, rabbit or something like it, thick with chopped vegetables and a tinge of honey. It was easy to eat and they sipped it gratefully from white glazed bowls in silence, as if afraid speech would break the spell of deliverance. Sparkling women dished it out to them at the door, as if they were wary to enter the barracks, their faces unsure but not above returning a smile when Mille's little brother, Dillon, now nine years old, offered them one in thanks. Behind them, though, soldiers kept watch and barred the Enskarans from leaving the barracks. Politely, but firmly.

Not that the colonists had anywhere to go.

They were tired and afraid and it took two days and five meals before conversation evolved above the basics.

"The beds are so soft," commented the Widow Lawrence. "I thought it was just my tired bones, but I've never had the like."

"Aye," Mr. Tomkins agreed. "A feather bed, I think."

"I had one in Vildeby," said Ms. Pierce. "I never thought I'd find another."

"And this is a jail cell?"

"Nay," said Millie. "This is a travelers' lodge. Pemioc is a trading village."

None asked how she knew this, but accepted it as true.

"With whom do they trade?"

"The exiles on the coast and the villages inland."

"Exiles?"

"Aye. The Rowdanae. They're separate from the rest of the people."

"Criminals?"

Millie had to think. "Nay. It was nothing they did."

"What then?"

"I don't wholly understand it," she said carefully. "It has something to do with these bees."

"Tell us what you can," they said.

They were fed and comfortable, a blessed respite from years of tension, so Millie allowed herself a little more room. "I don't understand it myself," she said. "But remember Mathew?"

Of course they did. Mathew was the Tirgwenian scout who'd traveled to Enskari only to return to his home planet to be murdered by the people he was trying to help. Her people.

"All he did was for the bees," she said. "The journeys, the trip to Enskari, the trip back, his sacrifice – all to seek their approval."

"Of the bees?"

Millie had said too much. Warm and sheltered they might be, and safer than they'd been in years, but they were not yet ready for all these things. They were God-fearing civilized folk, not a generation removed from the prophet and the Orthodox Saved. They were slender splinters of a splinter of that. More progressive than most, but still so far from the systems of this new world that even imagining this was to cause damage.

"It's a kind of caste thing," she said, putting it in terms they might understand.

"Oh." They nodded.

It was enough for now. Her people, Millie's people, had come a long way and she was proud of them. Not just in kilometers – millions across the system, hundreds across the planet – but they'd also come far in their thinking. She had high hopes for them, hopes of survival, inclusion. Evolution.

For two weeks they were sequestered in their house. Doctors visited, food was plentiful and rich, the days easy and calm. They were allowed to heal and grow strong but never allowed to leave.

They took their plight in stride, waiting unhurried for a fate they could no longer control. Only Millie sought to leave, to mingle with the Tirgwenians, but she too was barred.

She retreated into the company of bees. They were poor companions, pipes through which ideas flowed but were themselves empty.

The refugees gave her a wide berth – fearful or reverent, it made no difference. She was isolated and her only consistent human companion became her brother, Dillon, who alone among the denizens of the barracks sought her out.

"I don't remember ever having sweets this good," he said. "Ever."

Millie tasted one of the new little loaves of crescent cookies, yeast-raised, and honey-sweet.

"No sauce like hunger," she said.

"But I'm not hungry anymore and it still tastes good."

"You just like the sweetness. They cook with a lot of honey."

"Best thing ever."

"It's okay. But remember Mom's redgrape pudding?"

He thought for a moment. "No," he said. "I don't remember that."

Millie remembered how for a while, back on Enskari in Vildeby, it was all Dillon could talk about. It surprised and saddened her to think he'd forgotten, but such was the case. Those days – not even two years past – were from another lifetime.

Their clothes were mended or replaced. Their wounds seen to by a surgeon who poked them, and listened to their chests with tubes, bled them into vials, and gave them bitter bouillon that silenced pain.

Millie was given paper and pen and asked to provide a list of the refugees, names, genders, skills, and health status. This she did with a footnote asking for an audience with Lahgassi that received no reply.

On a bright morning fourteen days after they arrived, a young boy, earnest-faced and nervous, asked to see Millie at the door. He stood taller than her, but she knew he was younger. Only twelve years old. She knew also his name. Bost.

"I am to tell you—"

"Pax, Bost," said Millie.

The boy looked at her in surprise.

A bee spun spirals above her head and his eyes lit upon it and grew large.

"How?" he said. "Off-worlder…."

"Pax, Bost," she said again.

"Aye," he said with some embarrassment. "And to thee, Enskaran," completing the mannerly greeting.

"Call me Millie."

"Nay," he said firmly.

"Minister Gayle taught you my language, did he not?"

"Aye."

"And how are your parents, Jessya and Onuieg?"

"Jessya died of Enskaran pox," he said. "Onuieg is a slave."

She didn't know what to say.

"You will have no food today in preparation for the feast tonight," he said.

"What feast?"

"The Feast of the Fortnight."

"A decision has been made?"

"Aye," he said and in his eyes Millie could read nothing.

"Blessed be, Bost," she said.

"Pax," he corrected her. "Here we say *Pax*."

"Aye," she said.

And he left.

Dillon came and stood beside her and took her hand the way he would when he was nervous. "You're afraid," he said. It was not a question.

* * *

It was festive. Though guards stood by with lance and blade, they were not in war colors and there were fewer. The people of the village milled and danced and sang and laughed as the food was brought out.

The sky glistened with day shimmers in the late afternoon light, the planet's rings bright and milky, a path to heaven.

Though no one told them to, the refugees stayed together and took up two adjacent tables facing the central fire. Millie had joined them but was escorted politely to the head table, where she was now thinking about sweet smoke and spicy food and how her father would have loved this.

The music was joyous and celebratory. Millie understood some of the words of some of the songs. One, sung in part by men and then women, was a bawdy tale of a maiden who could not make up her mind and so married an entire village and populated a city. Another one was about an animal, a dangerous thing called a 'doa-kanti', who entered into an arrangement with the people to stop eating them in exchange for a yearly tribute and a promise to stay out of their forest. The animal spoke in howls and clicks, but the wisest among the people could understand them and the wisest doa-kanti could hear the people. And so a bargain had been struck. The latter was an old song, a folk tale and legend, popular with the children who howled during the choruses.

Millie recalled Hasin's feast in this same square and noted that this was more raucous than that and thought it a good sign.

Drums signaled the start of events. One pulsed a heartbeat, then was joined by another and another into a single rhythm. It came from behind and before, and the sides stepped up with a high song of strings. All spoke together in melody, a conversation that punctuated a moment, setting it apart from what was before, from what would come after. And it, a bridge between the two.

The Tirgwenians bowed their heads. Music rose for new instruments unseen, progressed like an avalanche, the sound hypnotic and telltale, and all at once it stopped. The final note lingered long and never ended, only eventually falling out in hearing.

And the people as one said, "Om."

Millie said it with them though she could not have said how or why.

Lahgassi arrived from some unknown place and took a seat next to Millie.

"Pax," said Millie.

"Pax," returned the leader, not looking at her.

Ceremony over, servants brought food. Fruits and nuts, broths, meat and warm bread on rough porcelain plates. Voices rose in conversation and feasting.

Millie saw Bost serving a distant table, scooping green berries from a bowl. Searching for him, she saw his father doing the same for picnickers some distance off.

"Is this a regular feast?" Millie asked.

"Nay," said Lahgassi. "It is a new custom and is done in your honor."

"'Tis very kind."

"The Feast of the Fortnight celebrates the prevention against your pox," she said and there was bitterness in her voice.

"A quarantine," said Millie, understanding. "This is celebration of the end of the time to watch for sickness?"

"Aye." Lahgassi didn't look at her.

Millie said, "I would speak to you about my people, what is to become—"

"It is decided."

"When may we know?"

"After the feast."

Millie's jaw quivered. "My father used to say that bad news always sits best upon a full stomach."

Lahgassi ate without reaction.

Across the courtyard, the refugees ate and kept their eyes on Millie. She offered them a reassuring smile that seemed to help.

It was a long meal, made longer by Millie's worry. It stretched out of the afternoon into the early evening when yellow-green auras arced over the horizon and the rings shone like glowglobes.

At a moment indiscernible from the one before, Laghassi raised her hand. Soldiers moved in around the refugees, who, seeing their approach, huddled together. Emme Mirrioth shrieked. Dillon began to cry and called to Millie across the courtyard.

"Lahgassi," said Millie. "You don't need to—"

Now the leader turned to face her and Millie's gaze was dark and rueful.

"You asked for life," she said. "You know there are debts."

"I understand," she said, tears welling in her eyes.

And then, another miracle, a smile of sorts crossed Lahgassi's mouth, a personal pleasure that belied the dread filling Millie's imagination.

Lahgassi turned to the square. "Enskarans," she said in a voice that silenced all but the crackling embers.

Millie strained to hear bees, seeking the calm they always brought her, but they too were quiet.

"Step forward when I call your name." Lahgassi produced a small bound notebook from a hidden pocket.

"Richard Berrye," called Lahgassi.

Mr. Berrye clung to his son, Ben, seventeen years old and wanting to be a space captain. He released his boy, and stealing a glance at Millie, stepped forward.

"Ragh'ohg," said Lahgassi.

A Tirgwenian woman came forward and inspected Mr. Berrye. She held a short knife in her hand. "Aye," she said.

"Huservus!" declared Lahgassi. The woman signaled for Mr. Berrye to come with her. The guard gestured with a spear. He remained.

Not noticing, and turning a page, Lahgassi called next, "Dillon Dagney o Yevrits a' Blos."

A man stepped forward. Dillon hid behind Mr. Tomkins's legs.

Lahgassi pointed to the hiding boy.

"Aye," said the Tirgwenian man.

A guard grabbed Dillon's arm and yanked him free.

Tomkins made to fight, but an aimed spear made him reconsider.

Dillon wailed, "Millie! Millie! What's going on?" He was tossed before the man, who regarded him coldly.

"Lahgassi," said Millie. "Huservus. I don't know the word. What is this?"

"Your chance at life," she said. "But you have a choice."

"A choice?"

"Huservus or death." Lahgassi signaled a soldier who lowered his spear and pointed it at Dillon's chest. Firelight reflected off its poisoned tip.

"That is death," she said. "He may take it if he would not have the other."

"The other is huservus?" said Millie. "What does it mean?"

Lahgassi creased her forehead in thought. After a moment, she said, "Slave."

CHAPTER TWO

We fought and did our duty. Now have we surrendered ourselves in sailorly fashion, all to the right. We were but following orders that our betters bade us.
Alleged last words of Captain Golick of the *Pempkin*
Captain Clelland's log, *Espina*
7, First-Month, 936 NE

21, Sixth-Month, 938 NE – Port Brandon, Almuda, Hyrax

Ships returned in ones and twos. The fast ones were first, a fortnight before, bearing battle reports and bad news. The bulk of them, though, the remnants of the great Hyraxian armada, limping and breached, broken and bleeding, harassed all the way home, were still a week away.

Atop the observation tower overlooking the capital's wide bay, Brandon watched. Prince Brandon of the Royal House Drust, sovereign of Hyrax, chosen of the prophet, he who lusted to be emperor, watched the threads of a dozen elevators burdened with pods rise and fall against his planet's raging sky. They held wounded men and salvage on their way down, medics, mechanics, and salvagers on the way up. The port elevators were overwhelmed, so those orbiting ships who were still able had dropped their own lines into the capital bay to rescue their men and save what they could.

There were fires above his planet. Vessels burned. Once in a while against the upper darkness would come a yellow flash as plasma spilled through a warship's heart and it would explode. An hour later it would shower the planet with debris that would skip and burn across the crystalline sky or slowly pierce it, to crash into his frightened world.

The great storm that had decimated his fleet was not past. It still buffeted Brandon's world along with the injured ships orbiting it. The flares tore sails, peppered hulls with meteors, bathed them in radiation, which sought the cracks left by Enskaran wrath. Each wave burned a little more, insinuated harm, promised death, and all too often found an opening to transform a mighty metal spaceship into a sudden yellow flash and a rain of amber comets.

This had all been explained to Brandon in long desperate reports from dying ship captains and wounded survivors, while planetside analysts, admirals, and generals excused themselves and their plans, citing the vagaries of Coronam.

The wreck of the armada.

The greatest war fleet ever assembled.

Lost.

Defeated.

Humiliated.

"So when do we expect the counter-attack?" Kolbert spoke from a buffet table where he alone seemed interested in the food. He balanced a glass of wine on a plate overloaded with cheese and fruit.

Sir Tom Kolbert, the prince's childhood friend and companion, tossed a redberry into his mouth with a pop, washed it down with half his drink, and laughed. "Am I wrong?" he said. "If I were that bitch on Enskari, at this point, I'd send my whole damned navy here and make Hyrax a colony. We'll all be in white makeup and satin garters within a week."

"Shut up," said Brandon.

"I don't know, sport," said Kolbert. "Do you still have a villa on Temple?"

"I said shut up."

The advisors shuffled their feet while the window filled with lights. Overflowing green auroras, smears of orange-red streaking across, ships dying on the shell of the planet.

"Is that a possibility?" Brandon asked finally.

Admiral Mola cleared his throat. "It is, Your Majesty."

"Can we repel it?"

Mola spoke with the confidence of a longtime soldier used to giving orders. "Of course, Your Majesty." Behind the admiral were two captains, Jeffries and Raynes. Mola's seconds. His 'think tank'. The architects of this disaster. They were in full dress uniform, navy-smart and nervous.

"Probably," said Tobias. The aged advisor stood like a scarecrow near a window facing in at the assemblage instead of out at the unfolding continuing disaster. "Reports are that less than ten per cent of our fleet is undamaged."

"For the love of God!" said Brandon.

D'Angelo, apostle to the prophet, sober for once, flinched at the curse. Minister Rendelle stood by him unfazed.

"However," said Tobias, "thirty per cent is serviceable."

"Battle-worthy and strong," said Mola.

"Usable," said Tobias.

"Enough?" asked the prince.

"With authority," said Mola.

"Enough," said Tobias.

"Good God," said Brandon. "We're vulnerable."

"Temple is nice," said Kolbert.

"We'll crush them. It would be their doom," said Mola.

Brandon looked at his advisors. Mola puffed up his chest while Tobias found a chair and lowered himself into it.

"What say you, lady?" Brandon said. "You know the Enskari. Will they attack?"

Lady Vanessa Possad looked at the prince with calm, as if not surprised he had asked her. She was a strange creature; a capable woman. It was a word he seldom used to describe anyone, let alone a daughter of a fallen house.

She smiled at him confidently. It was a warm, enduring smile that reminded him why he'd let her remain in his close court.

"They may well come," she said. "Zabel will be hesitant, but Sir Nolan Brett may well see the opportunity and send the fleet."

"Sommerled is in charge of their fleet," said Mola. "He'll see the foolishness of it."

"But Sir Nolan is the power behind the throne," said Brandon.

"Not quite that simple, Your Highness," Lady Vanessa said, not averting her eyes as she bowed. "But he is wiser and crueler than she, and may see the chance for your destruction when she sees only her deliverance."

Mola insisted. "Sommerled—"

"Will obey his superiors, as will mine," said Brandon.

The admiral froze stiff and straight. Behind him, Captains Jeffries and Raynes blushed in unison as if struck by the same slap.

The room fell silent.

Brandon tasted the tension in the back of his throat. The stress was not just his. It was shared by his court, his people – all the civilized worlds. Each had held their breath since he began his crusade to rid the system of the bitch queen, Zabel – the upstart, usurper, the parvenu – who against all social grace sat upon a throne. A woman. A lowly woman challenging God's own law. Delay became defeat, turned catastrophe, as the might of the greatest endeavor in human history was defeated by Enskaran pirates and fate's cruel hand.

Brandon knew his own stress was making things worse. His father, Andreas, had cautioned him about such things, but the dead old man had never faced anything as truly terrible as Brandon did now. The energy was dark, but it was energy and he would use it. There was more at stake than manners and morale.

This defeat – this catastrophe – was a system-wide shock. The repercussions of it would be felt for centuries. The danger of counter-attack was just the first threat. The invincibility of Hyrax was no longer a given. He could expect rebellion, close and far, high and low, his power challenged everywhere.

A descending pod exploded in an flash of pink light and black smoke, silent and sudden. The sound would come in time, traveling at its speed as the court watched the spot in the sky and then the water as it burst in a surge of froth and geyser. The blast had cut the elevator thread. The high-tension carbon filament anchored in the sea floor snapped like a ten-kilometer whip, cutting ships in half and sending a plume of water kilometers into the sky. In space, the ship on the other end would be thrown out of orbit. Depending upon its state – fuel, damage, crew – it might return, otherwise, another loss to Coronam.

"Your Highness," said Tobias. "A few details before Clelland arrives."

The shockwave hit the tower and bowed the glass.

"What is it?"

Tobias made a show of looking at the others in the room.

"Is it really something they don't know?" Brandon said.

The old advisor nodded and produced a stack of letters from his pocket. "The treasury," he said.

It wasn't a conversation Brandon wanted to have. He knew what was coming and would have put him off if he thought Tobias would let it go. Instead, Prince Brandon faced the bay and watched steamboats rescue survivors from sinking ships.

"We had extended more than we would have liked," Tobias said. "Our creditors were assured of payment from plunder after our victory."

"Enskari paying for its own destruction," said Kolbert. "The irony was half the battle."

"Hasn't there been enough Hyraxian blood spilled today, Kolbert?" said Brandon.

His friend smiled wanly, and poured more wine.

Brandon knew he'd just raised the tension another ten points. Good, he thought.

"Without Enskaran resources," Tobias went on, "the treasury is... troubled."

"The battle's not over yet, sire," said Mola. "We still outnumber the bastards."

"May I remind us, that the prophet has said the war must end," said Minister Rendelle.

"We don't take orders from you," said Mola, and to punctuate the phrase Jeffries and Raynes scowled at Rendelle in solidarity.

"Minister Rendelle speaks for me," said D'Angelo. "And I speak for the prophet."

"Hyrax does not take orders from Temple," said the admiral.

D'Angelo's face flushed from rage for once instead of drink.

"We cannot attack Enskari again," Tobias said. "At least for now. We can't afford it."

"How is it that the richest planet in the history of the species is so limited in what it can do?" Brandon asked.

"Money," said Tobias. "We've spent it all."

"Can we afford a defense?" said Brandon. "Might the treasury allow us, pretty please, a few crossbow bolts, a musket maybe, slugs for said musket – in the defense of civilization?"

Tobias waited stone-faced as Brandon felt his go red. He was not helping things.

"Options," said Brandon.

"The revenue streams will all need to be increased," said Tobias.

"The houses won't like their taxes going up again," Kolbert said. "Not one little bit."

"What have you heard?" said Brandon.

"The usual grumbling."

"Who? Eric?"

"You brother, sire? Nay. I don't associate with him."

Another ten points of tension.

"But, I'll keep my ears open," said Kolbert. "I'll shake a tree for Your Highness. See what falls out."

The last thing Brandon needed was to further alienate the powerful houses of Hyrax after the defeat, but to do nothing now was out of the question.

"Target the proletariat, Tobias," said Brandon. "Taxes, fees, levies. Defense duties. Explain the threat."

"Aye," said Kolbert. "How *are* we going to explain things?"

"Domestic taxes won't be enough," Tobias said.

"Of course not," said Brandon.

"I've taken the liberty of composing some levy documents," Tobias said. "Hyrax by county. Lavland. Silangan. I'd also suggest these tariffs on Claremond and Temple."

D'Angelo opened his mouth to speak, but couldn't gather the courage.

"What about Maaraw?"

"Hard-pressed there," said Tobias.

"Why?"

"Local trouble."

"That doesn't tell us much."

"If I may, Your Highness," said Lady Vanessa.

D'Angelo's expression went from scared to scandalized at the woman's voice.

"Proceed."

"I spoke with Lady Sonteyo, recently returned from Maaraw. She speaks of an uprising among the natives. A slave revolt targeting off-worlders engaged in the trade."

"I thought that was taken care of."

Tobias said, "We have been asked to send troops."

"We haven't any," said Brandon, looking at Mola. "Not anymore."

"The unrest on Maaraw is affecting everyone," said Tobias. "It's not just Hyrax dealing with it."

"Then let them deal with it. Resupply our ranks as we can and implement tariffs where we may. We don't want to look unfair."

"It shall be done, Your Highness," said Tobias.

Distant lightning arced sky to sea, tracing an invisible elevator thread announcing another orbiting evacuation.

"And will that be enough to shore up our finances?" asked Brandon.

"Nay," said Tobias.

"Nay?"

"It is twofold," said the old advisor. "Our occupations are expensive."

"They pay for themselves."

"Diminishing returns. Silangan has always paid for our military."

"And the parties," said Kolbert.

"And," Tobias continued, "if Enskari takes Tirgwenin—"

"We have plans for another invasion of Enskari," said Mola. "They shall never have the chance to set up a colony."

"Another invasion?" said Brandon. "With a rebuilt armada?"

"Aye. Grander than the last. Unbeatable."

"Unbeatable...." said Brandon. "Like the last one?"

"Unforeseen—"

"Shut up," said Brandon. "Tobias, go on."

"Sire, we must regroup."

"End the war with Enskari?"

"As the prophet has commanded," D'Angelo said.

"You would have us surrender? Before we've even been attacked?"

"I.... Nay.... We...." D'Angelo fell into a coughing fit.

"An end of hostilities," said Minister Rendelle, stepping in for the apostle. "For a time. To reassess."

"Direct action is too expensive," said Tobias. "We need to calm things."

"And?" said Brandon, knowing there was more. There was always more with Tobias.

"Perhaps we should consider pulling out of Lavland. Install a friendly king and let them police the world. We could still pull tribute and save our troops for other duties. Or discharge them."

Brandon turned on the ministers. "Does the prophet want that as well? Should we leave that planet of heretics to Gibbers, Millers, and Bucklers? Sit back and await the rise of a homosexual council to execute the gentry and give their manor homes to gutter scum?"

D'Angelo tried to explain. "I.... We.... I do not—"

"Shut up," said Brandon.

"We couldn't consistently pay the soldiers on Lavland before this new disaster," said Tobias.

Brandon saw a military steam carriage pull up below in the street. Black smoke mixed with white steam settled at the curb. Even from this distance he could see it jump and kick, backfire under heavy weight. Palace guards stood at attention as two men were escorted out of the carriage by active service soldiers. One was a minister of the prophet, the other an admiral. The admiral was in manacles.

"Triple the levies on Lavland to pay for their own security," said Brandon. "I would not remove our troops from that cesspool of reformation-minded heretics. There is the cradle of the blasphemies we fight now. It started there and bled to Enskari. We should raze them for that."

D'Angelo nodded in profound agreement.

"We'll increase production from Silangan," said Brandon. "Higher quotas – double them at least. It's a rich world. We have only to take what we want. Make it so. And of course, better convoy defense." Brandon shot a look at Mola. "What's left of the fleet can see to it that we can have another."

"Silangan is rich," agreed Tobias.

"Will you tell me now that there is also a revolt there?" Brandon said mockingly.

"Actually, sire...."

"You jest?"

"Reports are unclear...."

"Of course there's unrest," said Kolbert. "They're a planet of subhumans."

"Being worked to death by the thousands," added Lady Vanessa.

"Woman, know your place," said D'Angelo.

"You have contacts as far away as Silangan too, my lady?" asked Kolbert.

"Nay, just a view of that planet from several others."

"Enskaran propaganda," said Kolbert. "Let me guess – they're painting Silangians as pure innocent victims, and us, murdering monsters? Hair-raising tales of genocide in the mines?"

"Just so," she said

"They're backward savages made to advance civilization," said Kolbert. "A little work never hurt anybody."

"Like you'd know," said Brandon.

"Oh, ouch, sire."

The doors to the observation deck swung open, letting in two royal guards with Nicandus, Captain of the Drust House Guard. A step behind him came a high purger in holy robes and the black-and-white checkered sash of his order. He was followed immediately by a Hyraxian captain, and behind him, escorted by two more house guards, came Admiral Clelland, commander of the once-great armada.

"High Minister Tarquin," D'Angelo said, offering the purger his ring.

The purger knelt and kissed it.

Rendelle spoke. "May I present to Your Highness, High Purger Tarquin, late of the armada, Maaraw, Lavland, and Temple."

"Aren't you the well-traveled one," said Prince Brandon.

Tarquin bowed and retreated a step, perhaps sensing the mood.

"Clelland," said Brandon, stepping up to his admiral. "Report."

"We were undone by a storm and nimble ships, Your Highness."

"Not leadership?"

"That is not for me to say."

Brandon was surprised at Clelland's calm. Clelland was hated, not just by the Enskaran enemy, but also the entire system. Even on Hyrax, his name was spat and not spoken. Mola regarded Clelland with an open disgust that he'd been forced to hide when Brandon named him Admiral of the Armada.

Clelland had spaced the crew of the Enskaran pirate ship *Pempkin* to his infamy. Though the execution of pirates was a usual punishment, the manner of spacing – putting men in an airlock and opening the outer door – was an egregious maritime crime that horrified all spacefarers.

Now, the most loathed man orbiting Coronam stood before his sovereign calmly and soldierly. Not for the deaths of a few propaganda-played pirates; he was there to answer for the defeat of the armada – the loss of hundreds of ships, the deaths of tens of thousands of Saved, and the possible end of Brandon's aspirations to be the system's first emperor.

Unlike his superior, Admiral Mola, Clelland was not shaking or sweating, or even evasive. His voice was strong, his eyes clear.

"We've read the reports, Admiral," Brandon said. "Some of them by your own hand." The prince circled him like a bird of prey, studying his burned and stained uniform. "They tell of a disaster the likes of which God has never seen."

"I cannot speak of God," said Clelland. "Perhaps you should ask the clergy."

Brandon saw a smirk cross Rendelle's lips, horror cross D'Angelo's, and nothing but calm from Tarquin the purger.

D'Angelo was an apostle, one of twelve beneath the prophet. Only the holiest head of the Saved Orthodox and his two advisors outranked him, and yet Brandon sensed him tense when the purger entered – high purger, he corrected himself. He was not wholly versed in Temple politics, but he did know that the Holy Office of the Purgers were an order unto themselves and answered to very few. They were given the power of life and death and the means to carry out the latter if not the former.

"Was the battle plan ill-conceived?" asked Brandon, noticing the caked blood on Clelland's sleeves and smelling his soiled clothes. He was in battle dress, not a dress uniform as was custom. The cuts on his sleeves suggested age. He'd been in these chains for weeks.

"Nay. All was right enough," said Clelland.

Brandon saw Mola and his two captain shadows visibly relax.

"Only...." continued Clelland.

"Only?" said Brandon.

"Only there were more of those fast ships than we expected and they were better than anticipated."

"Better than our man-o-wars?"

"Better for the battle we had, not the one we wanted."

"And that is why you lost?"

"Nay, sire. Just a note. They were nimble but would have been little more than an irritant had it not been for the storm. They were quicker to maneuver. Truth be told, sire, we had two foes: the Enskarans and Coronam. The Enskarans had the advantage of speed and shadow. Nimbler ships to turn into the storm one moment and find our flanks the next. And of course, they could retreat to the planet's lee, where we were not so welcome."

"But you were given the strongest ships, armed with the most powerful weaponry mankind has ever seen."

"Aye."

"And you couldn't stop a few fast ships?"

"Not enough, sire."

"It is a matter of navigation, Your Majesty," said Mola. "It's about the angle—"

Brandon's look cut Mola's speech off like a sword slash. He and his seconds blanched and straightened their backs, the military response to most things. "Your Highness," Mola said, and shut his damned mouth.

"Clelland," said Brandon. "I expected you to say that the failure was due to your inexperienced captains. Did you not petition us for more time to train them?"

"I did," he said.

"Did inexperience play a part in the defeat?"

"It did."

"But you don't bring it up now?"

"Now being my trial?"

"There will be no trial," said Brandon.

Clelland nodded a confirmation. "It was a minor detail, my prince. Better captains would have helped, but we were unlucky. Had we sailed a week before—"

"So you blame defeat on the timing of our attack? You suggest we were foolish?"

"Unlucky."

"Damn you, man!" raged Brandon. "We have no need of luck. We have God on our side. Do you not listen to the sermons from Temple? The prophet himself directed us."

Clelland didn't respond.

Brandon turned to the purger. "What say you?"

"I may not interpret the acts of God," he said. "It is not my place."

Brandon felt his face grow red and watched the purger react not at all. He had a calm not unlike Clelland's. Nay, better than Clelland's. Clelland was resigned. Tarquin was certain.

Brandon surveyed the others. Tobias waited patiently for the scene to resolve. Mola, tense but proud, stood with his two aides at military rest. Kolbert was on his fifth glass of wine, nicely drunk but smart enough to hold his tongue. Lady Vanessa looked wary, as if she knew she had witnessed too much. But she had had been brought here as witness. This was only the start. Possad would report all this to the court in her clear and worldly way. It would do much to help.

Nicandus waited for the signal.

Through the window Brandon saw rescue vessels circling the wrecks cut by the severed thread and farther off to seaward, a geyser spout as another thread landed from space, another ship arrived.

"We are embarrassed," Prince Brandon said. "We are humiliated."

He watched the others in the reflection of the glass.

"We cannot blame the storm, for that is to blame God and that will never do."

D'Angelo glanced at Rendelle, who ignored the apostle's silent message and kept his eyes on Brandon's back.

"There must be an accounting for this tragedy," Brandon went on.

The purger, Tarquin, bowed his head, not quite in prayer, but near it.

"And the accounting must be with blood."

Kolbert shifted on his chair, a grin on his lips. Lady Vanessa raised a fan to her face.

"Nothing else will do."

Near the door, behind the others, Captain Nicandus stealthily drew his dagger.

"It is the duty of a soldier to die for his patriarch and planet."

"I understand, Your Highness," said Clelland. Not a hitch in his voice.

"I don't blame you, Clelland," said Brandon. "I bear you no ill will. Not for this, not for the pirates. You are a loyal soldier."

Clelland wavered as if his knees might buckle. "Thank you, sire."

Brandon said, "Captain Nicandus."

"For Hyrax!" cried Clelland.

Nicandus drove his dagger into Jeffries's back.

The blow well-struck and final, the man made but half a scream before dying on his feet.

Next to him, Raynes drew a secret pistol. He had it in his hand before his dead fellow was on the floor, as if he'd been waiting to use it, as if he'd known where the ax would fall and waited in defense. Perhaps they were not so stupid.

Nicandus had Raynes's arm before Mola's man could even aim. He broke it with a twist while pushing his own gun into the captain's groin and firing.

The magnetic slug shot up and out, exiting his middle back in a saucer-size blossom of blood and tissue. After passing through the man, the bullet shattered the glass two meters from the prince.

Mola pissed himself.

Clelland remained at attention.

Lady Vanessa turned away.

"Oh my God," said Kolbert and drained another glass.

"There is blood for this disaster," Brandon said. "These architects of our defeat have paid for this ignorance and pride."

"Tell the prophet Hyrax will act as it must," said Brandon. "Be gone, Templers."

D'Angelo opened his mouth as if to argue but Rendelle put his arm around his master and led him to the door.

Tarquin followed them out, his expression inscrutable. Brandon knew he'd have to watch that one.

"You too, Lady Vanessa," said Brandon. "We apologize for what you had to see, but you must now report this to our court. Be frank. Be honest."

"So that's why she was here," said Kolbert. "Bravo."

"You leave too," said Brandon.

Kolbert followed Possad out, wisely holding his tongue.

House guards carried the dead officers away.

Brandon picked up Raynes' fallen gun. It was a hand-flamer, a vile personal napalm shooter. Close range, painful, and lethal. A baby brother of the plasma guns his armada boasted. Once hit, the fire could not be extinguished. The fuel was glue and would have to be cut off the skin or burn itself out. Brandon held it up for Mola to see. "Proof your men were traitors."

"Your Majesty, I—"

"Shut up."

"What of me, sire?" Clelland asked.

"You are a soldier and a sailor, and man of worth," said Brandon. "And every breath you take angers Enskari. Good. Oversee the return of the fleet, Admiral. Give me a report on its readiness when you can."

"Aye," said Clelland.

"Aye?"

"It shall be done, sire." Clelland tried to salute but his chains would not let him.

"Nicandus," said Brandon.

The captain of the guard produced a ring of keys and removed the shackles from Clelland's scabbed wrists.

"Mola, meet your new superior," said Brandon.

"I am proud to serve," said Mola. "In any capacity, you—"

"Shut up. I want an honest report of Hyraxian potential by the end of the week."

"It shall be done, sire," said Clelland.

"Dismissed."

Clelland and Mola turned to go. Mola took a step to leave, but paused to let Clelland lead, to exit first through the door, as was his due by new rank.

Outside the sky flashed with burning debris like summer fireworks. Brandon stared beyond the light of his crashing fleet, seeing past his planet and its protectorates, across the system.

"I have it, Tobias," said Brandon. "One solution to many problems. We'll fight them over there. We'll take the prize, the riches, the world. We'll take Tirgwenin."

CHAPTER THREE

The information is there. Just because you don't know it or like it doesn't make it wrong.
Reykjavik Climate Crisis Press Conference
November 2, 2029, Old Earth

10, Seventh-Month, 938 NE – Vildeby, Enskari

The exhibition had been his idea but the materials came by Hyrax and Temple. Sir Nolan Brett, Second Ear of the queen, appreciated it when his enemies supplied him with ammunition.

Since before the battle commenced, Enskaran skies had been lit up with unseasonable solar flares and malevolent shooting stars. Then came railgun fire at first, long-range misses, sparks that flashed fear as precursor of the doom that charged for them unseen from distant worlds. Sporadic, then steady as the Hyraxian armada was met near orbit by Enskaran defenders.

Bursts of light – exploding ships laden with deadly bombs making second suns over their world, just as bright and just as deadly but blessedly unenduring. A kaleidoscope of flashes, glows, and cooling clouds. A rhythm of death. Repeating in broken time across the sky.

Behind them Coronam blew a storm of meteor and flare that lit the falling sky around the globe, auroras flashed from horizon to horizon, around the lee in green and yellow tendrils of leaking radiation and dazzling lightning, bright enough to read by.

The shower of debris from the now-darkened clouds, like fireworks of old, lit up the crystalline atmospheric shield in chaotic streaks of red and orange. Heaven ablaze with lights as the planet parried the shrapnel of dead spaceships – ten-meter metal shields, failed and twisted, furrowed with shot, melted by fire, crashing against Enskari's sky. Lifeboats and weapons, spools of nanothread, napalm, and men. Enskari turning the energy of each into light and lightning.

Such was the protection surrounding all the livable planets circling Coronam. Each had a wall against their angry sun. High-energy debris – solar or Hyraxian – was repelled in bursts of light and cracks of thunder, destroyed outright, or slowed to a speed that could permeate the miracle of their sky only to burn up in the lower atmosphere or, weakened, crash to ground when the planet's gravity could not be turned.

The lights over Enskari those days were a common sight for this or any world. Sporadic meteor showers, solar flares singeing the air in almost predictable ways, but the intensity had been awful, the duration unparalleled, and the cause beyond terrifying.

The battle was met, fought, and won in only a few days, yet the debris, caught in Enskari's gravity, would fall to the planet for decades.

Brett could use that.

The shooting stars of the defeated fleet would be a constant reminder of Hyraxian villainy and Enskaran favor. It was almost enough to make Brett believe in God. He himself had started the fad of calling the debris hits 'Brandon's Tears'. It would remind the people of their enemy and that was a good thing. The sky itself would be a gift for his government and queen, a bright reminder of the shared enemy for years.

It was from that sky that Brett had found the artifacts for this exhibit. Some had come from captured ships, the best conditioned ones, but others, surprisingly many, were found among ground debris to join the shocking exhibit at Government House.

"What is it about implements of torture," Sir Edward asked, "that makes them so obdurate that they can survive reentry intact?"

Sir Edward was Edward Kesey, First Ear of the queen. Together as counselors nearest the queen, he and Brett were the royal representatives on this opening day and stood vigil together in a balcony to see and be seen.

"It was the Temple ships," Brett explained. "The purgers tried to use their landing craft for lifeboats. We found most of these among their bodies."

"All the men died on landing?"

"Those that didn't died shortly thereafter, wishing they'd never come."

"Not Connor?"

"Nay, First Ear," said Brett. "It was the people. For the most part." And in this Brett felt some pride.

"How many prisoners do we have now?"

"Six hundred three and thirty on-world," he said, "maybe a thousand in orbit."

"The Hyraxian ambassador wishes to discuss return of prisoners."

"This I have heard," said Brett.

"He contacted you?"

"Aye."

"And what did you tell him?"

"I invited the Hyraxian ambassador to meet me here and we would discuss it."

Kesey looked out over the exhibit. Thousands of Vildeby's citizens, rich and poor, high and low, milled around the displays of deadly Hyraxian weaponry, uniforms, and gear intermixed liberally with Templer tools of torture carried to their world to punish them.

It was a vast public hall, full of people who moved in heavy silence, echoing only the scrape of dragging feet, broken here and there by soft weeping and low-voiced curses. A shared shock of public horror as Enskarans viewed rows of pokers and pliers, branding irons, and flesh renderers embossed with the checkered insignia of Order of the Purgers and the crest of Prophet Eren VIII. Of particular horror was a row of identical mass-produced iron-maidens, sixteen recovered so far. Hinged and full of spikes, they were special-made for their world – Queen Zabel's visage was crudely sculpted on their fronts, red-haired and harlot-clad, an insult to promised injury. Brett could not have invented a more powerful image to make his world unite against an enemy and around his queen.

"I do not believe the ambassador will make his appointment," said Kesey.

"Was that a joke, First Ear?" said Brett.

"Not on you."

The room was a sullen contrast to the world outside, which was still awash in jubilation for their deliverance. The planet was drunk with it. Not since the landing of the Unsettling had any world had such cause for joy as Enskari did after the defeat of the armada.

All things seemed possible. The rise of Zabel Genest, the first woman to hold a throne since Old Earth, was validated. Their people were graced.

The exultation had been so great and widespread that it had even eclipsed Connor's late-hour purge, officially decreed in *The Defense of the Realm Directive.* Hastily written and immediately enforced, it gave Archbishop Connor and his guard the warrant to arrest anyone suspected of being disloyal to the queen or the new Enskaran church.

And execute them.

It was meant to safeguard their world from traitors when the Hyraxian soldiers and Temple purgers invaded. It was a desperate measure in a hopeless time. But then, a miracle – they'd survived and not a single Templer had landed safe on their planet.

Brett knew the euphoria would fade and Enskarans would remember that the horror they'd feared had happened nonetheless by royal directive. It was a stain, a disgrace, a crime that could not be hidden, but it might be buried.

And thus on the heels of celebration, lit by Brandon's Tears, Brett had arranged for the display of foreign nightmares nearly met. Joy would bring hope, but fear would bring control. The first was spontaneous, the second would be stoked by Brett.

It was always strange to Brett that so few in the ruling classes seemed aware of how fragile everything really was. It was the same across the system. The forms of government, the houses that ruled them, the faiths and systems – though perhaps shifting and changing a degree in ten generations – were more or less the same since the Unsettling had brought them all here. It was a false sense of permanency people like him were in the business of creating in order to maintain it.

Scholars had marveled at how each of the planets, separated by seven hundred years of silence, had more or less come out the same. But Brett understood. The seeds were all from the same economic and ideological tree. He was not as versed in Old Earth history as he'd like, so much had been lost, concealed and burned, but he knew enough to trace a common ancestor in the fathers of the Unsettling. With the loss of advanced Old Earth technology to Coronam's rays, it was as easy as 'might makes right' to continue the feudal systems the old corporate houses knew from before. Silangan and Maaraw being the obvious exceptions, with Tirgwenin being a failure unto itself.

The Enskaran civil war had shown that those old systems could change. A woman ascended to a throne, and God, for all the rattle and threat from Temple and Hyrax, had not stopped it. There was much to suggest that permanency was the illusion Brett knew it to be, but the people needed reassuring that all was well, that their one change was all that was needed. A paradigm shift this far and no farther.

It was a slippery slope. A woman on the throne suggested female worth and the right to rise. It had been enough to start a war. But that was just the latest thing. Across the civilized planets, birthrights faded with fortunes, and merchants rose to stature above them, buying noble power with money. Slip and slide. Now Ethan Sommerled, the common-born, become knight, captain, and admiral – now savior of the world, challenged the very notion of inherited nobility and the quality of blood. It insulted the aristocracy and inspired the people.

Even before Sommerled, before the war, there had been rumblings and even strikes. These had shut down factories and crippled continents until Enskaran enforcers and Hyraxian terror put them back to work. These would come again. The people felt a new entitlement. It would need attention.

A door opened behind him.

"My lords," said Brett's secretary.

"Sir Edward, you remember my secretary, Jim Vandusen?"

"Blessed be," said Kesey.

"And to thee," responded Vandusen, a little flustered.

"What is it?"

"A packet from our embassy on Hyrax."

"Something that can't wait?" said Kesey.

"Apparently," said Brett.

They watched Vandusen rummage through a pouch. Brett noted a single-shot hand-flamer within it, a sandwich, and a book, before he came out with the official diplomatic pouch.

It was sealed with wax, addressed to Sir Nolan, and had a red stripe across one corner, meaning it was urgent.

"Spy stuff?" Kesey said.

"I have no secrets from you," said Brett.

Kesey laughed and the sound carried between the walls of the somber hall, causing many to look up and search their balcony for the source of the discordance.

The First Ear, old soldier that he was, fell to coughing to cover it, before returning to his stern pose as was befitting.

Brett retreated a step, leaving Kesey to keep vigil alone.

With a knife produced from a secret fold in his clothes, Brett cut open the pouch. Within it he found three letters. The first was from his man, Richards, in the embassy, explaining the other two. One, a familiar tan envelope denoting official state communication, was sealed with the crest of the court of Hyrax. Threats again, to be sure. The other was unique, written in an unfamiliar casual hand upon a brilliant white envelope of fine and scented paper. Its folds were sealed with the impression of the ring of the prophet, Eren VIII.

"Sir Nolan?" said Kesey. "You look…pained."

"Aye, Sir Edward," said Brett. "Excuse me. I must go. This might be important."

"Rubbish," he said. "You are just bored."

"True, First Ear. But this is your place. I work best in shadows. Allow me to return there."

"Blessed be."

"And to thee."

Brett left Kesey standing on the balcony in full military pose, medals from this war and wars before, the one of ascension, the ones he'd earned under Zabel's father. He was the symbol to be seen, not Brett, who needed to be unnoticed to be effective, the slither in the grass, the flash in the night. Kesey wore the shining armor, was the stalwart tree. He was a time capsule stretching across Enskaran history.

In an anteroom behind the balcony, glad to be away out of sight, Brett opened the missives and read.

"My lord?" said Vandusen. "Bad news?"

"Get my carriage. I'll be down directly."

The secretary bowed and disappeared. Brett folded the papers, happy for an reason to leave, but perplexed by the messages. Or rather, by one of them.

Within a quarter hour the Second Ear of the queen was nearing the palace.

The clattering hooves on cobblestones and the turning carriage wheels were a meditative song for Brett's calculating mind. He rode with his window down and watched the streaks of light and lightning as evening came. The news was strange but not urgent. Nothing he couldn't handle, but it was a fortuitous excuse to drop in on the palace, which was but a fifteen-minute gallop from Government House. He told the driver to take a longer route so he could think.

The unmarked carriage crossed the Reedy River past the wharfs into a poorer area of Vildeby, a place Brett had not visited in months. The streets were festooned with Enskaran banners, the queen's crest, the planet's symbol. Patriotism on display. Smiles and relief still evident on proletariat faces. Handbills for the exhibition papered the walls and were being read.

They turned a corner, and there upon the side of a building someone had painted a mural of Ethan Sommerled in battle dress and sword. The heroic stature was matched by skillful expression. It was a fair likeness of the man. The artist was talented. Brett would have to find him, to hire him, or execute him, because beneath the mural was written: *Sommerled – of the people, for the people.*

It was not a slogan the gentry would like.

Nor would they like the next one. A simple bit of graffiti, a heart scrawled on a wall, *Z.G.+E.S.* within it.

Brett mulled the uses and dangers of Sommerled. It took his mind off the letters, and then, when he passed an open blackened lot where Connor had burned bodies for all to see, he realized Sommerled had also taken the people's mind off the archbishop's crimes.

He still looked at his city with wondering eyes. It had survived. Brett's spies had told him that Vildeby was to be razed. Even if Zabel had given herself to the armada, had surrendered entirely, the city was to be razed with Hyrax's newest weapon. As an example. Like Connor's blackened lot.

The properties of the new plasma bomb were unclear. Only one had ever been exploded in atmosphere, that on Maaraw, and apparently by accident. Details of its effects were sketchy. It had been at sea level in a warm ocean, not lowered midair over a populated area. The Maarawan blast had been small compared to what Brandon had meant to drop on Vildeby, and still the Maarawan casualties had been staggering.

He took in his city's streets with reprieving eyes, awed by the ordinary because he'd thought he'd lost it. Soot-smeared and crowded, historic and vibrant, it filled him with surprised joy he shared with the people. Cobbler and peasant, tradesman, valet and soldier, lord and lady, each breathed rarified air for having come to believe they would not have it this day.

They passed a gallows strung with rotting bodies, looters caught and executed. Fifteen people, mostly men, but a few women and two children. More Enskaran casualties by Enskaran hands. But unlike Connor's sacrifices, these were on display. They'd hang until they fell from their ropes themselves as was custom. After deliverance, Brett had ordered the remains of Connor's work to be removed from sight. It was the first step to denial, the disappearance of the bodies. Next would come disappearances of other things and other people as necessary. Each a further crime to hide the first, but none as bad as the first.

The buildings thinned and then they were in the country, passing through orchards and past farms. Here too he was taken by the simple beauty of a farmer watering a starch apple grove. A rare smile creased Brett's lips, rare in that it was not intended, rare enough that he noticed it and though alone in his carriage, wiped it off his face. There was a reprieve here, a pause, a lull, but the war was still on. Or was it?

He again read each letter, and again, changing the order – Temple, Hyrax, spy; Hyrax, spy, Temple – to see if the impact changed.

Alarmed, expected, and curious. Very curious.

The carriage slowed at the first palace guard post and Brett leaned his face to the window and they were let in.

At the second guard post, he had to display his crest and face. A new guard panicked when he realized who was in the carriage. Brett heard him apologizing as they pulled away.

A little fear was a good thing.

At the landing came valets in red coats, white gloves, and orange helms who opened his door.

The master of the guard waited for him.

"Sir Nolan," he said, bowing low.

"Sergeant Faern," he said. "I'll see the queen."

"Nay, sir. The queen is indisposed."

Brett looked at the guard. "Tell the queen I'm here," he said and went inside.

Faern hesitated, then followed behind the Ear. He disappeared behind a service door that led to the queen's private wing while Brett retreated to the official office, too opulent and gaudy for his tastes, meant for receiving nobles, but today, he wanted to see it.

It was still gaudy and overdone. Gold leaf and marble statues, wide spaces and uncomfortable chairs. He'd been told that the desk was from Old Earth, but he didn't believe it. He couldn't see his ancestors bringing such a huge useless artifact across the galaxy. It wasn't even that attractive. It was black and heavy and scratched in a way that suggested age, but it was wood and wood didn't last a thousand years, did it? It had to be a reproduction. For the first time, with his relieved eyes, he found it not unattractive. It, alone in the room, he liked.

"Sir Nolan?"

The Second Ear turned to see the Earl of Nutorn standing in his doorway.

"Joseph," he said. "Come in."

The earl was dressed in court finery, silks and sleeves in a coat representing his title, warm in the winter, surely sweltering now.

"Second Ear, I'd speak with you about the Minister of Nature."

Brett nodded. He'd guessed the reason. "Is Sir Aldo at the palace?"

"Nay, Second Ear. As far as I know he's still in Austen. I am glad to find you here."

"Aye," said Brett, gesturing to a chair.

The man had no appointment. Brett was not usually so gracious in such circumstances, even to earls, but he had time waiting for the queen and his mood was strangely accommodating. He hoped it didn't show.

"Sir Aldo has sent me a missive," the earl said. He fumbled in his pocket and retrieved a handkerchief. He wiped the sweat from his forehead and then plunged his hand back into his coat and came back with a letter.

Brett took it across the wide desk and read it, acting like he didn't already know what it said.

"He demands my factories shut down," the earl said. "He says the pollution coming from them must be cut in half by the end of the year to be allowed to reopen. Then, each year thereafter, I'm to have a five and twenty per cent decline."

"Aye," Brett said.

"It is my factories that gave Enskari the power to fend off Hyraxi. Am I to be rewarded now by being bankrupted?"

"The realm is grateful."

"We ran nonstop, day and night, for the war."

"And we are grateful. Sir Aldo only takes umbrage at your fuel, not your patriotism."

"It is coal," said the earl. "What's there to take umbrage with? It built the empire. What are we to use? Wood? There are not forests enough on Enskari to run any of my factories at a tenth the pace I've been at."

"That was in lead-up to the war and now that the threat has—"

"Ended?" interrupted the earl. "You cannot think the threat is gone."

The earl was one of the richest people on the planet and his house had fought for the House Genest during the War of Ascension. For his loyalty, Brett would ignore the interruption.

"Nay," said Brett. "I meant to say, the threat has paused."

"And we must stay ready. My factories need to run."

"The Minister of Nature has the realm's best interest at heart," said Brett.

"I'll not follow this directive," said the earl. "I tell you, so you know. I feel it is my patriotic duty to keep producing the material – the fabric, the guns, the machines – Enskari needs to defend itself."

"Are you still running round the clock?"

"Aye."

Brett made a mental calculation of the possible costs of this to the treasury. The earl owned every factory in Nutorn and Nutorn was the heart of Enskari war production. He'd been tasked to arm the planet and no thought had been given to payment in the face of coming doom. Now, perhaps, someone would need to tell the earl to back off before he bankrupted the planet.

"You've done well," said Brett, pleased with the double meaning of the phrase. Of course, the earl did not see it.

"And this is how I'm repaid? When I first read this letter, I thought it'd been penned by a Hyraxian agent."

"That is a serious accusation," said Brett, flattening his tone to impart the necessary gravitas.

The earl tensed in recognition of his overstep. "I meant no offense," he said with careful confidence. "Only that it struck me that such an order, as Sir Aldo sent me, at this time, may benefit our enemies more than us."

Brett let the moment rest in the air for effect, then said, "It may indeed be premature. But it is not my position to overstep the minister—"

"But you are Second Ear."

Brett paused another moment and held the noble in his stare. Once he could forgive, but now the man's disrespect must not be ignored.

The earl stood rigid in defiance. It was a characteristic of his class. His eyes however, darting around the room, never finding Brett's, showed the Ear that the noble was aware of the transgression.

"It is the First Ear who would sway the minister from this course," Brett finally said. "It is not within my purview. I deal with…other matters." Then, taking pity on the man, Brett said, "Perhaps you might speak with the queen. I assume that's why you're here. It could not have been for me."

"Nay, it was only by chance I saw you."

"So it is for the queen you traveled all this way from Nutorn with your letter?"

"Nay, I received the letter only this morning. I am here to see Sir Ethan."

"Aye," said Brett, concealing his surprise, putting the pieces together. "You must excuse me now."

"Of course. Blessed be."

"And to thee."

With an appropriate bow, the earl left, pulling the door shut behind him.

Brett sat at the desk admiring it, thinking, wondering if it could be true. The last report he had on Sommerled placed him a thousand kilometers away at Fort Miller, just off the elevator and overseeing the rearming of his ship. That report was a few days old. A train could have delivered him to the capital by now. But what was not so easily done, at least should not have been, was to arrive here without Brett knowing it.

The earl was mistaken, Brett decided.

He leaned back and looked again at the letters.

Hyrax demanded the fair treatment and return of prisoners. No mention in the royal letter of having lost the greatest battle in human history, but that was to be expected. They were mostly concerned with a rumor that all Hyraxian and Temple invaders, wherever captured, would be transported into orbit and spaced. The letter didn't mention the rumor, but Brett knew it was behind it. The urgent appeal and mention of 'humane treatment', and 'obedient sailors', smacked of it. Brett had heard the rumor before the war and had considered what to do with it for a long time, whether to encourage it or try to stop it. His network of propagandists and informers could do either. In the end, he let it alone. He didn't want to give the enemy a reason not to surrender, and facing a merciless captor would do just that. Of course, 'Remember the *Pempkin*' remained a powerful motivational tool for recruiters, and gave their soldiers a reason not to surrender.

Brett was not overly impressed by that official letter, but the one from Temple, that one confused him.

Sir Nolan Brett. I, Prophet Eren VIII, personally take up pen and paper to write you, knowing you will share this information with your superiors.

Brett only had one superior, Queen Zabel Genest, and the prophet knew it. Funny that even in this letter, with this message the head of the Orthodox Saved had been unable to name her, to give his sovereign even temporary recognition.

It has come to my attention that there is a grave threat facing humanity. An alien menace that promises to destroy our culture, society, and species. So great is this danger that I have petitioned Prince Brandon of Hyrax to cease his war upon Enskari in order to prepare a defense against it.

We propose, therefore, a Prophet's Peace of Warring Worlds, a cessation of hostilities among us Saved in order to defend our way of life against the coming threat.

We trust you know the truth of what I say and will beseech your leaders to join us in this crusade.

Blessed be, Eren VIII.

Anointed,

Prophet of God,

Supreme Minister of the Saved.

Brett had to see this it as a diplomatic smokescreen of distraction and rumor meant to confuse Enskari, giving Hyrax time to rebuild. The play upon Brett's information was particularly clever, a game on his vanity, pretending veracity by assuming Brett's network must have uncovered the threat already, implying deficiency if it had not.

Mind games.

Brett's network of informers was strong, the best in the system, he was sure. If there was such a threat, he'd know of it.

He wondered if it might be an environmental danger. Sir Aldo had said the pollution problems facing Enskari, and which had led to Nutorn's letter, were not isolated to their world. All the civilized planets faced similar threats from weakening atmospheres and poisoned soil. But that didn't seem right, didn't seem to be what Eren was talking about, assuming the prophet was telling the truth, or indeed talking about something he believed. Environmental concerns wouldn't have come from the throne of the prophet.

Brett folded the letter and put it in a hidden pocket. He understood it now and imagined how he'd frame it to Zabel. Their enemies were vanquished, terrified, and panicking. They were grabbing at straws, drowning and done. The prophet's letter showed the desperation of defeated power.

A knock on his door.

"Come," he called.

The sergeant of arms entered.

"Faern," said Brett. "I'm ready. Take me to her."

"Begging your pardon, Sir Nolan, but as I said, the queen is indisposed and cannot see you."

"Cannot or will not?"

"Cannot," he said. "For I was not given access to relay your message."

"What?"

"Our sovereign is indisposed, is all I could learn."

"Ill?"

"I do not know."

"What do you know?"

The man stood at rest but kept silent.

"Speak, Faern," said Brett. "Speak to me now. Show me you are a noble servant. You know me to be one."

"I am torn between masters, Your Grace."

Brett drummed his fingers on the desk.

"In truth, Second Ear," said Faern, "I cannot speak as to what our queen is doing. I have had no word of her since Sir Ethan arrived this morning."

CHAPTER FOUR

They are truly savages. It is as if we've gone back in time, to some previous epoch where man was but a step removed from animals. They are brutal and cruel and lost. To call the Silangians human is a stretch of the modern usage, so far have they devolved since the landing. They are brutes. Our efforts here will be wasted.
Journal Report of Missionary Clive Batad, First Upon Silangan, 842 NE

11, Eighth-Month, 938 NE – Halle Village, upriver from White Coast, Silangan

It was midday when they arrived at the place. It was hot and moist and they were tired. They paused at the edge of the clearing, still in the shadow of the thick rubbery trees, just on the narrow trail looking in. No one spoke.

Minister Clavey had called Halle a city, but to Lund's eyes, after he'd arrived and saw it himself, he could think of it in no other terms than a village, a forest meadow filled with collapsing thatched huts and grimy humanity. No masonry, no metal, no cloth. No. Not a city.

Lund said a silent prayer before marching ahead. Eyletto held back with the others. After five confident steps Lund looked back at Eyletto. "Coming?"

Eyletto looked sheepish and afraid. "Aye, brother."

Lund gave him a confident wink that belied his own feelings and he hoped made him look wiser than his nineteen years. He strolled up the narrow path past low ferns to a space of collapsing houses and garbage piles, one difficult to discern from the other. Once in the open sunlight, flies stung his neck, beetles nipped at his feet, and gnats dove at his eyes only to get stuck on the sweat pouring out from under his broad-brimmed capello.

They passed a group of naked children tormenting an injured squirrel. The children looked up to study the strangers, unafraid and only a little curious. The squirrel was more reptile than mammal, but it looked a little like the creatures Lund knew from home and so he called it that. Its back legs were broken and its fur matted and bloody. It snapped at the children's bloody sticks and tried to drag itself away while they were distracted, trailing its viscera behind.

Lund tipped his hat to the children, not breaking stride. Four paces behind came Eyletto, followed by their three guides and six baggage bearers.

A woman squatted by a doorway and watched them with dull eyes. Her face was painted in red-sienna stripes of crackling mud. She was naked save for a thatch rag of a skirt she held up unabashedly as she relived herself on the ground. Lund noted the boxy jaw, squinted eyes, and narrow face of her race, black hair not unlike Hyraxian in color but coarse and untamable, short-cut and mannish. She snarled at them when they came close, gnashing broken and missing teeth like a beast.

"Pardon, ma'am," said Lund.

"Mind your own stink!" She spat at him.

Lund steeped to avoid the gob, but it caught the frill edge of his garments. Eyletto and the others gave her a wide berth as she shamelessly finished her business then returned to her hut, picking at her privates.

The trek to the village had taken six and twenty days of upriver sailing and then three more over land. Lund had been told in White Coast that there was a way to Halle by water, but their guides hadn't been able to find it. The closest they could do was come up a feeder stream off the Yolk River, beach their canoes, and cross the jungle mountains by foot.

The guides had nearly mutinied when Lund hired porters from among the river folk to press on after they failed to find the village by water. When contractual obligations failed to move them, he had to resort to threats of excommunication and then eternal damnation to get them to go on. Reluctantly they came, their family positions at stake, yet at every step they encouraged the missionaries to turn around and return to the coast.

Rutger Lund – Brother Rutger Lund – was called to this mission from his home in Sweetland on Temple. Along with his companion, Brother Manolo Eyletto, they were charged with bringing the good word of the Saved Church to the savages of Silangan. It was one of the most dangerous missions in the system and Lund had felt supremely blessed to have been chosen for it. Eyletto was not so sure. Though Lund was from Temple, fair-haired and bright-eyed, Eyletto was of recent migration from Maaraw, and had the tawny features of his ancestors and assumed that he'd been placed on Silangan because he was expendable.

"That is foolishness," Lund had told him. "The prophet saw our potential and chose us for this challenge. I have been here a year and no harm has come to me. None shall come to you. We are protected by God and the prophet."

"Aye, brother, forgive me my weakness," Eyletto said. "It could be worse, I suppose. We could have been sent to Tirgwenin."

"I didn't know we had missions there."

"We don't," said Eyletto with an air of something…resignation? Sarcasm? Lund didn't understand and so let the matter drop.

Eyletto replaced Lund's last companion, Cicsi from Lavland, who had served his two years and been sent home. Eyletto's arrival moved Lund from junior companion to senior missionary and he took his position seriously, seriously enough to seek entrance into the interior regions of Silangan to find converts.

Ministry on Silangan was problematic. The people were wild and yet human. They were people of the Unsettling like the folk on Temple, just far behind, thwarted by circumstance and fallen to barbarity while the rest of the planets – or rather most of them – maintained the true faith and systems of society that man cherished.

It was his calling to try to return these lost to the fold, to minister the word of God, the faith of the Saved, the religion of the Unsettling, which had once united them all. He did this by oath, 'for the glory of the prophet and the worship of God'.

Technology, though broken on all the planets at arrival, had never returned here. Nor had education, peace, learning, or God. Only

Tirgwenin with its millennium of decay was more degraded than Silangan. The only grace was that people still understood common language here, so Lund thought he had a good chance to succeed.

But it would not be easy. Hyrax ruled the planet and they didn't like the ministries. They didn't like the Silangians learning of the just God. It interfered with their mines. Hyrax had five and twenty silver mines on White Coast alone, six and eighty overall with fifteen gold, two and twenty lead, nearly a score of iron, and an assortment of miscellaneous other metal concerns he'd been warned not to interfere with. These were worked by Silangian laborers – people not advanced enough to be slaves like on Maaraw, but able to work when properly motivated by whips. They could dig, drag ore from holes, pound boulders to rubble, and load carts. More than that was not expected. It was bestial labor and the Hyraxians treated those that did it accordingly.

The Silangians had no use for their planet's metal. No sense to work copper or bronze, let alone iron. Gold and silver, mercury and lead, were curiosities only. Yet their planet had these metals in abundance and those metals drove the civilized economies. It was currency and shield for the spacefaring fleets. Hyrax exploited the mineral resources, worked the mines with the folk who by fate and misfortune had become little better than animals.

Though allies in theory, on the ground – on Silangan – Temple was at odds with Hyrax. Brandon's planet needed a workforce, while the ministers from the Holy World sought to unite humanity and expand the glory of God. Brutish the people were, but the missionaries had proved they need not be always so.

Past the defecating woman, the path widened, revealing a much larger community than suggested. The trees had been cut far back and the cluttered structures gave a sense of dense occupancy, yet besides the crass woman and cruel children, they'd seen no one else.

A hundred meters later they came upon a man standing square on their path flanked by four others. He looked to be waiting for them.

"Ministers," he called when they were close enough to hear. "We expected you much sooner."

"Expected us?" said Lund. He could sense his companions holding back.

"Aye. One does not approach the seat of Serlot without notice."

"So this is Halle?" said Lund. "And Serlot is the very man we wish to see."

The man smiled, a knowing, sly, and strangely disturbing turn of his face. He was Silangian, with the jaw and narrow eyes, long hair pulled up in a tangled knot. He wore leather robes of pieced-together pelts. He was barefoot and carried nothing in his hands and nothing hung from his belt. The others, however, looked to be soldiers. They held swords – clubs really, long wooden things with rock shards set as spikes at odd angles and edges. Never cleaned, they were rust-colored from past use.

"I am Bekulti," the man said. "Serlot has sent me to greet you."

"We have come from White Coast. I am Brother Lund. This is Brother Eyletto."

"Blessed be," Bekulti said.

"And to thee," said the others in unison.

"You speak well," said Lund.

"I'm from White Coast. I learned from the missionaries as a child."

"Oh," said Lund, brightening. "Under Minister Clavey?"

"Nay. He was after my time, I imagine."

"We are not ministers," said Eyletto finally, stepping up beside Lund.

Looking at their garb, Bekulti said, "Not ministers?"

"Nay. Only brothers," explained Eyletto. "Our powers are not as great as a minister. We are teachers. Missionaries."

"Representatives of the prophet, though?"

"Aye," said Lund. "We act in his name who acts in his." He gestured to the sky.

Bekulti grinned a thin smile. "You are expected."

Lund and Eyletto exchanged glances.

"Come," said Bekulti. "This way to the center. Things have begun."

The two soldiers led the way. Two more appeared behind the porters and took the rear.

Distant shouts carried over the plain but Lund could not discern if it was yelling or screaming. Chants or songs.

"I expected walls and gates," said Eyletto.

"This is Serlot's capital," Bekulti said. "He is the strongest on Silangan."

"Over the whole planet?" said Lund with a chuckle.

"As far as we know," said Bekulti. "Serlot does not need walls. He does not want them. Walls suggest fear. Serlot has no fear."

"But his people?"

"No fear."

"What of other tribes?" said Lund. "Do not the Silangians fight each other?"

"Aye. Often," said Bekulti. "Many bloody battles."

"But they dare not come here?" Eyletto said.

"They may dare come, but will never leave."

"We come in peace," said Eyletto. "Serlot must know that. We have no arms. We are peaceful."

Bekulti kept marching.

Lund had served in White Coast for his entire mission up until then, barely leaving the stronghold and shanty towns for a half-day trip to a farm one time. For sixteen months he'd done the prophet's work, converting and saving, and learning as much about the place as he could. A minister in the Hall of the Prophet had mentioned to him the day he was chosen for Silangan that the place was still a mystery and any information he could report would be a blessing. It was spoken as a casual aside, a form of congratulations as his parents wept at the news of his assignment, but Lund had taken it as an order from Eren VIII himself, sent by God for him. Along with his official duties, Brother Lund made it his purpose to chronicle all he found and relate with clear objectivity and divine inspiration whatever he encountered on Silangan. With less than six months left on the wild planet before his return home, he'd made the decision and approached Minister Clavey with his plan.

"I'd like permission to go inland and finish my mission there."

"To Magger?"

"Nay, not to another mining town. I want to visit wild Silangians. I want to see how they really are. Save them there, in their own homes. And report."

Clavey raised a finger but Lund, sensing a quick dismissal, pressed.

"I feel that I've done all the good I can here," he said, "or in any established mission – Magger or Jatt. I need to get among the savages, away from the mines. It's my duty to—"

"It's all well and good, brother," said Clavey. "I'll let you go."

"You will?"

"Aye. In fact, I've been pondering such a mission for a while now. Just the thing for you, I think. Keep you out for a few months, not too far, but among the wild natives. You should do some good and still return in time to greet your parents at the spaceport. They miss you."

Lund knew his parents corresponded with Clavey nearly as much as they did with him. They worried constantly and felt not unlike Eyletto about this assignment. Their entreaties to his minister were embarrassing.

"Go to Halle," said the minister. "It is a city a week or two upriver. Visit it. Spread the word. Baptize all you can. Come back and tell us what's happening there."

"Something's happening there?"

"The Hyraxians have heard of a new leader. A man named Serlot. We know almost nothing about him or what he's doing beyond his name and that he's upriver in Halle. Hyrax is concerned he might disrupt the mines."

"So it's a mission for Hyrax?"

"It's a mission for the Saved."

"And Serlot is dangerous?"

"Nay. No more than any savage, and the city of Halle is not unknown. They won't be shocked at seeing off-worlders."

"There's been contact? There's been a mission tried there before?"

"The Hyraxians visited."

"Raids?"

"Aye."

"Recently?" It was not an idle question.

"Nay, brother. Years ago. The incident is surely forgotten."

"How could they forget something like that? Wholesale kidnapping."

Clavey furrowed his face in a frown. "You forget who we're talking about. The Silangians are not like—"

"But we've—"

"Let me finish."

"Forgive me, Minister." Lund folded his hands on his lap. He recalled his vow of obedience and said the words silently to himself.

Clavey understood and paused long enough for him to finish before speaking again.

"I was saying that their society is not like ours. They live with violence and fear every day. They raid each other frequently – nay, *constantly*. They prey upon themselves far more than the Hyraxian wranglers do. I won't say they're used to it, but it is part of their life. They'll not hold it against you."

Lund had heard this before, it was part of the established narrative about Silangan, but after meeting the natives in White Coast, he'd become skeptical. He'd found them childlike and curious, not barbarous and brutal. That description might apply to the creatures working the mines, but that surely had much to do with the way they were treated. The tamed townsfolk were servile and calm, not unlike peasants back home.

"Reconsidering?" asked Clavey.

"Nay. Nay, I'm as stalwart as ever. Tell me more about Serlot."

"He could be your primary goal. Convert him and you will have the whole city."

"He's a king?"

"A strongman."

"A strongman? What's that?"

"A kind of king, a leader who rules by strength as opposed to divine right and noble birth."

"Will I be in danger?" Lund asked. "I'm still going. I just want to know."

"Missionary work is always hazardous, and in a wild place – going to the wilder areas still – the dangers must thus be greater. You will risk martyrdom, brother, but is that not the risk you wish to take? For glory?"

"Me? I seek no glory—"

"For God, Brother Lund. For the glory of God."

Lund felt himself blush.

Clavey's considered for a moment. "It might be too risky," he said. "Let us forget the entire thing. I would have you home safe after your mission. Your parents miss you."

The heat from Lund's cheeks migrated to his ears. He said, "I serve God and the prophet. I'll go immediately."

"All right, brother. Go with God, and blessed be."

"And to thee, Minister."

Every day since then Lund had felt a fire in his bosom, a fervor for his task. It was a certain knowledge that now more than ever, he was doing God's will. He saw the last meeting with Clavey as the point of no return and a rite of passage. It was at once terrifying and liberating to know he had the strength to claim his destiny. He felt the same exaltation traveling the jungle rivers as he had felt aboard the Hyraxian transport that landed him here, skirting Coronam's fiery reach en route to Silangan. Weightless and purposeful. Each time he'd left a home for the unknown, buoyed by faith, there was fear and excitement tempered by the certainty that he'd been chosen to do great things.

Lund scanned the ramshackle homes of Halle, taking in the filth and flies, and put it to memory so he could record it all later. He had many blank books with him and he planned on filling them all in the three months he would spend here.

"We have heard of Serlot in White Coast," said Lund. "A great man, I hear."

"Aye," said Bekulti.

"I'm told he is not Saved."

"In what sense?"

"In that he is not a follower of God and the prophet. What other sense can there be?"

"Children of the Unsettling," said Bekulti.

"Of course. Saved from the destruction of Old Earth. Aye." Lund smiled. Bekulti knowing the nuance of history went far to encourage him that Silangan could be brought back to the fold of humanity. They were not stupid. They were not unteachable.

"Are you close to the…to Serlot?" Lund asked.

"I help Serlot where I can," said Bekulti.

"Have you informed him of scripture? The messages of the prophet? The unity of man?"

"Nay."

"Why not?"

Bekulti laughed. "This is Silangan, Minister."

"Brother," corrected Eyletto.

"Oh, aye. That's right."

A smell of sweet rotting fruit and offal wafted from a ditch and Lund raised a handkerchief to his face. It was quickly soaked with his own sweat. He adjusted his hat only to have it free torrents of trapped moisture down his neck.

"The heat of this place is not to my liking," said Lund offhandedly.

Bekulti laughed.

Eyletto stumbled over some invisible obstacle and nearly fell into Lund.

"Careful, brother," said Lund.

"Aye, brother," said Eyletto. "Aye." He looked meaningfully at the armed men before them and behind and then back at Lund.

"It's all right, Brother Eyletto," Lund said. "As you say, we have come in peace."

Eyletto's eyes fell on something else.

Lund turned to see a clutch of old people. A half dozen bent over sticks and crutches, their faces painted in mud but still showing the oozing blisters of pox sores. Their arms were scabs and their rags stained with seeping feces and pus. They regarded the group with lightless graying eyes and toothless snarls. They smelled of filth, sweat, and the terrible sour-sweet stink of infection.

They walked between cluttered hovels. Lund was surprised that they never changed, that they didn't improve, not in size or construction or repair, as they moved into the interior.

"We've come to learn," said Lund to Bekulti. "About Silangian culture and your ways."

"I thought you came to convert Serlot."

"We will gladly give him lessons. I have books on history and mathematics, rhetoric and gospel." He gestured back to the porters carrying his boxes.

Bekulti smiled. "You would teach and learn?"

"Aye, exactly," said Lund.

"Proselytize and spy?"

"We are scholars and teachers."

"Aye," Bekulti said with a chuckle.

The paths were not straight, never straight. They meandered like snakes through a bog, turning this way and that, over short rock and muddy stream, without apparent order or planning. It made it difficult to see far ahead.

"These roads," said Lund. "Are they designed this way for defense? To keep the enemy confused?"

Bekulti laughed again and flashed his thin grin. "Nay. They lay as they are."

"No planning then?"

"As they are," said Bekulti.

Lund had heard Hyraxian bureaucrats discussing the Silangians' simple failures of feeding themselves, commenting on how leaders had no understanding or desire to provide safe water, roads, or sanitation. Leaders rose and fell often in bloody coups, reigns of chiefs measured in days more often than years. Most tribes, he'd been told, dispensed with naming a leader at all and relied on narrow family allegiances for support. Even then, he'd been told, they warred among their own, brother slaying brother, cousin, wife, and child – over trivial insults and shared scarcity which could have been easily avoided with but a little foresight and co-operation.

These tales came from Hyraxian wranglers. It was all hearsay since the Silangians had no written language, and only a broken oral tradition conspicuously lacking in history. One minister on Temple had said that Silangan had no past and therefore no future. Lund was beginning to understand.

"It's so different here," Lund said to Eyletto. "From the coast."

"What did you expect? The noble savage?"

Lund didn't answer but thought that was exactly what he'd expected.

The smell of wood fire wafted to Lund in smudges of tan against an otherwise brilliant blue sky. Close voices murmured and rose in a cheer.

Bekulti said suddenly, "Your god is not here."

"He used to be. And we bring him with us in our hearts." It was part of a speech Lund had practiced on the river.

"Your god is obscure. Ours are clear."

"Clear? How?"

"What they want and what they do. It is clear."

The slide to the plural reminded Lund of the rumors he'd heard about ancestor worship cults.

"And what god does Serlot…."

Lund's question trailed off when they rounded a corner and beheld a massive throng of people standing in an open square. There were thousands if there was one. They all had their backs to them, facing a low structure in the middle.

Bekulti was taking them there.

When they got closer, Lund could see that the platform was a crude flattened mound. Rock, and mud for mortar. It rose four meters above the ground, not high but enough to be visible by the entire gathering. The flattened top was perhaps three meters a side and three men stood upon it.

Ten meters from the mound, they stopped.

Bekulti gave a loud ululation that silenced everyone and drew the attention of the men on the mound.

"Is that Serlot?" asked Lund, staring at one of them.

"Aye, that is Serlot," said Bekulti.

It was difficult to tell size, but he looked enormous. He was dressed only in red paint, a wet feather necking, and a crown of twisting horns upon his head. His manhood hung between his legs, red and wet.

He held one of the terrible jagged swords and grinned when he saw the missionaries.

"Saved!" he yelled. "Behold!"

One of the men beside him descended a crude stone staircase and disappeared into the crowd. In a moment, he reappeared with three bound Hyraxian soldiers.

Eyletto grabbed Lund's arm. Lund instinctively went rigid in defiance of the fear pounding in his chest.

The Hyraxians wore rags that had been uniforms. They were scabbed and burned. Most of their fingers were missing; all of their ears. Their eyes were empty sockets.

"Enemies!" shouted Serlot. "Serlot's enemies! Silangan's enemies!"

The crowd roared, "Enemies die! Enemies die!"

Serlot grabbed the first prisoner by his ragged shirt and pulled his face up to his. The wild savage stood half a meter taller than the blinded Hyraxian.

"Blood! Blood! Blood!" screamed Serlot into the captive's face. "We know blood. We know strength. It is blood. Blood! Blood."

"Blood! Blood! Blood!" echoed the crowd.

Serlot pushed the soldier to his knees and raised his sword.

The crowd fell silent for the briefest moment, a telling time of anticipation and coming horror.

Serlot's sword swung down into the soldier's head, cracking it open, splitting the skull like a mashed melon. Pieces of his brain spattered with blood bathed Serlot in more red gore.

A cheer rose like an erupting geyser.

Serlot raised the sword and the cheer rose higher.

The next Hyraxian was served up the same and the next as well. With each strike the terrible sound of crack and squish made Lund's legs buckle. After the first, Eyletto bent over and vomited. The guides tried to flee, but their guards wouldn't let them.

Serlot kicked the corpses off the platform, their lifeless bodies rolling in a heap among others.

Lund noted that only the last three were off-worlders. The other bodies, he counted three and twenty on this side alone, were all Silangian. Men, women, children, and aged. There seemed to be no connection among them except that they had been alive and were now dead.

"You!" Serlot pointed into the crowd and three people rushed the platform fighting to be first. They scampered over the corpses fighting each other in their rush. One man finally crested the hill, his back a lattice of scratches where a woman had raked him in the struggle.

"Blood!" called Serlot.

"Blood!" repeated the man.

"Blood!" echoed across the square.

The man fell to his knees and spread his arms as if in supplication.

The sword found the crown of his head in a gut-wrenching thwack that finally caused Lund to stumble to one knee in Eyletto's mess.

So postured, Lund began to pray.

"Another off-worlder!" commanded Serlot.

Lund felt hands lift him up to his feet.

"Nay! Nay!" screamed Eyletto as he too was pulled to standing. "We come in peace!"

They were not dragged to the mound but made to stand and watch as another figure was put forward.

"A Tirgwenian?" said Eyletto.

"I've never seen one," said Lund.

The man stood as tall as Serlot, perhaps taller, but he walked with a stoop, as he'd been beaten. His skin was a golden yellow and reflected the sun in pinpoint flashes of light. He had blue tattoos decorating his face and neck. Though wearing whip marks and limping, bent and broken, he was otherwise whole – fingers, ears, eyes, and toes.

Behind him was forced another, a civilized, a Claremondian by the looks of him. Like his alien companion, he'd been beaten but was still whole. His hair was long, blood-matted and tangled. In the brilliant midday light, Lund could see the subtle hints of blue in his skin and hair, which was the character of the folk from Claremond. He wore a spacefarer's reflective vest, torn and streaked in gore and vomit.

The Claremondian caught sight of the missionaries and stared.

Eyletto shouted, "Who are you so I might say a prayer?"

The Claremondian said, "I am Gowfiko. But save your prayers for yourself. I'm not afraid."

"Bringers of bees!" shouted Serlot. "Bees!"

A general hiss rose from the masses, ugly and mean. Like a wave of hate, it crashed from the center out and then back to the middle.

"Blood! Blood!"

Serlot pushed the bound Tirgwenian to his knees.

The Claremondian pushed his way to a place beside the yellow man without being told.

"Mercy!" cried Lund for his Saved kindred.

"Blood!" shouted Serlot.

Up came the sword above Serlot's bloody head. It hung there, suspended in time and space for a long final moment before crashing down.

Lund screamed.

Eyletto sobbed.

The golden Tirgwenian slid off the mound to join the pile of bloody dead.

Up came the sword again and the Claremondian braced for the blow.

"This is our god," Bekulti told the missionaries. "The one with power, the one who teaches. The strong one. The only one we know. The only one there is."

"Blood!" came the call, and down came the sword.

CHAPTER FIVE

This indenture witnesses that ________________ (Servant) by these presents does voluntarily and of his own free will put himself to serve ________________ (Master) for a full term of ________________ standard years to be complete and ended on ________________ as payment of the Servant debt of ________________. During all which said Servant his said Master faithfully shall serve, his secrets keep, his lawful commands gladly and everywhere obeyed: he shall do no damage to his said Master nor see to be done by others without letting or giving notice to his said Master, he shall not waste his said Master's goods, nor lend them unlawfully to anyone, he shall not commit fornication, nor contract matrimony within the said term. At cards, dice or any other unlawful game, he shall not play, whereby his said Master may have damage with his own goods, nor the goods of others within the said term, without license from his said Master, he shall neither buy nor sell, he shall not absent himself day nor night from his said Master's service without his leave, nor haunt alehouses, taverns, or playhouses; but in all things as a faithful Servant he shall behave himself to his said Master and all his during the said term. And also shall find and provide unto the said Servant sufficient meat, drink, and lodging.

This contract and the term remaining thereto shall be deemed a negotiable instrument of value and the said Master may dispose of it for debts and obligations as tender per agreement between parties of transference.

For the true performance of all and every, the said covenants and agreements, either of the said parties bind themselves unto the other by these presents. In witness whereof they have hereunto interchangeably put their hands and seals this date of ________________. Witnessed and lawful.

Standard Indenture Agreement Form

26, Eighth-Month, 938 NE – Freeport, Dajjal

Dedikodu had been in a spacesuit once before – in lee orbit around Enskari doing maintenance on the *Hopewell* for Captain Upor while the rest of the crew went shoreside. He'd managed well enough, finished the work, strung mast cable from the bell to the head, pulling himself along the kilometers of shaft through his heavy insulated gloves, dragging filament behind him. It took hours. It was claustrophobic work, but not too hard. The silence was something else though. Only his own breathing kept him company for those many hours. It'd be the same this time, but for days probably, unless he could find a way to enter the elevator pod. He'd have to find a way into a pod and then the station in orbit, and then whatever ship was available. If there was a ship. In any event, he'd be off this shit of a planet, this dead rock of a cinder, Dajjal.

The suit he had now wasn't a true spacesuit. It didn't have radiation shielding. It offered only air and insulation. It was made for vacuum mining and had thick elbow- and kneepads and a reinforced helmet for the inevitable scrapes, bumps, and occasional cave-ins the work entailed. If anything, it was more durable than the one he'd been in before and as long as he didn't run out of air or expose himself to too much sunlight, he should be all right.

He carried it now in a duffel as he maneuvered through Freeport alleys in the fractional gravity of the dead world. He'd stolen the suit, of course. Took it when he took his leave of Carabat Station. With any luck he'd not be noticed missing for a couple more days. With no luck, which was more his way, there was already a report of a runaway indentured circulating among what little law there was in Freeport, and he was already a hunted man.

Freeport – the city, not the space station above the planet which shared its name – sat in an environmental dome between the frozen slagged walls of a narrow canyon. The planet moved in a tidal-locked orbit around Coronam, which was a fancy way of saying that one side of it always faced the sun while the other side, the side he was on, the side all human activity was on, faced away. Without even the semblance of an atmosphere, the sunward side of Dajjal was a deadly radioactive wasteland, a furious bubbling reminder of the ancient storm that had destroyed this planet and vaporized its neighbor, Kanluran. Kanluran was now nothing but a cloud of broken rock and lifeless ice while Dajjal was a stubborn cinder hellhole with just enough gravity and heavy metal potential to interest the more daring speculators. Using vast fortunes, they burrowed holes into the rock looking for gold and lead, iron and silver, at the very edge of exploration. Civilization was a theory here, not a way of life, and the mines were filled with the dregs of humanity, slaves and exiles, outlaws and the lost, toiling to their deaths in reinforced pressure suits for a place to sleep and a potato. Dajjal was the last stop on the western trade route, the jumping-off point to Tirgwenin if anyone was crazy enough to want to go there, and Dedikodu wanted to go there.

But he'd take any ship. Needs must. He had to get off this planet before it killed him.

"Do you have dust? An hour for a hundred pennyweight of silver," said a woman in a doorway. Her blazing red lips and plunging neckline gave little doubt to her occupation. "A day for half that in gold."

She looked clean, was not unattractive or too old. Maybe a few years older than his five and twenty, maybe ten more, but still a comely woman. She was pleasing to his tired, lonely eyes. It'd been a long time since he'd been with a woman. Four years at least. Twice that if he were to count only the woman he loved, that girl way back on Maaraw who had first embraced him. A spiritual exploration of delight and promises he knew even then had to be broken. A week then – nay, three nights, before he ventured spaceward as a free man. Now three times sold and here abandoned, as far from that girl as he could be and still feel rock beneath his feet, Dedikodu considered the offer of the whore in the door.

"Nay, lady," he said. "But I do very much appreciate the offer."

"Lady?" She laughed and her breasts jiggled beneath her blouse. "For that kind of manners, perhaps I can make you a better deal. Say, eighty pennyweight? I take dollars as well. Hyraxian or Lavlander. Anything, really. We'll negotiate the exchange rate."

Dedikodu had six coins in his pocket, two gold, the rest silver. No two alike. He'd taken them from a coat in the railway office when he'd smuggled himself into the pressurized sheep car. There'd been a hundred of the beasts – shorn, cold, and complaining. They bleated and smelled and tossed against each other in the lightless car in terror and confusion. The smell had been so bad he'd considered donning his suit after an hour, but instead bivouacked by the ventilator, and slept for most of the thirty-hour trip. After a while he stopped noticing the smell. It was only now in Freeport, wandering the back alleys and shadows, breathing petrol fumes and coal smoke, that he remembered the stench in his clothes.

"Might you offer me a bath instead?" Dedikodu said. "And a bit of laundry?"

"What you say?" The woman stepped closer and sniffed. "Oh, I see. The price just went up."

"Some soap and water?"

"Hot or cold?"

Dedikodu dug a silver coin from his pocket. He showed it to her.

"Where's that from, then?" she asked.

He looked at it. "It's an Enskaran twenty-dollar silver piece."

"Pure silver?"

"I don't know."

"What's silver go for on Enskari?"

He shook his head.

She looked up the alley. "Sure. Come on in, honey."

Honey.

He'd dreamed of honey for years.

Something moved in the recesses behind her that caused Dedikodu to hesitate. A figure in the shadows.

The woman gestured for him to go in. "Come on, honey dear," she said. "We'll get you out of those dirty things and cleaned right up."

"Cleaned right out, more like," he said.

He heaved the duffel over his shoulder and left double quick, thinking how easy it was for a pretty face to make him forget where he was. This was Dajjal. Freeport, in all its terrible irony. There was no comfort here.

Freeport was founded by Lavlanders and they, if anyone, claimed dominion of government. It wasn't much. A governor, tax collectors more crooked than the lava valleys in the Diamond Vale. A determined landing party could take the whole dead world in an hour. It had happened, but never lasted long. It wasn't worth it. An unspoken neutrality was over the place. Though war waged across the system – Brandon had suffered a defeat, he'd heard; his home world of Maaraw was in uprising – Dajjal was off-limits. Dajjal, at the edge, was reserved for people not politics. The need for harbor trumped the squabbles of kings and queens out here. There was something about that that Dedikodu found poetic, but he was unable to follow the thought far enough to determine why. When he tried, he found himself remembering terrible things on far-off worlds, bawling through tear-drenched eyes, yearning for honey.

A group of sailors passed him in the alley. They were five. Two looked Enskaran, one a Lavlander, and the others Claremondian. They regarded him with suspicion, perhaps never having seen a non-slave Maarawan before. Dedikodu ignored them, stepping like he had a purpose, and they passed him for the brothel he'd barely escaped.

He figured the terminal was near. He couldn't see the building, but by tracing a line from the dome airlock he could guess where the elevator filament connected to the ground. Elevator filaments were only millimeters thick, though he'd been told once, probably in a brag, that the shipyards of Lavland had ones that were over two centimeters.

There was no daylight in Freeport. Never daylight. Always night. Gaslights and corner coal fires lit the city. Lamps indoors. Diesel gel candles for sale on every corner, homemade and greasy. Glowglobes cost their weight in gold. The overhead dome was mirror and lit the city in twinkling constellations of cast-back orange spots. It wasn't much, just sooty and stained reflected light, but enough for Dedikodu to see that no elevator pods were moving up or down just then.

Out of the alley, steam carts chugged along cobblestoned roads, people milled about. There was a market in an empty lot. It looked like midday, but how they figured time in this forever dark was beyond him. He'd not heard a church bell or tower clock chime here in years.

Condensed water fell from the dome in a perpetual drizzle. The rain was oily and reflected rainbows in street puddles.

To his right Dedikodu heard the familiar bleating of sheep and saw herdsmen leading a flock to market. The animals' white coats were gray with oily rain. They might have been the same sheep he'd ridden with.

He tried to remember the port house, to think of his best approach, but he had seen it only briefly when Captain Upor had put him off here.

He still struggled with that betrayal. Upor had put him off. He, of all the crewmen, was the only man who actually wanted to go to Tirgwenin and he'd been put off at Freeport. Another mariner might have killed to be left here, to be free of the perilous journey through the cloud, exposed and endangered, not a planet shadow between worlds to harbor in if Coronam got angry. Nothing at the destination but savages and wild. But he alone knew there was something more there; he alone had planned to jump ship and remain on that planet in hope. And in penance.

He'd not had the chance. Upor put him off at Freeport and planted him in the torturous hands of Hyraxian agents for a bag of dust. He didn't know if had been silver or gold dust, a bag the size of a baby's fist. Probably silver.

Before selling him into slavery to Carabat Station to toil in the vacuum iron mines, the Hyraxians had tortured him and he'd told them all he knew. It was easy to turn on Upor's *Hopewell*, harder to admit the Bucklers under Minister Morgan and their plan to colonize Tirgwenin. Harder it was, but he'd done it all the same. Eventually. His back scarred with whip lashes, his chest red with brands, he'd told them all he knew. When they asked him how he knew the colony was to be put down on Rodawnoc and not Placid Bay as they'd heard, he told them Upor had told him personally. Though he'd since figured it out, at the time he didn't understand why his captain had done that. Then the ship left without him with Morgan's doomed colonists, and a few hours later, Hyrax asked him about it.

His captors surely believed it was false information, but Dedikodu knew, even before the first brand, that it was true. The planters were betrayed. More blood and more lives spent wrongly. Justice was a dream.

Since that last day in Pemioc, he'd been haunted by visions and the hum of bees. He had glimpses of order, rational, and hopeful. Flashes of understanding, snippets of ideas, enough to know they were there, but never enough to gel. Never enough to grasp, to make his own. A fleeting thing, like a will-o'-the-wisp, or a faith. For a moment in his life, at the worst moment of his life, he'd seen redemption and peace and then he left the place and with it, the chance. Since then, three years now with Hasin spattered with the blood of innocent people, he'd wrestled with that momentary insight. It was all memory now. Away from Tirgwenin and the strange yellow people, it was gone, and yet the memory of the memory lingered like a stain – or rather, like a clean spot on his otherwise soiled soul. It colored his vision as he saw cruelty as horror instead of a way of life, and people as potential friends instead of sure enemies. Stupid and simple, but a lesson so different from what he knew, it was truly revolutionary.

He'd been a tool of the colonists' demise, deliberately left on Dajjal for Hyrax to find. He knew where the colonists were going, had been there, and could provide maps, which he did with broken fingers. If by some miracle the colony survived without the food they needed, the salt they'd been promised, the timing they relied upon, and if the natives didn't massacre them – which was their justified action – then Hyrax would destroy them.

As he told his captors all he knew, promised to take them there even, meaning the promise, broken as he was, he'd remembered that there'd been a moment, an instant, a flash where he imagined he was more than a weak man giving up innocent planters. It was that flash on Tirgwenin that echoed and resonated, and though he was still weak and sinful, but a man, he felt he might be more. If only he could hear the hum again, he could be more.

The shepherds were in no hurry and seemed to take pleasure in blocking the road for the carts.

Freeport, beneath the elevator station, was the most populated place on the planet, but beyond it there were other places, domed homesteads, stations of various sizes. They called them 'stations' instead of ranches for reasons lost even to the inhabitants. It always confused newcomers who assumed that every little berg had a thread into space when at most they were lucky to have water recycling. They had all begun as mines seeking the heavy metals not vaporized by the storm that had scarred the planet. Most found it too difficult to mine and switched to some form of desperate agriculture. The ash made for rich soils after basic terraforming with microbes and fertilizers. Industrial glowglobes and plasma heaters turned domes into hothouses and Dajjal could sustain itself. Barely. Stiff grass grew best and fed sheep and cattle. Nut orchards and fruit farms kept the colony alive and offered a rare nonmetal export. Occasionally.

It could be months before a ship visited Dajjal. If Carabat Station was any indication, they didn't produce enough metal on the whole planet for more than three or four shipments a year scratched out of the rock by slave labor. He'd left three and twenty other souls at the station to their fates. All like him, former mariners pressed into service for debt or bad luck. Five years, the first two without pay. End-of-contract bonus, if you lived that long. Better terms than some places, but after spending months in the dark mines, kilometers below the surface, freezing, working in vacuum, he doubted many men saw the end of their contracts.

Knowing he looked suspicious standing in the half shadows, Dedikodu crossed the road to a food cart.

Producing his twenty-dollar Enskari silver piece, he handed it to a merchant. "I'll have four liters of filtered water, if it be truly so, and two kilos of mixed nuts. I'll take the change in coin."

The merchant took the money and studied it in candlelight.

"Two liters of water and one kilo nuts," he said. "No change."

"You thieving bastard. I'm paying twice what it should be."

"This is foreign money."

"This is Dajjal, fool. What else is there?"

Dedikodu knew from ports all over the system the way of bartering on the docks. For him to do anything else would draw attention. He glanced at the overhead telegraph wires and knew it was only a matter of time before his absence was noticed and bounty hunters sent after him. Might have happened already.

He needed the water. His suit's filters had been exhausted. Unlike the air scrubbers, he'd been unable to find new water filters when he fled. His purifiers were failing and a hint of urine flavored the output. Fresh water in the system would clean it and allow him to drink at least as long as the air scrubbers held, maybe five and seventy hours at exertion, twice that at rest. After that, the air would suffer and he'd eventually suffocate. If he remembered rightly, the elevator was near thirty hours without thrust, a short run for a small planet. If he couldn't get inside, he could ride the top, keep out of sight, not that anyone would be looking for a man clinging to the shell of a rising elevator pod like some desperate barnacle. Then, if he didn't freeze, fall, or have his equipment fail, with great luck, he might find a maintenance hatch, enter unnoticed, hide in the cramped orbiting station, and wait to stow away on the next ship that passed. What could possibly go wrong?

"Nay, it is you who'd rob me," said the merchant.

"Fine." Dedikodu reached to take back the coin.

The man pulled it away and eyed his duffel.

"You a sailor? Shipping out?"

"My coin, sir."

"Working the sheep?"

"My coin or four liters water and two kilos mixed nuts, with change."

The man looked up the street. There were no other customers. He weighed the coin in his hand.

"Where comes this coin?"

Dedikodu held his hand out while his other snaked into his coat pocket. The merchant noticed the move. "There won't be any change," he said.

"Fine. Water and nuts. And if your thumb's on the scale, I'll shoot it off."

The man showed his blackened teeth in a grin. "Give us a bottle."

Dedikodu rummaged in his duffel and removed the reservoir bag from the suit. He upended it in the street, draining the dregs onto the cobblestones. He passed it to the merchant, who filled it from a barrel spigot.

"Know you if a ship is at the station?" Dedikodu said casually.

"Aye, something's there. Pod came down this morning."

"Know its home?"

"Nay. But they're trading in the market." He gestured where the sheep were going, the flock now blocking two roads. Steam carts blared anemic horns barely noticed above the bleating.

"That's interesting," said Dedikodu.

The merchant turned over the now-filled bladder, noticed the Carabat Station stamp.

"And two kilos nuts," said Dedikodu.

"Got a bag for them?"

"Nay," said Dedikodu.

"I can let you have one for—"

"For my change?"

Another wry smile. "Aye," he said. He upturned the scale plate into a flour sack and passed it across. "Damn smell of sheep is putting me off me lunch," he said.

"Aye, the sheep," said Dedikodu.

It wasn't far, a block off the main road, before something like a city square opened up with merchants and bustling shoppers. It was tiny compared to the ones he'd seen on other worlds – even on Maaraw – but for Freeport this was surely the center of their economy.

The sheep were herded into a paddock. A shepherd proclaimed that the rams would be first to auction, then the rest sold in lots.

There were carts like before but also more permanent stalls with tin roofs that plinked beneath the falling water. The smell of cooking meat made his stomach growl while the hands of the beggars grabbing at his coat made him speed his step.

He found a row of crockery and glass, jewelry and pretty baubles the likes of which ships often used to trade. He meandered up the aisle, listening for accents, looking for spacefarers, short hair and reflective vests, men with canes against the gravity low as it was. Men who might help him for mercy's sake. He saw no one.

Dedikodu tried the row of grain merchants, thinking he might find a ship's quartermaster stocking up. Grain was prized in space. Bread would boost morale as much as grog. Still, he found no obvious off-worlders there. Thinking grog and rum might be another good try, he crossed an open area of caged butterflies and overheard lively chatter from among the onlookers.

"I'm telling you, my flutters save crops. Ain't no call to risk anyone's fields on some off-world gamble."

"But the butterflies don't give nuthin," said another.

"They give you crops, you damn fool."

"Gotta keep a patch of butterleaf for the caterpillars. A hectare at my station. Stinkweed we call it."

"Aye, stinkweed."

"Small price for the corn you grow, Master Thomas."

Most of the talking was being done by a man standing on a box before a sign proclaiming: *Lester's Butterflies – lest yer plants be unpollinated.*

"I'm for trying 'em. You can't keep me from buying."

"It's a pig in a poke," said the man Dedikodu assumed was Lester. "You don't know a thing about them."

The man he was arguing with shook his head. "They're bees. What's there to know?"

Bees?

"Lester, you have a damn monopoly. I'm all for giving the wench's bees a try."

"Aye, Lester," said another. "Less than half the eggs you sold me last year come out this."

"You didn't keep them warm enough, Master Brad."

"They're a fraction of your price, too," the first man said.

"She's a damn off-worlder. Got nothin' at stake here," said Lester. "She could be selling all drones. What does she care? She'll be gone before ye get home."

"I'll show you the queen in each hive," came a female voice.

Dedikodu looked to find it.

"I'm offering properly pollinated crops," she said. "Self-sustaining, stingless bees. A blessing on all fronts. And honey. Do any of you even remember honey? Such golden sweetness on the tongue?"

"They're full of disease," said Lester. "She got nothing at stake here. Taking your money and blighting your crops."

"You know me," she said. "You know me well."

"Aye."

"Who is she?" Dedikodu asked a man beside him.

"That there be Sadya of Jont. Captain of the *Lady's Rage*. A gunned and swift corsair, I hear." The man spat out something black and globous. "She's a pirate captain. She's something of a regular here. Lester's full of shit."

He found her then, standing not far from Lester on his box, a smallish woman, eight and twenty years perhaps, but those hard. She had a scar down the left side of her face from brow to jawline. The clear token of a saber cut. Her skin was pale, the sign of a sailor, sunless and wan, but even five meters away, he could see the bluish tint to it, a trait of the Claremondian folk. Her short hair too had the same bluish tint where he could see it around her cap.

"She's a captain? Freebooter or privateer?"

"No allegiance I know of," said the man. "She flies against them all. She's slagged Hyraxian treasure ships, Lavlandian convoys, and Enskaran transports. She's robbed shuttles off this very world too, I hear, but not in a while."

She stood with six men armed with muskets and sabers. There were five large crates on a flatbed cart with port house markings stenciled on the side. One was open and he could see a rope hive within it, the shifting shadows of waking bees.

Dedikodu moved closer.

"Ask her why she selling so cheap," said Lester.

"I'm selling them cheap because we don't have so many flowers aboard ship. Spoiling cargo."

"Where'd they come from?" said Dedikodu.

The captain searched the crowd for the questioner and when her eyes found him, there was a strange pause, as if she were trying to remember where she'd seen him before.

He was sure they'd never met. He would have remembered her, no doubt about it. He might have heard of her, though. Pirate stories were common, and tales of beautiful female pirate captains were often spun for the lonely mariner in the blackness of space. He'd never thought any of them real.

"Tirgwenin," she said.

An arm wrapped around Dedikodu's neck and yanked.

Before he could react, scream, or fight, he was flat on the muddy ground. He fell hard on his duffel and felt something break within it. A seal or a hard hose from the suit, broken. He could smell charcoal and figured it was a filter.

Another man stepped on his wrist, pinning his arm to the ground.

"Carabat will pay in cash for you, or rather you will, in time tacked on," said the man. He brandished a charged pistol and waved it in his face. "Or would you rather I free you now? Not worth as much as an example, but might be a mercy."

"What has he done?" said Sadya of Jont.

Oily drops blurred his vision, but Dedikodu could just make out the pirate captain standing, looking down at him held on the muddy path.

"He's a runner from a gang. Indentured for four more. Run out on his debt. A thief, too."

"He's a sailor," she said.

"Nay, a miner."

"A sailor," she said with emphasis. "I'll buy his contract."

"Not mine to sell," said the man. "We're charged only with his capture."

"Arrange it," she said, looking deep into Dedikodu's face. "I'll take him for his time and the year tacked on for escape."

"What?"

"I want him."

"I am a sailor, madam. Truly," said Dedikodu. "I have—"

"I know you, Dedikodu," she said.

"I'll work the gun batteries on the hull. I'll— You know my name?" He wasn't sure what words were to come next, what promises he was trying to make, what bargaining or beseeching he would do. His voice caught in his throat. His eyes filled with tears, his ears with a buzz as he saw the lone bee circling the captain's brow. Upon his forehead it landed and to his tongue came the taste of honey.

CHAPTER SIX

The heretic queen has sown her own destruction in the repudiation of the One True Church. Already in the midst of her so-called reformation, powerful and popular new flavors of religion – protestants of every description and abomination – are rising like weeds in infected soil. Gibbers, Gazers, Literalists, Brothers and Brethren, Cults of Nature, Bucklers, and snake healers of all stripes. With so much dissenting variety, zealotry, and free rein for free thought, it is only a matter of time before that throne is undermined by these dangerous infidels. This tolerance will be the death of them.

Personal journal of Jedediah Hunt, Temple Minister in exile
'Hiding under protection of sympathizers'
Somewhere on Dorothia, Enskari, 928 NE

14, Ninth-Month, 938 NE – Vildeby, Enskari

Sitting on the wooden chairs, again in official surroundings, Morgan waited to beg. His life was waiting; disappointment and waiting. Time's cruel play. Time was his enemy, but he had little else to spend.

He knew he looked desperate, a wreck of a man come to plead favors from the First Ear, when he'd exhausted everyone else. He sat among others, waiting his turn, and could feel their pity for him in sorrowful expressions that at once mourned but also hated him for whatever tragedy he brought. He stole glances at the others and saw them turn away. It was as he feared; his troubles were as visible as his worn coat. No question, he was a shell of his former self, a tired, wrecked refugee. There'd been a time when he could inspire from a pulpit, petition God with certainty. Now he'd lick the boots of anyone who could give him real hope.

He was approaching seven and fifty but he felt a century. Broken and tired, a husk of a man. His clothes hung on him like rags on a wire. He had no appetite and couldn't keep down what he forced himself to eat if only to keep going. The pleasure of dining was gone, as all pleasures and respites, and none more than sleep. Exhausted though he was, adrift in guilt and anguish, he could find no rest even there. His mind was troubled by nightmares in the darkness, and in the day, it was filled with memories of worse realities.

Recently his nightmares had a new face, a memory of a boy, his arms full of stolen silver, his one eye full of death. Not yet seventeen, he wore a stained leather vest under the official sash of an agent of the archbishop.

Through a friend of an acquaintance of a contact, Morgan had found the Yelkins. He'd appeared at their door and had been welcomed with mercy in their home on the eve of the day that Hyrax breached Enskaran space and Connor's purge began.

Morgan heard the commotion downstairs before breakfast.

Oliver Yelkin, master of the house, farmer and upright citizen, churchgoer and kind, burst into the room. "Alpin," he said in a panic. "A rider has come from Danton. Connor's guards are moving this way. The stories are true. They're rounding people up. They have a list. Bucklers are mentioned. They're killing people. We believe they're coming here for you."

"Oh...." was all he could find to say.

"We have a priest hole," said Oliver. "You can hide there until the storm passes. But hurry, they're on the very heels of our friend here."

Young master Dave, thirteen and a half years old, looked sick and worried as they passed him on the stair. Oliver led Morgan to the kitchen. There they found the lady of the house, Becka Yelkin, stationed before the large walk-in pantry.

"I heard it all, Oliver," she said. "Sound in this house carries so."

Oliver pulled Morgan forward. "We are in haste," he said to his wife.

"Nay. You shall not do this. Your good intentions will kill us."

"Move, woman."

"Nay. These are dark times. We must look to our family's safety.

Harboring this apostate is a crime under normal days. Now it's execution. What of Sarah and Dave?"

"Damn it, woman!" roared Oliver. "We must do what is right and this is right. We have a priest hole. It came with the house. It is as if God himself arranged this."

"Nay," Becka said softly but firmly, tears in her eyes. "Nay. It is too dangerous. These are evil times."

"And would we be as the times or be better?"

"Oliver, Dave's friend said they know he's here."

"And we will tell them he's gone, fled after we sent him packing through that door." He pointed to the servants' entrance. "There'll be horse tracks leading away to corroborate. He will not be found."

Seeing Becka's tears, Morgan began, "Oliver, perhaps I should—"

"Nay, Alpin. You will not last an hour. You are my guest and a countryman. We take but a little chance if you will be quiet and still. The room is safe and well hid, though sound does carry." He gestured for Morgan to come forward, but he hesitated, caught in Becka's dark, accusing stare.

Oliver said, "We are well known in the county. My word will carry far and the servants saw me lead you out this way."

Becka crossed her arms but didn't say anything.

Oliver Yelkin pushed past her, leading Morgan to the pantry. Behind a barrel of molasses, he removed a small panel.

"It is a tight fit," he said. "There is a ladder within that leads to a space above the kitchen. Go and be still."

The entrance was but half a meter square, and dark the instant the hidden panel was shut behind him. He found the ladder, climbed the short distance to the cubbyhole above the kitchen, and wriggled himself into it.

Silently as he could, he felt around the space and found a dusty glowglobe. He wound it a quarter, just enough for a weak orange light for him to survey his surroundings. The space he occupied was not a meter high, but several long and nearly two wide. He could lie comfortably. There was a mattress and a blanket, a book of orthodox scripture and a wooden bowl. They were dusty and greasy from kitchen smoke but not as old as the house. He turned off the globe and lay down upon the mattress, waiting in pitch dark, reciting silent prayers as perhaps another had done before. When that was done and the words lost all meaning, he waited and worried. His hands shook in impotent fear. How he wished he'd remained behind at Rodawnoc and sent another to plead their cause. To bring help. To save them. They could have done no worse than he.

Lost in his thoughts, adrift in time, he was startled by the pounding on the door that echoed like cannon fire. Sound did carry here.

Then came voices from the foyer. Quiet at first, helpful, direct. Then a gasp from Becka. "Nay nay nay!" she screamed, her voice rising to hysterical levels.

Oliver shouted, "David!" And there was a clash of metal. A scuffle. A fight. A scream and a crash.

A child began to cry, then scream.

Becka sobbed and begged. "For the love of—" A sickening thump and she was heard no more.

Boots on tile. Smashing furniture, shouts and objections. The baby, Sarah, silenced, a muffled cry to end the scream.

"Bring them out!" commanded someone with a country accent, slow with a snarl – from Southland perhaps. "Put 'em there. Or their pieces, least."

Noises moved outside behind a slamming door.

Morgan's fists broke open, unable to stay clenched for the shaking.

For maybe hours, minutes, or days, he heard indistinct sounds, steps far or close, something heavy dragged over something rough. The house settling. A possible cry. His own heart in his ears.

He remained in the hidden closet, silent except for his shallow breathing, quick and dizzying. The darkness around him close and heavy, he was unable to mark the passage of time. He might have slept, but if he did, he dreamt of suffocating darkness and horror unseen. It was no better than waking.

After what seemed like an age, he summoned the weak light from the glowglobe. He sat up and regarded the mattress, the silhouette of sweat he'd left there, and felt the damp on his back.

He crawled to the ladder, extinguished the light, and went down.

He pushed the panel and felt it give against the frame and then catch with a knock on something beyond, the molasses barrel, no doubt.

He waited and listened for the sound to bring a response. When it didn't, he lifted the panel aside and crawled into the Yelkins' pantry around the molasses barrel and into the kitchen.

It was as it had been, except for the silence and the dark. The sun behind the horizon told Morgan he'd hidden for half a day.

Moving as if through a sepulcher, he found the foyer a mess of broken furniture. A small pistol inlaid with the Yelkin crest lay charged and humming at the foot of a torn tapestry. It being the only noise rising above the deafening silence, Morgan went to it as if it were alive and speaking. When he picked it up, he found blood on the handle. From it, he traced a path of rusty drops to the door, which stood ajar. A breeze blew through the gap and carried upon it the sweet smell of cooked death.

Shuffling forward, his feet unable to rise above the floor, he moved to the entry and pulled open the heavy door. A red letter was tacked upon it with a shiny new nail just at eye level. The seal of the archbishop adorned the bottom like a bloodstained autograph.

In the courtyard smoldered broken chairs and tables, coal oil buckets and dead bodies. Black, charred, and interwoven – knotted in a fired embrace, Morgan counted at least four dead people: two large, two small. There could have been more. Individually unrecognizable, the letter on the door had named at least some of them.

According to law (Defense of the Realm Directive, Archbishop Connor, Church of Enskari) the Yelkin family of county Danton are judged and declared enemies of the state and are so sentenced. Condemned are Master Oliver and Mistress Rebecka (traitors, giving comfort to the enemy and ministers of the false church), their children David (sodomite) and Sarah (apostate follower of the false church). All are sentenced to die immediately by whatever means convenient. Their lands, holdings, and assets are hereby confiscated by the Church and Crown.

Perhaps somewhere there was a red letter with his name on it, but this horror here today had not come for him. The rider had come for the kind family whose reputation, good deeds, and public displays could not save them. The list of crimes bespoke grudges, rumors, and secret ledgers. The sentence bespoke of an institutional purge, a cruel madness, a hurry to domestic atrocity before foreign invaders took the planet and did their own.

Seeing a family destroyed so utterly, he reflexively summoned images of his own and this, doubtless, was where he drew the power to do what he did.

The young guard in the vest and holy sash of the archbishop must have been in the house. He appeared at the door with his arms full of silver dishes and serving trays, a teapot, and bag of clinking cutlery. A strongbox under his arm. Over his shoulder was slung a military musket and when he saw Morgan, he let fall the loot and reached for his gun.

Morgan did not know it was in him. He knew only that to die now, with his family in need, was to fail them. He was all they had. He could give his life – would happily give it – if it would save them, but this was not that. This was failure and death.

He'd never fired a gun before and was only partially aware that he held one.

The boy, a youth of seventeen, not even shaving yet, rushed his weapon to his shoulder, took aim, and died. A shot entered his head through his right eye just above the musket's barrel. Shot by Morgan with the Yelkins' pistol.

The sound of that shot had echoed forever and still rattled his mind.

He dropped the gun, feeling it peel away from his palm, still sticky in Yelkin blood. Without pausing, he helped himself to the strongbox and a horse.

Burdened with new nightmares, he returned to Vildeby and hid in barns and brothels until the Hyraxian threat was over and Connor's directive repealed. When new patriotism replaced old horror, he rose to start again, beseeching what few living friends he still had to help in the rescue.

Here he had failed and failed again, and he knew, sitting in the antechamber waiting for an audience with the First Ear of the queen, that he wore his failure on his face.

He'd arrived at Government House and found a place to sit near the Ear's door to wait and watch the auroras snake across the sooty sky in anticipation of another dawn, another day away from his family, separated from his congregation, the Bucklers – his ruined people. There was no beauty in the light. He could not even say that it was a blessing as he used to, thinking that the same light shone on his daughter, Daria, as it did him, for that was not the case. He was on Enskari and she and her daughter, his grandchild Diane, marooned and forsaken on Tirgwenin. Their light shone different than here. Their days were alien and cold. They'd endured a winter without succor and now, he'd like to hope, the summer found them well. But he did not believe it. If they'd made it to Placid Bay then maybe they'd have been all right. Maybe. But he'd left them in a crumbling colonnade at Rodawnoc, the only place on that entire planet where they were sure to be unwelcome. No provision, no resupply, no escape. He held out little hope, but still he did what he could and did what he had to do, blood on his hands and all. Watching the glow in the east, Morgan could find no warmth in the coming sunshine. It only reminded him of the bitter betrayal, deadly delays, and his own ineffectiveness at helping those who'd believed in him.

Today Sir Edward would open his doors to hear petitions from the public, as many as his limited time would allow. It was an old custom. Ancient. A formality. It was the lowest form of audience short of yelling at his passing carriage, and it was all Morgan could muster. Whatever reputation he might have had, whatever standing he used to enjoy as a noble and landowner, was no more. Ruined by his ruin.

He sat with thirty others smelling of sweat and unwashed clothes. A man sat at the edge of a bench with a stack of tattered papers. Deeds and legal writs. Probably not worth the paper they were printed on. A tradesman of some kind paced the floor holding a wrapped box, a present no doubt for the First Ear. A poor man's bribe. More than he had.

There were not a few there with envelopes from the archbishop, red warrants like the one tacked on the Yelkin door. The emergency over, these warrants now could be fought in the courts with favor and influence. Perhaps with a word from the First Ear, life and property could be saved. For some. These were the lucky ones, the people who'd not been caught, not been found at home when Connor's guards served the writ.

A woman come late kept drawing Morgan's attention. She was in her mid-twenties, later perhaps, with a babe in arms. It fussed and stirred and she fed it in turns, pacing among the supplicants to quiet its cries. Each coo and cry from the babe sent chills through Morgan's brain as he recalled the tearful farewell on that far-off shore, his daughter's face weak from labor, fearful and pale, her newborn, just days old, sleeping in her arms.

The door opened and a page stepped out. The people parted for the young official and silenced their whispers while he delivered a note to a waiting clerk, and, without waiting for response, returned the way he came.

The clerk opened the letter and read it. He looked up from his chair at the faces all turned to him and spoke. "Sir Edward is arrived. He has but one hour today. Urgencies of state compel him to be brief."

The clerk drew a finger down a list. "Mr. Morgan, go in."

Morgan walked briskly to the door. It opened as he reached it.

A page waited for him there and led him down a windowless white hall, bright with new glowglobes. At an open door on the right the page gestured Morgan to step through.

Sir Edward Kesey, First Ear of the queen, sat serenely behind an empty desk, a large window overlooking the inner court behind him. Seven other men were in the room besides: two more pages, a valet, and three armed guards, two by the door who'd stood behind him once Morgan entered, and one on the side of the Ear. A secretary sat with a clipboard in the corner, a quill in hand.

"Blessed be," said Sir Edward.

"And to thee, First Ear," said Morgan. He was surprised to see Kesey extend his hand to him but regained himself to take it and shake it strongly as he once had.

"How is it I may help you?" Kesey said, gesturing to a chair.

"Sir," said Morgan, "we have met before. I am Alpin Morgan. I was to be governor of the Crown's colony on Tirgwenin."

Kesey looked surprised and stared hard at Morgan's face. "Aye, I do remember you," he said. "You suffered trouble, I hear."

"Aye."

"And you fled the colony."

"Nay, sir," said Morgan. "That is a story spun by my enemies. My people – our people, on Tirgwenin – asked me to return to seek relief for them. A crime has been committed against us and I myself have been slandered. But I am not here for that. Not here for myself. I seek only the means to help them."

Morgan's reputation had been destroyed before he had even arrived back on Enskari. He'd been branded a coward, an incompetent leader, and a liar. It had poisoned all his efforts in court and favor.

"Was not that Sir Ethan Sommerled's charter you worked under?"

"Aye, sir."

"Why not approach him?"

"He is otherwise engaged," said Morgan. "And if I may speak freely, we colonists are Bucklers and some considered us treasonous during this recent time of war."

It was the obvious truth. Best to clear it now.

"I appreciate you having such regard for his position," said Kesey.

"He is a great man," said Morgan simply.

"And you were a man of some standing as well, if I remember?"

"I have suffered reverses, Your Eminence."

"And what can I do?"

"It is a simple affair," he said. "I arranged and resupplied rescue ships for the colonists on Tirgwenin."

"Did you land without plan for resupply?"

"It was all arranged, sir, but we did not land where we thought we would. We were, in fact, landed by a scurrilous captain hundreds of kilometers away from our true destination, in the very grip of an enemy."

He regretted his words even as he uttered them but they spilled out as if from a broken bottle.

Kesey's face twisted up in incredulity. "Were you not under Captain Upor? Admiral Aderyn's man?"

Morgan felt sweat run down his back, saw his hands begin to shake. "The same," he said then added, "forgive me and my…interpretations. I speak of how things appear from my position – but this is all water under a bridge. Sir. The matter before us is my ships." Afraid the Ear might cut him off, he explained quickly all in a single breath. "They were commandeered into the defense fleet before the battle began, only hours before they were to fly. Unarmed and fully laid on with supplies, they never left lee orbit and have languished there since. I received some promise from the Second Ear that they would be returned to me after the threat, and yet they have not been. They are the sum of all my efforts, all the wealth and privilege I once had."

"You have seen Sir Nolan?"

Morgan clenched his hands in fists and tried to hide them beneath his coat. "Aye, sir. Before the battle I had an interview."

"Why not return to him now about this matter?"

"Sir," Morgan said carefully, "I do not believe it is in his interest to see me again."

"He is a busy man, as am I," said Kesey. "Speak plain. What would you have me do?"

"Use your position – now that the threat is past – to release my ships. That is all."

"What are they?"

"They are the *Oracle* and the *Pitt*. Captain John Kebra is the master of the *Oracle*. I believe the captain of the *Pitt* has left his charge. I'm not sure who pilots that. I have had no word from them in months."

Sir Edward glanced at a page, who turned and left the room through a side door.

"Wait in the hall," he said to Morgan. "I might be able to answer you directly."

"Blessed be," said Morgan. Tears filled his eyes and blurred his vision.

He reached forward to shake the man's hand, but it wasn't offered this time. He bowed and said, "Blessed be to thee, sir."

"And to thee."

Morgan sat in the white hallway with trembling fingers as other pages brought other supplicants in and out of the Ear's office. Most came and left, but some were seated like him. They kept their distance from each other as if engulfed in their own tragedy and needing space for it.

Officials and courtiers moved past them, disappearing and reappearing through other doors, none paying them any regard.

From down the far hall came a message boy. He walked quickly, inspecting the people waiting in the hall, and then stopped before Morgan. "Are you the man called Morgan?" he asked.

"Aye."

"Follow me." The boy ushered him through a door that led down another hallway. "On the right just there, sir," said the page before turning on his heels and going.

Morgan clenched his fists and knocked on the door.

It opened immediately and a man stood before him. "Come," he said, pulling Morgan inside.

It was a small closet, a single settee, two chairs, and a carved table before a wall with a tall but narrow window diffusing outside smoggy light through sheer dingy drapes. It was a simple but a serviceable interview room. A door led out the back. The man gestured for Morgan to sit, but himself remained standing.

Morgan had not seen him before. Not in Kesey's office, not in the foyer, not in the hallway. He'd have noticed. The man was Hyraxian. His dark hair and stout stature could be from nowhere else. He was dressed in the clothes of a functionary: not a noble, but neither a peasant. No rank or purpose could be identified by his clothing, foreign or not.

"You are a minister?" said the Hyraxian.

"Not of your church."

"Nay," said the stranger, "and not of theirs." He cocked his head toward the door. "I am called Jasso. Captain Jasso. I am attached to the embassy. That is why I am allowed here. Just here. In these low bureaucratic hallways."

"Blessed be," said Morgan, not knowing what else to say.

"And to thee." Jasso bowed politely, if a little stiffly. "I'll make this quick," he said. "I was just in the naval office seeking word of some ships of ours when I overheard a page ask about rescue ships bound for Tirgwenin."

"What of it?"

"You won't like the news," he said.

"What have you done?"

Jasso smiled coldly. "Not us, minister. Nay, not Hyrax. Not us at all."

Morgan shook his head and hid his hands in his pockets.

"There is a new situation," Jasso said. "Not war, not peace. I won't pretend to understand it, but I am no fool, and this chance meeting might prove fruitful. I cannot make promises, but enemies of enemies and all that."

"What enemies?"

"The enemies that told my prince where to find your colony on Jareth's World. At Rodawnoc, am I right?"

Morgan's jaw fell slack.

"I see that I am. But we have done nothing about it. Enskari can do its own executions."

"I don't believe you."

"Minister, we had other uses for ships than sending them to that savage hellhole. We have not harmed your people. Yet."

"My God...."

"Calm down," said Jasso. "I meant only that I am not in charge of these things. I am but a lowly captain."

"I don't believe that," said Morgan.

Jasso smiled. "We've already spoken too long. Here's my card." He offered it to him and when he didn't take it, reached out and pulled Morgan's shaking left hand out of his pocket and thrust it inside it. "Perhaps we may exchange favors. Perhaps not. What harm can taking a card do?"

"From a Hyraxian agent? Plenty. I'm already—"

"Of course. Thus this discreet location."

"You're the enemy," he said.

"Minister, it is your queen and her archbishop and not my prince and prophet that have rained death upon Enskari."

Morgan put the card in his pocket with trembling fingers.

"Go, Minister. Blessed be."

"Aye."

Morgan returned to his seat in the hall and had barely sat down when another page called his name.

"Alpin Morgan?"

"I am here," he said, feeling a century old.

He followed the page back to Kesey's office.

The desk had papers on it now; some were clean and white and looked newly scribed, others were red and dangerous. Not offered a seat, Morgan stood by the chair he'd been in before.

"Mr. Morgan," said Kesey, not looking up from a paper he held in his hand. "It seems that your ships have been sent to Maaraw." He sounded out the name as he read. "Iq-ui-a-ni, to be precise. There's an elevator there apparently."

"What?"

"By necessity and command of the queen. Your ships were re-commandeered."

"I don't understand."

"There is trouble there. They needed supplies. Since your ships were handy and already loaded, they were sent."

"Nay…." Morgan fell into the chair. "It is worse than I feared. Nay nay nay…."

"We tried to find you, but could not," said Kesey, finally looking up from the paper. "We assumed…." His eyes fell on one of the red warrants. "Well, no matter there. It is done."

Clouds formed outside the Ear's window. The daily smog was gathering. Silent flashes of lightning caught on wires behind the soot. Morgan stared into the auburn cloud like it held an answer.

"Here." Kesey handed him an envelope.

"What is this?"

"It is a compensation certificate."

Morgan opened it and found the amount. It was a fraction of what he'd spent, what he'd need to spend again. It was compensation only for supplies. No consideration for the hire of the ships, the deposit, the crew, or time. Just money for grain and salt, nails, tack, and canvas.

"Blessed be," said Kesey as dismissal. "Good luck."

Morgan stood up but his eyes were fixed away.

"I understand you've had a run of bad luck, but perk up, and don't be paranoid," said Kesey. "Blaming other people for your own problems is a sign of weak character."

Morgan stared through the window behind the Ear, seeing a hundred kilometers off, seeing the dead boy in the Yelkins' doorway, the gap where his eye had been, feeling the blood sticking to his trembling fingers. Then he focused a thousand thousand more across space, past this glowering stare of a man who would not help, to a family he had to save. By any means.

CHAPTER SEVEN

The War of the Three Horses (155–159 NE) was the first and possibly most important political struggle in the history of Hyrax. The settlers of that world, still recovering from the landing crash and the loss of machinery, faced famine as population increased dramatically, as intended, but without the expected technology to feed them, which the architects of the Unsettling had relied upon in their planning. Social order had been kept by a corporate committee consisting of the three corporate powers who'd built the ship that had brought them from Old Earth. With the dissolution of the committee in 155, the War of the Three Horses ensued along corporate allegiances with each power vying against the other two for dominance.

For the next five years, pitched battles and bloody skirmishes were fought across the most densely populated continent, Konti. The war killed between fifteen per cent and thirty per cent of the planet's total population before DST defeated the other two factions at the Battle of Bannat.

The war is particularly notable for three key historical events.

First, the War of the Three Horses saw the end of gunpowder use on Hyrax. Last among the civilized worlds to outlaw the substance, it was finally deemed 'too dangerous to keep' after the Conflagration of Toseria (156 NE) when an electrical storm ignited a store of warehoused munitions, nearby caches, loaded cannon, and even individual weapons across an entire garrison, wiping it out and destroying the surrounding town, killing five and thirty thousand Saved.

Second, due to losses of personnel, particularly among the leading classes, rank and file soldiers rose to become commissioned officers, then knighted nobles, and so aristocrats, making the war the greatest social strata realignment in the planet's history until modern times.

Third, and surely related to the second, was the frequent and notorious changing of allegiances among the warring forces. Whole battalions would switch sides mid-battle, companies, platoons, and individuals defected to one army and then another, seeking the favor of a new consortium.

When the war was over DST made attempts to restore the original class order, punish its enemies and those who it saw as disloyal. However, these efforts were quickly abandoned in the face of overwhelming unpopular opinion. During reconstruction, however, DST showed a decided favoritism to certain houses, old and new, who'd remained loyal to their cause.

Our System: A Survey of Coronam Civilization
Chapter Fifteen: A History of Hyrax
By Dantes Moran, published Claremond, 920 NE

26, Ninth-Month, 938 NE – Jaletta, on Terel, Hyrax

Her ticket had been purchased with cash by an agent hired by a third party under the name of Lady Ava Clegg. To fit the part, Lady Vanessa Possad had altered her fashion, lowering the quality while raising the pretentiousness, until she stank of new aristocracy with cloying perfume and poor taste. Her lipstick was too bright, her cheeks a color just a step out of a brothel, her hair carefully done in last year's style. Rather than forge papers, she traveled without any, claiming to have lost them to a pickpocket. Her real documents had been sent ahead with her actual baggage in a plain pine crate to be picked up at her hotel when she arrived in Nutamanca.

She could not travel without baggage and so had assembled a collection to match her persona. Eight pieces, not including her travel bag and purse. Most were filled with lumber and rags, but her purse and travel bag were useful enough. Thus, by being obvious, she could pass unnoticed across a continent she'd never been to before.

Even this far from the capital, Hyrax reeled from the failed invasion of Enskari and the imminent counter-attack. People were fearful and suspicious, so she was careful and conscious of her role. Nouveau riche, the new nuisance class, was her cover. It offered her a unique invisibility. It was at once ostentatious and camouflaged. In the first train station in Jaletta, the real aristocracy ignored her with such rudeness she actually took offense, while the lower classes deferred so far that she couldn't get close enough to any to ask directions.

She'd finally cornered a porter who took her bags and directed her to the first-class lounge, where she had to show her ticket twice to the manager before he let her in.

There she'd found a seat alone and kept her nose in a book just to be safe. It was the book agreed upon and the title was clear in block silver type letters on the black leather cover, a dull historical survey, but a good signal and shield. Her recent ascent in Prince Brandon's court had brought her some notoriety, and though the chances of her being recognized in this backwater port city of the Hyrax's poorest continent were slim, they were not impossible. If she were recognized by someone, a courtier or a servant, she'd prepared a story to explain her presence: a secret liaison with a married ship's captain. The captain she'd name was dead, his destroyer torn in half by Sommerled's fleet three hours off Enskari, but he'd been of high enough station to justify the tryst, and news of casualties were sufficiently delayed to make her story a tragedy instead of a crime. She'd use this story if she were found out before her task. If she were to be identified after it, she'd simply have to kill whoever it was that recognized her.

In the last week, she'd sent three missives to Nolan Brett, the Enskari spymaster. Each contained sensitive and accurate information, news of the fleet, ships accounted for and lost, tonnage and morale. Weather reports. She included her most recent accounts from court, the mood and direction along with observations traveling across the planet to keep her appointments here. These she sent to the enemy of her world. They meant instant death if discovered, but somehow she felt the danger inherent in her spying a small thing compared to the hazards of her personal quest.

She'd been careful but not invisible. She'd been bold for this adventure. She'd bribed and borrowed, traded on information and favors, spent lavishly from her credit accounts filled with laundered Enskaran money, all just to glimpse a single trivial letter sent to a dying courtesan at the court of Almuda. In it she found an obscure reference that suggested a possibility for a little family get-together, which put her on this train.

Jaletta was a rich town, as was Nutamanca. The places between were farms, ranches, and forgettable. Jaletta was a fishing village that became fashionable due to its distance and clean air. Without heavy industry, there were few lightning strikes, and the vistas atop the coastal mountains inspired painters and avant-garde writers. Thus publicized in galleries and salons half a world away, the little town became an artists' haven and an aristocratic retreat. Nutamanca, the capital of Terel, was past its prime, the lead mines spent, but the money lingered on. The train, therefore, that connected these two places was opulent, well tended, civilized, and discreet.

Through a window she watched as porters carried in the train's provisions. Why should a little thing like an interplanetary war get in the way of luxury? It was a planetary tour on the loading dock. She saw crates of pruned Enskaran redgrape beside baskets of local strawberries. Silangian thunderfish on ice, flavored vinegars in Temple casks, branded bacon and whole sides of beef from Maaraw. Barrels of Lavlandian table wines under cases of Claremondian champagne. Feasts for a month, supplied for a fifteen-hour trip.

The second- and third-class cars were already boarding. At that end, there were no dining cars. Food would come from vendors who leased space in the crowded compartments and would raise their prices between stops and charge more for water than grog, knowing that the grog drinkers would need water later.

Already fights were breaking out for seats and baggage space in the lower-class cars. Few who traveled so poorly could afford the small cargo rate for their belongings and so carried their squalid things with them in their arms. Packed thick to begin with, baskets and bags pushed people to the limits.

A wall of soldiers along a low barricade separating the classed cars watched the ruckus but did nothing. Finally, a handful of nightstick-wielding policemen in tan uniforms broke up the dispute with kicks and blows. The screams carried all the way into the lounge.

Two marine officers in their blue-and-black uniforms but different unit insignia regarded the scuffle with practiced poise.

"What savages," said one to the another. "I wouldn't use such garbage to dig latrines."

"Did you see what caused it?" said the other, a decorated lieutenant with a medal of honor and sharpshooting badge. She didn't see any decorations on the other.

"What need they of cause? They're animals. Look at them. Filthy things. See how they crowd into that car? Have they no dignity? They're worse than dogs."

"I've trained worse to be soldiers. Good soldiers."

The first scowled at his companion. "Oh, that's right. Your family used to train dogs while mine was running a county. You're bred for it. Breeding tells all."

"You would know the worth of a true soldier if you'd ever fought. What is it you do? Clerk? Bookkeeping? Latrine digger?"

"Quartermaster corps," said the first through gritted teeth. "We—"

"Paper cuts are different than those from sabers," interrupted the decorated soldier. "Though I suspect the infection rate is higher in your case."

"You lowborn upstart—"

Their argument ceased when a conductor and an engineer entered the lounge. The soldiers retreated to opposite ends of the room.

The conductor looked like a ship's captain in his blue uniform with gold braid and round hat. The engineer wore white coveralls with the name of the engine, *The City of Tipp,* embroidered on his breast. His collar was adorned with the gold initials of the Hyraxian Royal Railroad.

They waited until their presence drew the attention of the room, then the conductor said with a low bow, "Ladies and gentlemen, you are invited to board the train."

Lady Vanessa heard the announcement with alarm. She'd expected to find her man here but he had not appeared. Somewhere, she had miscalculated.

None of this class were in a hurry. The men tipped their last drinks while the women adjusted bonnets, put away needlepoint, all careful to show that they moved because they wished to, not because a conductor had summoned them.

Slowly too, she collected her things – her small handbags, hatbox, and parasol – considering whether to carry on to Jaletta or return to the capital, when she saw him.

He looked like his nephew, narrow eyes, high cheekbones, the jet-black hair of Hyraxian descent. He was eight and sixty years but had kept himself well. He sported a mustache that harkened back to the previous century.

He was accompanied by a large man who seemed to be both a valet and bodyguard, armed with a sword at his hip and a pistol in a holster.

They hurriedly boarded the train.

Hearing her heart in her ears, Lady Vanessa found her compartment without assistance and locked the door. Through a crack in her window, she smelled the engine grease and the coal smoke. She thought she could make out the odors of rich cologne and boot polish among the frying fish and unwashed babies. She closed the window and pulled the shades.

Her information was right. He was on the train. The rest checked out too. He was traveling light, only the single servant. He was going all the way to Nutamanca, because there was nowhere else on the line that a man of his royal blood would be going.

Just to be safe, she wouldn't delay. Her information was incomplete; she did not know what his business was. She'd assumed a family visit, but was distrustful of that. Such a visit would suggest intimacy, fondness, and warmth. She couldn't see that family in those lights.

She probably should have checked with the others the day before, but in the heat of the wet moment, she had let the chance slip. She missed an opportunity there, but not her target.

She felt the train move. A sudden tug and a pause. The grind of steel on steel, a rumble and a stretch before the forward-heaving roll indicating they were off.

The salon was open now for drinks, but a meal was still hours away. She settled in to wait, thinking she might try to get a nap, but knowing she couldn't sleep. Instead she watched the landscapes, wild and dry, fly by her window as stars slowly appeared.

At dinner, she took a seat near the door in the corner. She ordered the bloom quail, from behind her book.

The first-class dining car filled with the same lack of urgency the train had – a slow promenade of the upper classes. Curtsies and bows, calm smiles as everyone measured themselves against everyone else. Fans a-flutter, ruffles riffling.

She herself was left alone, ostracized, her book and carefully uncomfortable fashion granting her that privilege.

Her food arrived and she poked it around her plate, eating only as much as she dared on her churning stomach.

She was contemplating dessert to buy time when the bodyguard valet finally appeared.

He stood in the door beside her and surveyed the room. Only at the end of his second sweep did he notice her. His eyes fell on her book cover for just an instant and his jaw tightened.

She felt the rush of nerves, adrenalin, and fear, and hoped it didn't show in her cheeks.

She lowered her book to her lap, reached into her purse, and took out a small black velvet bag, which she wrapped in her napkin. When the man was facing her direction – not looking at her, just facing – she dropped the napkin on the floor.

"Madam," said he, bending down and picking it up. "Allow me to fetch you a new napkin."

A waiter was already there and gave her a fresh one before he could speak another word about it.

"Thanks," she said with a twang in her speech. A nearby duchess winced when she heard it.

The man clicked his heels and followed the waiter to the kitchen car, her napkin in his pocket.

She ordered the sherbet for appearance but hardly had a bite. When she thought she could, she finally retired to her locked compartment and waited.

An hour later a note slid under her door, reading simply in bold letters: *A-6*.

This was the receipt for the five and thirty thousand dollars she'd put in the bag with the other thing four weeks before. Now she would test the famous Hyraxian loyalty, and bet her life on its caprice.

Outside, the landscape was a desolate gray-green, a pale desert lit by the auroras creeping over the horizon. Clean air and clear. Hypnotic vistas, ghostly and alive. She watched it for an hour darkening, waiting for things to take effect and for her courage to rise. Then she arranged herself and left for the *A* carriage.

No one challenged her as she moved through the narrow passageways. Porters rushed by, apologizing for being there, burdened with extra pillows and blankets, bedding down the passengers for the bulk of the ride across the continent.

She found A-6 and without hesitation opened the door and slipped inside.

"Madam," said a deep voice to her, "you have entered the wrong compartment. Why was it unlocked?"

"Nay," she said. "I seek you, Count Drust."

"You are Lady Ava Clegg, are you not?"

"And how would you know that?"

"My man Daniel mentioned you," he said.

Her stomach tensed. "What did he say?"

"Only that he thought you recognized me at the station, though to be honest I don't remember seeing you there." He surveyed her traveling dress, pausing for some time on her décolletage.

"Where is your man now?" she asked.

"I sent him to bed."

She locked the door.

"I don't think I know your family," said the count. "You come from new money?"

The bunk had been pulled down, the bed turned out. There was a glass of brandy on the little table by the window to Drust's right.

He gestured her to the bench beside him with a pat on the cushion.

"Enjoying exile?" she asked.

"Exile? Nay, I just want to stay out of my nephew's way. Court life is too full of intrigue."

"Are you not in disfavor?"

"A family quarrel. A trifle. Quite forgotten."

"You're returning to court, then?"

He swirled his brandy glass and sniffed before saying, "I have nothing against new money. If the old were any good, they'd have kept it."

"Is there any brandy left in the bottle?" she asked.

"Just a sip." He emptied the flask into his glass and offered it to her.

She shook her head.

He shrugged and gulped down his. "Not the way to drink brandy," he said. "But damned if this bottle isn't about to go off."

She grinned and relaxed a little. She sat down on the bench beside him but kept a little distance between them.

The count looked at the space and shook his head.

"You intrigue me, Lady Ava. I would know you better."

"I'm not as I appear, but you are much as I expected."

"What do you know of me?"

"You are Count Benjamin Drust, uncle of the ruling monarch, Prince Brandon Drust. One of only three surviving named heirs of the House Drust."

"Three?" he said. "Nay, there are five."

She folded her hands in her lap.

"There is myself, and Brandon of course, Eric his brother, Lady Sekari, my niece who'll pass the title to her son, Troy, if it falls to her, and cousin Shad."

"Shad died last month," she said.

"What?"

"The reports said it was a mugging in Caporto. It happened in front of a whorehouse. Two in the morning. He was stabbed seven and thirty times before his throat was opened from ear to smug ear and he bled out in the gutter. His royal blood mixed with the waste from the brothel on its way to the sewer."

"Oh, aye," he said. "I do remember that. Terrible thing. I don't know how I…was it seven and thirty? I didn't know that."

"Aye," she said.

"Who are you?"

"I am not as important as you, Count." She smiled.

He leaned back and nearly fell off the bench. He caught himself on the table with his hand. When he'd righted himself, he looked at his fingers, flexing them deliberately in front of his face.

"You are not in favor at court," she said. "Brandon thinks you a threat."

"You are an assassin for Brandon," he said.

"Nay. Put that right out of your mind, Count."

He smacked his lips. "I am no threat."

"It is not the future I wish to address," she said. "But the past."

"Who—"

"Three," she said. "You, Eric, and Brandon himself."

"Lady Sekari," he said, his speech slurred. "I just left her."

"She drowned yesterday with her son, Troy. Very tragic," she said. "Jaletta has a vicious undercurrent."

He shook his head, whether it was to deny the news or shake himself alert, she couldn't be sure.

"Her body will wash up soon. Or not. Her brat will not ascend."

"Who are you?"

"Vengeance."

He looked at her dumbly. His eyes fixed on her eyes now, not her breasts.

"Do you remember the wool future scandal of 927?"

He shook his head again, slowly, laboriously. His hand slid off the table and onto his lap.

"It really began in twenty-three," she said. "Wool was the export of the planet. It was because of its fine gloss. Your waistcoat is made of it, bleached and dyed, but the same stuff."

He looked down at his vest and then back at her.

"The price went up consistently. Futures rose, people invested.

Millionaires were made overnight. Get rich quick. Speculation was everywhere. None of this rings a bell?"

He opened his mouth, but shut it again.

"It was a bubble," she said. "That's a term economists use. Bubble. As in something that has to pop. People were trading on wool that wouldn't be produced for generations. The bubble expanded and threatened to burst more than once. One was stopped when Drust and his cabinet allowed partial shares. The price of a single wool future was out of reach for anyone save the most wealthy, but partial shares allowed not only the middle classes but also the poorer ones to invest. The bubble grew."

She felt the train slow. An even braking to minimize the disruption along the sleeping car. She didn't know the name of the stop, just that it was one of eight the train would make before dawn.

"Excuse me." She leaned over and pulled the blind down over the window, brushing her breasts against the count's face.

He didn't move.

She sat back on the bench a little more spread out than before – more comfortable, taking up more space than a lady should. She looked at the count and sighed. "I am getting better at this," she said. "My breathing is steady, is it not?"

"You are very calm," he said.

"I am not Lady Ava Clegg. She's not even real. I made her up."

"I see," he muttered. "Again, who are you?"

"I am Lady Vanessa Possad," she said.

"The courtier?"

"You know me?"

"By name only." His words came thick and slow.

"That is a little troubling, but no matter," she said. "The bubble."

"Aye, the bubble. Your family invested?"

"Assuredly so. Everyone did. It was the fashion. Nay, it was the *duty* of all Hyrax to invest. The king made it so."

"Brandon?"

"Andreas, the old king. Your brother."

"Aye."

"The bubble burst," she said and made a pop with her lips.

"Wait, wait," said the count. "I recall. There was relief."

"A bailout."

"Aye," he said. "The treasury was sorely put upon, but the crisis was averted."

"My family comes from old blood," she said. "First arrivals. We can trace our line back to Old Earth. We were not noble at landing but made so for our service in the Three Horses. We were loyal."

He shook his head and it moved as though it were heavy upon his shoulders.

"We never forgot our roots. We ruled a province for hundreds of years. We were very popular. The people trusted us and would do as we asked. My father asked them to invest as was his duty when Andreas bade him to do so. Then the bubble popped and all the province was bankrupt."

"The relief…."

"Only extended to noble houses."

He looked at her, not understanding.

"I can see the disconnect," she said. "It is endemic to your class and family. My father would not bear the shame of it."

"What shame?"

"I was but eight years old. I forced my tutor to explain it all to me, to make charts and make plain why my father was so unhappy, teach me what was happening. I'm sure my parents would have objected. But no matter. I was made to understand, yet I could do nothing. Then."

She rubbed her eyes as if staring into the past like this had taxed and dried them.

"I thought like you," she said. "We were fine. The treasury had made up our losses. Not all of them, but most. Silangian silver was plentiful and never-ending. The king spent lavishly so his friends didn't suffer."

"It could have toppled the throne," he said.

The complete sentence raised caution in her and she studied him for a moment, confirming his lethargy before she went on.

"I asked him. 'Father,' said I, 'why are you troubled?'

"'Because, my child, they trusted me and they are ruined.'

"'Who? The peasants?'

"'You're too little,' he told me, 'to understand the debt we owe them.'

"'We owe them?' I asked him.

"'Aye. It has been our family honor to protect them. We are elevated to our station not for us, but for them.'

"'We have our title and lands from the king and birthright,' I said.

"He shook his head. 'That is a fiction.'

"I became indignant. 'Father, they are dirty peasants, they can barely read,' said I.

"He caressed my hair then. I remember it clearly. He bent down, took a knee, and looked me straight in the face. 'Do you know I was chided for letting them read?'

"'Letting them read?' I said, surprised. 'We require it.'

"He raised a finger to his lips and winked. 'Our secret,' he said. There was a tear in his eye."

"Bleeding-heart class traitor," mumbled the count.

"Thank you," said Lady Possad. "I was beginning to pity you. It will be easier now."

His chest bounced in a laugh or a cough. One hiccup only, and then fell to shallow breathing.

The train took a turn and she felt herself pushed back. She hadn't noticed it leave the last station but they were well under way now. Another curve and another jostling. The count slid down a little on the bench, his eyes betraying his weakness, his hands unable to pull him back up.

She went on. "Letters arrived, people tried to see my father, to beg or accuse. He wouldn't see them or read the letters. Maybe he read a few of the early ones, but the stack I saw on his desk afterwards was tall and unopened."

Her throat dry, she poured herself a glass of water from the minibar.

"I should have drunk out of there," slurred the count. "Thought it would be too expensive."

"Always the cheapskate," she said. "And, of course, you should have paid your man better. I bought him cheaply and by mail."

"The brandy? I thought it tasted off."

"And yet you drank it anyway,"

He laughed and it turned to another cough, which turned to a gurgle, a wheeze, and back to slow labored breathing.

She swallowed her water and poured another glass, drank half of it.

"My mother explained it," she said. "After."

He stared at her, his eyes unblinking but shining still.

"My father wrote to the king and told him that he was going to give his money to the destitute of his province, those tricked and scammed in the bubble. The king forbade it. He sent a direct royal decree forbidding him from doing as he wanted with his assets. 'Bad precedent,' we were told."

"He killed himself," said the count. "With a pistol. I remember."

She nodded. "In the stable, so as not to stain the furniture."

"Coward."

"Before his blood was dry, my mother sold all we had to the auctioneers and gained control of the money. There was no decree naming her. She gave it all to the people, about every penny we had. She didn't have to. No one saw that coming. No one thought a woman would do that, would have that kind of moral courage. She followed my father's wishes, did the deed he could not. She sacrificed the House Possad for what was right. Thus, we were bankrupted. We were still ennobled, ranked and aristocrat, but we were broke. A fallen house."

"Father…betrayed…family."

"My father's family was bigger than just us three. My mother's larger than just us two. Mine, I'm figuring out, but I know who it doesn't include."

"You…doing…all right now," he said.

"My dowry bought me an education. The rest I did myself with a little help from new friends."

"Fool…."

"My father had to die to do the right thing, my mother had to sacrifice everything – all because House Drust wouldn't let a good man fight against a crooked system, not even a little bit."

"Traitors."

She kicked him, not softly, and he slid farther down the bench until he was mostly on the floor, his head resting on the cushion.

"Fallen house," she said. "That's what we became. One of the highborn brought low. Impoverished aristocracy given one generation of manners to redeem ourselves."

She carefully wiped the lipstick off her glass. "Your family destroyed mine," she said. "Seems like the least I can do is repay the favor. After you, there are only two left. My family will outlive yours."

She bent low over him to listen to his last shallow breaths. "I'm going to extinguish you, Drust. Your whole line shall be deleted. This is my mission. My life's work. For the good of the species, I shall erase you."

For an answer, through his slack drooling mouth, there was a gurgle in the back of his throat.

She smiled.

"You will be found in the morning. An old man dead of a heart attack. Nothing flamboyant. If any suspect foul play, they'll put it on your nephew and his sympathizers. Your family has no loyalty."

His eyes flashed to something on the wall.

She followed his glassy gaze to an attaché case beneath his hat. She pulled it down and feeling no hurry – she was an aristocrat on a train, after all – she went through the contents. She rifled through newspapers and investment reports, an engraved pistol, a bottle of aphrodisiac potion she knew to be bogus but expensive, a box of white powder that would get a commoner hanged. Telegrams and train schedules. And then she found something interesting; a small letter tightly folded, expensive paper, a cracked seal of wax bearing the Drust crest.

Dear Uncle, The people have never been more ready. The indignity of the armada's defeat was the final straw. Now is the time. I have the fifth army behind me. We need only vacate the chair for us to be elevated. Contact me when you are placed and we will proceed.

It was signed only with the initials *E.D.* but it could be none other than Eric Drust, the king's younger brother.

There was a second note in the same envelope, written by another hand and unsigned. It was a list of names – courtiers, nobles, and officers she knew from court. Those who had frequent access to the prince were circled. Hers was among them.

She read the first letter again and clicked her tongue.

"Now here's some family loyalty," she said.

Piled on the floor, the count stared into space with cold, glassy eyes, unmoving, lifeless, and dead.

She waved the letter in front of his face. "And then there was one," she said.

CHAPTER EIGHT

A working-class citizen, toiling to pay bills, appease creditors, provide for his family, is just as much a slave as one owned by a single master. It is only a difference in shares of his life. In both cases his work is stolen, its value underrated, and the difference between worth and pay is absorbed by the wealthy to make their wealth even greater. It is theft. It is immoral and a disgrace. It is servitude hidden under a blanket of normalcy and inevitability that an impressed slave doesn't suffer from. As such, such a deluded slave requires less effort to keep in line and more work to enlighten.

Jareth, *Notes on the Modern Economy*
Flame Tree Press, New York, 2328

12, Tenth-Month, 938 NE – Slaafaw, Maaraw

A bullet popped at their feet and spat stone dust into their eyes before they could duck for cover. The report came right after it.

"He's not too close," said Maylo from behind a cart, or rather the remains of one. "And he's not a great shot." He meant it to build up morale, but even in his ears it sounded like they'd just gotten lucky and luck was not something to rely upon.

"Can't see him," said Charlie. "But I bet he's on that roof there. The pub."

"Aye," said Maylo, reaching for his spyglass. "He'll be recharging. Who's got a line on it?"

"I have, Captain." It was Ursula. She was a crack shot with clear credit for eight and twenty kills, two for each of her fourteen years of life.

"Let's assume Charlie's right," said Maylo. "He usually is. Put a bead on that rooftop for when he peeks up again. Second squad, scope right.

First, left. Charlie with Ursula on the pub roof. Maybe that window there too."

"Aye, Captain," came the response.

Maylo didn't pull his rifle up as the others did but instead stared down the length of his scope. No one minded since he was a terrible shot. It was a poor trait for the commander of a revolutionary army, a position he'd earned by outliving the other commanders.

He glanced at Ursula, her hair pulled back in a bun, her tan face shining in the afternoon light, staring down the sights of her musket. She was beautiful, the flower of womanhood. A heartbreaker already, though still two years from majority. She might be too young to marry, but she was not too young to kill. And she was a killer. They all were.

His army, known only as the Liberators, had met little resistance so far. The bulk of defenders had all been pulled back to defend Iquiani, its elevator, and a large timber shipment meant for Hyrax, and another of corn for Enskari – hated rivals off-world, but all friends on Maaraw. It showed how little their enemy understood them that they thought the attack would be at Iquiani instead of Slaafaw. Slaafaw was the original slave port on Maaraw and though not as active now as Iquiani, for their cause it was more important than all the other ports combined. Economically it was not the prize Iquiani was, but symbolically it was unequalled. They were not playing for money, but for lives.

Three days prior, they'd entered the city in a rush. Just a few hundred of them had quickly pacified all the outlying suburbs, favelas, and camps, places where the locals lived and huddled, the natives staring in disbelief as their countrymen stood up to the off-worlders. The rich areas on the west fell just as fast. They'd expected a fight, but found whole neighborhoods empty of all but crying slaves, their masters having left them with the animals. They could see the fleeing ships on the horizon from the covered patios as they ransacked the mansions. The whole capture would have been over in a day had it not been for the fortified garrison in the town hall. It was only there that they met real resistance. Bow and flamer, musket and cannon. Snipers and supplies. It was anyone's guess who was in there; trained soldiers, off-world mercenaries, local zealots. Purgers.

Whoever it was had held out for three days already. Long enough for people to worry. Time enough for snipers to kill ten of them. Time enough for a relief column to be sent. Time enough for orbital assistance.

Three anchor lines had plumbed the sea that morning and another shook a field not ten kilometers from the town gates.

On the first day, the rebels had signaled the orbiting ships, suggesting that other ports might suit them better. Each, to a ship, had prudently cut their lines and were gone by the second day. They'd given them the time as a courtesy, but now there were four new lines, which augured true trouble, for they could be landing nothing but fighters.

Maylo had to commit a third of his forces to containing the garrison, forces he could be using now to cut anchor lines, forces he'd need to fight off any landing yet to come. Forces that were being whittled down now by snipers believing relief was coming.

They'd taken a boat-mounted plasma saw from the harbormaster. It should have been on its way out to sea to cut the three anchor lines there, but he'd ordered it jury-rigged to a steam cart and moved here to melt out the garrison. He'd been told it would take half a day to mount, and another half to move into position, provided there was a position to move it to. And all the while the clock was ticking. Their tenuous hold on the city weakened with each hour the garrison held out and the lines touched the sky.

Taking Slaafaw was a great idea, one that had been born at the very beginning of the movement. They'd dreamed of this moment, waited and maneuvered, and then struck. It had been a good plan, but now it hung on a knife's edge because of a reinforced building they should have known about.

Knowing the importance of situation and symbol, Maylo personally took charge of the situation, placing himself at the front line, where all the costs for freedom were paid in blood. It was perilous, but in all honesty, he didn't mind. He welcomed the chance for death. It would remove from him the terrible responsibility he carried as Andre Bruin's replacement.

A Maarawan man – tan and bearded – peeked over the lip of the pub's roof. His head exploded in a cloud of pink mist as Maylo jumped from the hypersonic boom of the killing shot. A musket tumbled three stories down to crash upon the cobblestones.

"Nine and twenty," said Ursula. "I don't suppose I can go up there and get his ammo, can I?"

Claps and cheers from the Liberators.

Maylo looked into the young face of Ursula, bright with accomplishment, and forced himself to smile. "Well done," he said. "Sure. We'll head up and take the ammo. We need all we can get."

"Nice," said Ursula, reloading her gun. It was a half meter taller than she was. She giggled as she slid in the slug and wound the cylinder for another shot.

"We shouldn't be far from second platoon," said Charlie. "Third has the other side."

"Right, right," said Maylo. "And it's eighteen hours before elevators land?"

"Soonest," said Charlie. "Best guess."

A day for the cutter to arrive, at least a day to remount it on a tugboat. How long would they have to cut?

An old woman in a shawl, her face lined with wrinkles, her eyes clouded gray, pulled open the drapes in a window behind Charlie.

Maylo's lieutenant spun around and leveled his pistol at it.

"Nay! Nay! Don't shoot me," said the woman, raising her arms. "I only want to see."

"You have a taste for death?" said Maylo.

"What? Nay. Nay. I want to see Maaraw standing on its feet. I want to see you drive the bastards out."

"Can you see with those eyes?" asked Charlie, lowering his gun.

"Enough to see a new day," she said.

"Stay inside, Mother."

"You are Xoan Maylo." It was not a question.

"Just Maylo," he said.

"You stand now for Bruin," she said. "Is it a weight?"

He tried to read her clouded eyes, to see if she were testing him or teasing him. He could see nothing there. Glancing at the room beyond, he saw shelves of jarred herbs and woven silks, pots and baskets, colorful and native.

"Shopkeeper?" he said for something to say.

"Aye."

"You are country born?"

"Born and raised in Vuyada."

"Is that far?"

"A world away," she said.

"Stay inside, Mother," he said. "And blessed be."

"And to thee, Maylo," replied she. "Be strong."

Maylo signaled first platoon to move forward.

Charlie raised an eyebrow and tilted his head to the old woman's shop.

Maylo shrugged, wondering how big the cart with the cutter would be.

Quickly and silently, they moved in two parallel columns, hugging the walls on either side of the lane, their heads pivoting up and around, surveilling for danger. Not all the people welcomed them. Not all were like the old woman. The dead sniper had been Maarawan.

They arrived at the pub front and Maylo signaled a halt. His squads took up defensive positions automatically.

Ursula knelt and examined the broken musket, shattered from its fall. She shook her head to Maylo and then glanced at the pub.

He nodded and signaled Charlie to come with them.

Cutlass drawn, Charlie kicked open the locked door and entered. Ursula came next, her gun ready but ill-suited for the tight fighting of an indoor battle. Maylo drew his pistol and realized it wasn't charged. He cranked it as the others moved on.

"Feel like a drink?" whispered Charlie. "Looks like they have redberry ale."

"Maybe later," said Maylo.

"Stairs here," said Ursula from the back wall.

Maylo knew they should search the whole building, every room and closet, but didn't have time. They were on a clock. Maylo had allowed this stop as a favor to Ursula, not knowing how else to thank her for giving up her childhood to a cause he no longer felt sure about.

Up they went.

The roof was arrayed as a patio: chairs, benches, even red checkered clothes on round tables.

A headless figure lay on its side. Ursula went straight to it, like it was a present to be opened.

Charlie pointed to the left to an open square and beyond that to a gray-block building.

"Had I known we were this close...." said Maylo.

"Aye," said Charlie. "Where's second platoon?"

"There." Maylo pointed to a far corner facing the square.

A figure holding binoculars to his face crouched behind a pile of rubble and waved.

"I think that's Luft," said Charlie.

"I think so too."

"That sniper couldn't have been up here very long," said Charlie. "Or Luft would have done something about it. Or the sniper him."

"Aye."

"Firebombs," said Ursula, looking into a rucksack. "Not homemade either. Enskaran, I think."

"Take them," said Maylo. "Leave nothing...dangerous."

"Leave nothing for an insurgency?" Charlie said.

"Right."

"The ammo is from Claremond," said Ursula. "The canteen's from here, though."

"Bully for the local economy." Maylo aimed his telescope at the garrisoned building.

It looked to have been made out of marble blocks, but that was only a veneer, the first ten centimeters or so. The marble, particularly around the door, had been shot away by Gauss fire, revealing a pockmarked composite metal barrier – ablative shielding. The kind of thing that protected spaceships against meteorites. It was at least a meter thick and had stopped all their small arms fire. Looking at the building now, Maylo thought it was obviously a bunker. Someone had planned ahead here.

"Who founded Slaafaw?" asked Maylo.

"We did. It was a fishing village."

"Don't be dense, Charlie. Who claims it?" He was embarrassed to have had to ask. He should have known.

"It was Lavlanders. For the slave trade."

"And how old, would you say, is that pillbox?"

"Goes back to the beginning."

"Before our cities were open to all their planets?"

"Oh, aye."

"So it wasn't meant to keep us out, but them."

"Always underestimating us," said Charlie.

"Luft is coming over."

"I'll bring him up."

"Nay, Charlie, stay with me. I want your eyes on this problem. Hey, Ursula."

The marksman looked up, her hands in the dead's man pockets. "Aye, sir?"

"Run down and bring Lieutenant Luft up here."

"Aye." She took up her musket and skipped back down the stairs.

Maylo studied the town hall, looking for angles. "Will the cutter burn that?" he asked.

"Definitely. Shouldn't take long at all."

"Really? What about the lines? Did not the harbormaster tell us that the cutter would take hours to cut one?"

"He lied. We could do it with a hardened steel cutter like they have in ships, but the pressures would need to be great."

"Uh-huh."

"Nanofilament crystalthread – anchor wire," he explained. "A tough animal, but not impossible."

"If you say so."

"Actually," said Charlie, "once we cut the first, we might be able to use that thread to cut the others."

"How do you know this?"

"Bruin told me."

"How'd he know?"

"Beats me. He knew some odd things."

That was something about Andre Bruin that Maylo couldn't explain either. The strange ex-slave trader who'd assumed the lead of their cause, grown it, driven it, was an enigma in death as he was in life. Before him, there'd been revolution coffee clubs, where ideas flourished but ended at the door. Maylo remembered the conversations, zeal and inaction. After they found Bruin, after the destruction of Coebler, it became a movement, and now an army. Bruin had led them mercilessly forward, driven by a moral authority that inspired and terrified friend and foe alike. It was like he could see into another place, hear voices from the past and almost communicate with the future. There was a desperate confidence about him. A nearly suicidal grasp of inevitability. He could sleep on a problem and awake with certain knowledge of a place or a coming storm, almost as if he'd telegraphed the question and the answer had come back in a dream. It was awesome. That was the only word to describe it, and those close to him used it among themselves in whispers and could only wonder. He was human. He was not perfect. They'd lost battles, lost men. He'd been betrayed and murdered. His final failure, his own capture and execution, had almost destroyed the movement. That it had not spoke to the man's influence even after death. Not for the first time, not even for the first time that hour, Maylo felt inadequate to the task his comrades had given him. Staring at the impregnable fortress, he again regretted accepting leadership. He thought perhaps after Slaafaw, if he survived, he might pass the lead to Luft. Explain and confess his cowardice. With any luck, he would be wounded and have an excuse. With a lot of luck, he would be killed and be freed of the struggle entirely.

"What's taking Luft so long?" Maylo said.

Still looking through the glass, Charlie said, "I think the door's got to be the weakest—"

The sound of shooting made them duck. The clash of swords beneath them made them run for the stairs. The roar of a flamer showed the portal in orange light and black smoke shadow.

More shots. Shouts and orders. The snick of a crossbow bolt, the clank of steel on steel, the chop of blade on flesh.

Ursula screamed.

They burst past, Maylo rushed inside, taking steps four at time, leaping to the next landing at a run.

The bar was on fire – tablecloths alight, a broken keg of spirits feeding the flames, which flowed like a snake from the bar.

Maylo saw three bodies on the floor near a back wall. Two were off-worlders, one was Maarawan. The local was a slave with a mark on his forehead just below the saber cut that had cleaved his skull. One of the foreigners was dressed in military livery and lay in an open door he hadn't noticed before.

Charlie plugged the keg.

"Where's Ursula?" said Maylo.

"That you, boss?" It was Luft from outside. "Get out, brother. The place is on fire."

"No kidding?" said Charlie.

"No kidding."

Charlie beat a burning table with his jacket. "We gotta put this out," he said. "Can't be burning down our city."

Luft and three others came inside.

"It's not our city yet." By the light of the burning beams, Maylo looked past the soldier to a descending stairway. "Who's hurt? What are our casualties? And where in the hell is Ursula?"

"Kim and Daniel didn't make it," said Luft. "The bastards grabbed Ursula and took her down there."

"What is this?" said Maylo, staring at the secret stairs.

"They're all over the place," said Luft. "They lead to city hall. This is the third we've found. There'll be more."

"So we can't even contain them in their bunker?"

Luft shook his head. "They're the guerrillas now."

"Explains how the sniper got up there without you seeing him," said Charlie.

"Sniper?"

Maylo shook with rage. He picked up Ursula's musket from the floor and remembered how she'd sought them out after a militia had burned her school. She'd had an old musket then, rusty but serviceable. She steadily upgraded her gear with each battle until she had this silver-embossed hunting gun bearing the initials *G.K.* in a Lavlandian crest. She'd liberated it from a plantation where it had never been fired. In her hands it had never missed.

He marched out of the pub as Luft piled up heavy crates to barricade the secret door. Soldiers of the Liberation waited and watched.

"She's fourteen years old!" Maylo screamed. "She shouldn't be here. None of us should. This is crazy. This is unfair."

Tears rolled down Maylo's face as he looked at his wounded men, blackened and charred. Their clothes burned off their bodies, their skin bubbled and scabbed from old blood and new.

"I'll be all right, Captain," said Charlie.

"Aye. Keep faith," said Luft, but lacking certainty.

"Maylo," came a raspy voice.

He turned to see the old woman from before. She was hunched over a gnarled cane, her fingers as knotty as the wood, her eyes as gray as the smoke pouring out the door of the pub.

"You're right," she said. "'Tis bad. And unfair. These are evil times. No doubt about it."

He knew the symptoms of shell shock as he reeled in body and mind.

"Maylo!" The old woman's sharp tongue recalled him to the street.

Tears rolled down his cheeks.

"Fourteen," he muttered.

"Times of change are not endured without suffering," said the woman. "You are here now and must act now. What would you do?"

Maylo faced the building in the square.

"They'll fight to the death," said the woman. "They were told to. Ordered to. The major – Traffen, his name is – made the order. Kill any man who surrenders. He thinks he's saving civilization."

"It's all right, Captain," said Charlie. "Luft and I can take this. Why not have a little nap. You haven't slept in three days." The last line he said loudly for the benefit of the listening troops.

"Millions of people were traded out of this town. Sold like pigs," said the woman. "Families split, backs broken. No choice for them. They suffered. We suffer. You suffer. End it. It is the way through."

"She suffers," said Maylo, thinking of Ursula in the fortified hall. Why would they take her except to interrogate her, torture her, rape her body until she was dead? It would not be the first time the militias of Maaraw had done such horrors. It was their hallmark. A terror to get the townspeople to stay in line, turn on the Liberators. Serve their oppressors out of fear.

A sonic boom shook the sky at the end of a whiplash.

"We cut an anchor line," said Charlie, pointing inland. "That could ruin someone's day."

Usually there would be a cheer following such a triumph, but none came from the waiting soldiers.

Maylo walked over to a medic and took up a roll of gauze from his satchel. He looked up the street toward the square as he wrapped the white bandages around the end of Ursula's long rifle.

"Charlie, Luft," he said to his lieutenants. "I am dead."

"Maylo—"

"Wait only until the cutter arrives. Then if I'm not out, burn that box to slag as fast as you can and get it back on a boat. Try to cut a few of the remaining lines. Keep the walls manned and—"

"Maylo!" interrupted Luft, but a sharp look from his captain cut him off. He rubbed his eyes and temples. "Okay," he said. "We know what to do if you don't come back."

"Aye. Good."

Charlie removed Maylo's pistol and checked the charge, checked its bore and weight before casually replacing it in his holster as if he were approving the line of his jacket. "Ursula?" he said.

"We are the dead." Maylo stepped toward the square.

"Wait," said the old woman.

"Stay me not," said Maylo.

"Not intended," said she. "Take this." And she pressed a bottle into his palm. "Open it when it's done."

"Perhaps you should keep it."

"P'haps, Maylo. P'haps not. Have faith. You may yet see."

He slipped the bottle into his pocket without looking at it. A single shot of whisky perhaps, a pinch of stoning herb, a bauble. What difference?

He marched to the edge of the square. He could see the other platoons staring at him from behind cover, confused expressions on their faces. Behind him his own squads took positions.

"If they shoot at him," he heard Charlie say, "they get one shot. Name the firing hole and we'll send something back through it, by God."

On his right, a steam cart lay in wreckage and two soldiers, both women he noticed, huddled behind it. A Gauss round had pierced the pressured boiler, bent the steel out like a flower blossom. If the garrison in the building did shoot at him, and he was hit, he'd be dead. Little worry then if Charlie returned fire.

Across the street he saw heads of other Liberators, freed slaves who'd sworn allegiance when no such promise had been asked. They'd offered their lives as their most valuable possession in thanks and wonder. He felt a thief, a trickster, taking their oaths. Like Ursula, they could have had days of sunlight and simple pleasures. They could have fled to the wild and lived free. But they had given their new lives immediately to him.

It was temporary. At best, he thought, their efforts would sow the seed for a future movement that would really free Maaraw, but Maylo always thought that eventually the other worlds would come back with terrible wrath and subdue their world regardless of what they did now. The more success they had, the more terrible would be the retribution. Taking Slaafaw would merit a terrible toll to be sure. Slaves would be crucified as warnings. Freed slaves in his ranks would suffer the worst. It had been promised and done. And yet, they joined the fight even before the shackle-scabs on their wrists had healed.

Bruin had told him it was because they understood better than anyone what they fought for. "Most of us can only imagine what they know," he said. "For us, it is an idea, however close we've been to it.

If we haven't actually suffered, we fight for an idea. Luckily, empathy is enough. Sympathy is powerful, and imagination is a force."

Maylo stepped into the square and waved the musket, flapping the flying gauze like a banner before a parade. Slowly he marched toward the garrison's door.

He'd joined the conspiracy in a pub because it promised excitement and he'd been bored. It was only later, after Bruin came, that the true weight sunk in. While Bruin talked about concepts of 'destiny of the species' and 'unity of minds', Maylo saw the dead piling up. The young, like Ursula, were particularly attracted to their cause. Bruin had said this would happen and continue because they had not yet been 'subdued by corruption', whatever that meant. With the young came off-worlders who voluntarily joined the depravations of a guerrilla war and fought and died alongside former servants. What terrible fate would they suffer when this was done, traitors to their class and world? And yet they were here, and more joined every day, smuggled in from Claremond, Enskari, Hyrax, and even Temple to take up arms with them.

And the goals had changed. Still foremost was the end of slavery, but now they just as often talked about self-rule as if their revolt could actually accomplish such a thing. There was talk of governing councils and blind justice systems. Shared resources. Even before Bruin's death these ideas had been common talk around their campfires. The great man listened but would only say that he was unsure how it would all pan out, almost as if he knew he wouldn't be there at the end.

If Bruin, for all his miraculous knowledge and faith, couldn't see how to do all this, how was *he* supposed to carry on?

Taking slow deliberate strides across the square, stepping over bodies of rebel and soldier alike, young and taken, he wondered if he was committing suicide. He felt spent, but more so, he was angry. It was Ursula that drove him forward. Snatched and taken literally under his nose. Insult and injury to come, horrible injury to that young girl. That one injustice he could not endure. In her life was his wrapped, and that – not politics, not strategy, not even suicide – moved his feet to the town hall.

Three meters from the door, he called, "I would parley!"

"We'll not come out," came a muffled voice.

"So I'll come in."

"Who are you?

The ablative shielding of the door had been pierced. Concentrated fire on a single point had breached it. A poor use of ammunition, but they'd put enough shots in the same place to create a twelve-centimeter gash. If he survived, it'd be useful information.

"I am Maylo. Captain of the Liberators."

A pause, then arguing and orders, curses, and finally a single voice. "Let us hear him," it said.

The door opened but half a meter. Maylo entered.

It was dark and gloomy. A single glowglobe illuminated what had been an opulent reception hall, marble floors and columns, sculptures and sconces. Maylo blinked for the darkness and counted roughly fifty people, and a few more lying on cots in an adjacent room. He could smell something cooking. Light poured in from hidden gun slits in the walls and a few stray holes where, like the gash at the door, gunfire had worked its way through.

Someone reached for his musket to take it, but Maylo pulled it back and they left him alone.

"Who is Major Traffen?" he said. "And where is Ursula?"

"I'm Traffen." A Lavlandian officer stepped forward, his curly hair showing beneath his gilded cap. Maylo couldn't read the rank of his uniform, he didn't know the symbols of all the off-world insignia. The man stood straight and aloof.

"You are in charge here?"

"Aye. State your business."

"Where is the girl you kidnapped this hour?"

"Why? Is she valuable?" Traffen's smile made Maylo grind his teeth.

His eyes now accustomed to the gloom, Maylo looked at the men staring back at him. No women, he noticed. Traffen's face might show confidence, but the others' shone with fear and worry.

"Is she valuable? Aye she's valuable." Maylo's head swam in rage. He suddenly whirled around and pointed his finger.

Soldiers defensively aimed their guns at him, but held fire.

"Aye, she's valuable. As are all of you!"

"Sentimental, Maylo?" said Traffen. "You are here to trade your life for hers?"

"Is that what it is? A trade? A commerce? Always a commerce. Of course. This is the place to trade on lives, is it not? The home city of the cursed slave trade."

Traffen shook his head as if disciplining a child. "There are much bigger slave markets in other cities—"

"Shut up!"

The room fell silent. Traffen's aplomb was shaken. A shadow crossed his face.

"I'll trade with you," said Maylo.

"I might just as well keep you both," said Traffen, regaining some of himself.

Maylo ignored him. Turning to the men, he spoke. "He'll have you all fight to the death."

The room stayed silent, confirming the old woman's insight. She'd been right about the major, too. Not even his own spies had identified the officer commanding this last holdout. She knew more than she should.

"He's trading your lives for his glory and our slavery. He's killing you because better to have you dead than on our side. And what are your lives worth? What is it you are buying?"

"Does this kind of thing work with your undisciplined troops?" asked Traffen. "Sergeant, arrest this rebel and put him with the other traitors."

A man with stripes on his arms stepped forward but was restrained, gently, by men near him.

"We're bringing up a cutter," said Maylo. "We'll have this building down today. A tomb of smoldering metal. All of you dead. Dead."

"Bluff."

"You heard the cut thread," Maylo went on.

"Poorly played, rebel. Sergeant—"

"To the death, men," Maylo said. "And what to die for? What are you *buying* with it?" He cast a disgusted look at Traffen.

"Aye, I'm here to trade, I suppose," Maylo went on. "I'm trading my life, here and now, and don't I know it. This is what I buy with my life – a chance to save yours."

"They'll never get a cutter—"

"I guarantee that we will melt you out. We might be driven from the city tomorrow or in a week or a month hence, but none of you will see it. This is not a threat. This is a certainty. It is coming and will be here long before relief. I simply ask, what is it you buy if you follow Traffen's order to the death?"

"Some things are worth the sacrifice," said Traffen.

"Aye," said Maylo. "Loved ones and friends. Comrades and family. How big is your family?"

The last line was an echo of Bruin's own motto and he felt weird for saying it, and yet within the phrase he'd heard so often and seldom contemplated was the answer to all this.

"You will die defending an obviously unjust system," Maylo said. "You are defending thieves, murderers, and liars. You will die and suffer that others may do the same."

Traffen clicked his heels. "I've had just about enough of this."

No one moved.

"Beyond these walls," said Maylo, "we die that others may have a chance to live. We live and we die for our family and our family is very large."

"So you want the girl?" said Traffen. "Sure. Take her as a sign—"

"Come out with me, comrades. See the true enemy. Imagine a better way and don't die for what you don't believe in. I would not kill you. I would free you. Let me free you." Tears streamed down Mayo's face.

"Remember your orders, men," said Traffen.

No one moved.

"I offer a choice. A chance."

Traffen's hand went to his holster. He drew a pistol and leveled it at Maylo.

Maylo didn't react. He looked at the young faces staring back at him; Maarawan, Hyraxian, Enskaran, Templer, all young and afraid. The choice of a lifetime stood before them. Courage and fear. He'd imagined these faces dead as he'd seen so many others, and mourned already the waste of their lives. And yet hearing the cock and hum of Traffen's pistol, Maylo knew that his own life, by this very act, had been well spent.

The shot did not come. Traffen coughed and staggered. His pistol fell to the floor. He turned and looked behind him. A dagger stuck out of his back.

"Peasants, traitors," he gasped, as blood gurgled out of his mouth.

Maylo collapsed to his knees. Life and death swirled in his mind, deaths and costs. Promises and hopes. It was like a gush of water, a ray of light, a trumpet and a song.

How long he knelt on that floor he did not know. When he looked up Ursula stood beside him. Her face was blackened and bruised. Her clothes were torn and bloody, but she looked proud and alive.

"It's over," she said. "Let's go."

And the faces of fifty men told him it was true.

Maylo stood up, wiped his face, and felt the bottle in his pocket. He removed it and held it against the light. Something fluttered within it. He unstoppered the flask and out came a bee that went up and out and then back, where it circled his brow.

"The lines are a bluff," he said. "They're the same cargo ships we let go pretending to be troop carriers." He knew this as though he himself had witnessed it from orbit.

CHAPTER NINE

One bee, two bee, three bee, four
Hover in the orchard, linger round my door
Five bee, six bee, seven and then eight
Sing a song of country roads
Reachin' past the gate
Nine bee, ten bee, eleven and a dozen
Conjure up my fancies
Hummin' with the buzzin'.

Enskaran Nursery Rhyme
40 NE

1, Eleventh-Month, 938 NE – Upaven, Enskari

Fall came later every year. She didn't need her scientists to know things were changing, that the planet was in flux. She had only to recall her early days in this northern estate to remember how things had been compared to now.

Eleventh-Month, the same month as this, just a dozen years before. She was a new monarch, the first queen, and still a child. The War of Ascension was in its infancy and she'd been brought here as much to hide as to educate her. There was a rush to make her regal. She was fighting against her sex, they said, so she'd have to work twice as hard to be just as good as a man. Every waking hour for those first months was an instruction in etiquette and statecraft, geography, science, and law. Never-ending lessons in placidity and aloofness, turn of phrase, and war. Always terrible war. She finally demanded an hour to herself each day to be left alone.

She commanded it as she'd been taught and did it well enough that she was obeyed.

She came to cherish that hour. She'd take it in the mornings or the afternoons as she might. In rain or sun, snow or fair, she'd walk in this garden. Early fall had been her favorite with a crispness she loved, like a coming of truth. Grasses retreating inward, flowers folded like sleeping cherubs. She watched the leaves change into colors as bright and varied as the stained glass in Vildeby Temple. She watched them fall in the breeze, to rest upon the path only to be gone the next day, the gardener keen to keep an uncluttered bower.

Walking now in her aristocratic gait, steady and smooth, gliding in her dress as if on wheels, she recalled those early times here and the energy she'd poured out on these paths. Often barefoot, even in snow, she'd run for the joy of speed and the burning in her muscles. Most unladylike. Unseen, or so she hoped, she'd danced in the arbors wild and native, soundless but for her feet on the ground and the laugh on her lips. The music within her and all around. She'd spin circles in the follies and skip stones on the ponds. She'd tease the birds with calls and often they'd call back and she'd laugh and feel like the trees without leaves – bare and alive.

There'd been years when she'd avoided this palace and its memories, never really knowing why. Once the civil war was over, though – a few years later – she reopened it and made it a regular part of her schedule. It was politically troublesome for the first houses of the capital, but they themselves often fled the smog of the winter for cleaner climes, and she could always hide behind the excuse of economy if she had to. With fewer courtiers to feed and fewer distractions to arrange, court at Upaven was much cheaper than in Vildeby. It was, however, always inconvenient for government having her so far away.

After the defeat of Brandon's armada, everything was different. To the planet and to her. It was as if they'd all been reborn. And maybe they had been. Each had looked death in the face, certain and terrible. Braced for it, had come to terms with it. And then it hadn't come. A planetary level of relief. Her world, people, society, body – all spared by a miracle none had felt worthy of, but each celebrated as divine grace with a new taste for time that had never been felt before.

Things were settling down, but nothing would ever be the same. Her attitude especially. As more demands were made on her, and duties returned her to potentate, she found herself frequently recalling days of her youth, and remembering this garden more and more. She put off meetings to be alone, and flat-out refused some requests and events, seeking ever more solitude. No, that wasn't correct. Solitude was what the press releases called it, but in truth, what she sought and what she had was love. A lover, at any rate.

The man singly credited with their salvation loved her. And she loved him.

And the world might love that too, if it could be, if it might, if it overcame itself.

The world had turned but not enough. It had turned at her ascension, greased by the blood of houses who couldn't envision a change. It had turned again with the creation of a new church, baptized in the blood of the Orthodox Saved. Still bleeding. And now with salvation, another turn and challenges to tradition. She knew the nobles would not accept a king born outside their class, even spoused to her, whom they loved. So they said. Her man, her lover, her world of late – Sir Ethan Sommerled. Hero and threat, raised to knighthood for his own deeds, the most popular man on the planet and also, possibly, the most hated.

She loved him, and he loved her.

But that was not enough.

They'd had to steal their hours away together. Keep out of sight. They could not stop the rumors, but there'd always been rumors. Since even before she bedded Sir Yates, her first, who'd taken her flower, there'd been speculation. At the time she was sure he was the one, but after he took a diplomatic post on Claremond, her interest in him faded and she saw him as a diversion. The first of a few. Not many, but not none. She was human and lonely. The problem came in finding courtiers discreet enough to approach, man enough to please, and wise enough to keep silent. Then had come Sommerled. And this time the rumors delighted the subjects but enraged the aristocracy. But as long as they were just rumors, with some distance and plausible deniability, they were safe.

The maples had barely begun to change, just a spot or two, a red gilt in a green leaf. The season had been slow to arrive. The inevitable turn was coming, but with such resistance now. The heat of her world was slowing the natural change of the seasons. The rose arbor was still a wall of coming buds, and not a yellow hint appeared on the locust bushes.

That would surely be on the agenda. The Minister of Nature was in the palace, doubtless alone in a corner, ignored by the others, worrying his handkerchief, practicing a speech in anticipation of this meeting with her full cabinet.

She took a pocket watch out of a secret fold of her dress and saw that it was time to return. She could be late; it was her prerogative. Many monarchs had made it a signature attribute of their rule to be late, but she'd always found it rude and her ministers had appreciated her for not doing that. Let the lower upper classes practice classist rudeness, she thought. She was above it. She'd be on time.

She'd taken her hour to wander this garden as she had in days past. Not as fast as then, not as free, but still open to its charm. She'd met Ethan here the day before, showed him her favorite folly, and they'd made love on the bench. Her knees trembled at the memory of it, and her mind filled with the beauty of the sky though the slatted roof, the fragrance of flowers, the thousand greens of the garden. The moment of ecstasy – hers and his. He was a considerate lover, her needs before his every time. Polite and unassuming but strong and protective. The joining, a thing beyond bodies; the heat, a passion of souls as much as muscle. In the silence that followed, she'd felt at home.

She was nine and twenty years old, hardly a young girl, considered an old maid for not marrying before twenty. She felt the years of lost opportunity like a weight. Still, it was unbecoming a woman of her status to be in love, to feel the longings of youth, the youth she'd lost, had sacrificed for station and kingdom. Lost, but not forgotten and now stirring in her like the bees on her flowers and the butterflies in her stomach.

Ethan was here for the same meeting as the others. As Defense Admiral he had a necessary and earned place there. Her Ears had warned her that certain classes, the better ones by name, were not happy with the admiral's ascension into their ranks. Gratitude didn't last long, apparently. Each noble, earl, duke, and count still breathed thanks to him.

She saw them through a fence, a naked tree amid yellowed grass, and realized she was at the edge of the garden and the ground beyond was untended and natural. They were plants native to Enskari. It was hard to remember that the roses and oaks, maples and vervain were not supposed to be here, and that an entire ecosystem had existed prior to their arrival 938 years, eleven months before. The bees too were an import, the original ones wiped out in the first century from pesticides the colonists had brought. The new bees were better, she was told, as were the crops and flowers. This palace garden was a celebration of that, where there'd been a conscious effort to exclude aboriginal plants. Seeing the stark black limbs and dried curling grass of the native growths, she thought it not unseemly to have included a few of them.

A vague thought. A distant idea. A thread she'd need to pull later. Her hour was up.

Fifty meters from the door she was met by ladies-in-waiting, pages, and guards who'd waited worrying for her return. They rushed to her like the return of migratory birds.

She ignored them as she'd been trained to, seeing them as function only, mobile furniture as she'd been taught, and entered her palace through the stained-glass doors of the rear portico. Chin up, back straight, hands cupped at her waist, she glided to the cabinet room in the far wing.

She passed a sea of people, waves, bows, and curtsies from distraction-seeking courtiers whiling away the time. "Your Majesty." "Highness." "My queen." Sycophants who seemed shallower than usual this day. Palace guards and soldiers, Connor's men in sashes, armed and stoic like upright columns holding up the walls. So many people and so stifling inside. So open and free without.

She took her seat exactly thirty seconds before the meeting was to commence. Perfect timing.

On her right was the First Ear, Sir Edward Kesey. On her left, the Second Ear, Sir Nolan Brett. Arrayed around the crescent table were her admirals, Aderyn and Sommerled. She caught Ethan's smile and felt a rush of heat to her cheeks driven by flutters in her heart. She held her features firm and trusted her makeup concealed her emotion.

Here were advisors and continental representatives. A dozen miscellaneous nobles whose place on the council predated her ascension and of questionable usefulness. Mr. Rose, the Collected Guild man, was there. On paper, at least, he represented millions of skilled workers across the globe. He cast glances at Archbishop Connor, while the head of her church looked old and tired, dour. He scowled as if he found the very air offensive. Perhaps someone had broken wind. Zabel smiled to think of it.

At the queen's nod a herald called them to order.

"It has been nearly six months since our deliverance," said the queen. "We would know the state of our world. But first, another thanks to noble Sir Ethan for his bravery and skill." Her use of the word *noble* was not accidental or light. She sensed the unease the word caused among the council. To their credit, they mostly hid their disdain as they rose and applauded the admiral. Even Connor saluted the savior of the planet.

"We'll begin with the reading of reports," she said. "Sir Edward."

Meeting participants were excused once their parts were done, thus limiting the comments and self-important rants nobles felt obliged to make on every subject. As such, the meeting diminished in people as the material being discussed became more secretive. Kesey, primarily involved with domestic projects, always began the meeting with a full house. Brett, her spymaster, would end it with a fraction of the present group, often only Kesey and herself besides him.

The meeting followed an itinerary and Kesey was vigorous in keeping to time. They heard about production yields from Southland and Austen and the capital continent, Dorothia. There'd been a setback on Whiteplain, the frozen, unpopulated, southernmost continent. The shelf where prospectors had set up base camp had broken free and the inhabitants had had to be rescued. Another attempt to start that mine would be made next year.

"How would the metals and fuels be discovered?" asked the queen.

"We thought we might start by blacking the ice to melt it."

Sir Aldo, the nature minister, looked positively apoplectic at that, and nearly spoke out of turn. Instead, he fidgeted in his chair as if it were on fire.

"We think that may not be the right solution," offered the queen. Sir Aldo relaxed. A little.

"Plasma then," continued the representative from the mining consortium. "We melt the ice with flamers and plasma guns. The very ones we use on our warships."

"The very kind Hyrax would have deployed upon our cities?"

"We must harvest our resources, Your Majesty. Enskari needs them."

"We are aware," she said and the man cringed at her tone. "Perhaps next year, your enterprise will have more luck."

The Earl of Nutorn was next on the agenda.

"Sir Joseph, Earl of Nutorn," announced Kesey. "You would address the council?"

"Aye, my lord," said the earl, who stood and bowed before the queen.

"We are pleased to see you in such good health, Sir Joseph," said Zabel. The man required special attention. His province was the primary industrial area for war production.

"I thank you, Majesty," he said. "But I am vexed."

"Pray tell."

"I am persecuted by the Minister of Nature."

Sir Aldo's face went red.

Kesey noted the time on a sheet. The earl noticed him noting it and got to the point.

"Nutorn is the heart of Enskaran greatness," he said. "We produce the armaments that grant safety to the planet. It is vital, now more than ever, that I be allowed to continue in this service."

"And how is our minister stopping this?" asked the queen.

"He would close the factories!"

His tone received a raised eyebrow from Zabel. She could do a lot with such a gesture.

"He claims it is polluting the planet," he said, softer.

"Are not your factories driven by coal and oil?"

"Aye—"

"And do these not pollute the air and streams?"

"It is a trivial cost to pay for the lives of everyone."

"We are asking you to clean up the pollution—"

"It is an impossibility," interrupted the earl before he could stop himself.

Zabel let the moment sit, let him feel her disapproval and the looks from the other subjects. He might have had allies in the room before the interruption, but they were hiding now as she looked to each man seated and measured their reaction to the slight.

"Begging pardon, madam." Nutorn wiped his brow with a handkerchief.

"Majesty," she corrected him.

His face went redder than the drapes.

She waited.

"Of course, Majesty."

It was upon such moments that her position as monarch rested. She could not allow any disrespect. Her position was too precarious.

She knew Nutorn's complaint. Brett had mentioned it.

"Half the pollution output by the end of the year," she said quoting the exact number Aldo had suggested. "Then five and twenty per cent lower yearly thereafter."

Nutorn waited a good long time before speaking again. "It is impossible."

"Have you made any improvements?"

"Nay, I would seek relief entire from the order."

"You have had months to comply and have done nothing?"

"Ma…Majesty, I would consult with you."

She sensed some of the nobles growing uneasy.

"So it is too late now to comply."

"Aye."

"We shall therefore order your noble service to us to continue."

Sir Aldo watched her intently. Nutorn smiled.

"Five and twenty per cent by next year," she said.

The earl flinched. Aldo didn't sit well either.

"We will address the matter again then."

"Aye, Majesty," said the earl. "Will the Crown assist in the expenses for the changes?"

Sir Nolan shook his head nearly imperceptibly.

"If we were to do that," she said, "we might as well own the factories. Is that not so, Sir Terry?"

Sir Terry was the finance minister. "Aye, Majesty." He rose. "Cut out the middleman."

The earl looked at the other nobles, who found other places to look just then.

"Five and twenty per cent pollution decrease is an achievable goal, Sir Joseph," said the queen. "You are clever and wise and not without resources. Perhaps you could invent a patentable cure."

That got him thinking. "Aye, Majesty."

A nod moved the agenda.

"Sir Aldo, Minister of Nature," announced Sir Edward. "You have the floor."

The scientist stood and bowed. "There is much to say," he said. "I have prepared detailed reports on all aspects of our ongoing research."

"Cut to the chase," said Kesey. "We are running behind."

He blushed and cleared his throat. He had a reputation of excruciatingly long lectures full of dry facts and figures that invariably set his audience against him. It was counter-productive. Pained though he looked at Kesey's instruction, her First Ear was doing him a favor.

"What the Earl of Nutorn said, though not an accurate representation of my order, is not hyperbole. It is worse. The factories of Nutorn must be shut down. When I sent the order to cut emissions, that was still a viable solution. Too much time has passed. They must now be shuttered. There is an immediate danger to the town and a long-term threat to the planet."

"Explain," said the queen.

"The parts-per-million concentrate of particulate—"

"We have your reports, Sir Aldo," interrupted Kesey.

Aldo cleared his throat. "An inversion, as we often have, might concentrate it to dead— To…to beyond healthy levels."

"And the only cure is to stop the factories? All of them or just Nutorn?"

"Nutorn is the immediate crisis, but, aye, eventually all—"

Jeers and knocks on the table. Discord among the nobles. A break in etiquette.

"Lords," said Kesey, a warning in his voice.

When quiet returned, the queen said, "We have read the reports, Sir Aldo. You are a noble and wise scientist. None better on all Enskari for what you do. But needs must, my friend. We are not free of Hyraxian threat. Our economy cannot function without production. It is a noble ideal, but too drastic. We must phase in such ideas with safeguards or we'll have no society to protect."

"My queen," said Aldo, "we are already headed for a rocky future. Lightning strikes and melting ice. Poisoned air and water. Eventually – and most importantly – the shield against our sun will fail. It is failing now."

"These are dire prophesies," she said. "And we will endeavor to allay them as we may. We begin with Sir Joseph's efforts to reach a quarter reduction."

"It won't be enough should the conditions conspire against them."

"Them?"

"The people of Nutorn."

"Let the government of Nutorn concern itself with the subjects of Nutorn," said Sir Joseph out of turn.

The queen let it slide. She already felt Sir Nolan signaling her to back down. The earl was a great ally and would be a dangerous enemy. Still, there was something about the way he carried himself that upset her, something about Aldo's warnings that worried her more than they used to. Catching Ethan's soft eyes in the corner of hers made her remember heat and love, the beauty of a garden well kept, the fierce passion of a wild one. It related to her actions and moods, memories and hopes.

Happy but uneasy, she said, "We thank you, Sir Aldo. We have your reports. We shall all read them."

"Majesty," he said. Dismissed, he sat down.

"I would invite the lords not privy to the war council to take leave at this time," said Kesey.

There were murmurs of surprise. The change in attendance was not unexpected but the looming question for many – the fallout of the Defense of the Realm Directive – would be left undiscussed, and forever forgotten, if possible.

None were brave enough to break etiquette and call the question, so each stood, bowed, and took their leave until only the inner circle remained.

It was the queen, her Ears, Connor, General Weir, and her admirals remaining. A couple of pages and personal secretaries. Brett's man, Vandusen, who had helped Ethan in a duel the year before.

"There is much to discuss," said the Second Ear. "We'll not address our newest intelligence singly or in any order, for it is thought to be all connected."

"Commence," said the queen.

"All reports from Hyrax indicate that they are in no position to renew their designs of invasion upon our world."

"Hear, hear," said the queen, smiling at Sommerled.

"Their economy is damaged. Their military blunted. The loss of men and materials, ships and treasure, will take years to recover from."

"So we are safe from without?" said Connor.

"No offense, Your Highness," said General Weir, "but must we have the archbishop here? Has he not done enough to strengthen our enemies?"

"What was done was done," said Sir Nolan. "There are agents and sympathizers still on-world. Fewer than there were, to be sure, but still many. The threats we face will now be more subtle and probably clothed in loyal garb."

The suggestion was not lost on the archbishop or the general of the army.

"Has not the prophet offered us peace?" said Weir.

"We are not sure," said Brett. "Before we discuss Temple, there are other matters we should make clear."

"Hyrax is vulnerable," said Sommerled. "That is the only matter that bears. The prophet would protect his puppet."

"That is a consideration, Sir Ethan," said Brett. "But I pray, allow me to continue."

"My apologies, sir."

"There is open revolt upon Maaraw," Brett said. "Most recently, rebels have taken the city Slaafaw."

"The whole city?" said Aderyn. "That's no small village."

Brett nodded.

"That's Lavland's problem," said Sommerled.

"Aye, but the rebellion destabilizes that entire world."

Kesey nodded. "I receive daily complaints from Enskaran merchants about it. It is affecting their business and our economy. Maaraw has been a reliable source of income for the Crown. It enabled our defense."

"It's been a symbol of system-wide unity," said Connor. "All the civilized worlds sharing dominion over a single savage planet."

Savages. The word struck the queen strangely this day.

"Did not Temple deal with this already?" said Aderyn.

Brett said, "A leader was captured and executed, but the movement didn't stop."

Weir fidgeted. "That's not good."

"It is there that the prophet would have us unite with Hyrax," said Brett. "To subdue the rebellion."

"Who benefits most from that world?" asked the queen.

Brett said, "Lavland, but each world shares in the spoils. All of us."

"Temple?"

"Aye. Temple to be sure, in tithing. Ten per cent from all the worlds, save ours."

"Therein lies the income of that world," said Zabel.

"Promoting foreign interests should not be our responsibility," said Connor.

"Let us table the debate," Brett said. "Let us look now at Silangan."

"What about it?"

"We have reports of a rebellion there."

"Now there's some good news," said Sommerled.

"Aye. It is not without reason that Silangan is called Brandon's bankbook. Any disruption there hurts Hyrax."

"Well done, Sir Nolan," said the queen.

"All thanks, but undeserved," he said. "We have had nothing to do with it. Like Maaraw, it is a wholly homegrown insurrection."

"Missed opportunity," said Kesey with a jovial wink. "But we won't let on it wasn't our spymaster."

"I did try," he said. "But truth be told, the savages there are beyond my methods. The nature of that rebellion is…strange."

"Go on."

"It is not as on Maaraw, where there is method and goal," he said. "The reports I received, from several quarters, are…disturbing. They talk of massacres and cannibalism. A bloodlust. Mass suicide and slaughter. The native attackers don't take loot, don't make demands, they seek only to bathe in the blood of their victims."

The room fell silent, the rustle of the queen's dress the only stirring.

"There must be more to it," she said.

"Savages," murmured Connor.

"They reap what they sow," said Sommerled. "I have seen firsthand the horrors of the lead mines. Silangan was bathed in blood from Hyraxian whips long before now."

Aderyn nodded.

"What has been the Hyraxian response?" asked the queen.

"They've sent what ships and troops they can. Mostly they're trying to downplay the rebellion. It is not big, only brutal."

"Terrorism?" asked Weir. "Is that their method?"

"Perhaps."

The queen could see her man was troubled.

"We can do nothing there now," she said. "Continue, Sir Nolan."

"Tirgwenin," said Brett.

"What about it?" asked Sommerled.

"My spies have told me that Brandon has set his sights upon Jareth's World."

"He has the means?" said Kesey.

"Excepting recent history, Hyrax is good at invasion. They have their best men lining up to lead."

"Who?" asked Aderyn.

"For the flight and defense, none other than Clelland."

"The man who spaced that one ship?" said Connor.

"The *Pempkin*," said Sommerled.

The queen vaguely remembered some story about Sommerled spacing a couple of Temple ministers, but put the thought aside as quickly as it arrived.

"He's been made an admiral," Brett said.

Aderyn laughed. "Atter the armada disaster? Damn, but Brandon's a forgiving sort."

"What of Lavland and Claremond?" asked the queen.

"Lavland is still occupied. Claremond is devoted to Temple. Both claim neutrality in our struggle, neither is in a position to change the course of history at this time."

"Just so."

"These are the events happening off-world," said Brett. "We are aware of our situation on Enskari. With all this in mind, let us now consider the letters from Eren VIII."

"Carry on," said the queen.

"I have been in touch with the Hall of the Prophet and received an official request to join in a concerted effort with Hyrax and the other civilized worlds to defeat the rebellion on Maaraw. After that, we should remain allies, and together, as humans, stamp out the alien menace wherever else it may appear.

"What alien menace?" said Kesey. "Does he mean the savages of Maaraw?"

"That is unclear," said Brett.

"The Maarawans are as human as we are," said Sommerled.

The queen was glad the admiral felt comfortable enough to speak up as he did, though she sensed Kesey growing perturbed at his continued presence in the conversation. And of course, Connor was angry at him constantly.

"I tend to agree," said Brett. "The prophet's men will not divulge what it is specifically that they fear, though they have led me to believe it is truly an alien threat, not man-made at all."

"And it's related to Maaraw?" said Sommerled.

"Aye," said Brett. "And Tirgwenin besides."

"Why there?"

Brett shook his head. "I have learned, through no little effort, that after Maaraw it is there they'd have our unified forces go next."

"That makes sense," said the queen.

They all looked at her.

"The Tirgwenians," she said. "We can see our connected roots in a Maarawan face to be sure. Even to those degraded Silangians we must claim kinship, but the yellow men of Tirgwenin, surely they have deviated far enough from the civilized to be called alien. Surely it is they that Temple fears."

"How can they fear a people so backward?" asked Weir.

"They can't," said Sommerled.

Kesey let out a loud irritated sigh. "Perhaps we should turn the floor over to the admiral."

To the queen's relief, Brett said, "Aye, what say you, Ethan?"

"It is an obvious ploy," said Sommerled. "Hyrax is unstable and failing. We have struck them a near-fatal blow. Brandon has impressed his puppet prophet, the charlatan on Temple, to divert our attention from our obvious counter-attack."

"It would appear so," agreed Aderyn. "It is the only way to see it."

"Sir Nolan," said the queen, "do you agree?"

"That was also my first reaction," said he. "And yet my spies tell me there is true alarm in the Hall of the Prophet. I think – and here it is as much my own hunch as any intelligence – that the prophet believes what he says. He believes there is an alien threat. He is sincere."

"That is never a word I would associate with Eren VIII," said Connor.

"What would you suggest?" said the queen to Brett.

"There is a strange wave of upheaval in the system. The trouble on Silangan is beyond our ability to address, not that we would. Maaraw hurts all equally and so it is in our interest to leave that alone too, at least insofar as not helping our adversaries. We have sent relief ships to our colonies there and they're as well protected as they can be for now."

"I have not heard a suggestion, Sir Nolan," said the queen.

"For us, it is Tirgwenin. We must not allow that world to come under dominion of our enemies."

"Sir Ethan," said the queen, "any word from your colony there?"

"Nay. None, Majesty."

Aderyn cleared his throat. "Sir Ethan, how long until your charter is lost for lack of success?"

"A year, give or take."

"Might you consider surrendering it now?"

"Why?"

Brett spoke. "There is a consortium prepared to take it on and defend the planet against Hyrax."

"A private endeavor?" asked Kesey. "No drain on the treasury?"

"Aye," said Brett. "Provided they have rights of conquest and colony."

Sommerled said, "Why not just impress this consortium and send it on with Enskaran warships?"

"I'm sure that would go over poorly with the monied classes," said Kesey. "We're already unpopular for recent…uhm…unilateral actions." His glance at the archbishop made it clear what that meant. "The rights of our citizens and all that."

"Could we take and defend the planet?" asked Zabel.

"Uncertain," said Brett. "But it is our best option. It would risk the least resources for the highest reward."

Aderyn said, "Are we supposed to stop our raids on Hyraxian treasure ships from Silangan?"

"Aye," said Brett. "The prophet asks that as well."

"There's the smoking gun right there," said Weir. "This prophet's peace is obviously meant to aid Hyrax. Aliens indeed."

"What of a counter-attack on Hyrax?" asked the queen.

"That would show that we're not going to conform to the peace," said Brett.

"They'll figure that out when we take the next convoy," said Aderyn.

"Not necessarily. Freebooters and pirates do as they will."

"That they do," said Sommerled.

"How soon can we have an attack?"

"Depends on our goals," said Aderyn.

"We can have something big enough to matter within a month," said Sir Ethan. "I've already begun."

"What is big enough to matter?"

"Destruction of stations and orbital shipyards. No invasion, just shipping. Cut a few elevator cords. Keep them rebuilding infrastructure instead of refitting another fleet. Hit them fast and hard and get out."

"We are still at war," said the queen.

"It might bring them to a real peace table," said Kesey, "not this phony ploy from Temple."

"I'd like to see them bleed a little," said Connor.

"I'd think you'd have seen enough of that," said Weir.

The archbishop turned on the general, but the queen cut him off.

"It has been a long day," she said. "Our nerves and patience are strained. Sir Ethan, prepare your fleet for counter-attack. Sir Nolan, play for time with Temple. See if we can find out any more about the distress in the Hall of the Prophet."

"And Tirgwenin?" asked Aderyn.

"Sir Ethan?" said the queen. "Have you created a permanent colony there as required?"

She watched her lover squirm and consider.

"Will you accomplish it in time?" she asked.

He hesitated. "My colony is lost," he said after a moment. "There is no hope for them or for another by my hand before the patent is up. I surrender it to you, my queen."

"Sir Nolan," she said, "I give it to you, to dispose of as you will."

He bowed in acceptance.

"Now leave us," said the queen. "All but my Ears. I'll see the rest at the banquet tonight."

"Blessed be," they said, rising.

"And to thee."

She couldn't stifle a tired sigh as the rest of the attendees left them. Nearly over.

"Sir Nolan," she asked, "who is leading this Tirgwenian consortium you spoke of?"

"Honestly, Majesty, it is I," he said. "I felt it was too urgent a matter to delay and so have pledged my own resources. There are a couple others involved, but the bulk is mine."

"And who heads the endeavor? We trust we are not losing you to an off-world adventure?"

"Admiral Aderyn is involved. If the situation merits it, he will personally see the thing through. Otherwise, he recommends Captain Smede."

"Have we met him?"

"I believe so. He is a good man."

"A self-made man," said Kesey. "Not of the noble crust."

"How has he advanced?"

"He served under Aderyn on first circuit," said Brett. "Got his captainship during the defense."

"Quite new," said Kesey, shaking his head. "Doesn't sound up to it."

"A new land might need new people," the queen said.

Kesey straightened up. "Aye," he said. "Of course."

"Something troubles you, First Ear?" the queen said.

"Aye, my queen," said Kesey. "If I may speak freely."

"You may."

"There is much talk about Sir Ethan."

"About Sommerled or about Sommerled and us?"

"Both," he admitted. "It is felt that he has too much influence over Your Majesty."

"And that is a bad thing?"

"Aye, it is," said Kesey. "It truly is. It smacks of disloyalty to the houses that supported your ascension."

"Disloyalty?"

"Aye," he said. "We must not allow the nobles to even imagine that their positions within this court are in danger from the lower classes."

"So we appear to be disloyal to our class."

"Exactly, my queen."

"But am I not also the queen of the commoner as well as the noble?"

"Aye, but it is a matter of etiquette and appearances. The better classes must be exalted over the inferior. Otherwise…." He shook his head as if unable to even imagine such an event.

The queen glanced at Brett, who kept a stolid expression, seldom betraying his inner thoughts. She was about to ask his opinion, but remembered instead the garden and her life before the throne. She recalled the paths of freedom, stolen hours as a child and then again – just as stolen, just as secret – with her lover the savior of her world. Kesey's word echoed in her head, 'loyalty'. But with it came another, one that was bantered around pretty freely during the War of Ascension. *Evolution.*

"We can see that these matters trouble you greatly, old friend," she said to Kesey. She reached her hand out and placed it softly on the old man's. It was spotted and gnarled. She looked at his face and saw the deep worry lines around his brow, the gray in his hair, and felt the weight behind his eyes. "You have served the throne long and well. We burden you with troubles and vex you at a time where your noble sacrifices should be rewarded and not added upon."

Kesey glanced down at the queen's hand upon his own and then looked up at her, confused.

"We release you, noble Sir Edward," she said.

"Release me?"

"Aye. Enjoy your remaining years in peace. We have been given new life. Of all my friends, I can think of none more worthy of being released to enjoy it than you. I release you."

"I shall not be Ear?"

"You shall not be in court at all," she said. "Be free of this mess. You have estates and family – grandchildren, great-grandchildren. We would have you spend time with them in these advanced years."

"I'm being dismissed?" His eyes were large and afraid.

"There shall be no scandal," she said. "We have some time to ease into this."

"Time? What time?"

"Time to make a gracious exit before we name your replacement."

Kesey fell back in his chair as if he'd been struck.

"And who, my queen," said Brett, "shall be the new First Ear?"

"After his return from Hyrax, I shall name Sir Ethan First Ear."

"Sommerled?" said Kesey, his face twisted.

"Aye. The hero of the world, our own symbol of unity, our own Sir Ethan Sommerled."

CHAPTER TEN

When the student is ready, the teacher will come.
When the student is truly ready, the teacher will go.
Zen Proverb, Old Earth

13, Ninth-Month, 938 – Pemioc, Tirgwenin

"We know a better way."

Lahgassi leaned over Dillon's shoulder as he shucked rodwheat into a bowl with a nimimi shell. Rodwheat was something he'd seen before, or the like, back home, but the shell, a yellow-and-blue pearlescent blade, tough as iron and shaped like sharpened knuckles, was as alien as the sparkling friends he sat among.

"This is how I was taught," he said.

"Who taught you?"

"It was Bost."

"Rowdanae," she said, as if that explained everything.

Dillon asked, "What am I doing wrong?"

She gestured to her missing arm. "I cannot," she said. "Have your sister explain."

"I never see her anymore."

She looked around the circle of shuckers and her eyes fell upon a young girl Dillon knew only slightly. "Maffrit. Show Dillon how do."

The leader's language skills came and went. At times, when addressing the colonists as a group, Dillon thought she spoke better than a minister. Other times, like this, wandering the village, overseeing the harvest work, she struggled with syntax and words, often asking Millie to translate. Millie was gone now, however, and it surprised Dillon that she had chosen to use his language instead of the Tirgwenian tongue.

"Ya, Lahgassi," said the girl. She emptied kernels out of her apron into a basket, stood, and stretched. Maffrit was a classmate of Dillon's and had picked up 'Saved Tongue' rather quickly. Ms. Pierce had several times congratulated her on her progress. Dillon had never spoken with her, however. She was, after all, a girl.

As near as Dillon could tell, their ages were comparable, both about nine, but she, being Tirgwenin, was ten centimeters taller, and of course, her skin was yellow, sparkled with reflective scales, and she had those unnerving inner eyelids. Not past the age of independence, she had no tattoos yet.

"Dillon Dagney, show me," she said.

Dillon caught glances from the others, little smirks from under blankets, knowing glances from under hats, as once again, the off-worlder didn't know how to do something.

Shucking rodwheat was a job for women and children. The men were doing other things involving smoke and holes which Dillon couldn't wait to ask about. Here at the midday fire, there were two men among their twelve. One was obviously courting one of the girls, sitting close and whispering in her ear whenever he thought no one was looking. The other was just a man who seemed to have the perfect temperament for the work and hummed to each cob as if he were courting it.

Maffrit gestured for Dillon. "Vis – show me."

Dillon picked up a new cob and drove the curved shell into the side and pushed. Purple kernels the size of his molars popped out and fell into his lap.

She sat behind him and wrapped her arms around his shoulders. She picked up a fresh cob and took the shell from his hand. Peering around his neck, she indicated a reddish patch at the nape of the stalk. "See?" she said.

"Aye," said Dillon.

She twisted the shell in the spot and dug out a single kernel beneath it. "See? This mother seed."

She put it aside and turned the shell around to the blunter side and pushed it down the cob. Kernels rattled off as if nothing held them. Five quick strokes and it was clean, the gathered the seeds whole and uncut.

"Why didn't Bost know to do that?" he said.

Maffrit turned her mouth up in a pout of concentration before saying carefully, "Rowdanae do hard things. Bost Rowdanae."

"Can I show him this?" Dillon asked, popping out the mother seed on a cob of his own and stripping it as she had done.

"Ya," she said. "That good."

She retrieved her own basket and sat next to Dillon.

The others watched her and smiled surreptitiously. The man hummed a complex melody.

"You like Tirgwenin?" Maffrit said. "You like Yevrits a' Blos?"

"Yevrits is very nice," he said. "She still mourns for her son."

"Ya. Him was nice."

"He was nice," Dillon said.

"He was."

"He died in the attack?"

"Yevrits no tell?"

He shook his head and took another stalk.

Maffrit blinked her two layers of eyelids. "Ya, he and many others be killed by off-worlders like you," she said.

"Not me."

"They looked like you." She gestured to his hair. "Red."

"Enskarans. If they'd had my skin but black hair like you, they'd be Hyraxian. They're worse, believe it or not."

"Uncivilized."

"Nay," said Dillon. "It's the other way around. Tirgwenin is uncivilized, like Silangan and Maaraw. Enskari, Hyrax, Temple – those ones, they're civilized."

She looked confused.

"Sorry. You don't understand other planets," he said. "I'm talking too fast."

"Nay. Nay, I do. I understand," she said. "I know planets. I know

Coronam. I know civilized. But calling you that does not make you that." She smiled with pride. "Good words?"

"You are very clever with my language."

"And no bee yet!" She grinned brighter.

He found the crimson spot and cut out the kernel.

"Dillon Dagney, save mother seed," she said. "Good to plant."

"Oh, sorry." He put the seed beside hers in her basket and she smiled like it was a great joke.

It was the kind of strange reaction he'd grown accustomed to in Pemioc. "They are nothing but surprises," Mr. Tomkins had said. "And not much to complain about."

It seemed like a long time ago, but Dillon recalled their coming to the village, the fear that had driven them, the hope they'd had for these walls. And the terror of the day of adoption, which they'd now come to call it.

They'd heard the words, *huservus*, and its translation as 'slave', but that wasn't correct. The concept of slavery among the people of Pemioc was more of a house-helper and not a toiling brute. Actually part of the family.

The colonists were separated. Child from parent, brother from sister, but still they were all in the village and except for the family times and work responsibilities, they were free to mingle and do as they liked with the other marooned Enskarans. Or not. More and more, they chose to not.

"There was method to the madness," Millie had said, quoting something he had never heard before. "They've put us in the homes of people who lost folk from before."

The village was still recovering from Hasin's massacre. It was fresh in memory and the newcomers wore the stain of that horror on their skin and in their language. Millie had said that it was a miracle they were allowed to live, and she was without words to describe what it was that had led them to be embraced by these people.

"Is that why Lahgassi chose you? She lost someone? A little girl?"

Millie nodded somberly but didn't elaborate. Instead she ran her fingers through Dillon's hair and smiled warmly. All the while a bee buzzed around her head like it was lost.

"How are the others faring?" she asked him.

"You're the leader. Ask them."

"I do, but they might not tell me everything."

"I think they're well enough," he told her. "They get sad sometimes, missing the people back home or who died. But not so much."

"Do you miss Mom and Dad?"

"Sometimes."

"And Yevrits? All good with her?"

"She likes this stinky cabbagey soup. It makes the whole house smell like farts. It doesn't taste terrible, but she eats it all the time. I liked it okay when we got here, was hungry, ate it all up, but it's gushy and watery and yuck all over. I prefer honey pies and such, but we have that soup all the time."

"I remember you eating that," she said. "I bet she thinks it's your favorite. Why don't you tell her you don't like it?"

"I don't want to hurt her feelings."

"I don't think that would happen."

"Look at Mr. Tydway."

"What about him?"

"He was put into that one house with that one woman and three little kids."

"And?"

He looked to see if anyone was listening. Seeing only late summer laziness of a sunny day, he said, "Remember when he rushed out of her house and the woman was crying?"

"Aye."

"Do you know why?"

"Why?" she said.

"Because she tried to kiss him – and more, probably, lots more. He's a widower. And in mourning."

"So is Jasnenay," she said. "They're getting along now, though, aren't they?"

"I guess."

"Lahgassi was asked to help with that," she said to him.

"Really? She seems like she can handle anything."

"Aye, but I was asked to have a word with Mr. Tydway."

"And you told him that he had to do it? Because I saw he went back into that house. We were slaves and if that's what we have to do to survive, that's what we have to do."

Millie blushed. "Not quite," she said. "It was more subtle." The bee landed on Millie's ear and buzzed its wings. She cringed like she was being tickled but didn't bat it away.

"When do I get a bee?" he asked.

"I don't know. So far I'm the only one of us to get one."

"Not many of them have them either."

"Nay," she said. "Not here. Not many."

"Why?"

She shrugged.

Millie's position in the village was peculiar. Once someone called her Krikhuia by accident and Dillon had to beg Yevrits to explain to him what it meant. After a long talk with plenty of gestures and some drawing on reed sheets with charcoal pens, he came to understand that Krikhuia was Lahgassi's dead daughter. How someone had mistaken his sister for a pure-blood yellow Tirgwenian princess was beyond him, but he'd seen it happen.

He knew that Pemioc was not an average Tirgwenin village. It was a trading post between the interior lands and Rodawnoc, and the two were very different. One was wild and hard, the other not. He didn't know what that meant or why it was important.

What he did know and what he felt was that he should be a productive member of the community. Yevrits a' Blos or Yevrits, the woman who adopted him, was kindly but stern with a hard face and slow to laugh, but so too was she slow to anger. She put Dillon to work immediately cleaning her little hut, which was nicer than the house he'd had on Enskari. He'd complained to Millie about the work, how he had to do stupid things that really didn't need doing, like raking the sand garden into shapes or collecting flowers for the table. She'd answered him with that same question: "Do you miss Mom and Dad?"

He'd thought that a weird answer and wondered if she'd been listening. When he hadn't answered she asked it again.

"No. I'm too busy."

And she'd smiled.

There was no school in the traditional sense, though the colonists set one up and it had been well received. Ms. Pierce was the teacher and taught anyone who wanted to hear her lessons. It started out as general education and language class, but then became more scriptural. She began to sound like a minister. This went on for a month as she spoke of Saved doctrine and the place of man among nature. After she lost her Tirgwenin audience she returned to language lessons to bring them back. Dillon once asked her about it.

"They were right to leave. I wasn't telling them true," she said. "It just doesn't seem real anymore. It's like the God we had back there didn't come with us here."

He thought about that. "My father used to say that God is everywhere and our true God loves us."

"That is so."

"But you said God is not here."

Ms. Pierce looked out across the village toward the distant hills and trees, the sky alight with green streaks of aurora. Her eyes fell upon the rings visible in the day sky, lights playing upon them in flashes and streaks. "God is different here," she said. "The old words from home don't do Him justice in this place. But be assured there is a God here. We will not be damned for loving this God."

It was a strange thing to say. Why should he be damned for anything? He'd done nothing but endure the trials God had sent him. He'd wanted to ask Yevrits about the Tirgwenin God but didn't know how to phrase the words. He was good at the language, better than most, but he'd not heard religious vocabulary. They didn't have church meetings. There were no ministers. Nobody told them what to believe or what would happen if they didn't. They had moments of silence that were explained to him as prayer, but no one spoke over them, entreating God on anyone's behalf. Even so, he always had the feeling that they all prayed for the same thing.

One of the things that had struck him was the absence of money. Aguirre and his selects back at the fort had pointed to that as a sign of the natives' backwardness, but he'd found no use for it since he'd come here. Food was shared, shelter provided, and he'd wanted for nothing. When there was something he wanted, he could trade for it. Usually by his labor, but sometimes with other things, a whistle or a shirt. Strangely though, he never really felt he wanted anything that much. And it was the same with the others. Everyone seemed to have enough.

For the longest time, Ms. Lawrence hoarded food under her bed. Everyone would see her steal table scraps in the folds of her dress. Dillon thought it strange that she'd do such a thing since Pemioc had such a good harvest that year and there was more than enough food for everyone. Mr. Hemmington managed to get his hands on a spear and slept with it beside his bed until one day he offered to give it to Lahgassi. She refused it and instead made three soldiers teach him how to use it. Ms. Lawrence too stopped her hoarding ways after a time and dumped a huge sack of meats and bread into the compost pile before the autumn field renewal.

The Tirgwenians watched all this with amusement. They noted it but didn't act, and if they thought it worthy of comment and derision, they did so in private.

And meanwhile the colonists, beaten and battered and thinking their lives were over, slowly came to understand that they were part of a community. They had enough to eat, were warm and sheltered, and surprisingly healthy. The food agreed with them. No one stopped them, the slaves – huservus – from running off, not because there was nowhere to go, which was true, but because it was not the place of the village to prevent them from going, which put a huge lie to the idea of slavery they all thought they endured. All that was expected of them was that they do their share. If that was done, and it was easy – for most work was done in a few short hours – they were treated like the villagers themselves and better than the Rowdanae.

He was unsure why they were a different class, but they decidedly were. His main playmate was Bost, a boy from the same area as their original encampment. A boy who'd witnessed all the Enskaran expeditions and survived them. Miraculously. He'd been slow to befriend the newcomers and finally had to be ordered to play with Dillon. That day had been awkward, but by evening, the two were best friends.

Bost was treated better than his father, Onuieg, but not as well as the Enskarans. If the Enskarans, relatives of the people who'd decimated the village, were welcomed, what terrible thing had Bost's ancestors done? Though all were referred to as huservus, the Rowdanae were truly servants, bearing the heavy trays to table and doing the washing up. They weren't beaten or demeaned, but they were surely different and did most of the burdensome work.

Thinking he finally had the right words, he'd asked Bost about it during the pollen harvest, but he'd gotten the standard reply: "Rowdanae," as if that explained everything.

Once a traveling band of men wished to test themselves against the village. Lahgassi stood with their emissary on a platform in the square and explained the challenge. Millie translated for the Enskarans. A nonlethal battle and the victor would win a prize. Their leader held up a pole hung with trophies from past victories and showed a polished piece of jade representing his nomadic clan. Several people spoke for and some against the conflict, honor and manpower being the concern, and then a vote was called. The Rowdanae looked on, didn't join the discussion, and didn't vote one way or the other. In the end the challenge was accepted, and in a field two kilometers from the village Pemioc lost after a ten-hour scrimmage that involved a half dozen leather balls, hooked rods, and fifty souls to a side, men and women. Many people were injured, some carried from the field, blood pouring from split scalps, but the game went on until the final score and a unified declaration of victory. There were no hard feelings, players hugged and laughed, compared wounds, and then all returned to the village for a feast. It had been a wonderful holiday. The entire village had watched the game – everyone except the Rowdanae, who'd missed every stroke, score, and play preparing for the feast and then cleaning up after. Bost was not happy about that.

There'd been many hours for Dillon to wander the village and play in the river. If he chose to linger by a villager, they invariably invited him over to see what they were doing and then tried to teach him something. It began as curiosity, moved to play, and then before he knew it, he'd spent half a day helping a fisherman find shellfish or sealing hives with a sap brush. His mentors would teach him vocabulary and tell stories about their work, why it was important and how they liked it. Before he knew it, he knew more Tirgwenian folk tales than Enskaran history.

As the summer drew to a close, the harvests began, and playtime was put aside for real work. Dawn to dusk sometimes, the village assembled the stuff it would need to survive the winter. The hunters left for weeks at a stretch while others tended the patchwork of fields, the last without fences or lines. One in four was harvested. One left fallow. One was turned and readied for the following year's planting. The fourth was wild and untouched to the untrained eye, as natural and untamed as at the birth of the planet, but it too was tended, watched, and replanted with hortmal and honey berries that the bees so loved and would feed the people in dire times. There was the home of creatures that shared the land with the Pemiae, and the caretakers entered those spaces quiet and reverent as if entering a church.

The rodwheat was the last of the major harvests. It needed a couple of freezes before it could be gathered. The pollen fields and the hidden orchards were replanted. Tilled fields offered beans and grapes and everyone gathered the wild varieties. Fish came from the river, was salted and stored. Oxen and pigs, wild tallstag and yellow-winged grouse were all cured in tall triangular huts that poured out sweet smoke like perfume flavored in autumn mists.

He liked the harvests. They were festive. They'd walk out of the gates in parade formation, songs on their lips sung in puffs of frosty breath as the sun crested the horizon. The work was hard but good and Dillon drank honey mead at lunch that made him dizzy-silly. The Enskarans joined the Tirgwenians in the work and sang their own songs, which the others learned and joined.

Though anyone could offer instruction and advice and frequently did, Lahgassi oversaw the work with Millie at her side. Dillon was terrible with a scythe until old lady Chasopi showed him how to do it properly. She had to be a hundred years old, all yellow wrinkles and purple tattoos, one eye white, the other slow-blinking. She worked with him until he was as good as anyone his size at the job. She'd given him a proud smile when he finished his patch, showing three missing teeth, and he smiled back, the steam sweat rising from his back into the crisp evening air.

It was a good harvest; everyone said so. They spoke of good omens at the community fires and said it was good they allowed the off-worlders to join them. They spoke of balance and debts, but to be honest, Dillon didn't understand it all.

"Your sister is good soul," Maffrit said.

Dillon snapped to, unaware he'd been daydreaming.

"Aye, aye," he said. "Millie, aye. She's always been that way."

"You will miss her?"

He looked at her trying to guess if she'd misspoken, or if not, what it meant.

"I don't see her as much as I'd like," he said. "We were all we had for the longest time."

"You not have others?"

"The other ones here? They were there but we weren't allowed to be…to…. There was a man named Aguirre," he said. "He took over the colony. He wasn't very nice. He wouldn't let us be like this."

"This?"

He gestured to the village, to the blanket-clad women popping kernels into baskets, bee tenders sweeping around the hives, a carpenter carving a greenwood bowl with intricate lines of netting.

She shook her head.

He sought for words. "We weren't like this," he said finally. "We were miserable and alone. We were treated unfairly. We finally left and came here because Millie knew the way. He said he did, but he didn't. He's out there still, I suppose, wandering around with the others like him."

"Rowdanae," she said and nodded.

Dillon shrugged.

A wind picked up and brought the smell of snow. He'd come to know it but no longer feared it. Back in the palisade, each storm presaged death and more deprivation. The scent still carried some of those echoes, but not nearly as bad. The village was prepared and he knew whatever terrible thing fate would send would first have to go through the village to get to him.

Laughter came from behind. He turned to see Jasnenay pull Mr. Tydway's blanket off his shoulders and run away with it. He was bare-chested beneath it and immediately ran after her, swearing that he was going to get her but laughing as he did. Dillon marveled at the man he knew from before, seeing his strong defined muscles where there'd been only bones and skin. He saw also the first lines of a purple snaking tattoo reaching out from under his arm.

Jasnenay shrieked as he scooped her up in his arms and carried her off toward the hay beds.

Maffrit smiled but kept her eyes down.

Dillon wondered at the display. He'd never seen the like among his people. Such behavior would have put Mr. Tydway in the stocks not just back on the island, but in Vildeby too. The tattoo particularly unnerved him. But somehow it matched not only the change in Mr. Tydway's physical form, but also his emotional one. He'd always been a very stern man, cold and emotionless. When his wife died of the pox last year, he'd not cried a tear. Now his laughter echoed off the huts and hives. This place was miraculous.

Maffrit slid her hand on top of his.

Dillon jumped.

"Feel skin," she said, her wide smile making him nervous. "See same?"

"What?"

"I think she wants to see how our skin compares to hers." It was Millie. She wore a traveling cloak of tan feathers and a padded leather jerkin. Her boots were colored in four shades of mud.

"Where have you been?" Dillon asked.

"Long story."

"I'd like to hear it. Do you have time today?"

She looked at him as if seeing him anew. "Aye, brother. Shall we walk?"

"I have work," he said.

"I do it so sister brother talk," said Maffrit. "Pax, Millie Dagney."

"Pax, Maffrit. You are very pretty today."

She blushed and turned away, stealing a glance at Dillon as she did.

"Come with me to the river," Millie said to Dillon.

They walked past the visitor barracks where they'd stayed the first fortnight. There was a group from upriver who'd come to trade fish for seasoned salts staying there now.

"So where have you been?" he asked.

"I went looking for Aguirre."

"Why?"

"He's been harassing some folk," she said.

"How?"

"He killed a family of Rowdanae."

"What? How do you know?"

She turned her hand up and the bee landed on her palm. "I wanted to know, and so I did."

"Do you understand it yet? The why or the how of these bees?"

"No. But I think I will soon."

"Why soon?"

She sighed heavily and waved to the traders making tea. They waved back but watched her warily. Her pale features and bright hair were surely strange to them.

"Can you explain to me what Rowdanae are?" Dillon said. "It's driving me nuts."

"It's complicated."

"I have time."

"Sorry," she said. "Isn't that Onuieg?"

Bost's father walked up their path, bearing a bucket yoke. He was headed toward the cesspool and didn't spare them a glance. Dillon could guess what was in the buckets.

"There, see?" he said. "I clean our bucket in our house, but Onuieg there collects it from like a dozen. Why?"

"It has to do with the bees."

"Of course it does." Dillon kicked a pebble.

"The bees come to people who are ready for them," she said. "That's how it was explained to me. But I kinda knew that already."

"How?"

"The bees."

"Why'd I ask?"

She smiled.

"If you're not ready, the bees stay away. If, however, you're Rowdanae, the bees will flat-out hate you."

"How do they show hate?"

"I'm not sure. I think they tattle to people with bees."

"Is being a Rowdanae inherited?"

"I think sometimes it is," she said. "At least Rowdanae tend to make other Rowdanae. Where they live is called Rodawnoc."

"I know. All place names end in *oc*. All peoples in *ae*. Pemioc, Pemiae. I learned that last summer."

"Not always, but yeah. Good catch."

Her smile reminded him of his mother's, though he was hard put to remember more about the dead woman than that.

"You'll get a bee yet," she said.

"So they're outcasts?"

"Aye, they're sent away or put into service where they can be watched. Both are a way to get bees."

"What? You mean you can get good grades at cleaning toilets and get a bee?"

"Aye. It's suffering. That's the key to it. Suffering brings wisdom and wisdom brings bees."

"That's how you got yours?"

"There's more to it. Suffering plows the field but the plants grow from sympathy, from feeling the suffering of others. It's a gift."

"A gift?"

"The bees think so."

"Do the bees talk to you, like in words?"

"Nay. They just show me things. I don't understand it, but I want to. And I will."

"You're not telling me something."

"That's true. But first the Rowdanae. As you know, this area was in pretty bad shape. The pox killed a lot of people and then Hasin killed more. Some of the Rowdanae who had been out there came here like we did, broken and dying, willing to serve rather than perish. They were brought on, but they can't escape their quest. They won't escape it. If they choose not to serve, they're no good to anyone, particularly themselves. The villages are trying to help them by making them work so hard. They'd starve them if they could, beat them if they thought that would help. They want them to go back into the wild, but the village is short of people, so they keep them on, making their lives easier than it might have been. It might not be a service to them, but needs must."

"And Bost?"

"Can still get a bee," she said. "At least he's not a true Rowdanae yet. The bees haven't made up their mind. He's still young. Not much to dislike about him. In any event, I bet he'd be welcome to stay in the village forever. Take a mate even. Maybe Maffrit." She gave him a coy smile.

"What is that look supposed to mean?"

"She likes you."

"Gross." He stuck out his tongue. "Did the bees tell you that?"

"Nay. But I'm not blind."

"I don't know what you're talking about."

"No matter."

"What about Onuieg?"

"With the bees? Possibly. The death of his wife helped."

"How can you say that? Bost cries for her all the time."

"That's the trade. Misery for wisdom. Stupid, isn't it?"

"Aye."

"Onuieg murdered someone," she said. "His wife's lover before Bost was born. That's the sin he carries."

"What? How do you…." He shook his head. "Why don't they just punish him and be done with it?"

"He was then."

"But not enough?"

"Nay. He doesn't think so."

"What about the other Rowdanae?"

"All of them have something like that. Some are much worse."

"Worse than murder?"

"Capable of worse. Further from wisdom."

"You make it sound like the bees are running the planet."

"Sometimes I think so, but they don't make decisions."

"They do too."

"Maybe."

He could see she was upset. She bit her lip, switching sides, upper and lower, twisted her face as if searching for a sum that wouldn't calculate.

The air, already chilled, was cooler by the river. There was ice in the shadows on the banks, and snow under the trees and against the huts.

Drying racks stood empty and tall, parallel posts and pallets set just off the dock. Fishnets and baskets waiting to be cleaned and put up kept them company near an upside-down canoe with a tear in its bottom. There was no one there to attend them.

"I don't think I've ever seen the river so deserted," Dillon said.

"We are happy here, aren't we?" she said to the river.

"We are," he said. "It beats starving to death, that's for sure."

"Aye, but more than that?"

"Isn't this exactly what Mom and Dad were looking for when they took us here? A place to be safe and healthy? A community?"

"There were other motives, not as simple, but I'd like to think this was what their idea ultimately was."

"How was theirs different?"

"Ambition," she said. "Conquest. Changing the place to suit them rather than the other way around."

"Well," said Dillon, "that's good, isn't it? I mean, we have to make this place civilized, don't we?"

She closed her eyes and inhaled deeply through her nose.

"You can smell the sea," she said. "Just a hint of salt, like a memory from before."

"Gives me the willies," he said. "Reminds me of those terrible times."

"Me too, a little."

A group of green water birds glided by like so much driftwood. They curved their long necks to watch the two and floated downstream a meter above the surface toward the ocean.

"Do our people talk about civilizing this place?"

Dillon heard a weight in the question and so thought before answering. "Nay, I've not heard those kinds of things since before. Aguirre said them a lot. As did the others. Dad too."

"Do you think the plan has changed?"

Again he paused and considered. "Because we don't have a church anymore?"

"Do the people ask for one?"

"Nay," he said. "I've not heard mention, but I assumed since.... We used to have church every day – several times a day," he said. "Strange how we don't miss it."

"Do you miss it?"

"Nay, of course not," he said. "But if we don't have one, aren't we forgetting something?"

She looked much older, suddenly. There was sadness in her eyes and a depth to them. They seemed to take in so much more than his. Dillon wanted to see with her eyes, to see what she saw, because he knew she saw things he did not and might never. Now she looked at him as if delving into his mind. A bee circled her brow and he started to think that maybe she was.

"We honor our parents with life," she said. "We must grow. That is what they would have us do."

He thought he understood. "Do you think that the others will try to, uh...civilize these people?"

"They might try," she said. "And if they do, they'll probably be exiled like the Rowdanae."

"Really?"

"Or worse," she said.

Dillon looked back toward the village and tried to see it as a threatening place. It had been once, when they first arrived, spearman surrounding them, bowmen and soldiers, but now it was home. And that was strange. He'd never felt at home in the ship traveling here, and never in the fort. But here, after just a few months, he'd found his place and it was good. He tried to imagine these people throwing them out. It was hard until he remembered his own people mistreating theirs, then with a mirror, he could see the danger.

"I don't want to be civilized," he said.

"That comment might win you a bee."

"Really?"

"I don't know. But I liked it."

"When will you know?"

She shook her head.

"But you're learning?"

"I am," she said.

"Good, because you need to teach me. And everyone, really. They all look up to you."

"Still?"

"Of course."

"They're all settled in and can speak for themselves," she said. "They'll be fine. They can do without me."

Dillon didn't like the sound of that. "Feeling sorry for yourself?"

"Perhaps a little."

"You're being weird. Are the bees teaching you to be weird?"

"Nay. The bees aren't teachers. Not like that. They're more like a telegraph or a library."

Dillon harrumphed. "This is so confusing. So you have a library but no teacher?"

"Lahgassi has tried to teach me, but she can't help me fast enough."

"Fast enough for what?"

Millie's eyes were drawn upriver where the current bent around a bluff. A shadow crossed her face, a deeper worry. Dillon squinted to see, raised his hand to shade his face and looked. He saw only the river. Water and current, smooth and roiling.

"Why are we here?" said Dillon. "At the river?"

"There." She pointed.

As if by her gesture, a long canoe rounded the bend. It was wider than the ones from the village, sturdier, better in every way. It had straighter lines and rounder curves. It took the current as if up on blocks and barely nodded to an eddy as it crossed over. It was adorned with color and shine. Engravings wreathed the sides, curved and straight, tribal and deep, like the tattoos of the Pemiae but different – like a dialect. The bow glinted in gold and silver, sparkled in red, blue, and green gems. There were no oarsmen. It moved as if by motor, but there was no sound or smoke save for a humming of bees in a cloud of insects hovering over a hive at the stern. A single man stood at the prow, tall and straight. He was clad in a simple pale blue robe draped over one shoulder. His other showed his yellow skin in the amber rays of the autumn sunlight. He wore a broad-brimmed hat of a darker blue that would shelter his shoulders from rain. He raised his hand in greeting.

Glancing down at his own pale skin, Dillon felt ashamed and vulnerable. He slid behind his sister, who had straightened up, raised her chin, and turned upriver to face the coming crisis.

"Who is it?" said Dillon.

"His name is Bouer," she said. "He's my new teacher. I'm going away."

CHAPTER ELEVEN

It fell to the lot of Elder Wells and myself to penetrate the thickets along the river and up the mountainside to find a passable way through. The events of the previous days where the scree had fallen and sent to God eighty-seven faithful brethren and wives weighed heavy on us. We picked our way through the narrow gorge, looking for the path that would safely bring the people across.

We had only to look at the sheer walls around us to know that God had led us here. After the crash and the regrouping, after traveling months across the plains, God had put us directly before this wedged canyon as a promise. It stood stark and high, light-filled and full of wonder, like an open door in a granite wall. The prophet declared it a miracle and called back the scouts. Together, four weeks ago, we entered with glad hearts and took the challenges as they came, cutting the road in bare rock and river bottom, thicket and briar on the slopes. Four weeks of challenges and graves until this blessed day when Elder Wells and I broke through to the valley beyond.

Journal of Elder Clayton Willemsen
Saints Gate, Temple
22, Seventh-Month, 2 NE

05:00, 16, Twelfth-Month, 938 NE – Saints Gate, Temple

Saints Gate was a single V-shaped canyon, narrow and sharp, cut into a soaring wall of granite as if someone had plunged an ax through it.

The mountain range had craggy peaks and jutting pinnacles that poured debris down their steep sides into lower narrow valleys. These other canyons held secret paths that were easy travel but discovered late, long after the settling and the establishment of Zion City, home of the Hall of the Prophet and seat of the sovereign of the Saved. When the first peoples had arrived from their crashed ship of the Unsettling, they'd seen the pass as a gift from God, a way through an impenetrable obstacle. Proof the divine loved them.

Jessop knew the story of the pass and trek. It was told with ever-increasing zeal each Pioneer Festival. Every child knew how the faithful had carved roads in the cliff side and how many scores of souls had fallen to the raging glacier-fed river below. The road was still there, but seldom traveled. Rail tracks through Mill Canyon and a cart road along the Tanner River were the safer and surer paths, but Jessop could not fault the pilgrims for rushing the gap. Viewed straight on, from the west as he did now at dawn, Saints Gate was a shining open split through the highest mountain range on the planet, walls of stark white granite two thousand meters and more recalling Moses's walk through the sea.

The prophet's Second Advisor exited the train in the little town that bore the name of the famous pass behind it. The stationmaster met him on the platform.

"Advisor Jessop," he said and bowed so low that Jessop thought he'd tumble over. "Saints Gate is truly honored to have such a holy and noble official as you visit us."

In the distance were the far spires of Zion City. It was not even five and twenty kilometers from where he stood, just a few minutes by rail, but seemed much farther.

"I take it the presidency doesn't visit here much," Jessop said.

"Nay, they are busy and we are but a small place."

"But an important one."

The man beamed with pride. "I have alerted the mayor and town council. I just heard of your coming."

"Nay, Brother Smith," he said, reading the name off his badge. "I am not here officially, and contrary to your kind and reverent welcome, I am not noble. I am but a servant of the Lord." He'd meant it as a modest confession that unlike the other apostles, he indeed had humble roots.

The man bowed again, and seemed at a loss for what to say.

"I'm here to visit the archives," Jessop said. "I won't be here more than the day."

"The mayor will be disappointed. He is at this moment arranging a feast. We have not had anyone from the first presidency here in over three hundred years."

"Truly?"

"Aye," he said, almost ashamed. "But we travel to the Hall on all the holy days. We are devout and true keepers of the vault."

It was the town motto: *The Keepers of the Vault.*

"Then it is only right that I make time," said Jessop. "I will remain at least until tomorrow so I may meet you good people at the feast. In the meantime, can you find me a guide to take me up the pass?"

"Aye, Your Holiness. I'll see to it at once. Have you luggage?"

"Only my case."

"I'll see to the guide immediately. Blessed be."

"And to thee, Brother Smith."

The stationmaster lit up as if he'd been given the keys to heaven.

Jessop had wanted to make this visit in secret. He'd traveled second class without escort, servant, or soldier, and wore only walking clothes under a warm plain coat, nothing unusual or suggestive of his station. Nevertheless, he'd been recognized. What had doubtlessly given him away was his foreignness. He was from Claremond and he wore the blueish hazel hair of that place and its freckles still from his youth. In a sea of silver-haired Templers, he stuck out like lint in milk. He was not the only foreigner on Temple but he was by far the most famous. Second Advisor to the prophet of all humanity. His picture was probably hanging in the stationmaster's office below that of the prophet.

He was not worried, however. The only man in the system he had to answer to was the man he wanted to ask questions of. This at least might strike up a conversation. In the meantime, he was Second Advisor and there were not many doors his word would not open, nothing he could do that would not be pardoned. Even this breach, should it be discovered, would be unpunished. He'd not been given permission, but forgiveness was a certainty.

At the door of the station he found a cab while the stationmaster sought to have the mayor's personal carriage brought up for him instead.

"This will be fine," he said and got in.

The stationmaster acquiesced but was clearly unhappy. Whether he'd lost respect for the advisor or thought he'd failed him, Jessop could not say. It was so tiring trying to live up to everyone's idea of him.

"To the church vaults," he told the cabman. "And pray you, do not worry. I have a pass to enter." And with that the cabbie clicked his horses and the cab pulled away.

The calm lazy morning drive past fields of gleaming snow and idyllic farmhouses was far removed from the turmoil engulfing all of humanity.

"We are fighting for our very existence," the prophet had said. It was how he opened every meeting of the inner sanctum now. He said it the day before in the progress meeting and spoke it with a terrible and frightening zeal that was contagious, though none save Eren himself seemed to know what the threat actually was.

Eren would reveal his prophecy in good time, but it had been months now – half a year – and still Jessop knew no more of that pivotal moment than he did the day it happened. He had been there, had witnessed Eren coming out of his sanctum, holy fire burning in his soul, touched of God and purpose. Just after the defeat of the Hyraxian armada, the prophet had demanded to see the records of an ancient and disgraced monastic order and in the same breath issued a holy edict that mankind must stop fighting themselves. There was a greater threat, he maintained. But what that was, he didn't say.

The prophet had weekly meetings with all his advisors and any apostles who cared to join. Few did. They kept the functions of the church running smoothly while the prophet dealt with this crisis. Most of the apostles were too old to do more than nod. The prophet must have seen this too, since he surrounded himself with more vibrant ministers and functionaries. Men of power and intelligence who brought news from all around the system, offering information and gossip as if it were an offering upon an altar.

"We are unclear what to make of the Enskaran reaction to your holy dictate." Minister Bensen had become the central liaison for the intelligence agencies and the prophet's primary adjunct, closer than even his advisors. He was a capable man, a Templer, an old school friend of the prophet in his late sixties. He had left a congregation in Havilah to serve the prophet upon his ascension. He had no official title beyond minister and before the recent crisis had provided for visiting dignitaries. Jessop always suspected he was a spy, relaying what he learned in the quiet of Visitors House to the prophet at their monthly lunches. "They parade the purger tools in a publicity tour, rallying people to their queen and painting Hyrax and this holy planet in the worst possible light."

Grand Purger Greguri looked on unashamed. His face bore a smooth acid scar on the right and he did nothing to conceal it. His black-and-white checkered sash was bright and crisp-pressed. He sat with the air of a man beyond judgment. Many whispered he was the power behind the throne, but Jessop knew that to be a lie. Still, his powers to guarantee orthodoxy by any means meant that he might, by virtue of his office and army, threaten even the highest among them.

"What of Maaraw?" said the prophet. "What help have they sent there?"

"A small Enskaran fleet – three to five ships – was sent some months ago to relieve their colonies. They arrived unhindered."

"Hyrax let them through?" asked First Advisor Hansen.

"Nay," said the envoy. "We suspect they were never challenged. They snuck by. Probably rose above the well and skirted the civilized worlds."

"That's dangerous," said Jessop.

Hansen shrugged. He'd never been off-world and at his age, eight and seventy, it was doubtful he ever would.

"Did they send troops to squash the rebellion?"

To this, Minister Halley, a Maarawan himself, one of only three non-Templers in the room, rose to speak. "Some arms, a few men. Enough to garrison their Z colony."

"Z colony?" said Jessop.

Minister Halley looked embarrassed. "We call it that."

"What do they call it?"

"Zabelland," he said. "After their accursed heretical queen."

"That's not enough," said Eren. "We need troops there. We need a purging. We need to squash that planet, end the rebellion. We need to control its ecosystem."

"We lost thousands of purgers over Enskari," Greguri said flatly. "It'll take us years to recover."

"We don't have that much time!" Eren slammed his fist on the table and the entire room jumped.

"The loss of life from the loss of the armada is staggering," said Bensen. "The reports from Hyrax suggest that it might boil over to threaten Brandon himself."

"I read D'Angelo's report," said Jessop. "Our worthy brother apostle said nothing like that. Has there been a new missive?"

"Nay, Brother Jessop," said Bensen. "But I have found that letters from Minister Rendelle are generally more accurate."

"Ah," said Jessop, recalling D'Angelo's drinking.

"What other word from Hyrax?" Eren asked.

"They have sent less than Enskari to Maaraw, Your Holiness. They're leaving the defense of their colonies to the merchants and nobles who have interests there. I suspect Brandon is hesitant to send troops off-world."

"Fear of Enskaran counter-attack?" said Hansen.

"That and…." Bensen glanced at Eren.

That was the moment Jessop decided to make the trip to Saints Gate. Bensen knew something that he did not. He shared the secret with the prophet. Not a secret, but *the* secret. Humble as Jessop was, he could not let obedience get in the way of service.

"Every planet is endangered, Kendall," said the prophet, using Jessop's first name. "Everything we have is perched on this precipice."

Jessop waited then, like he'd waited countless times before, for the prophet to explain the terrible threat, but again he did not. Bensen spoke instead.

"So, Brandon would keep his forces close to home. There have been assassinations, members of his own family recently murdered. And now and always, social unrest. The levies upon the people—"

"Are nothing new," said First Advisor Hansen. "Brandon must not be such a coward. The prophet has asked him do a thing, and he must do it. The prophet speaks, he must obey. From this planet, this city, this hall and table comes law for all humanity. We are the shepherds of man. This is the seat of the king of men, speaker for God, the divine connection. We are the governing body of the Saved."

"Hear, hear!" went the affirmation around the table. Jessop added his while watching Eren, who seemed unmoved by the unanimous adoration.

"What about mercenaries?" he asked.

"They are in short supply," said Bensen, referring to a report Jessop had not seen. "And of course the slave trade from Maaraw is nearly nonexistent."

Eren turned to Greguri. "Why wasn't this ended before?"

"You read High Purger Tarquin's report," said the grand high purger, and Jessop saw then that Greguri too knew the secret.

And he didn't.

"The war continues, Your Eminence," continued Bensen. "It will be fought on Tirgwenin now."

"How so?" asked Jessop.

Again referring to papers and reports he, Second Advisor, had never seen, Bensen said, "Hyrax is sending a landing force to claim Jareth's World."

"They're going to destroy the Enskaran colony there?" said Jessop.

"Nay. That colony has already failed. In fact, Sommerled, the queen's plaything, has lost his patent to it."

"It was an illegal patent," said Hansen. "The prophet gave that world to Brandon and Hyrax."

"Even so," continued Bensen, "Enskari has granted the rights to that world to Aderyn and Brett. They must set up a permanent colony. There are already ships en route."

"Admiral Aderyn?" said Greguri. "One of my childhood heroes. He'll not be caught unaware."

"I doubt he'll go himself," said Jessop.

Bensen said, "We don't know how many ships, or what they carry."

"They'll have the shorter voyage than Hyrax either way," said Jessop.

Eren VIII ground his teeth, his face red with worry.

"What is it, Your Eminence?" asked Jessop.

"That world..." he said. "It vexes me."

"Hyrax needs it," said Bensen. "Their coffers are empty and Silangan is in upheaval."

"Another revolt?" said Hansen. "Savages."

"Nay. Not anything like Maaraw. I'd call it an upheaval." Bensen found a paper among the others and scanned it. Speaking over the top of it, he said, "It's not organized. It's wild and bloodthirsty. If there is hell in our system, it might be Silangan. There are wholesale massacres of people and animals. Whole forests afire. Savages on savages, savages on Saved. Half the mines have closed. The others are in lockdown."

Jessop watched Eren for a reaction to this new terrible news, but he saw nothing for Silangan.

"Social stirrings on all worlds," said Bensen.

Jessop asked, "What do you mean, 'social stirrings'?"

Bensen looked at Eren, then said, "I'm trying to take the measure of our flocks."

"For?"

"Stirrings."

Jessop laughed.

"Raise an army of Templers," said Eren. "We'll do this ourselves."

"Do what?" said Jessop.

"Defend the Saved."

"From what?"

"The end of the world," was all he said.

The meeting ended. Jessop cleared his calendar and bought a ticket to Saints Gate to seek answers.

The Maarawan revolt challenged Jessop's beliefs. On the one hand, it was a brutal bloody affair. Plantations burned, Saved slaughtered, a reign of terror. On the other, it was a fight for freedom, a noble struggle like those told of in scripture, a people throwing off their chains.

After the Unsettling, before the planets communicated again one to another, each world had varied in their faith and practices. Some more than others. Silangan was nearly unrecognizable. Claremond, Jessop's home, was not far from what Temple itself had become. Orthodoxy and unification came with the arrival of missionaries, and the civilized worlds quickly righted themselves to the one true faith. Maaraw's deviation, however, was deemed great enough to label an entire people subhuman, with the asterisk that some could be saved, but most, particularly those from the interior, were now little more than animals. And the slave markets opened. Lifelong, generational slavery in all its ugliness was born and maintained by the other worlds whose technologies had fared better than the Maarawans'.

Jessop often mused at the strange quirks of history and chance. Humanity had fled a dying world, leaving Old Earth in the misery of pollution, disease, and disaster. Each fleeing ship had arrived and been stricken dumb by this sun's power, crashing each upon a world. There, each separated from the others for three quarters of a millennium, nearly identical societies were born. Nobility and caste mirrored upon each colonized world much the same, with the exceptions being Silangan, which had now gone mad, and Maaraw, where natural religions replaced the True Word and damned them all. How unlucky to be Maarawan. How terrible to be Silangian. How graced to be civilized.

When he was a child he'd asked his minister about Maaraw.

"Are they not people too?" he'd said. "Should we not treat them as we would be treated?"

"Some are born to lead, others to serve."

"But they have done nothing wrong."

"God has made them for this. All is right and as it should be. Do not pity them. They are blessed for their toil. It is their work that builds civilization. When their work is done, they will be brought back to the fold if they are worthy. The prophet himself says so."

"Could not the prophet free them all now, with a word?"

"Aye. And one day that will happen."

"When?"

"When they are ready."

In the carriage up the canyon, he remembered that moment now, recalling Eren's rage at that planet's rebellion. What better sign of being ready for freedom could there be than actively warring for it?

It was an ugly thing. Maarawans were already stigmatized. Even Minister Halley, able and bright, freeborn and wealthy, devout Saved, would never rise to the heights of those born on civilized worlds. It had been for the prophet's sake and for his local knowledge that he'd been allowed in council at all, but Jessop knew that the other ministers and apostles saw him as some kind of trained monkey, mimicking the niceties of society, not really human.

He'd grown up thinking that any moment the prophet would free the slaves, raise all of humanity by raising the lowest. How could the church ever fulfill its promise of heaven incarnate when there was inequality, caste systems, and worse – racial slavery?

His family for a while had been affluent, and owned Maarawan slaves. He remembered how the new ones would cry at night, but the old ones were worse. Jessop never forgot how truly broken they were, accepting every indignity and offense offered them. He tried to defend them, demanding of his fellow countrymen and Saved that they at least be shown compassion. They had laughed at him for that, stranger and friend alike. "Whose side are you on?" they asked. Animals weren't treated so badly, but animals wouldn't tolerate what the slaves were made to. They could bite and flee, but the marooned Maarawans on Claremond were trapped. The spirits were driven out of them if not in the first generation, then by the second.

There'd been that terrible time when a maid, who no one had known was even pregnant, gave birth and drowned the child in a washbasin. The father never came forward. It was never known if he had been Claremondian or Maarawan, so young was the child that no marker had shown yet. It was just a baby, innocent potential lost. It could have been Tirgwenin for all anyone knew. They hanged the maid in the square. From the moment she was discovered to the moment her neck snapped, she never said a word. Jessop had been ten years old and he could recall her dark lifeless eyes unchanged by her dying.

The prophet had to free them. No one else could. For all Brandon's ambitions, if there was to be a central government in the system, it would be in the Hall of the Prophet. Jessop had seen this in Eren's new mania. Directives across worlds, information gathered and acted upon, however incomplete. Enskari was lost to the heretic queen, Silangan never in the fold, Maaraw possibly one day. The prophet acted for the good of all, for all the Saved across the civilized worlds. He alone had the authority – moral and traditional – to end the human trade, but could he? The planets had come to rely on Maarawan labor, some more than others. On Temple they were menial servants. On Lavland, harvests wouldn't happen without them, and of course Hyrax marched them before their armies to absorb bullets.

But the size of the horror protected it. The sudden emancipation of millions of slaves would destroy worlds. The prophet could dictate, but as shown by Queen Zabel, he could not enforce. Should he dare free the slaves, he'd have four apostate princes instead of one.

But that was not what haunted the prophet now. No. It was Tirgwenin. *"That world…it vexes me."*

The realization that the voice of God was afraid sent a chill down Jessop's back.

The certainty of this steeled him in his errand. It might not make him a heretic, though he approached the border of that dark land; this visit to Saints Gate made him disobedient. As the highest ranking non-Templer of the church in the history of the Saved, he was risking much for this trip.

The ministry had not been his first career choice. He'd expected to join the hundred-year-old family glass-making business. He remembered, when he was very young, the little shop bursting with people, workmen and buyers, trained craftsmen and apprentices. These were the times when they'd have servants at home. It was the high time, the halcyon days.

He remembered the first cracks in their happiness in a whispered conversation between his parents. His father speaking too quietly to hear in their kitchen as young Jessup studied music in an adjacent room. His mother he remembered saying, "It'll be all right, dear. Quality will win out."

Within a year, the threat was plain to all, and even young Kendall Jessop could see it. A new glass factory went up not two kilometers from where their little shop stood. The third son of the noble House of Broglie threw it together with the proceeds from a temporary levy the county put upon the merchants.

The new factory brought in a hundred Maarawan slaves for labor and collected indentured servants from across the planet and beyond. Lavlandian glassblowers were installed in barracks on the factory grounds. Their own trained workers were poached away, some suddenly having their mortgages called and signing contracts with Broglie to keep their family under a roof. The price of jars plummeted. Some said that the factory lost a dollar on every jar it sold. Which was a trick for a five-and-twenty-cent piece of glass. With such competition it did not take long before Jessop's glass business no longer made jars. Once they'd pulled out of that line of business, Broglie cornered the market, secured long-term contracts, and tripled prices.

But by then Jessop's family's business was well and truly failing.

The servants were sold and the family moved first to a small house on the west side, a lower rent district. They lasted there a year before moving again to an apartment in a worse part of town, and finally, to a converted shipping shed behind their shop.

His father had taken to drinking and his brothers grew wild. He remembered the day he'd told them he was leaving for Temple, that he'd been accepted to study on the holy planet.

His father looked on, half-drunk. His mother started to cry. His brother was livid.

"You're selling us out," said his brother, Andrew.

"There is no work here," he said. "This is the best future I can make."

"Aye, but what of our future?"

"One less mouth to feed."

"Go and do some good, son," said his father. "You have a good heart. Use it."

Andrew shook his head, his face red with rage. "You can do more good here. We need you for the fight. There's injustice here. This is a blood feud with the Broglies. They have ruined us." His brother gripped a long carving knife and shook it. He raised it above his head like a signal, a threat.

"It is just how things are," Kendall said.

"Then things need to change," said Andrew. "What happened to us has happened to others and will happen again if we let it. The few grow rich on the suffering on the many."

"God's will—"

"Man's law," he said.

"What would you have me do?" Kendall asked.

"You are smart, little brother. Think of something and lead."

"Lead who?"

"Those who would fight against this injustice."

"One man's injustice is another man's fortune."

"Must it be so?"

"Revolution?"

"This can't go on. Look around the city, the planet. The middle class is dying."

"It's progress," said Kendall, repeating something he'd heard.

"It's theft."

"It's how things have always been."

"I disagree. Things are changing for the worse. I see us lower than Maarawan slaves before long – toiling to have a blanket and a mouthful of maggoty mush, while the aristocrats drink redberry wine in my stolen goblets."

The goblets were always a sore spot for Andrew. Broglie had copied Andrew's popular design and mass-produced them at a tenth the cost of his handblown version.

"I am sorry, brother. Fate has not been kind."

"It's not fate."

"We wish you well," his mother had said. "Don't we, Andrew?"

Kendall followed his brother's eyes as they fell on their mother, despair and hope, sadness and ruin written there. "Aye," Andrew said, putting down the bad. "Aye. Make us proud."

"I'll try," he said.

"We'll keep going here," said his brother. "I'll marry and make some babies. Keep the name alive. Maybe stir things up."

With the money Kendall sent home, his parents lived out their lives in some measure of comfort. Andrew had his family, a son and a daughter. He'd wooed and won a round woman named Heather after signing on as Broglie's foreman. He kept that job for two years until the factory burned down under suspicious circumstances.

Had he stirred things up? Were these the kinds of 'social stirrings' Bensen had mentioned? He could see no reason to connect the two moments of his life beyond the casual word, and yet here he was.

There was a small coal stove in the cab just big enough to keep the worst of the chill away. Jessop poked the smoldering orange lumps and warmed his hands near its sides. The chimney rattled in the roof and sizzled for the snowmelt as the carriage bounced over the uneven roads. The window had fogged from his breath and Jessop wiped the glass with a sleeve and looked out again.

Already the tiny town was lost in the distance behind hedges and walls. Before him the great crack in the mountains that was the pass rose up like a sentinel guarding a gate.

They drove along the same road as the first emigrants. In places it had been cut out of the very stone in the sheer canyon walls. Out one window, within arm's reach, was the gray rock of the mountainside, while through the other, one icy meter beyond the wheel, was a thousand-meter drop.

They met no one coming down as they ascended, which was all for the best. Jessop could not imagine how two conveyances could pass each other on that narrow road.

Before today, Jessop had always used the libraries in the Hall for his research, occasionally going to other offices to see their collections if he needed something obscure. The archivists had always managed to direct him properly and he'd never been left wanting. His rank brought privilege and there wasn't a collection on the planet he been unable to access. But now he was not so certain.

The vault was a gold mine repurposed for long-term storage, supposedly based on a tradition dating back to Old Earth. Cut deep into the granite mountainside, safe from flood and wind, radiation storm and human attack as much as possible, it offered a safe temperature-controlled repository for important books and records. There was talk of treasures there, ancient artifacts and original copies of scripture. It was rumored that the great houses of the system stored their family records there – genealogy trees, journals. Secrets. It was said that there were caverns within the vault that even the prophet himself could not enter by treaty and custom. Jessop did not give much credence to these stories, and for his purpose he'd not need to test them. He was here to seek local records, forbidden knowledge of the church itself, documents deemed too dangerous to share but too important to destroy. Within the vault he planned to trace legend to page and discover the prophet's secret.

The cab left the road through an open iron gate and rounded a final bend into sunlight, which blinded Jessop for a moment. When he'd blinked away the contrast, he found they were upon a large open ledge, a hundred meters by fifty, with buildings and a loading dock set against the mountain wall. A plain metal door ten meters tall and as many wide marked the entry to the vault. On either side of the door were small wooden shacks, snow-topped, with smoking chimneys. Two soldiers exited them in tandem and moved before the door in step and ritual, crossbows in hand.

Jessop got out of the cab and was struck by the cold. It was dry and penetrating. He pulled his coat around him and stomped his feet.

"How high have we come?" he asked the cabbie.

"Least five and twenty hundred meters above the town, sure 'nuff. Likely more, sure 'nuff, Your Eminence."

"You have borne me sure and safe, kind friend," he said. "Blessed be."

"And to thee."

A door within the door of the mountain opened, and an archivist minister appeared. Jessop saw the gray robes of his office beneath his thick winter coat. His breath, like those of the soldiers and his own, showed in white puffs.

"Welcome, Advisor Jessop," proclaimed the archivist with a wide gesture and a low bow. "We are blessed and happy to have you. I am Gartrall. How may I serve?"

In reaction to Jessop's confused expression, the archivist pointed to a pole with a wire. "I received a telegraph from the mayor," he said. "He asked that I not keep you too long, for he has a banquet planned."

"Quick work," said Jessop, embracing the minister. "I did not mean to bring inconvenience. I would not be a burden."

"It is an honor to have you," he said. "I am at your disposal."

Two young men emerged from the door and rushed at the carriage. "May we take this cab? We have a train to catch."

"Mind your place, students," roared Gartrall at the two. "You are in the presence of the sacred. Do you not recognize Advisor Jessop?"

Recognizing him, the two threw themselves to the ground bowing so low. "Apologies," they said. "We meant no disrespect."

"Scholars?" said Jessop.

"Aye, we usually have a dozen or so here each day."

"I thought access was limited."

"Aye. They have dispensation. We have, as you know, the biggest library on Temple."

He did not know that. But it made sense.

"You may take my cab, brothers," said Jessop. "I will stay here awhile. I assume when I need another, one can be arranged?"

Gartrall pointed to the wire.

"That will be fine," Jessop said. He took out a billfold and offered the cabbie a fifty-dollar bill.

He refused it. "Nay, it is my honor to bear you."

Jessop looked at the man's tattered coat and work gloves, his hat stained with oil spots. He was missing two teeth.

"Then I shall pay for you to convey these gentlemen down."

"I do it for your asking."

Jessop said, "Cabbie, brother, friend. I order you to take this money. Argue no more or I shall grow angry."

"I can't make change for such a sum. Have you a fiver?"

"It is all for you."

"It is a fortune."

"So blessed are you," said Jessop, pushing the money at him.

Tears tinged in the cabbie's eyes. He glanced from Jessop to the archivist and slowly reached his hand out to take the offered bill. "You are truly a great man," he said. "Blessed be."

"And to thee."

The two scholars, young Templers, college-aged and city-fashioned, watched the exchange with awe. Poorly clad, they shivered in the wind, clutching their satchels to their chests and averting their eyes. Jessop waved them off and turned to the archivist, allowing the two to board the cab. With a click of the cabbie's tongue the horses deftly drove down the hill and out of sight.

"Let us go inside," said Jessop. "It is bitter cold."

Gartrall led the way. The two guards ceremoniously turned at the last step and returned to their shacks.

"Those two were here for three days," said Gartrall casually.

"Is that customary to stay so long?"

"Oh, aye. That was a short visit. Little can be done in a week. We have rooms and cots. A simple board for a fair price."

It was not much warmer inside but at least the wind was less. Jessop's breath still showed in mist as his eyes accustomed themselves to the low-light glowglobes set along the corridor.

"It's easy to lose track of time here," went on Gartrall. "No sunlight."

"And fascinating tomes," added Jessop.

"Aye."

"I seek the records of the Brother of Apis," he said.

Gartrall pulled up a step. "Those are forbidden," he said automatically. "The purgers have control over those."

"Just the same, I would see them. You know where they are?"

"Aye," he said. "I have just put them back not these many days ago."

"Excellent. Bring them to me. Is there a private closet, warm and bright, where I might peruse them?"

"It is forbidden."

"Also bring me the records of High Purger Tarquin upon Maaraw. Last year. You will probably find those papers also among the purgers' forbidden archives."

Gartrall shifted his weight uneasily. "There are terrible penalties associated with those texts."

"And rightly so," said Jessop. "I advise you not to read them."

"Oh, I have not – will not. I haven't the right."

"Then go fetch them. Will those acolytes show me to a closet? Tea would be nice. I'll probably like some of your modest fare around lunchtime."

"One must have the right," said Gartrall.

"Did not the prophet read these books?"

"Aye. They were sent for and we delivered them. Under guard. Militia and purger."

"I'd not so inconvenience anyone," said Jessop. "Thus, I have come here. Afterwards I will attend the mayor's banquet?"

"Advisor Jessop," said Gartrall, "I do not mean to be impertinent, but there are strict instructions about those texts."

"Did not the grand high purger peruse them?"

"He has the right."

"As does the prophet?"

"Of course, but it was he himself who—"

"Very good. All is as it should be. You are a faithful servant."

The archivist rolled his hands together. "The prophet's orders were very clear," he said. "Very explicit. None but he may have immediate access. I cannot—"

"Be easy, Gartrall. Here is a letter from the prophet."

He produced the missive from an inner pocket. The letter was in Jessop's own hand, but he could explain that if the archivist asked. The signature, of course, was a forgery, traced from a framed letter hanging on Jessop's office wall calling him to be the prophet's Second Advisor. Though Eren's signature was less firm today than then, the lines were the same.

"Oh, oh," said Gartrall. "Of course. I shouldn't have... please forgive—"

"Nothing to forgive. I should have given this to you first thing. Forgive me for making you uncomfortable. I will tell the prophet how diligent you are."

To that Gartrall beamed.

"I shall retrieve the records myself," he said. "For, to be honest, no one else can." He shook a ring of keys for effect.

"Excellent."

Gartrall insisted that the advisor take his office for his work. He ordered two acolytes to attend him, bring tea and bread, and then he left to retrieve the records.

Jessop sipped tea, admiring the woodwork of the archivist's office, wondering how he'd get the letter back. He was on his third cup when Gartrall arrived bearing three small leather-bound books, an official report envelope, and a tall glass jar full of dead bees.

PART TWO
PRELUDE: THE PRIORY OF APIS TEMPLE (FOUR HUNDRED YEARS PRIOR: 512–515 NE)

'The past is never dead. It's not even past.'
William Faulkner

CHAPTER TWELVE

Abstract: Higher than basic education is not serving the Saved. It is a privilege and not a right. It is a boon given to those who have shown, by virtue of heredity and placement, a requirement to possess an above-basic education. Those unworthy to have it are prone to misuse it. Be it among laymen or clergy, the threat of open access to information is not to be underestimated. Rebellion, unorthodoxy, and apostasy are the inevitable results of free-thinking and unfettered access to unregulated knowledge.

Decree: To diminish this threat and to protect the faith and the faithful, it is hereby ordered by The Divine Prophet Benjamin IV that all books save those listed as approved primary works are to be returned to the Hall of the Prophet for storage, dissemination, or destruction.

(See attached list of approved primary works.)

Apocrypha Edict, 511 NE

3, Fourth-Month, 512 NE – Priory of Apis, Temple

Prior Thomas felt the duty of decision expand in his mind like a blooming bud as he walked in the morning air. He moved slowly down the green grass path beneath pink eaves of peach blossoms and imagined he was in a tunnel. He strolled slowly, deliberately, giving his legs no cause to be angry, his mind no reason to worry. He opened himself to the beautiful day. Ten paces into the trees he paused on his cane and was still a moment. Worried as he was, he loved the renewing beauty of spring.

He turned his face to the filtered sunshine and closed his eyes.

The air was a murmur of sounds; the whisper of wind in the leaves joined the buzzing of spring bees in the flowers. He inhaled the fragrance of the peach blossoms and smiled despite himself. A cool breeze from the mountains touched him then, and carried from those heights the memory of snow. It was crisp and clean but in its pauses gave way to the nearer earthier scents of mud, grass, and those gorgeous sweet blossoms.

Tilting his head to the sky, he opened his eyes against the brilliance. The morning sun shone in a pure gleaming heaven, veined with fragile vestigial auroras and day sparkles peeking out from the deepest blue. Everything seemed clear and bright, a blessed relief from the problems he faced.

He walked the grounds of the priory to clear his mind. He needed to find the connections that would, if not make sense of the new directives, then at least allow him to accept them. So far from Zion City and the Hall of the Prophet, so small and alone, he could not sway opinions where it mattered. His options were to conform or disobey. His holy vows made the latter impossible, but the first went against his heart.

He waved away a flitting bee and admired the healthy trees. He relished the thought of upcoming fruits, ales, and pies. It was a good sign that the crops would be better this year. The monks would have enough to eat, and with any luck, so would the peasants.

The orchard led into the cemetery and in only a few steps Thomas was among the past brethren. There were trees there as well, but not so dense, not so beautiful and pure. They were haphazard and old, relics from the earliest days, and when these died, they would not be replanted over the holy bones. Among them was an apple tree whose seed it was said stretched back to the Unsettling and Old Earth. There were a pair of cherry trees with similarly fabled origins. There was a plum tree in bloom, one of the last, and next to it and thriving like no others were a pair of starch apple trees. Hearty trees those, slow-growing and hard to kill. A weed by many reports, but it fed man and beast alike with its hearty fruit. He was fond of its pulpy red-orange meat secret beneath its yellow skin. It tasted like sweet potato but was stringy and juicy. You could make a bread of it and it would keep you regular. He knew it to be a native plant, one of the few they cultivated. It was popular among the peasants in Apis, the little village whose name the monastery had taken, but since it was not of Old Earth, it was shunned by the higher classes.

That it was here at all was a testament to the priory's position as a bridge between all, between peasants and nobility, between old and the new, between man and God.

At the end of the orchard he walked alongside the gray brick wall. He felt the old brick chip under the pressure of a fingertip, noting how two hundred years had weathered them. He thought about the men who'd made this wall and remembered he was standing now among them. He adjusted his cowl and scapular, cinched up his robe and said a silent prayer for the dead.

Looking back the way he came, he saw the gray abbey rising above the pink trees in similarly cracking brick, but from this far away, with its red ochre tiled roof, it looked like a scab-topped mountain. The shingles were bright as blood or faded to near gray depending on when they'd last been replaced. The random arrangement of their shades held his interest longer than he thought it should.

Between the bakery and the bathhouse, he could make out tawny-robed monks strolling among the colonnades, heads bowed, hoods down. He imagined he heard the click of falling devotional beads as they prayed in the open air. More likely it was an animal cracking nuts or a wild bird beyond the wall, but he liked to think the sound carried as far as the wall, if not farther.

He'd put off his decision, knowing that he had time and that everything was more hopeful in spring light. Things moved slowly here and he felt that speed right and proper. They were small and far and time was their friend.

In good weather Apis was a month from the next village and half a year from the Hall of the Prophet. *No, that's not true*, he thought. That road had improved since he'd last used it five and sixty years before, for the letter he'd received from the prophet about their library was dated only four months prior to him receiving it. The world was growing close. Still, no one in Zion City expected a timely reply.

Down the valley slope floated fingers of white smoke from village chimneys. He could see the clutch of houses with roof tiles the same orange-red as the abbey's, the same mismatched aged colors blending at this distance into a washed-out rust. The storehouses and squares, tradesmen and stables were all grouped gayly like geese on a pond, the water – cultivated fields – surrounding them. Figures walked the morning roads out to waiting farms; a dozen men, two oxcarts, and three horses. They filtered out the side ways, none taking the highway road past Doclen Castle. There were some optics at play that made the fortification look bigger than it was, some refractive illusion that smarter men than he might understand. The village looked small beneath it – another illusion, for he knew the castle to be several kilometers farther and a fraction of the relative size of the clustered buildings, but from here, all lined up and set upon the distant hillside, the castle loomed. The light had not reached around the side of the castle facing Thomas, and the walls seemed dark and menacing. It was built of the same gray brick that made the monastery and town, but in the shadow it looked alien and dark. He'd never understood why the castle had been built as a fortress. There were no marauding bands, no enemy armies. No dangerous wildlife that could challenge a fence let alone a stone wall, and yet from the beginning, it had been intended to be defensible. He'd learned it was of an ancient design, ancient even at the time of the Unsettling, a mimicked relic of bygone times. Now it was a modern ruin, eroding like the walls of the monastery.

A new breeze brought a louder hum to his ears, and he turned toward the vegetable garden and saw beyond the patches of melon and tammygord the back of a monk sitting near the beehives in his yellow robe.

He'd given himself the day to collect his thoughts that he'd been careful not to organize before. Tomorrow he would decide; today he would be left alone, but recognizing Brother Lerer, he thought he might visit the young monk.

"Prior Thomas," said Lerer, turning to see him. "I was just thinking about you."

"Praying for me?"

"Actually, I was wondering what the difference was between a prior and an abbot. We have an abbey, but we call ourselves a priory."

"What about a monastery?"

"Aye, what about that?" The young man smiled a teasing grin. "Come sit," said the young monk.

"On the ground?"

"Or there on the bench." Lerer gestured to a low plank between the hives. The buzzing was constant but soothing.

"Don't these things bother you?"

"They don't have stingers," Lerer said.

"But still."

"I find their sound palliative. Sometimes they land on me, and I let them. That too is restful. Would you rather we talk elsewhere?"

"This is not a formal interview, Brother Lerer."

"Nay, but I would not have you uncomfortable."

Thomas waved his scapular, raised a cloud of sunning bees from the bench, and sat down. "I seem to recall a homily about bees and stinging. A parable, full of warning."

"Those weren't this local variety," Lerer said.

"Nay, from Old Earth most likely. I remember them growing up."

"I remember them as well. Nasty things. Had to wear a suit just to get near them. I like these better, but to be sure they're not as hearty as those we introduced. The Old Earth kind drive these out. This native breed is more sensitive to pesticides and herbicides."

"I didn't know we had any of those."

"We used to. I found mention of them in the gardener's book. The original monks brought them. Barrel of chemicals and seeds. The seeds didn't make it, but the poisons did. It's all long gone now, but the reports of the bees dying out from them are quite clear."

"The bees made a comeback."

"Glad for it. The town is named after them."

"Apis?"

"Means bee. In an ancient tongue."

"How do you know that?"

"It's what the townsfolk say. It might be a rumor, but I saw it referenced also in a log."

Something about the way Lerer spoke made Thomas doubt this, but the day was too warm and his thoughts too muddled to make more of it.

"I never thought of you as a gardener, Lerer, more the bookish type. All this time you've been looking at agriculture? Have we found the hard labor your father requested for you?"

Lerer leaned back and Thomas saw that he sat cross-legged and shoeless on the bare ground.

"I'd like to think my father was joking about that," said Lerer. "But to be honest, Prior – or should it be Abbot? I think he was serious and thought that manual work was the only cure for me."

"Do we not work you hard enough?"

"Not like he'd have me worked."

A bee crawled across Lerer's fingers. He turned his hand to keep it upright and finally blew the bee back into the air.

"The House Melk had no need of me," Lerer said. "I was the youngest son of three. At least, I was then. Dad might have sired a platoon by now."

"As youngest son…."

"Aye. Someone had to join the clergy."

"And we welcomed you."

"I stirred things up back home," he said. "Dad wanted me as far away as possible and Apis is far. In fact, if there is a priory, abbey, or monastery farther away from my home than this, I'd be hard put to name it."

"There are places farther away, my boy."

"Hermitages," Lerer said. "Not orders. You can't send someone to a hermitage. You have to go on your own, but one can pay the flesh-tithing of a son and impress him into a faraway order. Thus getting rid of a problem while rising in local estimation because of the sacrifice."

The bees collected on Thomas's dark scapular. He thought to shoo them away but held back. "I'm having to remind myself these aren't flies."

"You get used to them."

Thomas shrugged. "In ancient times the three were quite different."

"Bees? What do you mean, Thomas? Three what?"

"How is it you talk to me so casually, Brother Lerer?"

Lerer recoiled. "Oh, I am so sorry, Prior Thomas. I meant no disrespect."

"Nay, I mean not to chide you, only to wonder at your reaction to superiors."

The droning rose to a pitch then fell back, small, but present. Thomas scanned the area for what might have aroused them.

"It might be the place, sir— Thomas— Prior, Prior Thomas," Lerer said. "Among the bees I am most relaxed. That surely contributes to me speaking so informally. I have been chided for it before."

"When we are together, Thomas is fine. Refreshing, actually. It's strange we haven't talked much together these three years."

"Five," said Lerer. "I've been here five years. Six in Eighth-Month."

"That long?"

"I am more contented now. I no longer miss the busy streets of Clearport or the luxuries of my father's house."

"I wonder if you are really so detached from them."

"I'd not lie to you."

"Perhaps to yourself."

Lerer appeared to ponder this for a moment. "They seem distant now, and everyone else closer."

"The years have more weight when young. What are you? Eight and twenty?"

"Four and twenty."

Thomas shook his head. "How time has tested my timekeeping. Forgive my forgetfulness. I am three— No, four and eighty now."

"It is of no matter, Thomas. It's relative and insignificant."

"Wise beyond your four and twenty."

Lerer shrugged. "I had a good education before. Our library was well stocked." Here he shot Thomas a hard glance. "I've found something here."

"You speak of God?"

"I'm not sure what, but there is something to all this…peace."

Thomas couldn't control a laugh. "Is this the runaway monk telling me this?"

Lerer smiled abashedly. "Aye. Sorry, Prior. I know I was a problem."

"How many times did you run?"

"Not once this year."

Thomas smiled.

"Four times, the first year," said Lerer. "Once the second. I came back on my own that time."

"You would have died, so ill-prepared for the climate."

"Aye, and there was no place to go. So, see? I've settled down to become a good little monk."

"And yet this morning I find you out here among bees instead of at work."

"And yesterday I was in Apis."

"And missed afternoon, midday, and evening prayers," said Thomas.

"I wouldn't say I missed them."

"Is that a jest?"

"A little one. I spent the day watching a cobbler make shoes."

"And that makes up for missing daily devotions?"

"That *something* was there."

"God?"

"Something."

"In the making of shoes?"

"I've been feeling that something a lot lately." Lerer's eyes fell on the beehives and followed an insect into the air. "A feeling. Or an idea."

"That something has a name," said Thomas. "God."

"I'm not so sure."

"Of course it is."

"What I know of God comes from the scriptures and pulpit."

"Of course."

"But I am not sure that is the same thing I'm feeling. Actually, Thomas, I'm pretty sure it isn't."

The bees flitted in and out, round and away, their low hum a soothing undertone.

"I was explaining priories," Thomas said, "abbeys and monasteries."

"Oh, aye."

"In ancient times they were distinct, but not so much now. Originally a monastery was more like those hermitages you mentioned, except communal. The monks removed themselves from the laymen and sought spirituality that way. A priory was the home for an order of monks. They could be monastic or not. We were founded as a priory. They had more to do with laymen, but still their primary goals were the goals of the order, whatever they might be. And finally, an abbey, headed by an abbot, was more related to the laymen still. An abbey often housed a monastic order but always served the community first. The abbot is leader of not only the order, but to the laymen, much like a bishop."

"What is the goal of our order exactly?" said Lerer.

Thomas laughed. "Honestly, Lerer, I don't think anyone remembers what brought us out here. My guess is that we are the product of the church falling behind settlements. When the population boom happened and people spread out over the planet, they often did so without clergy. Missionaries were then dispatched to established places to bring to them back into the fold. I suspect that's our origin."

"So it was for control?"

"Control? Nay, it was for unity. The church unites and stabilizes. It keeps order. It keeps us together through shared history and belief. We bring civilization and knowledge."

Lerer smiled knowingly and Thomas nodded in appreciation. "You're thinking of the directive from the prophet," he said.

"Aye. And…?"

"I have not decided yet."

"What is there to decide?" said Lerer. "It is an order and the roads are open. But what of the school?"

"The edict spoke only of books, not education."

Lerer raised an eyebrow.

Thomas felt his face flush. "The order—" he said. "The order itself asked for books. It didn't demand the end of schools."

"The intent versus the letter?"

"The prophet says what he means. It's not up to me to know his mind."

"I've offended you," said Lerer. "I apologize."

Thomas noticed the bees had arranged themselves in a circle and were sunning themselves on his lap.

"It took a certain kind of man to come out this far," he said. "I have nothing but respect for the people of Apis. Over a year it took them to get here and here they remained. Five years after the first, we showed up. The road was already done, the crops waiting, the people healthy. I like to think that our order too has that kind of intrepid spirit."

"Self-sufficient?"

"Aye."

"And out of the prophet's control?"

"Brother Lerer, you tread too hard."

"I meant no disrespect, Prior. I only made an observation that our priory has been more independent than most."

"We have had to make our own decisions without higher counsel, that is true," said Thomas, "but that has been our hardship, not a blessing."

"I think it's good that it takes a year for a message to come and be answered."

"I can speak to that better than you," said Thomas. "It is a burden. A heavy responsibility. When you are older, you'll understand."

"Aye."

"Control is the wrong word," said Thomas.

"You don't need to explain. I was out of line."

"It's a teaching moment," he said. "If I may?"

"Of course."

In the warming air, the humming of bees became a soft bass note of life under the fragrances of spring becoming summer.

"Guidance," Thomas said. "That is what the prophet offers."

"Do we not have the scriptures for that?"

"Aye, but as the voice of God, the prophet can better tell us how to interpret the writings and which to use for each occasion."

"I thought we weren't supposed to talk about scriptural contradictions?" said Lerer.

"You're testing me."

"Apologies. Again, I am so—"

"It's all right, brother," said Thomas. "These are questions a young man must ask. I was the same."

"So…you found answers?"

"I found faith."

Lerer rolled his eyes and looked horrified when he realized Thomas had seen him do it.

"Say what you would," said Thomas.

"Nay. I'm—"

"Say it."

"I'm glad our order doesn't do corporal punishment," Lerer said.

"We used to."

"Aye," he said and nodded knowingly.

"You are a trial. Say what you would."

"I would only say that faith might be misconstrued as abdication of responsibility."

Thomas sighed. "Four and twenty you are?"

"Aye."

Thomas shook his head. "Tell me about the bees. Would you be a beekeeper?"

"I wouldn't hate it," said Lerer. "There's something about them."

"That same something?"

Lerer bit his lip. "Aye."

"And you find it good to pray here."

"I wouldn't say I pray as much as I listen."

"To the buzzing?"

"That and then the silence in between."

"What silence?"

"It comes when the buzzing is internalized."

"I don't understand."

Lerer raised his hands in a helpless gesture. "I can't think of how better to explain it – but I'll try." He clasped his palms together on his lap. "I sit and close my eyes and listen to the buzzing. I try to think of nothing. Truly nothing. Emptiness. Then comes the silence and then…

then things…change." He waved his hands again as if trying to pluck the words out of the air.

"So no prayers?"

"Not as such."

Thomas furrowed his brow at this. "Doctrine says prayer is prescribed. Free prayer opens the way of lies."

"The Three and Twentieth Article of Belief. I do remember, that's why I don't call it prayer."

"A purger might call it something else, might suggest you are treading paths of apostasy."

"And what say you?"

"You are striking again at the same wound with me," Thomas said.

"The order to lose the library has something to do with my sitting in the sun collecting my thoughts?"

"You see no connection?"

"You're saying the rules are different out here, so far from the center."

"Aye. But they shouldn't be." Thomas felt old. The bench was more comfortable than any plank should be. Just looking at Lerer's posture made his knees hurt and the challenges coming from the young man's mind did the same to his head.

There was a time, as recently as a few years after he arrived, while Spencer was in charge, that this kind of conversation would never have been allowed. It took too much license. Was disrespectful of authority. Now, even as head of the priory, Thomas not only allowed it, he sought it out. He felt the time in his joints and rubbed his neck.

"I'm not sure I like you visiting the village unaccompanied," he said.

"Brother Minnar came along."

"Brother Minnar? He accompanied you or you accompanied him?"

"What's the difference?"

"You try me so. I know who Minnar sees in the village. It is unbecoming of a monk. This has all gone too far."

"Nothing happened. They spoke in the square. He's giving her lessons, at least while he still can."

"Can I expect another visit from Tresza's father?"

"Nothing happened."

Thomas sighed and stood up. The startled bees rose in a purring cloud and flew in elliptical lines around his head. He shooed them away. "I've got to get control back over this priory."

"There's that word again," said Lerer.

"Do you not have work to do, brother?"

"My task was copying manuscripts in the library."

"Go see if Franco has any other work for you."

"So we're sending them?"

"Go!"

Lerer stood and bowed to the prior. "Blessed be," he said.

"And to thee."

Thomas watched Lerer walk away and disappear around a barn. Birds took to the air as he passed the aviary, two geese, a clutch of red pigeons, and a few nighteaters not yet asleep.

He thought to follow Lerer to the library, to walk among the shelves seeking inspiration to his dilemma, but he'd done that enough this winter to know he'd not arrive at any answer he wanted there. Besides, the library would be crowded today with monks reading as fast as they could, relishing the last moments before the books would be gone.

Not for the first time, he wondered if he shouldn't have kept the edict secret from the others, at least until he was ready to act upon it. Like the casualness among the brethren and the free time everyone had, his democratic counsel was not in keeping with normal church policy or even the ancient habits of the order. He'd read the journals of previous priors and seen the strictness that was equated with the church. Those books would need to be sent off with the others, he thought. And, if anyone in the Hall of the Prophet read them, they would see the decay of discipline and the ad hoc reactionary methods that defined the priory now. If that were to happen, Thomas had no doubt he'd be replaced. A new man would come up, disciplined and harsh, probably accompanied by a purger who'd straighten the order out quick. Gone would be the lively new songs, replaced with chants of obedience. Gone would be the summer festival of Saints' Day. The talk would be about the Saved instead of the people. God instead of good. Regardless of what happened to the rest of the library, Thomas recognized that there were certain books that should never leave the valley.

He crossed the garden to be among the fragrant blossoms again. Walking slowly, easing his old and tired knees, he let gravity guide him toward the gate, thinking about the two thousand five hundred six and twenty books he was meant to give up. Of course the presidency didn't know how many they had. It was a fraction of what the great libraries had or even a well-stocked abbey closer to Zion City, but it was a formidable collection out here, and the jewel of the valley. They'd had two centuries to accumulate and copy. No traveler crossed the river without being asked if they carried a book. If they did, the priory would invite them to a feast of shamble-sheep mutton and honey mead in exchange for time to copy them. The library so constructed was a marvelous eclectic record of different subjects and handwritings. Reading the books took some getting used to, the changing hand and line. Often the most popular books would be recopied by a single monk with a fine clear hand, like Lerer's, made more beautiful, a gem among gold. The books were treasures. Though some were of questionable quality and use – base tales of sex and violence, little merit but great lust – and others dry as bone, records of family histories, all were valued and kept. Among them, thus, at the lowest, was the grunting voice of man, and at its highest, the inspired word of God. Histories and journals, tales fanciful and real, were collected by the chroniclers. Whatever the order was originally designed for, it had become the mission of the brothers now to collect, keep, and share their accumulated knowledge.

And that apparently was not a good thing.

Thomas could not wrap his mind around the prophet's edict. To this, Thomas had sent no response yet, not even an acknowledgement of having received it, though Chronicler Franco recorded its arrival in his log. That log might also need to go to Zion City if he were to read the order literally. How were they expected to function?

Thomas did not know Benjamin IV, but neither did he know his two predecessors. In a calm and beautiful garden with a hundred others, he'd sworn his vows before Samuel II, an old man with kind eyes. What had happened since then, to that peace in Zion, to require such a drastic order as this was beyond his imaginings. But it had to be something. The prophet had his reasons and those reasons must be from God.

In his two and thirty years as prior, he'd received no direct contact with a superior except the occasional letters of introduction for new monks sent to Apis to be forgotten. Lerer was right, this was an exile and he was the head of the exiles.

And he liked it that way.

His childhood recollections were far from fond nostalgic memories. They were cloudy and fearful, full of uncertainty and grief. Details were unclear, lost in time, but what he knew was that it was much different than here. He remembered more strife, more cruelty. He recalled skies full of coal smoke, dead men in cages at crossroads, disease and poverty. Though not unheard of in Apis, those things were not the norm here as he remembered them there.

A hundred paces from the courtyard he heard the clatter of hooves coming up the road. The horse was at gallop, being pressed to mount the hill at speed. Either an emergency or an aristocrat needing to show their importance. The aristocrats spent horses that way. Peasants only pressed their animals when they had to.

Ahead, he saw the tall tan horse pass under the gate. It was an aristocrat. There weren't many within riding distance of the priory: three estates some kilometers off, three houses in town, and the castle on the hill. The rider was from the castle. Upon his cape was embroidered the Doclen coat of arms – a winding snake around a vertical tree branch – but Thomas didn't recognize the man.

The rider pulled up and skidded across the cobblestones. Thomas entered the square, saying a prayer of patience before he spoke. "Who comes here?"

"Minister," said the man, finally getting down from his horse. "Minister Thomas?"

"Aye."

"It is me, Finn Doclen. I've come to announce that my father has died."

Thomas saw no sign of sadness on the young man's face. "Oliver Doclen dead? That is indeed grave news."

"It is what it is. And what that is, is that I am now the master of Doclen Castle and governor of the province."

Finn was Oliver's only male heir and so it was right what he said. Two and twenty years old, fidgety, raising a haughty air. Thomas felt a wave of fear and knelt to offer a prayer for the future, and also for the memory of a good man who was Oliver Doclen.

"He fell off the tower," said Finn. "Tragic, but it is what it is."

"Oliver fell?"

"This morning. He fell from the high tower."

"And how is your noble sister, Deserey?"

"She is away with friends."

"So it was just you and your father in the castle?"

A shadow crossed Finn's brow. "I was asleep," he said. "What the old man was doing up there is a mystery."

"A tragedy," said Thomas. "I grieve for your loss."

"Loss? Oh, aye. See to the funeral," he said. "I've got to get this place in order."

"In order for what?"

"In order," he said. "Let's bury him tomorrow."

"Will Deserey be back by then?"

"Nay, not for a fortnight."

"Then perhaps we should wait."

"Tomorrow," he said. "Bury the old man tomorrow. See to it." He glanced around as if valuing each stone and shrub.

Thomas recalled Finn had last been here for his baptism at eight years old. He'd been back in Apis a year after graduating in Orsin, but hadn't visited. The Doclens had a chapel in their castle and Thomas was told that the family took their worship there, even though old Oliver still made it a point to visit the priory on holy days, often with Deserey. Never with Finn. Rumors were that the young noble spent his time chasing barmaids and gambling. It was well known that he didn't like the little town his family governed. That Deserey was out of the castle while Finn remained was a reversal of the usual arrangements.

"We might not be able to put together a funeral of such importance as your father's in so short a time," said Thomas.

"I remember when a weaver died. He was in the ground the next day."

"He was but a weaver," said Thomas. "Your father was…of greater stature."

Finn seemed to think on this for a moment, twisting up his lip. He'd shaved that morning.

"It is what it is," he said. "As you would have it. But make it soon."

"Aye."

"Aye, my lord," Finn corrected him.

"Aye, my lord."

CHAPTER THIRTEEN

It happened all at once in a moment of stress. I was exhausted, sleep-deprived, fearful and joyous all at once. Lerer called it empathy. It is as good a word as any.
Personal Journal of Brother Franco, Chronicler of Apis 505–515 NE
21, Tenth-Month, 513 NE

21, Tenth-Month, 513 NE – Apis, Temple

It was well after midnight, hours still to dawn, in the time he could never judge, when the boy appeared at the gate. Franco knew immediately that it was an emergency because of the hour, and instinctively that it was secret for the boy didn't shout, but called to him in his hut.

"Brother. Are you awake?"

Franco had asked for the shift to catch up on his record keeping. He'd already cut a third quill and was working on the arithmetic of their diminishing stores – calculating rations, guessing what the town might still tithe to them, praying for the fewest missed meals.

"I am awake," he said. "Who is it there?" He took up the lantern and looked to the locked gate.

The boy said, "I come from the village. I need to speak with Brother Minnar right away."

Franco recognized the boy, Gebbert's son, Eric. Tresza's brother, a lad of but eight or nine. Strong and strapping until recently.

"Is this about your sister?" asked Franco.

The boy's eyes were wild and worried. He was thin, emaciated – starving, as were most in the valley. He didn't answer.

"I'll get him," Franco said. "Wait here."

"Can I not come in?" asked Eric. "Perhaps get some refreshment. It was a hard walk."

"Nay."

Franco's robes hung on him but he was nothing like the skeleton waiting at the gate. He wished he could invite the boy in, feed him, give him a moment of satiety – a longer life – but he understood the danger better than most. There'd be a line from the gate to the town square by morning if he were to give this boy a morsel. The food wouldn't last a week, and once the stores were open to the masses, there'd be a rush. There could still be, but the sanctity of the priory with its threat of divine retribution still kept them safe. In any event, as his math testified, there was not enough for a fraction of the town, possibly not enough for the priory. Charity at times like this was dangerous.

Minnar's bunk was empty. Even as recently as when Prior Thomas still lived, early in his tenure at least, leaving the dormitory in the middle of the night would be punished, a caning at best, but such discipline was another one of those forgotten traditions the priory had discarded in ever-increasing degrees for as long as Franco could remember. Luckily, he had a good idea where he'd find Minnar. He went to Lerer's room and saw light leaking under the door.

"Brother Lerer, is Minnar in there?"

"I am," came the monk's voice.

"There's a boy for you at the gate."

"Eric?"

"Aye."

The door burst open and Minnar stood before him as wild-eyed as the youngster outside. Behind him, Lerer sat on the bare floor, cross-legged, a bowl in his lap, bees buzzing in the room.

"At the gate, you say?" said Minnar.

"Aye."

Minnar rushed down the hall and they heard the crash of furniture after he rounded a corner.

"Hold up, Minnar," called Lerer. "Bring us, or at least take the lantern with you. You'll do no good with a broken ankle."

Lerer rose to follow. Franco saw he was barefoot beneath his robes and nearly mentioned that perhaps the acting prior should put on sandals, but figured it was not his place. Places weren't what they used to be around the priory.

Lerer gestured to Franco to lead the way, politely but firmly. They found Minnar on the floor before a toppled table, grasping his knee. Sand from a broken incense bowl spread like an alluvial delta of ashes and dust. They helped him up and after a few limping steps he could hold his own weight.

Franco led the way with his lantern. Outside, the air was cold and still, but bright with low clouds finding and filtering light from somewhere.

"Minnar," said Eric. Franco noted the lack of title. "Tresza's time is here."

Minnar's face lit up for a moment, but then seeing Eric's not reflecting his emotion, fell. "What is it?"

"It's a breach birth," he said. "Though I don't know what that means exactly."

"It means trouble," said Lerer.

Minnar reached for the gate and made to open it. Before the crisis, it would have opened easily, but now, for fear, it was chained and locked.

"Franco, fetch the key. We're going to town."

"I'll come with you," he said, showing the key from his pocket.

"Why?"

"I'm the chronicler," he said as if that explained everything.

Woken by the crash down the hall, several monks looked out on them now.

Lerer said, "Brother Cray, take watch."

"Aye, Lerer— I mean Prior."

"Lerer's fine."

The gate was thrown open and the three followed Eric down the path toward the city as swiftly as they dared.

"How did you manage this path without a light?" Lerer asked Eric as they stumbled over the rocky road.

"It was easier before your light," said Eric. "The sky was enough."

The skies had been unseasonably quiet. The green-yellow auroras that often bathed their nights had been absent or small all year and the nights had been darker for it.

"Dare we?" said Lerer, mostly to himself. "Let us pause a moment, friends. Franco, extinguish the light."

"Lerer—"

"Do it, brother. We'll catch our breath for a minute and let our eyes adjust."

Franco felt in his pocket for matches and found none. Once their light was out, they couldn't relight it. He wanted to argue but blew out the lantern as asked.

The monks had the advantage in stamina. They still got calories every day, vitamins – even wine. Minnar paced like a caged cat casting his gaze down the steep road. Lerer watched him, his face calm but concerned. Young Eric sat with his head between his knees, trying to catch his breath and wheezing on the intake.

"I'm going," said Minnar. "I can see well enough." And he was away.

Lerer watched him go then followed at a measured pace. "We'll meet him there."

Once his eyes adjusted, Franco was surprised he didn't need the cold flames of milky auroras to see. The stars were enough. They trotted the rocky path without a stumble or stop and soon found themselves crossing the dark square of a far farmhouse.

Eric fell behind, out of breath and weak, but Lerer knew the way. Franco stayed between the two, his dark lantern swinging at his side. Off in the distance were twinkling lights on the Doclen Castle battlements. He counted ten before he stumbled over a root for not paying attention.

"Why does the town not light their streets anymore?" he said.

"They've eaten all the oil," Lerer said without hesitation.

Franco felt ashamed for not knowing this and wondered how Lerer did. He figured it was the weird bee-knowledge he'd talked about, but then remembering his frequent visits down the valley, realized there could well be a simpler reason why he knew the town's problems. Franco told himself to record the event in his log; the peasants drinking their lantern fuel was the kind of detail that would really spice up his reports.

They heard the wailing when they were still twenty meters from the door. A lone flickering light shone in a window of a humble farmhouse on the edge of town.

Lerer sprinted to the house, knocked once, and went in. Franco followed.

It was simple and clean, sparsely appointed with sturdy furniture: chairs, table, cupboards. A fireplace threw off the only light.

"Brother Lerer," said old Gebbert, rising from a chair.

"Blessed be," said Lerer.

"And to thee."

"Where's Minnar?"

"In the back with the womenfolk. Couldn't stop him."

At that moment a low stunted moan rose from the back of the house, a wail rising in volume and anguish until it was a scream that rocked the very windows before falling to gasps to sobs. Minnar's voice, soft and soothing, cooed beside it. Franco could not hear the words, but the emotion was clear. It was accompanied by other voices – womenfolk, who urged and soothed alongside Minnar.

Gebbert gestured to a man in the corner, shadows over his torn uniform. "Brother Lerer, you know Allen here of the guards?"

"I do," said Lerer. "Mr. Allen, what brings you here?"

"Illegal birth," said he.

"What?" said Franco.

"Tresza ain't married. She's giving birth. That would mean an illegitimate birth, wouldn't you agree?"

Gebbert's face, already wan and thin, darkened as his eyes fell on the acting prior.

"That's an archaic law," said Lerer.

"Still a law."

"Doclen sent you?"

"It is the opinion of our ruling lord governor that it is his place to restore law and order to Apis since the church has been negligent both socially and spiritually."

"I've heard his slogans."

"In this time of crisis, he intends to exercise his lawful authority for the good of all."

"He's already taken our stores," said Gebbert. "What does he intend to do with my daughter?"

Allen shifted in his chair. Franco knew the guard from before when he was but a potter's son. When Doclen reinstituted the guard, he was one of the first to volunteer. Franco saw that he had put on weight since he last saw him, a feat few had accomplished this year.

"Master Doclen will do what is lawful," said Allen.

Another scream.

"Allen, could you wait outside?" said Lerer.

"It's cold."

"So much the better," said Gebbert.

Allen shot him a look.

"Allen, leave," said Lerer.

The guard held his stare to Lerer's for a moment and then found something more interesting nearer his feet.

Lerer's rise to lead the abbey and become the presiding minister of Apis, and thus the spiritual, if not the official, leader of the community, was not a church-recognized rank, but his position was beyond question. He had authority that belied his age regardless of title. Franco had tried to explain it in his journal, to suss out what it was that made the young man from Clearport such a force. He'd been unable to put his finger on it though he'd dedicated countless pages to trying. In his fifty plus years of service to God and man, Franco had nothing to compare it to.

He remembered when Lerer arrived, full of indignation at being so far from civilization. He'd run off a couple times, been returned by brothers, and came back on his own at least once. He'd settled down eventually, working in the scriptorium and library, helping in the orchards. A change came over him, slow but clear. He kept his friendly outgoing attitude, became introspective and seeking. *Seeking*. That was the word that Franco had lit upon most recently.

Franco remembered how the old prior, Thomas, had taken a particular interest in Lerer. The two men spent many hours together after Oliver Doclen's death, taking long evening walks together, or visiting around a warm stove. Franco suspected Thomas sought a confessor for his guilt at not returning all the priory's books to the Hall of the Prophet as directed. It was a decision that weighed on him for the rest of his life. Though supported by most, Thomas had suffered for his decision. "Distance from authority should not mitigate law," he told them. "This I know, but my heart makes me disobey. Perhaps I'll repent." And Franco felt that Thomas wanted to repent, but never got the chance.

Franco in particular grasped the magnitude of the problem and his sympathies were decidedly toward keeping the books. They were his life, and had the prior sent them away, his life's work would be over. Even with such vested interest, he'd not spoken his feelings when it was clear that Thomas was wavering on the prophet's order. Others lobbied vocally to keep the books while some kept silent, remaining truer to their vows, watching and waiting. Franco always felt that his silence put him in the wrong camp because, though his tongue was loyal, his heart was not. When Thomas announced that he'd send some books back, but keep those 'necessary to the survival of the priory', Franco nearly cried for grief. Then when the list of surrendered books was released, penned by Lerer, he nearly cried for joy. Only copies of books the priory had multiples of were sent to Zion City. And so the collection remained intact.

It was for the good. Books were needed. The priory had the only library for three hundred kilometers in any direction. To be without them would be to destroy their purpose. Franco felt for Thomas and the burden of his decision. He'd been an honorable man, and though in the whole scheme of things it was difficult to put too much weight on any decision about a minuscule collection of books in a little priory at the edge of the frontier, yet it was a personal and spiritual crucible that Franco was sure contributed to the old man's death. Franco's position as chronicler was saved by Thomas's spiritual sacrifice, and he knew it.

When the famine came in earnest this year Thomas's health turned. Though the priory had better stores to weather the crisis, Thomas took the barest ration and rumors were that he was giving that little bit to other monks. His communication with Lerer increased and was often held behind closed doors. Franco had been present for many of their earlier talks about theology and society and noted in his personal journals – not the official ones – that their talks often took them to dangerous places, approaching blasphemy and apostasy. He speculated what was said in secret and shuddered to think ill of the 'two priory lights', as he'd called them in his official account.

It was assumed that Thomas was grooming Lerer for leadership, but Franco felt that the instruction went the other way. He didn't have any proof, only a feeling built from the few moments he'd been present at their talks during that winter. Lerer knew things that he really shouldn't know, like the religious practices of Old Earth and the condition of the other survivors of the Unsettling – knowledge from worlds beyond communication. These could have been ignored as fanciful tales, and usually were, but Franco thought they had an uncanny ring of truth, as if Lerer had studied them somewhere or been told firsthand, or – as was whispered – as if they had been told to him by angels.

When the old man finally died this last spring, the brothers unanimously chose Lerer to be their new prior. Even the assistant prior cast his vote for him. His age made Lerer ineligible; thirty winters at least were required by charter, but the brothers were willing to postpone official ritual and let Lerer assume the duties immediately. The town, too, took him as their leader.

The guard, Allen, looked at the other men in the room. Franco followed his eyes over himself, old Gebbert, and Rolden, Tresza's other brother, the older one, who split stumps with an ax bigger than a wagon wheel. Or at least used to. Rolden was much diminished, but still half a meter taller than Allen.

"I'll check back in the morning," said the guard.

Allen opened the door and stormed out. Franco closed it behind him.

"Warm autumn, don't you think?" said Franco after he'd gone.

Lerer laughed. "Aye, very mild," he said. "Beautiful weather. Blessed night."

Another scream. Minnar's voice unbroken now, cooing and praying.

"How long has this been going on?" asked Lerer. He lowered himself to sit on the floor, upon the packed hard earth near the fireplace.

"Began just before supper," said Rolden.

"It speaks," said Lerer.

Rolden gave him a look.

Lerer winked at the big man. Turning to old Gebbert, he said, "And what did you have for supper?"

"We had the last of that cheese," he said. "And some barley soup. Found grain in the floorboard that the rats had missed."

"Did you not get the honey I sent?"

"Oh, aye," he said. "Rolden had all that yesterday."

"All?"

The man blushed and looked away.

"Don't be judging him, Prior," said Gebbert. "We others had plenty and Tresza would have it no other way."

"And Eric— Wait? Where's Eric?"

Franco realized the boy had never come in. "I'll get him."

Outside, the night was still bright but his vision had been compromised. He stumbled to where he'd last seen Eric but couldn't find him.

"Eric," he called. "Eric Gebbert!"

A breeze caught his words and spirited them up toward the priory.

His sight adjusted onto several outbuildings – a shed, an empty sty, a privy – and he made for those. He'd gone only two or three steps when he saw a lump on the ground.

The young boy was in a heap. "Have you fallen asleep?" He knelt down beside the boy and turned him over. His face was dark in the pale light and this confused Franco for a moment until he smelled the blood. He touched the boy's cheek and felt hot stickiness.

"Help me," said Eric, his voice weak in the wind.

Franco scooped him up in his arms – he weighed hardly anything – and hurried back to the house.

"Lerer! Lerer!" he yelled.

Rolden opened before he got there and Franco bore the boy to Lerer by the fire.

"I think he fell," he said. "I found him by the wall."

"Ouch." Lerer examined a cut over Eric's ear. "Can you hear me, boy?"

"Aye."

"You clumsy goon," said Rolden.

"It was Allen," said Eric.

"What?" said Gebbert.

"Allen," said Eric. "He hit me."

"Why?"

"I was out by the gate eating bread."

"What bread?"

"I gave him some honey biscuits," said Lerer.

"You did?" said Franco. "When?"

"On the way down."

"Allen clobbered me with his truncheon."

"And took the bread?"

Eric nodded.

"Before you say a word, Franco, or write something I wish you wouldn't, know it was my personal ration. Okay?"

"Of course," said Franco.

"The bastard clobbered my son for a cookie?"

"I think he just hit me and took the food after. I don't think he saw it before," said Eric.

Another scream from the birthing room.

"You'll be fine, lad," said Lerer. "A big goose egg and a call for a bath. No need worrying the womenfolk about this, eh?" He looked at Rolden and Gebbert. The two men nodded slowly.

"Go wash up, Eric," said Gebbert.

"I never got to thank you for the bread," said Eric. "I had most of it. It was worth the whack."

Rolden helped Eric to the water pump outside.

When they were gone, Gebbert said, "We're better off than most. I think Allen sees that, and knows why. Which means Doclen knows too."

Lerer lowered himself back down beside the fire, his bare feet sticking out toward the embers.

"The other villagers might also suspect," Gebbert went on. "With all of Doclen's taxes, they're getting pretty hungry. We lost the Widow Pirit today."

"Nay...."

"Aye. And two from the Eggers clan are about done. You know they lost Mark."

"Isn't Jeff bringing them food?"

"From his guard rations? Nay. Doclen would have him horsewhipped. They're just glad one of them will make it through."

Lerer closed his eyes and it was then that Franco saw the insect orbiting his head. His first thought was that it was a fly, since this was a farmhouse, but he'd seen bees so much in the priory that he recognized it as one of those. Besides, flies were gone this time of year. Bees too, usually, he thought.

He turned his mind to what he was hearing, remembering his charge as chronicler. "Has the tax increased?" Franco asked.

"Nay, but they've not diminished either. Weekly pound of grain. No one's had a pound of grain for a month. He's taking liens against homes now. Percentages of markets. He's already foreclosed on the livery. Half the county is already indentured and we're not even to winter yet. Wait until Doclen starts selling the people back their own food. There'll not be a free man in the village, or a parcel of common land."

"Common land?"

"He's made claim to all the commons."

A long sudden wail filled the house.

"One thing at a time," said Lerer. "One thing at a time."

"Her screams are getting closer," said Franco. "I think it's nearly time."

"You have a lot of experience with this stuff, have you, monk?" asked Gebbert.

Franco felt himself blush. "Nay, not personally, but there are records of it in our books."

Lerer smiled. "I think he's right, Gebbert. It's nearly time."

"I'm not saying he's wrong, just asking how he knows."

Rolden and Eric came back in. Eric's hair was wet and his face clean. He held a bloody rag in his hand. Before the door was shut, Franco saw a sliver of light in the east.

Grunts. Moans. A scream.

Minnar's voice carried through the wall. "My darling, my sweet strong Tresza, one more push, and I—"

Another scream.

"No? No!" Minnar's voice.

Something fell over and broke with a clatter and splash.

"My darling…my darling…."

A silence where Franco held his breath.

A new voice, another cry, small and shrill – peeved at being alive – wailed its first breath.

A red-faced woman peeked out from the room and said, "It's a girl."

Old Gebbert lifted himself out of his chair with some effort. There was light in his eyes.

"A girl?" he said. "A girl. A girl! It's a girl." He teetered for a moment and then stumbled back into his chair heavily, crying for joy and relief. Rolden was there to ease him down. "Son, go get the bottle of port I've been saving. We need to drink to this. Lerer, you and the brothers must join us."

"We'd not take your stores, Gebbert," said Lerer. "I know you haven't much left."

"Nonsense. We're related now – yours and mine."

This was of course a reference to Brother Minnar being the father of the child in the next room. It was a poorly kept secret. The whole valley knew of the relationship between them even before Tresza grew gravid. Nevertheless, the priory named it rumor because to name it otherwise, to say what everyone was sure of, and Minnar himself would never deny, would be to destroy them all. The penalty for a monk breaking his vow of chastity was death for everyone involved.

Minnar wanted to be released from his vows, to be made common so he could marry, but that was also impossible. It could only be done with an order from the prophet, and to even petition such a thing would bring purgers to the valley and expose more than Minnar's transgressions to the judgment of the cloth.

Beside the famine, Minnar's situation was the first true crisis of Lerer's tenure. Minnar was one of the inner circle, together with two others, Hoopes and Eugene, who all had an affinity for the docile bees that were kept in the garden. The four of them seemed to have worked something out by midsummer because Minnar's mood was sharply improved then, so much so that Franco remembered recording in his daily log that *today Brother Minnar has thrown off his melancholy and seems to have found new life.*

Lerer gave a wan smile. "Of course we will drink with you," he said to old Gebbert.

Rolden again left the house. Eric took the stool in the corner, his head cradled in his hands.

The sounds of the new baby subsided amid the noises of motion and soothing talk. After a moment, Minnar stepped out, his face wet with perspiration and tears, his hands sloppy and red. A grin spread wide over his face. "It's a girl," he said.

"Aye, a blessed thing," Lerer said. "How is Tresza?"

"As well as can be expected. It was not an easy birth. There is some bleeding."

"Can she travel? Can the baby?"

"I don't think so. Why?"

"Allen was here."

"Allen?"

"Aye, lad," said Gebbert. "He was sitting right there, where Eric is now, when you burst in."

"I didn't see him."

"Distracted, I suppose."

"Why was he here?" Minnar's tone suggested that he knew the fearful answer.

"Bastard birth," said Lerer, rising to his feet. "Doclen means to carry out the law."

"He'd never...."

"He'll use this to get at the priory," said Franco, explaining it to himself. "He'll use it to break into our stores. He'll try to break us. Move the power from our sanctum to his castle."

"Aye," said Lerer. "I do suspect that's his plan."

"And he calls that child a bastard," said Gebbert.

Surprising himself, Franco said, "We can try to bribe him to look the other way."

"That law is stupid and ancient," said Minnar. "It's one thing to punish me as a vow-breaker, but the child? And Tresza?"

"Doclen will press for the maximum penalty just to get our attention," said Lerer.

"And to break us."

"What are we to do?"

"We can't wait until spring. Get to the priory. You, Tresza, and the baby. We'll give you sanctuary until we can smuggle you out."

"Where will they go?" said old Gebbert.

"Away," said Lerer. "If you know, you could tell."

"They'll punish us all if Tresza runs," said Eric. "Doclen will pillory the town. He'll ruin us for sure. Father, there will be consequences."

"The boy's right," said Minnar.

"What if we get one of the peasant boys to claim paternity?" said Franco.

"Aye," Gebbert said. "We could say it was Mark."

"No one would believe that," said Minnar.

"They don't have to believe it," said Franco. "We just need an excuse to save...."

"Me," said Minnar. "Tresza will still be punished. The blow struck. We won't fool anyone."

"We'll think about it," said Lerer. "First we get to the priory. Doclen won't dare break the sanctity."

"Father, think what you're doing," said Eric. "Tresza made her own decision and these people aren't family."

Franco thought about the precious rations Lerer had given Eric and how little loyalty that had bought.

Gebbert looked from his son to the monks.

"How big is your family?" said Franco, feeling he was quoting something, but couldn't remember where he'd heard it.

"Aye..." said Gebbert.

Franco felt like crying. His lip quivered as he heard through the door the murmuring of a newborn in its mother's arms. As the moment's silence stretched out, the murmur turned to a low buzz. His soul filled with amber warmth as he lost his breath and stumbled.

Lerer caught him before he fell and lowered him onto a bench with Minnar's help.

"Brother..." Franco said. "Something's happening to me. What is this? This...?"

Lerer smiled at him. "I'll try to explain later," he promised.

"Take them, Prior," said Gebbert. "Doclen will do what he'll do. Now or later, he'll do what he intends. Save my Tresza. Save my grandchild, and I'll give Doclen a good fight here, by God, when he comes."

"Minnar," said Lerer, "gather them."

The monk hurried to the birthing room.

Franco sat with his mind awash in emotion. It was like being drunk without the haze, asleep without the rest – alert and receptive, telepathic and exposed. He felt like he was on an ocean, adrift in a warm bath of undulating currents of potential and passion. Plural emotions, echoes from the room and a connection to a well of infinite others.

It's all right, he heard Lerer say to him. *This is the connection I've been talking about. Get your feet beneath you. We need you now.*

But Lerer was not talking to him. "Where's that boy of yours with the wine?" he was saying to old Gebbert. "We're going to have to drink it fast."

The woman argued behind the door, objecting to the sudden move, begging Minnar to see the condition of the mother.

Franco fought the dizziness and powered his way out of the honey-sweet hum that was the roiling sea of his mind. He found footing in the house and blinked his eyes as clear as he could. When they were washed of visions, they were still wet with tears. Those he wiped on his sleeves.

"My God," he whispered. The recall of the moment caught the breath in his throat and his eyes rolled back in his head.

"Steady on, brother," said Lerer, holding him up.

Franco shook his head as if breaking a dream. He slapped his own face and clenched his fists. He rose and jogged in place. "Aye, aye, Prior. I'm with you."

"What's wrong with him?" said Eric.

"Empathy," said Lerer. He threw open the door and looked around at the brightening sky. "Where'd that boy go?"

"The barn," said Gebbert.

"I'll fetch him," said Eric. "No one listens to me here anyway."

Franco pressed his palms against his eyes until he saw lights. He thought of Minnar behind the door and was filled with fear and happiness mixed in a tumultuous flood that hit him all at once like a gust of wind, and spun him to its vortex. It was Minnar's emotions, but he shared them as his own. He swayed on the stool until he remembered he was Franco and not Minnar. He opened his eyes and focused on the dawn light creeping closer.

"I'll check the barn," said Lerer, getting up.

With a start Franco saw the room was now dawn-bright. Time had passed unreckoned.

Then it was just him and Gebbert. He couldn't remember Lerer leaving.

Thinking of Lerer, his mind traveled out to be instantly filled with his friend's fear and trepidation. It was as consuming as the wave from Minnar, but perhaps because the emotions were not in such opposition, or maybe because he was learning to control whatever was happening, he was not so overwhelmed by the sensation this time.

He became sensible of a bee circling his head in a crowning orbit. Hearing the soothing buzz brought it all under control and discernment. He was still dizzy but he could separate himself from the others if he tried, at least partially, for he suddenly knew that they were not separate at all. The revelation stuck him dumb.

He opened his mouth to say a word, but found nothing. Instead, he laughed and felt the tears pour down his face.

"You all right there, brother?" said Gebbert. "What's happening?"

He was the chronicler. His life was words – describing, recording, expressing – and here he was mute, unable to connect what was happening inside to the world around him, or perhaps better said, unable to disconnect long enough to utter a single syllable about it.

The best he could offer was a wave of his hand, indicating not to worry and strangely knowing it to be a true statement.

"What's taking them so long?" said Gebbert.

A pause like the moment between lightning.

There was a low knock on the door. Then a harder one.

"I said I'd be back," said Allen. "And I've brought friends."

CHAPTER FOURTEEN

Nothing fuels revolution like hunger and hangings.
Old Earth Proverb

21, Tenth-Month, 513 NE – Apis, Temple

He'd sent the alarm to the priory as Minnar gathered his family for escape. Outside, looking for Gebbert's sons, he sent another message, a warning of possible trouble. Then, at the barn, finding Rolden and Eric bound and gagged, two crossbowmen over them and Allen strolling toward Gebbert's house with four more, he ordered the entire priory to town.

"This is not our wish, Prior," said one of the guards.

"Did you hurt them?"

"Nay," said the other. "Just bound them as Master Allen ordered."

"Master Allen?"

"Aye."

"Master of what?"

The two men looked at each other and then at the ground.

The two sons were tied back-to-back on the ground. The guards raised their cocked weapons. "We have orders," one said.

"To kill me?"

"To shoot anyone who interferes with lawful orders."

"I would check them," said Lerer, gesturing to the boys. "Allen clobbered young Eric earlier tonight. Let me see to his wounds."

The two shared a glance and then one of them reluctantly nodded.

Eric's head was bleeding again. His hair was a mat of wet and hardening scabs. Over his cloth gag his eyes were full of accusation.

Lerer offered him a consoling smile, the best he could manage, and turned to Rolden. Like his brother's, his eyes were big and accusing, angry and stern. Unlike his brother's, they were not meant for him, but for the guards and their crossbows. He gnawed on his gag, sawing his teeth across it while pulling at the ropes binding his wrists. There was blood on them.

Shouts from the house. A crash.

Rolden kicked to get to his feet, but couldn't.

Lerer could understand Rolden's rage and also Eric's indictment.

Recognizing one of the guards, Lerer said, "You are Jasper's boy. How fares your father?"

"Better than most," said the guard.

Lerer nodded. "No harm here," he said, pointing to the hostages. "And take off the gags. I already know."

As if in answer, a woman's scream shook the night and a child cried an anguished response.

Jasper's boy set his bow down and went to work on the gags.

Lerer left the barn.

He didn't know all the townsfolk, not half of them really, a fraction by name, many by sight, but they all knew him and that was something. Perhaps that was enough.

He said a prayer in a language that had never been spoken on this world and went to the house. There were many men there now, a dozen on foot, more on horseback.

He could not see the future, but he knew enough of the past and the present to have guessed that this crisis moment was inevitable. Evolution he knew took two forms: there was the slow erosion of mountains by breeze and rain, steady and seasonal, that shaped gorges and valleys. And then there were sudden landslides and earthquakes when the world could hold its old shape no longer – not for an instant more – and whole continents would break and reform – mountains brought low, plains raised up. Like all peaceful men, Lerer had hoped for the former but saw now, if there was to be justice here, the latter needs be.

These ideas were birthed in him long before he came to Apis, coalescing back in Clearport among the prostitutes. At first it was just a lark, a use of his privilege and money. He and his friends would go drinking and take women as dessert. Though attacked from every pulpit, prostitution was everywhere. Mostly, they gathered in the squalid areas among the shanties, along the ditches of black oil-topped water that ran foamy and rancid from the factories to the sea. The women, desperate for money, needing it for sick children or crippling drug habits, would frequent the taverns to trade where his class slummed among theirs. The church would not cleanse society of that evil for fear of showing the roots of it – but that was a thought he had later. Then, he only noted that after coitus, alone with the women in their dingy shacks or backroom rentals, he'd found true souls. He'd ask about their lives and they would tell him, thinking it was part of the game. They might embellish or hide, but after a while, soliciting the same three women, he gained their confidence. He learned the names of their children, their histories and dreams. He'd overpay them and became a favorite.

He considered not using their bodies, to just give them money, but somehow he thought that such action would be insulting. The women were not seeking charity. They were working and this was their job. Law and morals might stand against them, but history and necessity gave even their base occupation a nobility they would not easily discard. And so he grew gentler and more generous in all ways he might.

His friends thought him a fool and he played the role for cover.

"I get exercise and a story," he told them. "Always interesting to see how the other half lives."

"Sluts or the poor?"

"Both."

Lerer Melk, of the House Melk, might not be an heir, but aristocrat he was. He instinctively sensed a hard limit to how far he could take his sympathies for the lower classes and so kept his thoughts to himself.

What haunted him most were not the differences between the classes – the haughtiness, humbleness, wealth and poverty – but the similarities. It was how the best of the poor and the best of the aristocracy were brothers, the same character, just different circumstances. Equally so the lower values; the base among the poor were as terrible as the tyrants among his class. Regardless of station, there was a family resemblance.

Such a simple idea and yet so revolutionary.

He'd give to charity, sometimes ostensibly, but most often secretly, until his family's accountants noticed how he spent his money.

"Our finances are otherwise engaged," he was told and had his allowance cut.

Worse, there were times when he'd betray the consciousness of his class. After a drink or two, he might say something derogatory about his family, caste, or society. Since society was overseen by the prophet, his comments always had an air of blasphemy to them.

But his privilege meant his words were allowed but not unnoticed and they set him up for his ultimate exile.

It was a sign of status for great families – and his family did see themselves as great, at least in their province – to give a son up to the clergy. It was a duty of a lower born son who'd just be a drain on the family to join an order voluntarily – under pain of disinheritance and apostasy. And, because of his giving money to prostitutes, arguing against their God-given birthrights, he'd been sent as far from Clearport as possible, to the mountain frontier town of Apis.

Before he went, he secured a promise from his friends that they'd rescue him.

They didn't.

They hadn't even tried.

He was surprised he'd ever thought they would. He'd given them twenty thousand dollars and a challenge to betray everything they believed in.

When he realized they weren't coming, he swore revenge.

Such was his thinking then. It gave him energy for a while, a few months, a few years, leading him to run away to seek his vengeance and then…what? He didn't have a plan after that. He harbored some amorphous idea to flee to a far-off province and start again. It'd been a whimsical thought he'd had in the orchard, listening to the wind. The thought merged into the vision of Apis around him, the trees, the grass, the bees. This he saw was the far-off province, and it was here, he realized, he had to start again. He fell to laughing then, a good hard belly laugh, tears in his eyes, a stitch in his side, and all that was needed to allow the bees into his mind.

He recalled the moment while he walked to Gebbert's house and found Minnar bound and struggling against two guards. Tresza, half-naked in the morning cold, a soiled blanket only around her shoulders, clutched the baby to her breast. She was driven forward at the end of a sword. Franco stumbled after them on unsteady legs as if drunk – his awakening arrived. The sun was low over the horizon and Lerer followed his long, jagged shadow, reaching for calm in the recesses of his memory, recalling his first moments of enlightenment.

It was like vertigo then, not the sympathy it became later. That first moment was like discovering a window in the air and looking through it to a swirl of ideas. It removed him entirely from the world. His senses, mind, and at the time he thought maybe even his body, were drawn through the crevice into that other dimension. He didn't know how long he'd been there, outside himself, at that window, through it – becoming it, becoming ALL – before he retuned to the orchard. It felt like days, but when the ethereal rent shut itself with a purring exhale, he found himself still on his feet, firm on the ground, in the light, the wind blowing his hair and a bee circling his brow like a crown.

And then all the feelings he had for the whores in Clearport rushed into him like a pressured hose. Their faces flashed before him in transitions of tolerance, to friendship and even love, as their time together changed them all. He felt their pain and trials as if his own and shook with them. Then his legs failed him and he melted to the grass and wept, wishing there was some way he could give himself to them, wanting to sacrifice everything he had as penance for generational injustice. He remembered his politics and hated his cowardice. He knew all the universe was beautiful, or rather, he knew it could be.

"What do you think you're doing, Allen?" he said.

"Following my orders," said Finn Doclen from atop a tall horse. Lerer hadn't noticed him before.

"What do you think you're doing, Doclen?" he said to the governor.

"You will refer to me properly, monk," he said.

Old Gebbert stood in the door, a guard barring his way. Blood ran down over his eye.

"What is your plan, Governor?" Lerer stepped toward Minnar, but Allen stood in his way.

"Carry out the law," Doclen said. "As is proper and right."

He found Eugene at the priory, in the bell tower, watching the other monks flood out the gate running toward the town. *Ring the bells*, he told him.

And Eugene rang the bells.

"What's going on?" said Doclen. "Why the bells? Is it a holy day?"

"Nay," said Lerer.

"What game do you play?

"Do you not recognize the alarm?"

"Alarm?"

"Aye."

Doclen shook his head. "You've gone too far this time, Lerer," he said.

"I was about to say the same thing, Governor."

"Me? Too far? For arresting criminals? Oh, how the church has rotted here."

The chimes rang in a song never heard in the valley before. It was not for prayer or passing, but an urgent sustained din. Lerer recognized it, though he'd never heard it himself. Eugene must have discovered it in his travels to the library and used it now. It woke the townsfolk, who sensed its urgency. Perhaps they had some race memory of that song from Old Earth. Lerer liked to think things like that, that the visions the bees brought to him might permeate other minds through other means.

"So it was all planned?" said Doclen. "You knew I was coming?"

"Nay," Lerer said.

"A signal then?" His eyes tracked a circling bee.

"Something like that," said Lerer.

Doclen nodded like he understood something.

A cart rounded the road and Tresza and Minnar were herded into it.

From the doorway Gebbert yelled, "It was Eggers. Mark Eggers. He's the father of the child, not the monk. Tell them, child. It was Eggers."

Minnar kicked at the guards and grunted against his gag. Tresza, now standing in the cart, looked at her father. Their eyes met in a long terrible moment that flooded tears into Lerer's eyes, fluttered his heart, burned his soul.

The baby gasped and fidgeted. Tresza closed her tear-filled eyes, and said, "Aye, it was Eggers. Mark Eggers."

"It was, was it?" said Doclen. "Not what I heard."

"It was," said Gebbert. "And I'd challenge any man a liar for saying otherwise."

Minnar broke free for an instant but was brought down by his heels. He fell hard on his face with a crunch. Lerer felt the pain in his own nose.

Townsfolk, already awake with the dawn, alarmed by the bell, arrived gawking at events in Gebbert's yard. And the bell pealed on, calling all and everyone to witness.

"I should fine you for disrupting the peace," said Doclen, "but I think you have done us a favor."

"We're 'us' now, are we?"

"Sergeant," he said. "I've changed my mind. Don't bother taking them up to the castle. We'll do this now since the town is awake. Assemble in the square."

"Aye, my lord."

"Oh, and find this Eggers fellow."

"He's dead," said Allen.

"Already?"

"Aye, just this week."

Doclen looked down his nose at Lerer. "Did you know this?"

"I heard of his passing today."

"And you confirm that he was the father of that bastard with that whore?"

Guards lifted Minnar to his feet. He begged Lerer not to forsake them.

Lerer silenced the passage to Minnar's mind and focused on possibilities and probabilities. There were no good answers here.

"I was not present when the child was conceived," he said, hearing Minnar's screams in his mind. "I cannot speak to it."

Doclen laughed. "A cowardly answer to be sure, monk. But good enough for now. I'll have my flesh and your spirit too. And soon, I'll have that priory on the hill, its cellars and orchards. I've heard tales of honey ale. I'll pour a draft of it on your pyre."

Lerer barely registered Doclen's threats after he'd called him a coward. It had hit too close to home.

Echoes of conscience. Warnings of mayhem. Upturned tables, mess and flood.

Earthquakes and streams.

The cart pulled away with guards falling in behind. Minnar, bound and gagged, drawn on a leash. Franco staggering, the guards laughing, thinking him drunk. Doclen led the way atop his horse like a general entering a conquered city. Townsfolk who didn't know what was happening ogled the overfed horses, gnawing hunger twisting in their bellies.

The journey took a quarter of an hour to the heart of the little town. When they got there, at Lerer's instructions, the monks were all assembled. Also too were most of the townspeople. Lerer told Eugene he could come down now and the bells went suddenly silent.

"About time," said Doclen. "Really, Lerer, you should have more consideration for the good people of Apis. They need their rest."

"What they need is food."

"Times are hard. That's no excuse for lawlessness." He raised his voice to address the crowd. "Lawlessness is the issue here," he said. "There are laws laid down by the prophet and God – we have gone far from both."

All was silent save for the rattle of leather and buckle as horses waited impatiently for breakfast.

Doclen continued. "By birthright it is my duty to see that the law is followed. I must cleanse the moral rot fostered by the supposed spiritual shepherds of this valley." He pointed up to the priory.

Pockets of low murmurs.

Doclen silenced them with a glance.

"My family has some responsibility for this, I admit," he said, holding his hand over his heart and bowing his head slightly in feigned contrition. "My father was too lenient and allowed the rot to fester. God saw to his punishment."

Laughs and scoffs.

Doclen turned his horse to see if he could identify from whom it came. His horse snorted and threw its head.

"They're hungry, Finn," said Lerer. "You shouldn't have brought your fat horse here. They see you sitting on a meal."

Doclen snarled and addressed the crowd.

"You are hungry? And why is that? Why is there famine here? Why indeed? Why, Brother Lerer, did God forsake this valley now? Why did he slow the rain, ruin the crops, and curse this place?"

"The valley has had famine before," said Lerer.

"You know this?"

"Aye."

"How?"

Lerer looked at the young noble and shook his head. "It's in the histories. Men have kept records. People remember."

"Oh, I thought perhaps you'd had a vision," Doclen said with a sneer. "Aye, I've heard of your stories, *Friar.*" He said the last word with so much mocking that it brought laughs from the crowd, who didn't understand yet what was happening. Doclen thought they were for agreement, but Lerer knew it was because he had sounded like a three-year-old.

Still, Doclen wasn't wrong. Lerer had had visions of times before. It was early in the process, when he was still unsure what was happening. He'd thought he was visualizing what he'd read in journals, but as the hum of the bees eased access to that other place, he found himself in the minds and lives of the actual people from centuries before. Having seen them, learned their names, he'd checked them against birth registries and chronicler history only to learn that his visions were accurate where he could connect them. In this way, his skeptical mind learned to accept as truth the other things he felt and saw. But most of all, he allowed himself to feel them. It was like a fever with highs and lows, whole lives spent in struggle. Some tragic, others beatific. And as he felt and became, his access expanded across time and space.

The first living mind he touched was not on his world, but from another. She called herself Maya and claimed to be a child of Old Earth but not of the Unsettling. She was a denizen of another planet circling Coronam called Tirgwenin. The only one with rings. She looked like an angel to him, golden and sparkling, alien and yet familiar. She assured him she was not divine, only a human like him who'd evolved a bit. She was an elder among her people, but would not tell him her age. She welcomed him as the first from his world to reach them.

She showed him things that made him hopeful and fearful at once – the shape of Old Earth when they left it, and the name of their leader, Jareth, who she said led the first human pilgrimage to Coronam. She told him to explore the library, naming the place where the knowledge was kept. It was an old name, she told him, ancient even on Old Earth. She called it the Akashic Library and within it were the records of everything that was, is, and would be. Access was limited by merit and wisdom, but the bees – the wonderful miraculous bees – created a conduit that saved lifetimes of work and allowed for their strange conversation.

This was a riddle to Lerer, then and now. Much of what she said was a riddle.

Keep seeking, Templer, and you will find answers, she told him. *Ask always the question, "How big is your family?"*

Lerer had sensed a dismissal.

The bees are allowing us to communicate?

Aye.

So what's to prevent us from speaking again?

We are far apart.

But the bees care not for time or distance.

Not that kind of distance, my dear Templer. We— I would not disrupt you.

How?

I can tell you things you are not ready to know.

But the library—

Will show you what you are ready to see. I have not that wisdom. I only wanted to show you that you are not alone, you are not insane.

I never thought I was, he said.

Then you are a rare one. She'd smiled and Lerer had felt it pull his own cheeks wide.

Search the library, Maya told him. *Ask the questions and* the *question. Teach others so that the bees may find them.*

To what end?

Aye, she said, laughing.

And was gone.

Lerer had reached out to Maya many times since then, but never again had she answered. He tried again now, but came only to silence.

Looking over the townsfolk, soldiers, and monks, Lerer said, "Before, in Apis, when times were hard, when crops failed and famine came, we helped each other." Each word he spoke, simple to itself, was a stone falling from a wall, a break in time, a place in history piling upon him. He felt the weight of it. But to his right, men came carrying wood to the square.

"This is about a crime," Doclen said, "not about hard times. This woman is a whore." He pointed to the nursing Tresza in the cart. "She bears in her arms a bastard child. It is against the law. Our law. God's own law!"

"Don't do it, Finn," said Lerer.

"As lawful governor and judge, I declare the obvious verdict. Guilty of fornication!"

A tall three-meter stake was slid between the ancient rocks in the center of the square. A similar one had not been placed there for over a century. The wood fell into place with a hollow knock.

"I am told that the father of this child is dead," said Doclen, looking at Minnar, who was on his knees weeping. "Mark Eggers was his name, so I'm told. But this is rumor. Does anyone know otherwise? Would the Eggers clan care to refute this base accusation?"

Doclen looked for the Eggerses. Lerer did the same. They weren't here. He at least knew who to look for.

Doclen's gaze fell again to Lerer. "If it had been a monk, God forbid, what disgrace would there be on your priory?"

Lerer touched Minnar's mind and heard prayers to God.

The townsfolk looked from Doclen to Minnar to Lerer and back. The monks watched only him.

"I would ransom her," said Lerer.

"You have no money."

"The priory has stores. We'll give them up for her life. Exile her. You are allowed to make that verdict."

A sliver of a grin cracked Doclen's face. Lerer remembered the governor was only three and twenty, but that grin made him look half that, so petulant and cruel. On a toddler it would have been concerning, on an adult, with power of life and death, it was terrifying.

"Your stores mean nothing to me," said Doclen.

"They could mean everything and you know it." Lerer glanced around at the hungry faces waiting and worrying. Withering.

"Are you raising the rabble, monk?" said Doclen.

"This is about control," Lerer went on. "It's about resources. It's about us not questioning inequality. It's about the powerful oppressing the weak."

Bundles of sticks, stolen from sheds, were piled around the stake and Tresza was brought forward and set to stand by one.

"This isn't necessary," Lerer said.

"It is," said Doclen. "You people need to understand who's in charge here, who wields the power. Who is the law. It is there along the road to progress." He pointed to his castle. "Not there on the dead-end hill." He pointed to the priory.

Tresza still held the babe in her arms, but weakly. She looked around as if in a dream, a defensive denial of the horror she was experiencing. Blood pooled between her legs. Guards wrapped ropes around her body regardless of the child, strapping the babe across her breasts as they wound her from foot to head, fastening her to the stake. The baby cried and gasped against the pressure. Tresza held it and found breath to pray.

Pointing to the stake, stepping his horse away from lighted torches, Doclen said, "This whore is just one symptom of a misguided populace.

You have wrong ideas of so many things. This will remind you of the truth. When next the taxes are due, you will remember. I am Apis."

Doclen signed for the fire to be lit. No one moved.

Lerer saw that Jasper's boy had brought Rolden and Eric to the square. They were more bound than before, but their gags were off. They went slack-jawed at what they saw.

"Burn the whore and bastard!" Doclen ordered.

A guard with a torch took a step but stopped.

"Burn her!"

The guard looked around the square, at Doclen and the people, at Lerer, and didn't move.

Doclen pulled the torch from his hand, nearly trampling the guard as he did.

He threw the fire to the kindling.

It caught quickly and bright.

The people gasped.

Guards circled the burning stake as a barricade, and let the fire rise unseen behind them.

"Nay!" screamed Gebbert.

"Have you burned all your bastards, Finn?" cried someone from the crowd.

"Who said that? Find the man and arrest him."

No one moved. The fires rose to Tresza's blanket and it flared in flame.

When the baby screamed, Tresza hummed it a lullaby until quickly, so quickly, both were silent.

Lerer felt the mountain weigh him down, paralyze him. Fear stopped him from moving, from speaking, from taking the fire before him and lighting the future.

He knew himself to be a coward.

He was not the man he'd hoped to be, the evolved creature the universe wanted.

Let the stream do the work.

The whole of the stake was engulfed in fire, the flesh new kindling to the flame, meters high in the burning daylight.

Minnar screamed and the bees carried his anguish across the universe. He kicked and pulled away and ran at the flame. He wrestled his hands free and leapt into the fire.

In an instant flames were about him, his robes alight, his body new fuel. He threw his arms around the charred girl and baby, nestling his face into her smoldering neck, and remained there while the fire killed him.

Once entwined around the girl, the bees conveyed a solution and end, a feeling of serenity, joyous reunion, and rest.

All went quiet save the popping of flesh and the cracking of wood.

Franco collapsed to his knees and buried his face in his hands.

Other monks rose in prayer and anger.

The crowd waited, horror-struck.

Lerer stared into the fire and traced the moment of Minnar's death, of Tresza's, of the baby's. He felt his fear harden to outrage, his cowardice become purpose.

"Nay," he whispered.

"Nay," he said louder.

"Nay. Nay!"

"Shut him up," said Doclen.

Allen cuffed him across the back of the head and he stumbled forward.

"Nay!"

Lerer turned, paused, resolved, then ran at Doclen, who watched him come, disbelieving.

The prior pulled the governor off his horse to the hard stones, between the ring of guards and the hellish pyre.

"Release me! I am your lord!" Doclen screamed.

Lerer pummeled his face, feeling the skin of his knuckles split on the man's jaw and loving the feeling.

The crowd closed in.

The guards lowered their pikes and left Doclen to fight the monk on his own, sensing the coming storm.

Allen rushed to his master's aid, but Franco tripped him by the ankle. Squirming away, he drew a sword but Rolden, now unbound, stomped on his wrist, relieving him of his weapon with a satisfying crack.

"You'll hang!" screamed Doclen.

Lerer stood him up and slapped his face.

The noble whimpered, entreated, "Remember your vow of peace, your pledge of obedience."

"I know what this is," said Lerer. "I have seen where this goes. A repeat of Old Earth. A world murdered! It can't happen again."

He spun Doclen around like a dancer twirling a partner, a speeding waltz in daylight and flame until he released him, flinging the bejeweled and be-furred nobleman by his own momentum into the raging human fire.

CHAPTER FIFTEEN

They trap the road and hit us at night. The water is poisoned; the fields burned of fodder. Our resupply never arrives, disappearing between two checkpoints, never to be seen again. We're lucky if we make ten kilometers a day and for those we pay with our lives.

Letter from Sub-Lieutenant Arlson, Third Cavalry, to his wife
Marching to Apis
12, Twelfth-Month, 514 NE

21, Seventh-Month, 515 NE – Apis, Temple

"I can't speak to everything. I was but a witness. Me and my kin – my boy. He was a guard."

"Just tell me the facts, Jasper."

The mason cocked his head. It was a casual matter-of-fact indication that he understood the direction. Nothing special, except that it was so casual. So calm. So serene. The man was not intimidated by Stokes, not his bearing, his brow, his breeding, clothes, guards, or exalted position. He was not directly disrespectful but it was far from the expected atmosphere of power relations Stokes was used to. He was an apostle of the prophet, one of the Twelve, direct servant of God. He was in the highest ruling body on the planet – in the universe – and yet this peasant couldn't care less.

It was a condition throughout Apis. He'd met no one since arriving who hadn't acted the same in some way. In the three days he'd been here no one bowed to his authority willingly. It was unnerving. He'd had the first dozen flogged for the perceived disrespect, two to death, before realizing that if he killed everyone who didn't show him the respect of his office, he'd massacre the entire town.

"Well, after the prior—"

"Lerer?"

"Aye, him. Lerer, he done it."

"What did he do?"

"He tossed Doclen into the fire. Just like that." He snapped his fingers and the sound made Stokes jump.

Stokes was jumpy and he hated that he'd just shown it to this peasant. His nerves were shot, his sleep troubled. Just the night before he'd dreamed he was in a field of grain watching weeds push up between the crops. He knew the weed would take over the field, the valley, the world, and he didn't know how to stop it. He pulled some, only to have more sprout a few meters away. The air was alive with the sound of pests while the shoots pushed up from unseen depths and threatened everything. There was something wrong in Apis, something worse than a rebellion, something beyond his imagination and fear – something insidious and apocalyptic. He felt it like a vibration of the air, a tone just below hearing that resonated in his small bones and sent chills throughout his body. This morning, in the pale daylight after his unsettled night, he'd dubbed it a world-wrecking weed.

Stokes glanced to the two soldiers, the one behind Jasper and the one by the door. They stood ready, waiting for a single word to end the interview in the quickest, most permanent way. Thus comforted, Stokes turned back to the peasant.

"I remember this room from before," said Jasper. "Used to be wall-to-wall tapestry. What a shame that was. It's much better now."

"You disapproved of the Doclens' wealth?"

"Nay, sir," said Jasper. "I meant only that it was a shame to cover those stones. That's some good work there. I should know."

"Aye."

Again his nerves were showing. He'd blurted out an obvious question that would have condemned this man. Such gracelessness was unbecoming a man of his breeding. The peasant wouldn't be caught so easily.

"Lerer was not the prior," Stokes said.

"Not officially, but many called him that. He was the center of the priory, later the town. It was a title of respect."

Stokes recalled that Jasper had not referred to him with anything more reverential than 'sir' since the start.

"What did the guards – your son – do when Lerer murdered Doclen?"

Jasper regarded Stokes for a moment. "Nothing. Some were of the mind to do something, but the crowd was lively. Everyone knew then that things had changed and the tide, at least for a while, was turned."

"No one tried to pull Doclen out of the flames? He was a noble."

"He burned like any other man," said Jasper. "A little faster perhaps than Minnar or Tresza. The baby. Probably because of his thick furs. Or maybe it was his body fat." The peasant held his cold eyes insolently on Stokes.

"What happened then?"

"I'm sure others have told you." Jasper leaned back. His chair creaked and the sound stabbed into Stokes's nerves.

"I'm collecting information," said the apostle, waving his quill. "I'm trying to be thorough."

"What will you do with the information?"

"That's really none of your concern," said Stokes.

"Nay?"

"What happened then, stonecutter? Or do you need some help remembering?"

Jasper didn't flinch at the threat, which again unnerved Stokes. The purgers had been at work on the captured militia since they'd retaken the valley. For two weeks Apis had been under their control and they were as unbowed now as they'd been when they'd held off the third and sixth cavalry battalions for two months. Two hundred peasants against a thousand mounted soldiers in pitched battles and open warfare and they'd almost won.

"That bonfire was the spark and the fire spread quick. The tinder was always there, the idea too, but it took the prior's action in the face of Doclen's to set it ablaze."

"What happened?"

"We marched on the castle."

"Just like that? Spontaneously? Without direction?"

"Lerer said some words. Some good ones."

"What were they?"

"Don't remember exactly. Something about freedom, food, and family. It didn't take much. We were starving and we all knew food was at the castle. With Doclen a smoldering heap, seemed like the obvious thing to do."

"And the guards did nothing?"

"Some did, actually."

"What happened to them?"

Jasper smiled, knowing that Stokes already knew. Several people had been hanged already for it. "They were killed," said Jasper. "They got in the way of the greater good and were removed."

"Your son?"

"Went with us," Jasper said plainly. "He helped us storm the gate, overpower the remaining idiots at the castle, not that there were many. Doclen had brought most with him to help with the murders."

Stokes thought to correct Jasper, to explain how it was a lawful execution and not a murder, Doclen, the governor, being the law of the valley, but he knew it was a waste of time. The man was a peasant, would probably be hanged like his son. And besides, he'd already tried explaining it to several of higher station with no effect.

"After the looting of the castle, what happened?"

"We were free."

"But you were a freeman already," said Stokes.

Jasper laughed. "Doclen had mortgaged the valley and indentured most. I was not long from that fate. Starvation and slavery were the only things on offer before the bonfire."

"Lerer took dictatorial control over the valley?"

Jasper smiled a wry grin. "We were free. Lerer led us because he was the best of us."

"Because he was a noble?"

"Nay," laughed Jasper. "Because he made sense. He fed us and opened schools and taught a philosophy that made sense."

"What did he call this new religion?"

"He called it family."

"And everyone followed him because he fed them?"

"Didn't hurt, but his ideas were right and everyone saw it."

"Everyone?"

The mason shifted in his chair and the creak boomed through the room. A bee flew in the open window. Jasper saw it and smiled. Stokes's stomach knotted up.

"Not everyone," said Jasper.

"The wealthy and noble didn't?"

"It was mostly them, aye."

"And what happened to them?"

"They were put aside."

"Put into the dungeons of this very castle?"

"We had to keep them from running off and bringing you folks," Jasper said flatly.

"And the rest of the village?"

"The village? Well, we prospered like we never done before." Jasper held his hard gaze on Stokes so long that one of the soldiers stepped forward.

A bee landed on Jasper's arm and the peasant smiled to see it.

"Tell me about the bees," said Stokes.

"They can sense good and evil," he said.

"That's blasphemy."

"Proof is that this bee is on me and not you."

Stokes raised his hand and the guard slapped the mason with his gauntleted fist.

The blow put him to the floor. When he rolled over, blood trickled from one ear; his jaw was misaligned.

"Take him," said the apostle.

As the guard dragged the heretic away, Stokes stood and stretched, and remarked that the walls were indeed expertly fitted.

* * *

Later in the garden he found a seat near a blossoming tree beside a fountain and sat. The tree was some local thing, scarlet bark and white flowers emitting a subtle but sweet nutty perfume. A bandaged soldier stood at attention twelve paces down the path.

Apostle Stokes found old Prior Thomas's letter and reread it.

It was I and I alone who disobeyed. The brothers of Apis, truer to their oaths than I, only did as I ordered. They are good and godly. Their hearts may or may not have been with me and my choices, but that is irrelevant. Sworn to obey, obey they did. It was I who disobeyed. It was I who kept the library. Let the guilt be all mine for this transgression.

I do not excuse. My crime is clear. What I feel compelled to do however, is explain.

We have a brother here who has, for lack of a better description, been touched. His name is not important, though I suspect if someone is reading this confession, he is known to you. This brother has knowledge far beyond his means. He speaks with a wisdom beyond his years and a certainty beyond this world. He is not mad. Of this I am sure. He knows secret things that can be verified, and wondrous things that will be uncovered one day. He is modest about this, speaks of having access to a celestial library where all God's knowledge is kept, though he would disapprove of this description, wishing to distance his miracles from deity.

When asked how he came to be chosen for these gifts, he is also modest. He credits education, imagination, and empathy as the qualities that led the bees *to notice him. He is clear that when he speaks of bees, he is not metaphorical. He refers to the physical insect, the native breed for which our priory is named. He explains, and I must believe him, that the bees are part of a miraculous unseen web of connections that link knowledge to mind. He says the bees will come to anyone who is ready to receive them.*

With his uncanny awareness, this monk, this teacher, could be anything, but all he wishes to do is serve mankind. Let me be clear here: this man with whom I have shared many hours of counsel desires nothing more than the advancement of the species and works toward that. This is the root of his knowledge, and the seed of what has blossomed in my soul.

For my entire life I have strived to understand God and his will. Never before my talks with this monk have I even approached a fitting answer to the questions

I have struggled with. A fervor grew in me, and my heart and mind came together in it, like magnets properly aligned, and I realized then how opposed it is to the church to which I have sworn allegiance.

Here then my second sin, that of apostasy, as I rationalized and justified my first sin of disobedience with the books. I have broken with the church, the prophet, and our law, which I see is unjust and detrimental to the greater goal I'm beginning to understand.

The sixth precept of my priory oath is to remove myself from politics, and here then is my third sin, for I see a direct connection with politics and faith and cannot be true to Truth in the abstract without action in the world. To love is to act and there can be no separation. I have worked actively against our governor, Finn Doclen, as he has taken advantage of the hunger here for his personal gains. The law is on his side. But the law is wrong. These laws bear the crest of the prophet but are clearly unjust. If his words come from God, it is not the God I would serve. But I do not believe that is the case. I see now that a system has entrenched a man – the prophet – to maintain that system, and here see now my fourth sin: I disbelieve the prophet's infallibility and divine mandate. I challenge the divine right of the nobles to enslave the peasant. I see no need for the neglect and violence we must endure. There is enough for everyone. My family is big.

My death is near. I grow weak with the valley. My physical frailty is in accord with my conscience. The promises I made as a youth battle the knowledge I have now as an old man. They will not be silent. I have chosen a path and though I know it is right, and know it will spread and free this world and others, I feel also that I am damned for aiding it. There is uneasiness in me. I want to repent. There is a man inside me who counts my sins and challenges me to return to the path. He measures my weakness and blindness against my God and prophet. He condemns me for what I have done and what I have allowed this priory to become. It is this man, I am sure, who keeps the bees from me even now and makes me write this confession. It is he who would send this letter to the Hall of the Prophet and summon righteous correction from the holy church for my misdeeds. Even now, I struggle with this man and as the lights grow dim, I pray against all hope of grace, that I will be forgiven for my disobedience and its results, while simultaneously rejoicing in the glory of them.

Stokes wondered what would have happened if the letter had been sent when the prior had written it instead of being discovered now among the priory rubble. Less pain, surely. It was clear the old prior foresaw this crisis, the correction that now tortured and killed the flock he was charged with protecting.

"Add this to your sins, old man," he said aloud. "This blood is on you."

These debts were compounded by the loss of so many soldiers needed to breach this valley. The apostle of God went cold to think what the cost would be if these events were repeated elsewhere. How great the prior's sin then?

How could the old prior have believed such a story? It was one thing for the ignorant peasantry to buy into a tale of miraculous insects, but that an educated prior would fall prey to a designing conman spoke to the man's dementia and a decline in moral standards.

He'd seen it before, not with convenient local bugs, but with other props. There was a woman who said she could read the future in the entrails of animals. The better the animal, the better her sight. The town had her reading the guts of noblemen and children before the purgers shut her down. It seemed to be a symptom of the borderlands. Pioneers had gone too far afield and away. Many outposts had fallen out of touch. Missionaries helped, but there was no guarantee that they, like Prior Thomas, would be immune to the blasphemies they met.

Gullible old men, stupid peasants, conniving troublemakers with a history of rebelliousness. Add that mixture to a weakened moral atmosphere, returning government authority, and a lean harvest; the recipe was complete. Just another pretender who would be king. The only surprise was that it had lasted so long; nearly two years.

He turned his face up to the sun to feel the radiance of God upon his cheeks and fell into silent prayer, as was his way. Bees flitted above him, crossing his vision, streaking the pink-yellow light he perceived behind his clenched eyelids with shadows.

He stood up with a start and took a step away from the tree. Bees in the blossoms, bees in the garden. Bees in the mind?

Could it....

Across the courtyard, a woman was led in by two soldiers. She moved gracefully, her posture erect, her eyes keen. These things belied her simple linen dress and shoes. It was his next appointment.

Stokes looked around him for a better place to talk. He'd thought the garden a good choice but now feared it, questioning his own reason.

He said a prayer, and laughed to himself. He sat back down on the cool bench beneath the blossoming tree full of bees and scent, and signaled the guards to bring Deserey Doclen to sit with him.

She was beautiful. Peasant clothes could not hide her pure breeding, which showed in her narrow nose and high cheekbones, firm chin and firm blue eyes. Those noble features were as good as a passport into any great house on Temple.

"Mistress Doclen," said Stokes, not getting up.

"You are the apostle?"

"Aye. These are my casual clothes."

The light caught in her disheveled hair and made a flaxen glow around her head. Bees roused by her coming rose from the branches and coursed through the air.

"I expected purgers, why you?" She held him in her gaze. Was that her breeding or was she just another haughty criminal?

"The purgers remove the cancer," he said. "I am here to heal the body after the infection is gone."

"We'll be welcomed back into the flock?"

"That's why I am here." He painted his face with his most saintly smile. "Sit." He patted the bench beside him. "You are a lady. Act like it and you'll be treated as such."

She sat down in the shade of the tree.

"What is this delightful tree called?" said Stokes, seeing her eyes searching the flowering boughs.

"It is a mistbegone," she said. "It pulls moisture from the air. It can dissipate a fog cloud."

"The bees like it."

She hesitated before saying, "It's in bloom."

"Where were you during the revolt?"

"I was asleep in my room when they came, awakened by the clamor of fighting. I looked out that window there." She pointed to a tower.

"You must have been terrified."

She moved a wisp of hair from over her eye. "I was not afraid. Nor was I surprised. I'd expected something like it for a long time."

"Why?"

"Finn was cruel."

Stokes waited for her to continue but she didn't.

"How did they get into the fortress?" he asked.

"They knew a secret way."

A bee landed on her sleeve and she regarded it. Stokes felt a rush of worry.

"The bees?" he said. "The bees told them?"

She looked up at him with a placid expression. "Nay. I asked Lerer about it later and he said the guards took them through it."

"Which guards?"

"I don't recall," she said and smiled.

She was lying. She wanted him to know she was lying. She could have lied without him suspecting, so collected was she.

"Were you raped?" He tried to shock her.

"Nay."

"How did they coerce you into joining them?"

"They asked me how big my family was," she said.

"Ah, the rallying cry of the false prophet. And you knew your life was endangered if you refused?"

"I see what you're doing," she said. "I don't need your help. I don't want it. I won't be returning to the flock. Have many come back?"

"We're not at that stage yet," he said. "Explain to me how someone of your breeding and class could be made to serve the rabble?"

She collected the insect off her sleeve onto her slender fingers. Her hands were graceful but dirty, her nails bitten and chipped.

"I volunteered," she said.

Stokes cringed. He was trying to save her from the fire. She was not making it easy.

"The years had been lean but would not have been life-threatening under my father. Under Finn, they were deadly and destroying."

"So it was penance for the perceived crimes of your brother?"

"You call them crimes?"

"Wouldn't you?"

"I would, but I'm surprised you can see it."

"Perceived. I said perceived crimes. I'm still gathering information."

"After the uprising, not another soul died from hunger."

"Because Finn was gone?"

"Because there was enough for everyone. More than enough. It was a distribution issue. And no one missed Finn."

"Not even you?"

"He murdered my father," she said.

Stokes took a breath. "That is quite the accusation. Patricide is a serious crime. You know for a fact your brother killed Oliver Doclen?"

"Aye."

"How? The bees?" He forced a wry smile.

The bee on Deserey's finger lit into the air and flew a circle above her head. "Nay," she said somewhat dreamily. "I didn't need them to know that. Plenty of coincidence—"

"Coincidence is weak evidence to convict a noble of so heinous a crime," he burst out. "Are you aware that even suggesting such a thing against a noble is a criminal – nay, capital – offense?"

"Plenty of coincidence," she repeated, "to back up the servants' accounts."

"Lowborn servants?"

She shook her head in pity.

Stokes felt his checks redden. "Your brother, Finn, was the rightful lord and steward of this land. He was your kin and a noble. Of the highest pedigree. How can you besmirch his name – *your* name – in this way?"

"Class before creed, eh, apostle?" she said.

Stokes heard his teeth grind.

She went on. "I wasn't surprised Finn had been killed, nor that a monk had done it. Finn was a monster. Lord he might have been, but he was no steward. He was selfish and cruel and stupid."

"But he was of our class."

"Yours."

"Lady Deserey, Deserey, I'm not sure you understand the gravity of this interview."

She glanced around if the conversation was boring her. "There were those in our household who fought the uprising," she said. "Ignorant slaves dying for a dead master."

"Many people died."

"A fraction of what my brother had done."

Perturbed, Stokes returned to his questions. "So you were captured?"

"I volunteered."

"To join them?"

"To feed them. I remembered my father's oath of stewardship. There was need. People were starving. It was Finn's doing. And he was trying to destroy the priory."

"Another accusation?"

"Aye," she said. "He was literally taxing the people to death and trying to blame the stewards of the holy church."

"They were lawful taxes."

"Lawful but unjust. Patently, cruelly, and obviously partisan. He was on his way to own all the land in the valley. There wouldn't be a free man in Apis, or a farm without rent, when he was done. All would be indentured to pay their lawful tax."

Stokes had never met Finn Doclen, but he'd met people like him, shrewd businessmen who knew how to take advantage of tragic situations. The Hall of the Prophet was full of their lobbyists, seeking favor and legal cover for when their masters overstepped their natural advantages. He'd always thought that such men were dangerous but secretly envied them their boldness and ruthlessness, traits he felt he needed now in Apis.

Lady Deserey went on. "We had so much food in our cellars it was rotting. It was a very easy thing for me to turn over the stores. It was moral and right."

"And then?"

She leaned back and caught a sunbeam on her cheek shining through the luscious leaves. "And then we made a society as near to heaven as there's ever been on this planet," she said.

"You blaspheme?"

"What else could be paradise? We were happy. We were peaceful. We were united and growing. It was as easy as being fair to one another. That's all it took."

"And Lerer set himself up as a new prophet?" he said.

She gave him a look that would have gotten a peasant beaten. "He showed us how to be quiet and how to gather the three jewels to bring in the bees."

"The three jewels?"

"Compassion, moderation, and humility."

"Where'd he get that?"

"From Old Earth."

"How?"

"The bees."

"You believe that claptrap? Oh, lady, I thought you more refined."

"I am glad to disappoint you. Will I be killed?"

"This isn't a trial." Stokes grew aware of a silence in the courtyard, then a feather tickling up the nape of his neck and hum in the back of his head. "You would seem to be a traitor," he said, shaking it off. "To your class, family, and God."

"Not my family. Not my real one. But this isn't a trial." She smiled mockingly.

They regarded each other for a moment, then Stokes said, "Tell me about the bees."

"Ask Lerer."

"I plan to."

"I'll tell him," she said and closed her eyes for a moment. When she opened them, she laughed to see the expression on his face.

He blinked, washed the shock away, and laughed back at her, though not as honestly.

* * *

He found Lerer where he'd left him, bound naked in the stocks in the town square. He'd been whipped and beaten. His broken leg was wrapped beneath him like a rope, blood caked down his back and face, a black pool of scab where his right eye had been.

"Deserey said to expect you," he said when the apostle approached.

Stokes counted two dozen guards on duty standing a picket to keep the commoners away. He found a stool by the trough, brought it up to Lerer, and sat down in front of him.

"Tell me about the bees," he said.

"Why?"

"Life."

"You'd spare my life? I think you're a little late. I won't see midnight."

"Not yours, Lady Deserey's."

The monk regarded him with his one eye. "And what of my brother monks?"

"Only a dozen—"

"Eleven," said Lerer. "Franco died an hour ago. Bled out on the purger's table."

"The chronicler? I was not done with him. But how— It doesn't matter. The monks are forfeit, as are you. But I could save Deserey Doclen, traitor that she is."

"I just have to tell you about the bees and she'll be pardoned?"

"If you tell me truthfully, you have my word."

"I know she gave you no reason to pardon her."

"Thus it is up to you."

Lerer craned his neck and looked at the sky. Stokes followed his gaze, not sure what he expected to see. It was only a blue canopy of warm summer sunshine. The lightning storms that had lately begun to vex Zion City were nowhere to be imagined here.

Stokes said, "You came from a good family, I can understand how your ambition was challenged out here."

Lerer shook his head. "You have to unlearn that kind of thing for them to come."

"How did you unlearn it?"

"I didn't. They came anyway."

"The bees?"

"Aye, the bees. Keep up, Apostle. We're not going to get many redos today."

"The bees are real?"

"As real as the three on me now and the six above my head."

Stokes bent, looked, squinted. He couldn't see anything on Lerer's body for the gore and filth, but scanning the air above him, he counted the half dozen.

"They're the weak local variety of pollinator," said Stokes. "How'd you choose them for your crusade?"

"They chose me."

"They're insects."

"They're a miracle," he said. "And they're the most threatening thing in the universe for you and those like you."

"How?"

"They link us together."

"A symbol?"

"More literal, Apostle. A conversation. Distance is nothing. I have communicated with other worlds."

"How?"

"They give access to a network that exists below the surface of perceived reality. If two people are connected, they can connect."

"And through these connections you've talked with people who know of Old Earth?"

"Who've you been talking to?"

"Prior Thomas. He left a confession. We found it in the rubble of the priory."

Lerer twisted his neck in the stocks. "You didn't need to burn it down, you know," he said.

"He said you knew of Old Earth. Was that from books in the library?"

"A little, but what I learned, I learned through the bees."

"I don't understand," said Stokes.

"I can't explain it better," said Lerer, his speech going thick. "And don't think I haven't tried."

A bee landed on Stokes's thigh in the sunlight and paced a circle on his knee.

"This is preposterous. You'd kill the Lady Deserey to keep up this mad tale?"

"Did they tell you I was mad?"

Stokes watched the bee and felt a throb in his forehead.

"Nay," said Lerer, smiling. "They said I was sane. That's why you're here. Because I couldn't be dismissed as a madman."

"You can now with this insect fiction."

"As God is my witness—"

"Don't you blaspheme."

"What oath can I use that will convince you? The bees are the key. Spare Deserey."

Stokes grinned, liking the note of desperation in Lerer's voice. The smile faded a moment later as he considered what he was hearing.

"Your story doesn't add up," he said, rubbing his temples. "You say you have to be worthy for them to come, the three jewels and all that, but they came to you without them."

"Aye," he said. "That is true."

"Why?"

"I asked that," he said. "Not that there was anyone to ask."

"Did you get an answer?"

"A hunch," he said. "I think they came to me because they wanted to. I didn't draw them, they came because they were tired of waiting and I was the closest thing they could find. I had the imagination, stamina, and foundational philosophy."

"What philosophy was that?"

"Love, though thanks to my upbringing and class, I struggled against it. It was in a moment of surrender they found me. A simple laugh that opened the way."

"You're saying the bees have an agenda?"

"I don't know," he said. "But they seemed eager to get started."

"Get started doing what?"

"Connecting," he said. "Evolving."

"Rebelling?"

"That was my idea, but knowing what they taught me, it really was the only thing to do."

"Revolting against holy authority? Murdering nobles? Attacking centuries of order and tradition?"

"Aye. Millenia, actually." Lerer laughed and it caught in his throat. He coughed and convulsed until he vomited blood and bile.

Stokes watched and waited.

"You killed noblemen," said Stokes. "Priests killing nobles. Shame doesn't describe it."

"People killing people," said Lerer. "People defending themselves. People defending each other."

"The Lord of—"

"Finn was a murdering bastard. Temperament and position put him square in the way of progress. I would have liked things to be more peaceful, and easier, but it was not to be."

The line made Stokes smile. "That's the usual rallying cry of the rebel."

"Because it's usually true."

"Do you know how many people were killed since your little rebellion?"

"I do," he said flatly.

A shiver shook the apostle. "Well, how does your philosophy of love and sharing justify the death you caused?"

"We didn't commit suicide, Apostle. There were soldiers on the other end of the lances that killed my brothers and sisters."

"Knowing what you know now, seeing how it all ended, would you do it again?"

"A hypothetical question? Interesting."

"I'm curious," said Stokes. "Are you broken? How was it that your bees didn't foresee this disaster?"

"I can't see the future with the bees, though honestly, I suspect that some can."

"Would you do it again? Would you drench your hands in so much blood, monk? Noble Melk?"

"I would, Apostle. Because as Deserey told you, we had paradise here for a while. It wasn't lazy rest, the way your folk tales relate, but a thriving community of fellows, growing better and stronger by the day. Those you kill will be martyrs and will be remembered by those to come. The survivors will carry our story, and the bees will be there to start again."

"Blasphemy."

"Get used to it. I was the first, but won't be the last."

"Your paradise was feeding everyone?"

"That's the heart of it. You don't let your family starve. I extended my family out a bit."

"To the village?"

"To the species, you idiot. This is bigger than the valley, bigger than Temple, bigger than the system. The bees will unite all. The archaic, cruel systems of caste and church will be toppled for a better ideal. It's coming. It has to. Our survival depends on it. We will follow Jareth's path because it's better."

"Who's Jareth?"

"A teacher."

"This is exactly why the prophet ordered all the books brought back to the Hall. Can you not see how your education has radicalized you?"

"You're not paying attention."

The wind shifted and Stokes covered his nose for the smell of the captive.

"I wrote some of it down," said Lerer, "but I suspect you burned it."

"By God I hope we did."

"Blaspheming?"

"Praying, heretic."

"What about Deserey? The light dims."

"Don't be melodramatic."

"I'm being literal."

"I can't believe the bees are what you say. You're spinning a yarn."

"Be still."

"What?"

"I said, be still, Apostle. Listen."

Stokes straightened himself and listened. Before him Lerer slackened in the stocks, his head lolling at the end of his fettered neck.

Stokes heard nothing, but then corrected himself. The nothing was something. It was silence. He'd gone deaf. Nothing reached – not the sound of wind, the rustle of armor, the labored breathing of the prisoner. Nothing. Silence. And the eerie calm, as if he were underwater. He searched his mind for an appropriate prayer when the hum began.

It was low and distant and he turned his head to locate the direction, but found it was everywhere and nowhere. It was in his head. The bee on his leg lifted off and dove around his forehead. The humming became a buzz, a soothing low drone that linked his ears to his head.

And then the others came. Lerer first. Stokes felt the pain where his eye had been, the remorse for failing now and the certain knowledge that others would come and finish the work.

He felt flesh burn and heard a scream within his mind, seeing dungeon and purgers bending over him with branding irons. "Tell us, Eugene, who were your co-conspirators?"

Lady Deserey in her room looking out a window across the valley, watching smoke wisps rise from the priory and thinking there was some kind of optical illusion over the valley, for the rubble looked so close.

A peasant far away, hiding in a lush thicket, waiting for the purgers to go, wondering if his mother survived, hoping his children would.

All these minds and more rushed in on him, breaking down his psychic defense, his wall of prayer, his devotions and prejudices. He saw an innate inability to reconcile that pain to the beauty the church presented to some, promised to all, but delivered to few.

Here were the masses. Here were the people. Station and birth were lost to empathy – to love one another. A communal struggle. The ancient call of the ancient saints. His words. All their words. A thousand messiahs across a thousand centuries – Old Earth and beyond. Unification and justice that went against the church. Where was the quality if a beggar could be a saint and a governor the devil?

"Save me, God!"

Stokes staggered and swatted a bee out of the air, knocking it into the dust. He crushed it beneath his boot.

"It's just a bug," Lerer said. "A lowly common insect. And they're everywhere." He spat of glob of horror into the dust. "You can't kill them all. It would destroy the planet's ecosystem. Everyone would starve."

"How was that visited on me?"

Lerer's words came out in spurts. "I did it. It took something out of me, though, I can tell you that."

"Abomination!"

"Remember your promise about Deserey." The false prophet's body's slumped and settled. The bees around him hovered for a moment and then flew away. It was their departure that convinced Stokes that Lerer was dead.

The apostle wiped sweat from his face and neck, soaking his handkerchief. He heard wind in the trees and movement of men and horses, and the distant but lingering buzzing of bees.

"Bring me the master purger," Stokes said to the first guard he came to. "Bring him to me now."

The guard sped to the castle as Stokes found a shady spot under an awning. He looked up the hill to the burned monastery, the timbers still smoldering. He remembered seeing beehives up there on the far side in the orchard. They'd not gotten to those. They would be next. Then the town. Then the people. All of them.

PART THREE
ASSEMBLING

'To change something, build a new model
that makes the existing model obsolete.'
Buckminster Fuller

CHAPTER SIXTEEN

By revelation and direct commandment of Benjamin IV Holy Prophet of the Saved, it is hereby commanded and ordered that all departments, agencies, and peoples of Temple take immediate steps to eradicate a certain native infectious species which threatens all Saved.
Infectious Species Eradication Edict (ISEE)
515 NE

15:30, 16, Twelfth-Month, 938 NE – Saints Gate, Temple

Jessop read the four-hundred-year-old reports of the cleansing of Apis with horror and shame. He was appalled at the reports of the human fires that burned for weeks, fat-fed and spurting. Not a soul in the entire province was spared. Estimates ranged from five thousand, an impossibly low figure, to eight and fifty thousand killed, sacrificed. Murdered. The official count was three and thirty thousand, two hundred eight and fifty. It was called a cleansing, but Jessop saw it to be what it was. A massacre.

The deaths were all numbers and lists, as cold and clinical as a laundry inventory, and had he not read the histories, the journals and reports, they would not have connected as actual human beings. He thought himself a sensitive person, sympathetic and kind, but when faced with faceless figures and crimes beyond reckoning, he could glaze over such horrors as well as any modern man. But he had read the papers, and as he looked down the names of notable deaths – the peasants were numbered only – he fell quickly upon Deserey Doclen and caught a gasp in his throat. Of course the monks were listed: Franco, Hoopes, Eugene, Lerer, and also Minnar. Tresza and the baby, he assumed, were the 'whore and bastard' that burned before the official order of cleansing.

Even after the uprising, Brother Franco, the priory chronicler, served his office with accuracy and art. There were gaps in his records, notably about the nature of the bees and his own experiences with 'the deeper understanding that they brought', but the record of the day-to-day work of Apis after the revolution was clear and complete. It was a confession of treason. The lands were in common, as were all resources 'known and unknown, that the land, air, and sea might offer'. They were far from a sea and yet it was written in their charter that way. They obviously had plans to expand.

They opened schools, nine and thirty of them to be precise, and these were egalitarian – noble, peasant, and slave – welcomed into 'the family' as friend and comrade. The chronicler admitted his own perspective had been forever altered by the coming of bees and the 'sympathy that had brought them to him', and had wondered if he, or anyone so touched, could objectively witness what he called the 'beginning of a new age of human hope and wonder'. Through his writings, Jessop felt he knew the man intimately, and through him, the enigmatic Lerer – at least enough to mourn the monk's cruel death four centuries before.

And that had given the Second Advisor to the prophet pause.

He felt ashamed knowing he should read these reports with the eye of an elder, one charged to defend the system, a ruler sworn to order. Like the Apostle Stokes, he should side with the nobility. But he, the third highest ranking soul on the planet, couldn't agree with anyone but the poor people of that tortured village.

His mind made parallels to Claremond, recalling his father's advice, his brother's murmurs of revolution. Man's laws versus God's. He knew what misery the aristocracy could inflect. His own family had been so damaged. As he studied the reports of the chronicler, the journals of the monks, Thomas's diary, even the tale of the revolution from Lerer's own journal, his heart bled at the injustice they'd endured and rose to applaud the righteous revolt against it.

Suspecting he'd been manipulated by a clever scribe, Jessop turned to reports from the other side, from Apostle Stokes, from the purgers, from the military commanders who'd lost half their commands to a fifth of their number, but he found nothing there to change his heart and with each mention of torture, execution, and holocaust, he cringed and mourned. He felt a growing distance from his office and rank, until he shook with anxiety. He questioned his life and purpose, wondering if he hadn't been struck with divine revelation under the granite mountain.

"You look peaked, Holy Adviser," said the archivist appearing through the office doorway. "Shall I fetch you food?"

"Aye, Brother Gartrall. And cool water would be nice."

Gartrall bowed and left, moving down the stone corridor with some speed, his shoes scraping on the gritty stone, his shadows cascading from the rows of dim glowglobes. How he had come up to the door without Jessop hearing him was a mystery.

Jessop felt the hours of sitting challenge his legs. He stretched and walked to the threshold, looked out upon the darkened hallway, and pulled the door shut before returning to his work.

The cleansing of Apis was overseen by an apostle and not a purger. That was strange. Stokes had not abdicated the responsibly for the slaughter. He'd demanded it, and stayed until it was complete. He even executed soldiers and officers who'd grown close to their prisoners. The Doclen house was completely destroyed, its lineage erased. Stokes had come to rescue and redeem an ancient family but ended up wiping it out.

Stokes admitted in his letters to the prophet that he had all along intended to free Deserey Doclen, the last of her family, but once the bee touched his mind, he knew the evil there had to be contained 'at any and all costs'. His fear was palpable in every paragraph and sentence. It was the devil, he was sure; 'none other could have that kind of power'. Jessop wondered why the apostle had attributed the acts to infernal forces instead of God. He found his answer in a later confession:

What poured into my mind was the vision of destruction, the end of religion, of the prophet, of order and rank. The end of law. The end of government and authority. A social madness where the ignorant and low would tread down the holy and noble.

Egalitarianism was not a new concept, but what made this event so terrifying to Stokes was that the political notion had a decidedly spiritual, or at least psychic, element that challenged not only the governing systems of the planet, but its religious ones as well. Standing in opposition to what everyone knew was the only way to live, such a confrontation could only come from hell. It was truly an apocalyptic vision for Apostle Stokes. Whereas Franco had described his first communion with the bees in beautiful transcendental language, Stokes spoke of an assault, a mental rape. But of course, the bees had not come to him as they had the others. Nay, if Stokes's version was to be believed – and Jessop tended to believe it – the bees were forced upon him by Lerer, a thing so hard to do for the weakened monk that it had killed him. Was it meant to be an attack or an education?

Jessop rubbed his eyes and looked around the cluttered office, wishing for a window.

A low knock came from the door. "Holy Advisor Jessop?" Gartrall fumbled with the latch and entered carrying a carafe of water and an earthen cup. He was followed by a page with a tray of roast beef sandwiches. Jessop thought he saw another figure out in the hall, but couldn't be sure. The thought of someone there spying made him remember his forged permission to be here.

"Archivist, would you be so good as to bring me a copy of the *Prime Doctrines of the Saved*, earliest version possible."

"That is under glass," said Gartrall.

"Please."

"Of course."

"Oh, and *The Principles of Noble Living*. Any copy will do."

"We have many."

"Blessed be," said Jessop as dismissal. He poured himself a cup of cool water and raised it in thanks.

"And to thee," replied Gartrall, pulling the door shut behind him after the page had slipped through under his arm.

Jessop had no interest in reading the official moral codes of the Saved, but it might give him cover for being in the vault. He could say he was working on a talk for General Conclave.

A lie.

He was planning lies. Who was he fooling? It was easily checked – the same man who would verify he was interested in canonical texts was the man who'd report his investigation into forbidden ones. What had happened to him?

He thought of his position. He was not from Temple. He was Claremondian, holding the highest rank in the church ever for anyone not born on Temple. He had a place in history. He was already a hero to millions of faithful, a new man in an old institution. And of course, he was distrusted by some because of it. Was this not confirming that prejudice?

He picked up the report from Maaraw, the one from High Purger Tarquin. The name filled his stomach with knots. He knew the name. The man was the beast the prophet had sent with Brandon's fleet to cleanse Enskari. Had the armada succeeded he would have killed millions of people in the name of purity. More lists and numbers in a ledger to bury the horror of a genocide under unimaginable figures. He thanked God it had not happened – and realized in that instant his faith in God went wholly counter to his trust in God's messenger.

He read Tarquin's report and fidgeted in his chair as the man described in clinical detail the tortures he had put the rebel leader through before the end. And then he described the final blow and told about the bees.

The bees.

Again the bees.

Tarquin had suffered Stokes's experience – a mad intrusion into his mind at the feet of a dying man. Tarquin shared also the bloodthirsty reaction as his ancient predecessor, ordering the execution of a – he wanted to say 'martyr', knowing it was the right word, but Jessop forced himself to call him a rebel instead. A political mover, with a similar humanitarian philosophy. Nay, more than that. The same philosophy as Lerer. He'd even used the same terminology, the exact same question, 'How big is your family?'

It was right in front of him. He'd not seen it for the torture of good men, the execution of noble blood, and the soul-searing smoke rising from a burning baby.

The bees.

A jar of dead bees.

A knock.

"Come."

Gartrall entered, carrying two books, one old and handwritten, big as a desk, the other small, modern, and well bound.

"How is your history, Gartrall?" asked Jessop as the archivist put the books down.

"Passable," said the archivist.

"When did we discover Jareth's World?"

"In 655," he said. "It was the last of the planets to be observed by our astronomers. It completed the system map. It was called the Ring World until Aderyn, that damned Enskaran heretic, visited it in 922 I think, and discovered it to be an Old Earth colony predating the Unsettling by a century. Pity it didn't thrive like the rest of us."

"When did it get the name Tirgwenin?"

"That's what the native savages call it. I first heard the name a few years ago. Sounds barbaric, doesn't it?"

"And it is the only planet with rings?"

Gartrall looked confused. "Aye. I thought everyone knew that. Didn't you make a mobile of the system for science class? I remember using glass balls and paper rings, string and a sunfruit for Coronam."

"We had no science classes on Claremond," said Jessop.

The archivist blushed. "I meant no disrespect, my lord holy advisor."

"Where did you go to school?"

"I come from a good family. Sixth to the title, so I joined the church. We had tutors. I studied with the nobility of Jerum."

"When was this vault made?"

"Work began in 512 and was completed, or rather, opened for storage in 520. It's still expanding."

"In reaction to Benjamin IV's Apocrypha Edict?" said Jessop.

"Just so," said Gartrall. "Now it is the safest repository of information in the system."

"And very well maintained," said Jessop.

Gartrall looked at the jar of dead bees on the desk. "Benjamin IV was the one who eradicated those parasites."

"He killed the bees?"

"The native version carried disease. In 515 he ordered the eradication of the entire species. A very successful campaign. It was wiped out by 550, planetwide."

"What was the disease?"

"I don't know exactly. The Old Earth bees are a heartier variety anyway. The other planets attest to that."

"The other planets?"

"Aye, the native bees – *Apis Coronaman* – are found on all the other worlds, except Silangan and the dead ones. Can't speak to Jareth's World, but I assume there too."

"So would I."

"The human variety – meaning those that came with us in the Unsettling – have nearly wiped them out on the other worlds too. God's mercy there, since they spread disease."

"So I shouldn't open the jar?"

Gartrall looked at the container as if seeing it for the first time. "I hadn't thought of that," he said. "I suppose it's safe. Those have been here for four hundred years and many people I am sure have opened that jar."

"Or not."

"Or not," the archivist conceded.

Jessop felt a chill more of anxiety than atmosphere. "I'm nearly done," he said. "Call a cab for me. I'm sure I must leave soon if I'm to make the mayor's feast."

"I'll see to it," he said and left.

Jessop reread Lerer's pages, which mentioned the name of a planet that was still a century and a half from being discovered and five hundred years from being properly named. He could think of no moment of prophetic revelation in the history of the church as concise, clear, and accurate as Lerer's. This knowledge had come, he claimed, from psychic contact with an alien mind across space. Maya. This was not the raving of a madman, claiming to converse with seraphim or saints. It was too coherent. Was it logic or a leap of faith Jessop felt as he realized he believed the dead prior? Maya had been real, a living, breathing person like Lerer himself, like Bruin on Maaraw, like how many others touched on other worlds by this phenomenon. Here before him was proof of… of…of something. Something divine, demonic, supernatural? Something beyond modern understanding. More he could not name.

So of course it was secret.

There was an old adage in the church that God values faith above all else and so keeps His miracles to a minimum. It was stated differently in every town and province, but that was how he'd learned it on Claremond. If God were to show himself, through certain revelation or full-on miracles, it would weaken one's love for Him. It never made sense to Jessop but like the rest of the Saved he figured it to be one of the deeper ineffable mysteries that defined the one true religion. Having faith that faith was enough, was enough. Yet here before him was record of a miracle. Not a great miracle, not a parting of a sea or the curing of a plague, but a simple throwaway tidbit of knowledge that the writer had no business knowing.

He wondered when it had been recognized as the miracle it was. Immediately, he realized, because the details of the affair had been concealed from the beginning. He saw the official order penned by Benjamin IV himself sealing the records and putting them in the custody of the church's most zealous and cruel order, the purgers.

He made a quick inventory of who knew the secret. The records were in the purgers' care but that order was not known for their scholarly pursuits. High Purger Tarquin obviously had no idea what he was dealing with on Maaraw, but he was sure that Grand High Purger Greguri knew. He sensed it at the last council meeting. The prophet knew and had known to ask for the records. That is, he knew where to look. Beyond those two, Jessop couldn't think of anyone else who knew before the current crisis. He was an advisor to God's messenger and no one had briefed him.

Lerer hadn't claimed divine guidance as the source for his

enlightenment and cause of the revolution, as so many others had done. Franco hadn't linked the experience to God, and old Prior Thomas had died believing his faith in the church had actually kept the miracle from coming to him. It spoke clearly to the danger of the miracle; the bees' arrival was accompanied by a renunciation of the current social order of which the church was paramount. They were incompatible.

The end of the world, was what the prophet had said.

He opened the lid of the jar, shook one of the ancient dead bees onto the table, and studied it.

He'd seen them before. Back home, they'd been called honeybugs, not bees, because bees had stingers and these did not. They were fuzzier than transplanted Old Earth bees, and their sheen was more enamel than flat, though the colors were the same black and yellow.

On all worlds except the dead ones and Silangan. And Temple.

Remembering the mayor and the party, he knew it was time for him to leave the mountain.

As if summoned, Gartrall appeared at the door. "A cab is waiting," he said.

"Very good." Jessop put on his warm coat, and wearing a placid face that belied his inner thoughts, he exited the vault to find the heated cab to take him to Saints Pass.

"I know where to take you, Most Holy Lord," said the cabbie in a twanging accent. The title was one Jessop had not heard before, surely inaccurate, but who could keep track of the right ones?

It was dark, an hour past sunset and the sky was its moonless black. Temple had no moon. Claremond had one and Jessop missed it often, looking into the black abyss above his new home. A single wisp of green aurora slithered from the north, slowly spreading its strange light upon the mountain.

A chill breeze caught Jessop beneath his collar. "Blessed be," he said to the cabbie, stepping inside.

"Aye, thanks. Thanks aplenty."

Jessop warmed his hands on the little stove inside the carriage as it maneuvered down the steep and now icy road. He closed the drapes as much to contain his thoughts as to keep the warmth.

He fell into a silent reverie and was surprised when the cab stopped and he found himself in front of a tall granite house lit by burning lamps and a glowing sky.

"Here, m'lord," said the cabbie, opening the door for him.

Jessop looked up and saw that the tendrils had reached halfway across the heavens, a testament to the time he'd been brooding. He marveled at the light, the broad and multiple ribbons of green, yellow, and amber waving on unseen particle winds.

"Second Advisor, I welcome you to my humble home." A man in formal dress, crimson coat and gold buttons, bowed low before him. "I am Mayor Neslen."

"I am welcomed," said Jessop, returning the bow. "I hope you have not gone to too much trouble."

"It is my absolute pleasure. I have long wanted to meet you."

"Oh?"

"Aye, I served a mission on Claremond many years ago, and wanted to say hello."

"A noble undertaking," said Jessop. "You have a handsome house."

Jessop noted the three-story granite structure complete with front pillars and several outbuildings all done in similar fashion. He couldn't see any neighbors.

"I'm only borrowing it," said Neslen. "While I'm mayor. I have a ranch at the mouth of the canyon. The house there is twice as large, but not half as historic."

"Are you related to the Apostle Neslen?"

"A great-grandson."

A group of nobles milled together on the steps leading into the house, their rank clear from their fine clothes. A red carpet stretched out the door to the curb, and gray uniformed servants, spaced every two meters, held lamps above their heads while staring blankly ahead.

"Let us come in from the cold," said Jessop, noting a shooting star above the house scratching a brief light across a lavender ribbon.

Neslen led the way over the carpet and up the stairs. The nobles took formal places on either side and all bowed and curtsied. As often happened at moments like this, Jessop thought of how far he'd come as a middle-class merchant's son to have aristocracy bow to him. He also felt very underdressed. He thought he caught snide looks from some of the nobles regarding his clothes, caught their up-and-down scan of his dress and the subtle sneer of their lips. He'd felt such looks before, even when decked out in his holy finery. His pedigree, which inspired the common folk, was held against him by the upper classes. He'd been born to a middle-class family – not the lowest by any means, but anyone not born of a genealogically verified patrician pedigree was lowborn to those who were. It wasn't that they saw him as subhuman, but themselves as superior humans. He'd grown used to it – the disdain. He was never sure if it was racism for him not being a Templer or classism for him not being blue-blooded. The two looked pretty much the same. It was his job to endure it. He was a symbol of the new church, a reaction to the reformation movement that had flared up across the system and had even taken over an entire world, Enskari.

Inside, the house was ablaze in glowglobes and crystal chandeliers. Ribbons had been hung from the high ceiling and looped lazily to wall sconces just above eye level. The opulence of the building spoke of formal reception while the ribbons spoke of a casual party, a wedding perhaps. It was a strange blend but Jessop decided he liked it.

Chamber music floated from one side. The smell of rich meat and spicy sauces perfumed the air from somewhere else, and Jessop caught a glimpse of a long banquet table though an open doorway, servants already standing at attention there.

"You have done far too much, Brother Neslen."

"It is our honor."

The guests filtered in as Neslen showed Jessop portraits of the past mayors, all of whom he was related to. Jessop listened politely and nodded, but his thoughts wandered and he found himself studying the backgrounds of the paintings more than the hard-jawed silver-haired oligarchs staring out of them. Each had the canyon or the vault pictured behind them, the standard backdrop for Saints Gate. Many showed people toiling with stone, loading it on trains and oxcarts, or carrying them on their backs as the pictures got older.

"All the stones for the Hall of the Prophet came through Saints Gate," the mayor bragged.

"All of them?" said Jessop absently. He peered at a small figure in a particularly busy picture. The artist had gone to pains to fill the background and borders with activity, even to the diminution of the illustrious man the portrait was about. Jessop was fascinated by it. Busy old-time streets full of livestock and plain dresses on one side, men working stone on the other. He focused on a singular figure. A man in tattered clothes and broken-brimmed hat, barely a centimeter tall on the canvas. A cut stone was strapped to his back and a band secured it around his forehead. Even so small, Jessop could see the sweat on him, the tension in his muscles and the hunger on his face. Looking back at the other side, at the townsfolk milling around, he saw there too a gauntness. The man in the center with a broad mustache centuries out of date was round and robust, his cheeks bright, his two chins clean-shaven.

"Well, not all," confessed Neslen. "But most."

Jessop had forgotten the question. "What's that?"

"The stones for the capital, not all were from here. That was an exaggeration. But most were. And all for the earliest buildings." He seemed genuinely embarrassed.

"Is that mutton?" said Jessop.

"Aye, shall we dine?"

"Refreshments would be most welcome."

"Would you like a drink?"

"I would welcome a glass of strong amber wine."

Neslen's face beamed. "I have just the thing. Come." He called to his guests, "Let's eat!"

Jessop had to smile at that. Noble he might be, and only a few minutes from the capital, but Saints Pass and its mayor had a rural informality that Jessop liked. Before sitting down, Neslen introduced all the guests to

Jessop in turn. Each kissed his hand, bowed, and then the whole party took seats in the banquet hall, Jessop at the head, Neslen to his right.

He was toasted many times with Neslen's favorite port, which was over-sweet but powerful and good. Jessop slowed down after his third glass, when the food was served and the conversation turned to the kind of frankness only strong port could elicit.

"You are a credit to your race," said a blustery man.

"My race is human," Jessop heard himself say before thinking.

When he could, Jessop studied the faces of the servants. In each he could see the clear purebred Templer lines of nose and silver hair. Any one of them could be a child or cousin of any of the nobles at the table. Many of them probably were, and yet he observed the same callous disregard for them he'd seen in the biggest metropolises. These elite had the same learned helplessness of higher classes everywhere – an inability to reach salt on the table, wash their own hands, or put their own napkins on their laps. Rural and homey it might be, but in Jessop's frame of mind he saw the terrible useless and callous living divisions that had brought on the death of Apis.

And the bees.

"We've heard talk of war," someone said, pulling Jessop out of his thoughts. He found the woman's face three to his left. Someone related to a member of the Seventy, involved with grain, he remembered, but he couldn't recall her name.

"Enskari has not accepted Eren's peace with Hyrax," said Jessop. "It is very sad."

"Nay," said the woman. "Temple at war."

"There're rumblings, Counselor," said Neslen. "We thought you might have a thought about it."

All eyes turned to him then and Jessop realized it was a question the entire night was built around. How quickly news travels.

"What has happened?" he asked.

"We got a notice today," said Neslen. "The militia has been called up."

"I have a son," said the woman. "A lieutenant. He's never held a gun in his life." Her voice shook nervously. The mood was shared around the table. Even the drunken man who'd tossed offhand racism was interested and as attentive as his drunk mind could be.

"Is there a threat?" said Neslen. "To Temple?"

Jessop was careful not to let on that he had no idea about the militias. It made sense considering the prophet's position, but it still stung that he was so far out of the loop. He was seldom consulted in local – meaning Temple – matters, so he shouldn't have been surprised.

"We live in dangerous times," said Jessop, trying to find something mollifying to say. "I am sure it is just a prudent move of preparedness."

No one seemed satisfied with that and the stares made Jessop add, "There are places where the valor of Temple might be needed to improve conditions."

"My son was a purger," said an older man with twisted gray whiskers. He was easily the oldest one there and spoke with the hearty voice of one who had little to lose. "He died over Enskari aboard the *Marco*. How much must we sacrifice?"

"That is not for us to ask," said Jessop, reciting the prescribed answer to such questions.

This too didn't go over well, but this time Jessop let the silence remain and ate some carrots.

"Temple has never had war," said Neslen. "We're a people of priests."

He thought about the war at Apis and how little people knew their own history. But he didn't correct the mayor. What he surely meant was that Temple didn't have a standing interplanetary force the way every other civilized planet had. And as for the people of priests, they were bureaucrats, merchants, and aristocrats – only he here was anointed.

"Do not fret, my friends," said Jessop. "Temple is safe. Who would threaten us?"

His mind went to honeybugs, but Neslen said, "Enskari."

Jessop shook his head. "Nay. Enskari hasn't the—"

His speech was cut off by a boom from outside. It rattled the glass.

Everyone froze, stunned for a moment, and then all got up and ran to the door, Jessop following the mayor.

The sky was alight in shooting stars. It was a meteor shower, a wonderful spectacle. This was a big one, but they were common enough. They set off the flowing auroras beautifully.

Jessop was about to invite everyone to have a final drink together under the lights before he had to go back to the capital, when a bright blue-yellow explosion flared overhead. It blinded him for a moment. He blinked away the images as fast as he could, and when he could see again, he saw the sky filled with streaks of fire and pops of light and a slithering blue plasma stream streaking down toward them.

"What is that?" cried a woman.

"The space elevator strand," said Jessop. He watched in disbelief as the liquid light sped down the invisible filament from hundreds of kilometers in space to stab the heart of Zion City. When it touched ground there was a white flash and some time later a shockwave that blew granite dust into the partygoers' faces.

A siren went off, low and wailing. Bells chimed and echoed from horizon to horizon.

Jessop looked to Neslen for an explanation.

"We're under attack," he said.

CHAPTER SEVENTEEN

Although it would often be faster to navigate between some planets by going above or below the solar plane, it is an unadvised practice. Coronam's gravity well is as intense and unpredictable as its storms. Planer navigation – skipping between planets along the planetary ring – provides ships near shelter should a sudden storm arise or a malfunction occur. If something like that were to happen while 'sailing the well', as it is called, a ship might be cast into the depths of space, unable to return, or be sucked into Coronam's fiery surface, a fate surely as bad.
Educational Pamphlet: ***Taking Your First Space Trip***
Dorothia Travel Board, Enskari, 930 NE

3, First-Month, 939 NE – Aboard the Merry *over Hyrax*

"Do we turn?"

Sommerled gritted his teeth.

"Do we turn?" repeated Mr. Kyle. "Sir?"

Three elevator platforms and half a dozen ships were all laying fire on his squadron. He tried not to take it personally, but he couldn't help but wonder if they hadn't figured out which ship was his and shot accordingly.

"Can we get any kind of shot off?" asked Sommerled.

"We could throw some phalanx slugs their way," Mr. Paul, the weapons officer, said. "Should get there by morning."

"Don't we need those to defend the ship?" It was Mr. Ralston, first lieutenant and Second Earl of Katansby. The fear in his voice did nothing to hide his youth and inexperience. His father had pulled strings to get him a bridge position on the Enskaran flagship. As a favor to his queen, his friend, lover, light of his life, ember of his soul, Sir Ethan Sommerled had accepted him, but had prudently not given him any real responsibility.

"He was joking, Mr. Ralston," Sommerled said as patiently as he could. "I'd not waste the ammunition."

"Still six minutes to firing solution on the first man-o-war," interrupted Mr. Paul. "Six minutes."

"Do we turn, sir?"

"Aye. Aye aye – turn the ruddy ship out of the volley. Full thrusters. Signal the squadron just in case they're not watching."

"Full up Z 20!" declared Mr. Kyle. The order was transmitted to the engine room while the helmsmen above the navigator swung the rudder wheel and chimed, "Full up Z 20, aye!"

Sommerled braced as the *Merry* fired its thrusters, nearly pushing Ralston out of his chair. Sommerled had warned him about loosening the straps. A couple more pressure bruises and the boy might learn something.

The veteran crew held better than their aristocratic mascot. They were used to the zero-gravity battle bridge, which could shift and shove in any direction at any time. Above him, below, and to the sides, Sommerled looked at the sober brave faces of his shipmates and felt strangely and peacefully at home. In life-threatening danger over Hyrax, he felt more at peace here than he had in the palaces of Enskari.

His mind slipped back to his queen, to her face, her shoulders, wrists, fingers, breasts. He imagined her scent, her taste, her touch, and he forgot for a moment where he was and what he was doing. With a strange and sudden start, he realized he was vulnerable. And afraid. For the first time, facing railgun and plasma cannon, he was scared because now he had something he was unwilling to lose.

He remembered where he was, recalled this trip of vengeance, or was it ego? An unnecessary risk, he realized now.

Ralston stared at him, fear writ large in his eyes, reflecting something he'd seen on his own, no doubt: a worry, a love. A weakness.

Sommerled winked at the young officer and listened to the signaling clicks going out to the other ships. He spelled out the abbreviated messages in his mind, imagining the lights on the aft and sides of his beloved *Merry* flashing bright and clear. It was an old trick to keep calm in stressed situations – and the sound of cable strain from a full-thruster off-vector turn was indeed a stressed situation.

And he had something to lose.

"We're not going to clear it all," said Mr. Andrews, at damage control. "That big man-o-war anticipated."

"Then why did we go this way?" said Ralston.

"I suspect because any other way would have been worse," said Sommerled. "Am I right, Mr. Paul?"

"Aye aye, sir."

"*Cuffly* and *Douglas* in line and formed."

"Very good," said Sommerled. He'd fought with the *Cuffly* for years and knew it nearly as well as his *Merry*, but the *Douglas* was a new ship, freshly built and captained by, of course, a nobleman seeking glory. At the queen's request, he'd welcomed the Duke of Gravny to the mission and had given him command over second squadron. He'd been difficult, questioning the admiral's orders over relay. Two of his ships were directly lost to hesitation, so Sommerled moved Gravny to his command squadron. Sommerled's original command squadron had begun as seven ships, seven captains of superior experience and skill. During the well maneuvers, as the Enskaran armada fought Coronam's polar storms, he'd sent all but the *Cuffly* to other groups to lead them through. Even so, they lost twenty per cent. Some had turned and limped for home, some were destroyed, but worse were those lost to the void, pushed below the solar plane into infinite darkness from where their engines could not return them.

He'd sailed the well before, risen above or below the plane for stealth and cheating speed, but never before had he gone so deep and long as this journey. There was an eeriness about it that transcended the usual loneliness of space. The dangers were greater, the stakes higher than ever. The gravity pockets and radiation plumes were more violent than he'd ever experienced, but also there was a ghostly presence he could not describe.

He'd hidden his fears behind an enthusiastic veneer, eager and solid as ever. But then, as they reached the lowest point, readying to turn up for Hyrax, in the deepest depths of the well they would ever reach, far off but visible, set against an infinite blackness behind a spurting polar jet, they glimpsed what could only be described as a graveyard. At first, the scouts thought it a debris field, rock and metal, but soon everyone could make out distant sails and still-flashing lights of unnumbered and unnamed unmoving ships stuck in some gravity hole beneath their star. There were scores of them, perhaps hundreds. Sommerled had tried to signal, but though lights shone on some, nothing was returned or acknowledged. Sommerled had visions of starved and skeletal crewmen, bound to their stations like his own men now, death finding them fixed in Coronam's weird physics, haunting their hulls forever.

There they were when Gravny had nearly lost his entire squadron and two of his ships had to turn for home. He'd only had to follow the others and take no shortcut to pass but he'd done something else. The crisis had drawn Sommerled back to the present and he put the terror of the dead ships behind to keep his from joining them.

When the armada reformed, Sommerled brought Gravny and his staff aboard the *Merry* for a briefing and reassignment. He'd set a grand table, which was the best in the fleet, but still surely far beneath what the duke was used to. The two men tolerated each other and toasted the success of their mission. Finally, Sommerled found an opening to challenge Gravny about his behavior. He broached the subject as calmly and politically as possible.

"Ethan," said Gravny. "I only pause to compare your tactics with the classic stratagems of our greatest generals. You should be grateful to have my knowledge and education for advice."

Sommerled, biting back his rage, had calmly replied, "In times of crises please follow orders promptly. Lives depend on it. And please call me Admiral."

"Of course."

The *Douglas*, with Gravny at the helm, was now defending his right, and Sommerled had something to lose, something to live for, something wonderful waiting for him.

He would get home.

"That battered destroyer on the Caporto elevator is moving," said Mr. Croom, the lookout.

Sommerled glanced at the young officer, barely two years older than Ralston but with more space time than most of the fleet. "I thought it was missing half its hull."

"Can still maneuver, apparently."

"Can still maneuver, apparently, *sir*," corrected Mr. Ralston as if he were helping.

Sommerled ignored him and peered out his periscope. "Running for cover or coming to fight, Mr. Croom?"

"Can't tell yet. *Sir*."

Sommerled winked at Croom and several of the bridge officers chuckled. A good release of tension, but Ralston looked scandalized.

"Who's that at 133 mark -20. Nay, -30?" asked Ethan.

Croom swiveled to another periscope.

"I have the destroyer," said the weapons officer, his face pressed to a lens. "Want to move in for a shot, Admiral?"

"Hold, Mr. Paul. Do you see that, Mr. Croom?"

"Aye," said the lookout. "That's fifth squadron. Looks like the a… ah…1-3-1-2…who's that?"

"That's the *Margaret*," said Sommerled.

"Aye, the *Margaret* is steering for the destroyer."

"And it's looking for a fight," said Mr. Paul. "She's turning side for a shot."

"Incoming. Sixty seconds," said Mr. Andrews.

"Already?" said Ralston.

"The shot's from the man-o-war, Mr. Ralston. Not the destroyer. Yet," said Sommerled. "Spin to face."

"Aye aye!"

The helmsmen redirected the thrusters to angle the ship into the barrage, pointing its tapered nose at the incoming fire because that was where the armor was thickest. New vectors of force and false gravity pulled the crew askew. The battle bridge was the heart of the ship and its physical center. Hatches led in all directions. Periscopes and wires, switches and lights, glowglobes and handholds pocked the walls and hung like treasured art. From any perspective men hung from the ceiling and were stuck to walls, while visitors floated free and bounced between hatches and holds. Sommerled noted that Ralston was again punished for his loose straps as his uniform tore beneath one and squeezed blood into the air, where it congealed in a constellation of red before being absorbed into his shirt.

"Phalanx guns firing," said Mr. Paul.

Sommerled heard the rattle of interceptors like distant popcorn as the men in the hull pods let fly clouds of shot to wall the ship from the guns of the man-o-war.

There were two loud clucks and then a sound like rain on a tin roof as debris pelted and smashed into the hull. In a moment, all was quiet save the engine and the low humming tension of the straining sail cable.

"Report."

"Grapeshot?" asked Ralston.

"Debris," said Sommerled.

"Tears in two, three, and four mainsails," said Croom, realigning his scope. "Navsail two has a hole in it."

Clicks of teletype rattled at damage control.

Mr. Andrews said, "Confirmed. Hull damage to quadrant three; skid, divot, and breach. Crack in section three. Containable. Battery six unresponsive. Confirm?"

Sommerled swiveled to a side scope. He took a quick intake of breath as he saw the gash through the gunner's pod, a meter wide, twice as deep. The sides of it glowed in melted slag, cooling but still red, atmosphere escaping from several places. The seat where the gunner had been was split and dangling. His legs were still in the chair exposed to vacuum but his upper body was gone along with the meter of metal that had failed to protect him.

"Confirmed. Battery six destroyed," said Croom. "One casualty."

There was a moment of silence for the dead man, probably a slave or convict working off his sentence. None knew his name, but he was a sailor, a shipmate lost in the darkness. It was Mr. Andrews at damage control who broke the moment. "Noted," he said.

"I see atmosphere leaking from the *Douglas*," said Mr. Kyle. "Must have gotten dinged too."

"And *Margaret* shot early," said Mr. Paul. "Sure to miss unless that destroyer defies all laws of physics and remains right where she is for the foreseeable future."

"Give us patience," murmured Sommerled.

"Third squadron—"

"There is no third squadron anymore, Mr. Croom," said Sommerled.

"Sorry. I saw the *Clark*. What squadron is that part of now?"

"That's part of eighth," said Ralston, referring to a clipboard. "Six ships."

"Four now," said Croom. "One's dark, the other is running."

"Who's running?"

"Can't tell. Heading out plane, into the black."

The battle was being fought on the lee side of Hyrax, with the planet between them and the sun. It was the safest place to moor ships and that was where Brandon's fleet was.

"Could just be maneuvering for a better approach," offered Mr. Paul.

"Signals from the rest of his squadron are less than supportive of that claim," said Mr. Baker at communications. "They're using profanities. *Sir.*"

A ripple of shot plinked the hull, glassy and bright, metal on its way to rip their sails.

Mr. Andrews reported, "Eighty, fifty, and seventy per cent effect on two, three, and four. Navsail seven is still gone."

"What? Didn't it grow back on its own?" said Sommerled.

"It's the weekend," said Mr. Andrews.

Ralston stared with disbelief while the crew chuckled nervously.

Sommerled clapped his hands and rubbed them. "All right. We're still in this. Get us a firing solution on a platform, Mr. Paul. Any platform."

"Aye aye."

It had been a good plan, a counter-attack on Hyrax to destroy Brandon's damaged fleet once and for all. It should have commenced at the heels of the failed invasion, but Enskari had needed to recover from its near annihilation.

But that was all right. Spies on Hyrax had reported preparations for the expected assault, including a wall of orbiting unshielded gun platforms, maned by men in suits, absorbing fatal radiation with their fingers on triggers as they slowly died. These preparations cost Brandon plenty and Enskari drew its vengeance by sucking Silangian silver out of their treasuries for it. Rumors reached the court that damaged Hyraxian warships were sitting idle and untended in the off-world shipyards for lack of payment.

For five months Brandon bled money and then stood down, believing the attack had been called off, and they were considering the prophet's cynical plea for peace after all.

That plea had naturally been ignored. Enskari and her queen remained unbowed and had agreed to no armistice. Enskari assembled her fleet, sneaking ships away, pointing them off-vectors and then dropping below plane and planet, to sail the well for a surprise attack on the hated Hyraxians this day.

Sommerled's hatred for Hyrax had grown beyond anything he had ever known. He'd despised them before, as a patriot, but now it was personal. He dreamed of delivering Brandon's severed head to his queen. His feelings, he knew, stemmed from his love of Zabel. Every moment he spent with her, the strong soul of Enskari, made him want to protect her the more. Her enemies were his enemies, not for him being an Enskaran – though that was enough – but because his devotion to her demanded no less. He would follow her to hell and throw himself on the flames that she might take another step because of it.

He realized now, with something to lose, that his love made him vulnerable. He had to return alive, to serve his sovereign, not only as a man to a woman, a friend to a friend, but as an advisor to the monarch – First Ear of the queen. His death would hurt her.

He had much to lose.

She'd told him her plans in private, in her bed, after a long, warm and hungry night. He had only to return to share all she could share with him. All was possible now, even the impossible dream of marriage.

And here was the fear.

And for the first time in his life, he questioned his capabilities. Now, he saw, he feared defeat more than he longed for victory. A toxic mindset.

"Caporto elevator run plotted," said Mr. Paul. "I figure we have to get within fifty kilometers to get through. Which means we'll need to get around that big boat to make the shot count. Shall I relate the plan to the squadron?"

"How's the rest of the fleet?"

Mr. Baker spoke, a new man, brash and blunt on communications. "Taking good shots. Still should have an hour to disengage."

"Losses?"

"You want that now?"

"Nay. But an idea."

"I'd say we're fighting with half of what we brought," said Baker.

"Let's make them bleed," he said. "We'll take out the famous Caporto elevator platform. They'll write songs about it."

"Aye aye."

They'd not caught the Hyraxians unaware. The diversionary attack on Temple had been effective, the destruction of an orbital elevator and a score of Temple ships sent to their God, but it hadn't drawn the Hyraxian fleet to their defense the way they'd hoped. Seeing the sky now full of plasma fire and shot, streaking magnet shells, and burning Enskaran ships, Sommerled realized it'd had the opposite effect: it had told Brandon they were coming.

Still, he'd make them bleed.

New fleet reports: ninth and tenth squadrons had taken out something big and explosive near the lower pole. Fourth squadron was damaged but doing work on a repair yard it had found hidden behind a fifty-kilometer bubble of black sailsilk. Expensive camouflage ruined by a telltale elevator pod that drew attention and now their fire. Should be some good tonnage evened out there. Locally, his crew reported the *Merry* fit and fighting. They'd sealed the atmospheric breach on three but battery four was no longer communicating. Worse. It was no longer firing.

"Roll to compensate," said Mr. Andrews and unseen thrusters turned fresh guns toward the enemy. Meanwhile the sails were filled to swivel the ship around, bringing their gun platforms to bear on the orbiting station.

Sommerled always looked for the carbon fiber thread that linked platforms to planet, tracing an invisible line from one to the other, hoping he might see a glint of reflection, but he never did. This time, he did see an elevator car rising, thrusters decelerating the pod in orange fans beneath the potato-shaped station, slowing it to dock. Sommerled would cook that potato if he could. If they managed to come in close, knocking out the gun emplacements, he would happily torch them with plasma cannons, but he was doubtful he'd get that close. It was well armed and ships were streaking over the horizon to protect it. He'd just have to enjoy its destruction at the end of his tons of magnetically fired projectiles instead of radiation flame.

It would be a glorious wrecking.

His appointment as Ear had not been announced. It would follow his triumphant return from Hyrax. Nevertheless, rumors had escaped and it was not a popular move among the aristocracy. Ralston and Gravny attested to Zabel's concessions for him to serve in the stead of the venerable Sir Edward Kesey. Doubtless she was even now assuring some nobleman that he, hero of Enskari, was worthy of the station. Among some, his low birth spoke against him more than the salvation of the planet spoke for him, Sir Nolan had explained.

"They were never in danger, Ethan," Brett said. "If Brandon had landed, they would have just switched loyalties to him. There's no money in dying for a cause."

It was at a private dinner, just the two of them, in a side room of the palace Sommerled hadn't known existed before Brett led him to it. He'd been served a plate of pasta, which smelled rich and creamy, but was afraid to taste it. "But they denounced the church and stood against the prophet."

"Aye. The purgers would have killed a few of them, cut off their heads so they died quick and painless. They'd have paraded Zabel and myself across every civilized planet before killing us quickly, as is our right. They'd have murdered you to be sure, but the rank-and-file nobility are the wheels of commerce, the keepers of culture and society. God's favorites. They would be forgiven and returned to their stations after suitably long looting by off-worlders."

"But what of all the torture devices the purgers brought?" Sommerled asked.

"For your class, not mine," said Brett between bites of his dinner. His eyes fell upon Sommerled's untouched plate and he frowned. He poked his fork into a cluster of Sommerled's noodles, scooped some up with a piece of brown chicken and ate it. He washed it down with a deep drink from Sommerled's goblet, swallowed, stifled a belch, and wiped his mouth on a white linen napkin before looking the admiral in the eye. "Don't insult me, First Ear," he said when he'd finished. "I don't want you dead, Ethan. The queen doesn't want you dead. She…likes you. I like you."

"And if you'd wanted me dead, I'd be dead?"

Brett only smiled and returned to his own food. "The uppity ones who started the reformations came not from the gentry, but from the rising lower classes who didn't know their place. The ones who had the nerve to better themselves while the purebreds rotted. The new queen is a symbol of that. An able woman. You and your Bucklers are another symbol. Neither can be tolerated by the old order. It's how it's always been."

"Until now?"

"Until now."

"But they didn't land," said Sommerled, tasting his food at last. It was excellent. A little rich perhaps, but very good. The noodles melted on his tongue.

"Aye, thanks to you."

"And God."

Brett raised an eyebrow.

"Coronam and luck?" said Sommerled.

"We are not far into our reformation, Ethan."

It was strange that Brett now called him by his first name more than anything. He could not bring himself to call the Second Ear by his. He tried it nonetheless. "What are you saying, Nolan?"

"I'm saying that many nobles think the queen is moving too fast. Some still harbor resentments and pine for the prophet's church. They long for security. Certainty. Consistency. The War of Ascension is still clear in their minds."

"Weren't those disloyal families purged?"

"Nice word," said Brett.

"*Connored* doesn't have the same ring."

"Connored. I like that. For Connor's guards. Aye, they did clean up much of it, but not all. Like they'd have done if Temple had landed, many families swore new allegiance, were forgiven and spared. We couldn't get rid of them all. Society can't work without them."

"So they think," said Sommerled.

Brett stopped chewing and regarded him for a moment, alerting him that he might have offended the Second Ear.

"I meant—"

"Nay. It was well spoke, Ethan. Don't apologize for being frank with me."

Sommerled knew that if there was one person on all Enskari he should be careful around, it was this man.

"You see a future not many do," said Brett.

"The queen does."

"Aye, she might."

Brett went on. "Things are moving fast. She mentioned evolution to me. Perhaps that is what is happening, but evolution is a slow thing, I'm told, by and large. Slow and steady. Sudden changes bring sudden reactions. Dangerous times. We've weathered the worst on the planet with the civil war and – God be praised—" He winked. "—we may have weathered the worst from without – Hyrax and Temple. But these are only temporary respites until time has buried the energy to go back."

"You are a philosopher?"

"Nay," said Brett. "I'm trying to warn you. If you think being the Ear of the queen will protect you from the nobles' jealousy, you're wrong. Dead wrong."

Sommerled had never trusted Brett. No sane man would. But he respected him. His loyalty was beyond question but the spymaster's methods often made people doubt them nonetheless. His loyalty was to Enskari and the queen, and Sommerled wondered what would happen if those two interests were ever not aligned.

"The queen is living proof that a woman can do a man's job and do it as well, if not better. It's a blow to egos. You've shown up the nobility. A commoner doing a noble's job and doing it as well, if not better. That might be one blow too many. It strikes at the very core of privilege. Hyrax, Temple, or here – you are the real threat in the system."

"And here I thought I'd just need to win over Sir Edward's friends."

"Oh, you'll have to do that," said Brett, pushing his plate away, only half-finished. "Kesey is well loved. He was the last holdover from the time of Theodore the Thrice. Replacing him is worse than if you'd replaced me."

"Are you not well loved?"

Brett smiled wide. "Nay."

"Why are you telling me all this?"

"Why am I warning you? Would not my devotion to the queen be enough for that?"

"Is it?" asked Ethan.

"Come back home in one piece and with Hyraxian blood on your sword. More than that I cannot ask of you now."

"Now."

"Aye. Now."

A loud snap and twang rumbled the deck.

"Mainsail cable," said Mr. Andrews. "Number three again."

Sommerled spun the periscope to face aft. He traced the long mast past the navsails in the middle to the mains at the end. The silk sails of a spaceship were always beautiful to him. They were like flower petals at the end of a stalk while the manned bullet-shaped hull of the ship pod was like an anther and stamen rising out of the bloom. When the sails were full aglow with solar wind, it was an inspiring sight, full of raw power and hot wonder. Now, with only the wisps of background radiation seeping around the dark side of Hyrax, they had shown but the dimmest glow against a dark starry background.

He found the damaged sail with some difficulty, but he recognized the problem immediately – a cable had snapped and the freed sail had sprung ninety degrees off alignment. It was fouling neighboring sail and threatening to take them down, listing to the side.

"It's pulling us," said Mr. Kyle.

"Jettison number three," Sommerled said. "Do it now."

"Cutters!" said Croom.

"Where?"

"X 50, Y -230, Z 60."

"Fire boats. Fast. Plasma cannons," said Mr. Paul. "Close range only."

"Tell the *Douglas* to take them. We'll stay on the platform. Ask the *Cuffly* to deal with that destroyer."

"We're listing. It's the sail."

"Cut the damn thing already!"

"Ralston," said Mr. Kyle. "Mr. Ralston."

"What?"

"You need to confirm at your station."

"How?"

"There underneath," said Sommerled, pointing to the lower central panel of Ralston's auxiliary support station. "The switches. See them? Look for the number three."

"Got it."

Mr. Paul said, "On my mark. Three, two, one – pull!"

Paul and Ralston pulled their switches simultaneously with a grunt. There was a turn and a squeak of neglected pulleys, but the mechanism engaged as designed. The ship was rocked by a loud conclusive click. Deep in the rigging decks, a pinch of pressured blade severed all the cables to the problem sail, including its hold on the end of the mast. The sound was a twang and rumble, then the ship lurched as the sail flew off and tumbled into space.

"Aligned for clear fire," said the weapons officer. "We can clear out some of those buoys."

"Firing away."

"I'll get us in close now," said the navigator.

Sommerled was pushed into his seat. It was a reassuring feeling; it told him he was in command. The captain's chair was placed to have the most comfortable ride when going forward. He'd been in all the other stations, but this one suited him best.

Ralston shrieked as the seat strap caught him across the neck and burned him.

"*Douglas* out of alignment," said the navigator.

"She's saying something about Admiral Aderyn."

"What?"

"*Shepherds Gate*," said Mr. Baker with a sigh.

"For the love of God."

"He's off," said Mr. Croom. "Gone vertical."

Gravny was going rouge. Gavny was breaking the formation. Gravny was endangering the entire enterprise with a vain, bravado mimic of a better man's heroics.

Sommerled had read the famous battle, as had every good Enskari captain. A sudden rise and plunge from up axis had surprised a pirate ship called the *Shepherds Gate* off of Ravan. Aderyn had immobilized and captured her. It was a stroke of brilliant captainship at the time, but since then every captain in the system knew its simple countermeasures. The coming attack was easy to dodge if you knew it was coming. And as Sommerled turned his lens toward the cluster of cutters, their plasma cannons hot and seeping, he knew they saw it coming.

On his left, the *Cuffly* turned hard to try to take up the space between the nearer attackers and Sommerled while he bore down on the platform.

"Platform firing," said Mr. Paul. "And that destroyer is turning on us."

"Turn to take the destroyer, sir?" asked the navigator.

"Nay, Mr. Kyle. Stay on the platform. This might be our only run."

"Aye aye."

The ships flew on. Sommerled watched the streak of plasma thrust from the end of his mast, and the burners on the *Cuffly* as they realigned to take on the greater threat.

"Destroyer is firing," said Mr. Paul. "Six in a round."

"How's their aim?"

"We should shift."

"Shift."

"Aye aye."

Sommerled felt himself lifted out of its seat as the *Merry*, still at full burn toward the platform, shifted out of the fire. It lasted for nearly five minutes and then weightlessness returned.

"How's their aim now, Mr. Paul?"

"We're not on top of it anymore," said the weapons officer, "but I think we can hit a three-quarter profile."

"My best side," said Sommerled.

"A little closer and I'll have a hundred per cent solution."

Ralston fumbled for his straps and finally tightened himself into his seat.

"Do you need a medic, Mr. Ralston?" asked Sommerled, seeing the blood patch bigger on his shirt.

"Nay, sir. Fit and fighting."

Sommerled liked that answer and gave Ralston his first unforced nod of approval. The earl seemed to sense his sincerity and grew a little in his chair.

"There goes the *Douglas*."

"Let me guess, there're no cutters there for Gravny to attack anymore?" said Sommerled.

"Not a one," said Mr. Croom. "And our flank is wide open."

"We should be getting grapeshot soon," said Mr. Kyle. And as if on cue, they were.

"One minute to fire."

"Make final adjustments," ordered Sommerled.

"The *Cuffly* couldn't make the turn," said Croom with some urgency. "My God, their sails."

"Stay on target," said Sommerled, but turned his scope to look back.

Five close cutters armed with plasma cannon poured hell into the *Cuffly*. Its sailsilks were flaming rags, its mast a smoldering matchstick. Fire arced and flashed up the spine and then the hull went dark.

"*Douglas* turning to run," said Croom. "Destroyer is realigning. They'll be damned close to us when we arrive at firing point."

Sommerled studied the destroyer. Its mast was burned. It had half its sails. The hull was ripped and torn, several decks were exposed, but its guns were bright and menacing, safe and sure at the rear of the pod. It looked like a cornered animal turning to fight.

A bolt of fear surged through him. Sommerled suddenly knew, as certainly as he knew anything, that if that ship got a shot off, it would kill him and he would not get home. He was no longer willing to die. He had too much to live for.

"Take the shot," he ordered.

"Sir?"

"Take the shot on the platform now. Best solution."

"Aye aye."

Console lights dimmed and there came the feeling of wind in the room. Sommerled felt the hair on his arms prick up as the magnetic guns fired two tons of hardened metal and hate at the orbiting space station. The ship trembled and gasped, a fever shake, and then went quiet.

"Get us around!" said Sommerled. "Signal fleet, we're heading home."

"Aye aye, sir."

The ship dove for cover between platform and planet, looking to use the gravity to spring them into space.

Sommerled turned his scopes behind him to where the *Cuffly* stood dead in the darkness, hoping to see it fly free, or failing that, to see fuel plasma pour out of the gunner's pod. That was how they'd scuttle the ship. All would die, a blessed thing, saving themselves from the purgers' tools and the ship from the enemy. But it stayed dark and still. Sommerled bit his lip to keep from screaming, tasting blood on his teeth.

The Caporto platform erupted in spilled atmosphere and fire. They'd hit it and hit it hard. What wasn't broken and burning was tossed into space as the platform spun from the impact. Debris whirled out in arcs of searing gas. Sommerled knew some of that debris was human and for that he was glad.

The fleet was in no mood to remain and followed the *Merry* back down the well. It wasn't necessary to go that way now for the secrecy, but fear of the well might give the Hyraxian captains pause.

In any event, there was no pursuit and in four days the fleet rendezvoused around the flagship. Sommerled invited all squadron commanders to join him and told Gravny to come.

The others captains arrived in uniforms, but Gravny had his official robes and sashes on and struggled to keep them in place as he moved between gravities.

Sommerled met him with the others in his banquet hall. There were eighteen of them.

"Gentlemen," said Sommerled. "It was a harder thing to do than we thought, but we have done it. We have bloodied the nose of Prince Brandon and revenged the queen. It has been a successful campaign."

The men looked uncertain of this. They all knew the cost. They'd lost thirty per cent of their fleet outright plus another twenty so near destruction they'd need complete overhauls if they made it home at all.

"It could have been better," said Gravny. "I have—"

"Hush," said Mr. Ralston. "The admiral is speaking."

All the captains looked at the dandy noble, who twitched his lip but kept silent.

"It could have been better," said Sommerled.

Gravny rolled his eyes.

"Gentlemen," said Sommerled. "I hereby accuse Captain Gravny of insubordination, failure to follow orders, and indiscipline that tangibly resulted in the loss of a capital ship and all aboard. What say ye?"

"Aye!" shouted the group to a man, loud and strong.

Gravny looked on with complete surprise.

"Surely you're not sug—"

"Shut up!" said Ralston and smacked him hard across the back of his head. "The admiral is speaking."

The weight of the moment finally settled into the noble as he looked from the young Ralston to Sommerled and across the accusing faces of the other captains.

"There are other charges," said Sommerled, "but these are enough."

"Ethan...." He trailed off like a parent reminding a toddler of the rules.

Sommerled felt his ears grow hot with rage. It was a heat that'd smoldered since he'd had to leave his wingman in Hyraxian orbit, its crew to be murdered – spaced possibly, its captain, his friend, tortured and killed, paraded in the capital of Hyrax. Shamed. Disgraced. The noble *Cuffly* to be repurposed against them.

And worse, it had nearly cost him the *Merry*. His ship, his crew, his life and future.

Gravny straightened his posture, tipped his head ten degrees, and looked down his nose. "Do you all not know who I am? Do you not know my family? Our connections? Our heritage and rank?"

"I sentence you to death," said Sommerled.

"You cannot be serious," said the Duke of Gravny.

"Mr. Ralston?"

The young noble stepped forward with a quick step, and in military fashion handed Sommerled a cocked and ready crossbow. The men in the room stepped back.

"I demand an appeal," said Gravny. "My class and station—"

The bolt went through his head and lodged in the far wall.

Gravny stood upright for a moment, bewilderment on his face. Then the final understanding seemed to come to him just as he melted to the deck beneath the pull of its false gravity.

CHAPTER EIGHTEEN

Empathy leads to justice, which leads to sacrifice, which leads to renewal. We all die, it only remains how and why.
Lerer Melk, Personal Journal
16, Fourth-Month, 515 NE – Apis, Temple

18, Second-Month, 939 NE – Beleksha, Tirgwenin

The moon was shattered, torn and bleeding. It was the final insult, the final death blow as the Unsettled fled its poisoned, crippled, and dying planet.

Millie saw the moon. Not as a visual phenomenon, but a memory, immersive, full of sound and emotion. A tableau of all her senses. She saw the broken moon from a continent of Old Earth. She felt hunger in her belly, fear in her mind, betrayal in her soul. Transferring, refocusing, finding new minds to witness, Millie found repeated those feelings at that moment – pain, sickness, fear, betrayal. A collective experience. A common horror.

The ships, the last vessels from Old Earth, had left for Coronam, rats fleeing a sinking barge, leaving everyone else to die. The Unsettling. As a final insult, they wrecked the moon itself and their fleeing curse played in catastrophic tides and gravity wells, falling debris and more misery. It was a final act of tyranny from the wealthy.

She opened her eyes. Tirgwenin's rings were bright on the southern horizon, casting shadows with reflected light. From on her hill, she watched the sunset settle upon the town. Coronam had painted the sky pink and orange like autumn leaves and love, caressing it with green tendrils of aurora like grass in a stream. All this over a plain of freshly fallen snow. It took her breath away.

The soothing buzz of bees was so constant now that she barely noticed the three circling her head, bobbing up and down, alighting on her shoulder.

Down in the village people moved in the final light, cloaked and booted, arms bare, faces bright in the chilling wind, their golden skin catching the odd reflection and sparkling their way.

"Did you see?" asked Bouer.

Millie turned to look at her mentor and guide, as he called himself. The Tirgwenin word was 'groo' and she liked it better, but Bouer insisted on using Enskaran words, even though they both knew they were inaccurate approximations.

"I did see," Millie said.

She'd worked for two weeks on Old Earth through the library's connections, experiencing other human minds singular and collective – long-dead but living echoes of truth – centuries of social movement and decay. Bouer said it was the most important lesson she had to learn now, the one she needed to understand before she moved on.

She was on a path others had taken, an education and initiation as old as this civilization and anchored as the truths she touched with the bees, but delving so deep into Old Earth society was a particular addition for her.

The wind caught Bouer's long sable hair and fluttered it like flags across his face.

Millie pulled her hood up over her own strawberry-red locks when she realized her ears were numb from the cold. She'd been lost in the threads for hours. The bees were tired. She released them all and they burrowed into her clothes for warmth.

"This cold isn't good for them," she said.

"The bees? Nay. This time of year, most hibernate. We keep a few awake in the greenhouses." He pointed to a cluster of glass-roofed houses to the west, their windows ruby in reflected sunset.

She knew this already and thought it interesting that Bouer would tell her again. "Why do you keep taking me out here to work?" she asked. "Why can't I use the longhouse like the others?"

As he often did, Bouer looked into her face as if it would grow transparent and show him her soul. A bee rose from within his collar and took flight.

"You are more productive up here," he said.

She felt a tickle as one of the insects nestled in her neck. "Why do we care so much about Old Earth?"

"You know why."

"History lessons with moral undertones."

"Overtones. Aye."

"But I know the morals already. The bees wouldn't have come to me if I didn't."

Bouer shook his head. "It's not the same. Wisdom is not knowledge. Knowledge is not wisdom. Wisdom is better, but you need both."

She tried to see the two and eighty years he said he was, but Bouer looked no older than her father was when he died. Late thirties. He was thin and tall, as were all the people of this world. He had a dark tattoo on his neck that disappeared into his long hair, and he had a way of not losing focus when he blinked his inner eyelids.

She'd spent three months in his company away from her people. It had been hard to leave them, but she knew she had to. She understood by the eldritch truths that the bees brought her that powers beyond the little border village of Pemioc wanted her. If she had refused, it would have been…impolite. She could imagine repercussions if she refused. Like her people, she knew distress, want, hunger, and fear, things removed within the walls of Pemioc. If her sacrifice would secure for them a place, a life for her brother and the others, it was a bargain. But this was fancy and fear. For truth, she'd felt no danger since Bouer took her away, only weird undercurrents of worry and suspicion.

She received reports from Lahgassi. The leader of Pemioc would reach out to her every week to pacify her guilt with uplifting stories of new success and wellness among the community. The connection was always weak compared to what she had with Bouer and others – many of whom she'd never met face-to-face, some she was afraid to. Lahgassi always told her about her brother, Dillon, how he missed her but was kept busy with chores so had little time to worry and fret. Most recently, he had been seen near the honey hives kissing little Maffrit, the precocious girl Millie remembered. Lahgassi made light of it, but Mille could feel some concern about that relationship, but also joy. Richard Tomkins had stepped up to 'lead' the Enskaran colonists.

Millie asked Lahgassi to tell Dillon and the others that she was doing well. That she was happy, well treated, and warm.

Make sure they know I am no prisoner, she said. *I am where I need to be. Tell Richard Tomkins that I am being taught things that will better help our people assimilate and to be gentle, always gentle.* This was what she'd been told but she sensed there was more to her being here, much more than that. There was a hanging unsettled question between her and these people that had not been communicated or addressed. It hovered like a star just below the horizon. *Do not let Tomkins worry so much about me. Tell him I have seen him drunk and remind him to keep his boots on.*

The final bit of the message, a reference to the time he stepped in an ox pile while drunk, was meant to prove the message was from her and not made under duress. With any luck, he would listen and relax. She was calling in a favor. She still had authority over the colony, even in far Beleksha, eight hundred kilometers away. She'd delivered them to safety from hell. If that weren't enough, her eldritch connection to the bees set her even higher. Among the Pemiae, she was special; among her people, she was a messiah. She resisted any divine attribution to what was happening, but it was useful and saved a lot of time in fruitless explanations to those who could not understand.

Richard Tomkins was not as wise as she would have wished. He was a little hot-headed and spent more time worrying than doing. While she was still there, she'd sensed his unease for her – a fatherly affection. Since her leaving, this knowledge was reinforced with visions and feelings that came to her in the limbus of sleep, between waking and dream, when her mind was most open. His feelings must have been strong, for he had no bee. The feelings came to her unfocused and also unaddressed. It might have been Lahgassi or one of the other acolytes slipping the thought to her accidentally, or it might have been Tomkins himself sending out psychic signal loud enough to be sensed. She's been unable to verify this one way or another.

In any event, Millie knew that Tomkins needed to be reassured. Now that the Enskarans' bellies were full, their bodies warm, they could slide into old habits of inflexibility and distrust. She could not let that happen. She witnessed the charity of these people every day and was amazed by it each and every time. Nevertheless, she was aware of a darker undercurrent, a wariness just below the surface of their smiles. It was why she was taken to this hill to work, away from the others. There was suspicion and distrust on both sides.

"Are you cold?" asked Bouer.

"If I say I am, you'll tell me I lack discipline."

"The mind can overcome much physical distress."

"I am toasty warm. You could cook on me," she said and chattered her teeth for emphasis.

Bouer's face lit up in a smile. "Shall we go in then?"

"Nay, I want to watch the light play out," she said.

Her groo glanced at the sunset. "How is it different on your world?"

"The sunset? More violent. The weather was always violent."

"How?"

"Deadly lightning storms are not uncommon. Cities are protected by steel nets, and even so lightning often gets through. People and livestock die all the time. We're told it's just part of the planet. A natural result of Coronam's energy."

"We all share that, so why does Enskari have it so bad?"

"All the civilized are that way," she said. "It's not just Enskari."

Bouer shook his head. It always amazed Millie, the strange holes in his knowledge. Her teacher could explain how spaceships traversed the skies with carbon silk and plasma streams. He knew the names of all the planets and their moons and continents. He could explain their tides, their seasons, and point to each one at any time in the sky or beneath his feet. He could accurately map their cities on a globe, connect them with rail lines and canals that she had no reason to doubt. He knew Silangan and Maaraw, the structure of the Kanluran

Cloud, and the composition of the ash of the dead worlds, and yet he knew nothing of what any of them looked like, who ruled them, or why, what their people were like or their histories. He was interested in learning, however, and after her lessons were over, he would often take a few from her.

"It is from the smog?" he asked. "The lightning?"

"Aye," said Millie, applying what she'd learned from Old Earth's collapse to modern Enskaran weather. "I believe so."

"And you have ministers of weather to fix this?"

"I don't think so."

"The pollution is allowed to go unchecked?"

Here, she felt, was more than curiosity at work. Here was a test. "Aye," she said. "Those in charge allow it because they are rich and can avoid the worst of it."

"I see."

"The same as on Old Earth."

"Aye."

Lately, most of Millie's education had come from guided mediation through the library. Bouer would send her in search of an idea, a time, or a place, and she would follow where it led. She suspected that the curriculum was not his idea and speculated from where it came.

On the journey from Pemioc to Beleksha, Bouer was a more traditional teacher, lecturing and answering questions, challenging her with ideas. One of his earliest and most important lessons was to explain the divide they were crossing.

"Pemioc is a border town," he explained in common tongue. "It separates the places of the outcasts from the lands of the civilized."

His accent was peculiar with a strange guttural interpretation of normal words. 'Outcasts' spoken as if he were swallowing it. She had gotten used to it, but sometimes his word choice was unusual and wrong for modern usage.

"How are you using the word civilized?" she asked.

"Did I use it incorrectly?"

"It's a loaded word," she told him. "We call our worlds civilized

– those with technology and spaceships. While the others are savage. Maaraw, Silangan, and Tirgwenin are savage. Uncivilized."

"What if I told you we had technology? Better technology than your civilized worlds."

"I'd say you hide it well."

"We do," said he.

"You appear to be far behind."

Bouer thought about this for a moment while his bee did loops above his head. Then his face twisted up as if remembering something and Millie knew he'd just touched a thread.

"Civilized and savage?" he said.

"Aye. It's also related to the idea of the church. The Saved. Those who follow the prophet."

"So Enskari is savage?"

"Oh, nay. We're civilized. We have technology."

"But no prophet?"

"We threw that off."

"Would you say we are savage?"

"Technologically, aye," she said.

"What about socially?" He smiled at that and Millie had no answer.

Bouer said, "In order to be part of our society, the higher society—"

"The civilized?"

"Something akin," he said.

"Go on." She was testing his patience.

"One must have the acceptance of the bees. One does not need the connection you and I have, but you cannot be one that the bees abhor. If you are like that, you are not welcome in the civil— non-Rowdanae society."

"Rowdanae means exile?"

"Aye."

"Forever exiled?"

"Nay. Only until they learn enough to return."

"That seems unfair."

"It is our way."

"Little Bost, the boy I knew in Pemioc and Rodawnoc, was born there. How can he be so condemned?"

"He would not be if he showed affinity."

"What would you do? Go get him?"

"Aye," he said. "Like we did you."

"Oh."

"In the meantime, they suffer."

"That's terrible."

"It's necessary."

Her excitement for the trip had waned after that, and Millie had fumed about this injustice of the Rowdanae as they traveled into the interior of Yimfall, the Tirgwenian name for the major continent they were on. What made the injustice of the Rowdanae worse was how Bouer explained the simple arrangement of the Tirgwenian society.

"Everyone is guaranteed the necessities: food, shelter, medicine, education – everything that a human needs to live. Even art."

"Everyone except the exiles?"

"Aye. They must suffer."

"You let them starve?"

"Aye, we do."

"And die of disease?"

Bouer had looked at her in that certain way then, that condescending way that suggested pity and patience. It was not the first time he had looked at her that way, but this was the first time Millie had not looked away from it.

"Your people brought disease. It threatened the entire planet. When we found the cure, we shared it with them."

"Why didn't you let them suffer then?"

"Our inhumanity knows some bounds," he'd said wryly.

"You needed to inoculate them to save yourselves," she said.

Bouer's surprise was subtle but definite. He changed the subject and they traveled northward.

When they arrived in the small but bustling town of Beleksha, Millie confirmed that everyone had the necessities of life. She was told it was one of the oldest settlements on the planet, but the age was hard to see. There was a timeless quality about the buildings and streets that carried over to the people. There were industrious people, and some lazy ones, but no poor ones, at least not poor the way she knew poverty, starvation and sickness, loneliness and squalor. No one was hungry or walked the streets naked for lack of clothes. Some were clearly smarter than others, some more refined. There were servants and masters but these were not made by wealth or coercion but by necessity. A rancher needed help to tend the land and animals; a leader, advisors and aides; a chef, cleaners and waiters. Rank and position were not inherited, though sometimes a son of a diplomat might follow in his father's footsteps, but this was in no way expected. There were police of a kind, but she never saw anyone arrested. Strong drink could make someone wild or some emergency might arise that called them. There were a hundred classes and each had its place in society in an equal tier – except those who actively had bees.

Everyone in Tirgwenian non-Rowdanae society had been accepted by the bees, but not everyone had access to them. Few did, in fact. It was rare to have one – maybe one soul in a hundred would make contact; maybe one in a thousand could call them and use them. The numbers went exponentially higher as the number of bees increased and the powers they brought were realized. Such people were revered and leaders were chosen from among them. Having more bees did not equate to leadership; an ability to call and connect was enough. A thousand bees or one made little difference. As was explained, what mattered was temperament; the bees proved the necessary empathy but also provided the necessary link to communicate across the planet. Tirgwenan was made of far-flung villages all linked by the bees.

Millie noticed that most leaders were women and even though it was not required, most had several bees. She'd asked about that.

"Temperament," Bouer had told her.

"You mean their nature. They're protective? Caring?"

"Just that."

"How big is your family?"

He'd smiled. "Aye, just that."

"Can a man not be the same?"

"Of course he can," he said. "But the tradition of female leadership is hard to break. It's worked for us. It's not law. We have some male leaders, lots really, but there is something to the feminine that allows more to survive."

She didn't understand this, but let it go. "And more than one bee?"

"Just so," he said cryptically. But the next day he challenged her to connect to two bees at once.

"Why?"

"Try," was all he said.

She tried and failed and tried again and failed, and then all at once, last week, it happened.

She'd undergone a two-day fast and a half-day meditation unaided by the insects. Atop this very hill, Millie had called and connected with five bees. One was a connection to Bouer, who monitored her upper thoughts as a distant observer. The second she sent to Pemioc and Lahgassi to look upon her brother. The third to a nearby park to see the pond through the eyes of the old woman called Tyey, who called her 'Miee', unable to find the *l*'s in her name when she spoke it. The other two connected to the library where she plundered visions of ancient seas, wooden boats, and flying ships. A volcano tragedy and the birth of a child, black as coal in a warm dirt-floored hut on a winter's day, to a mother who beamed with a light of love so bright it shone across millennia and gladdened Millie's heart.

All the links were alive and she felt each play upon the others. She could maintain them all with a half consciousness, skipping from one to the next in her mind, most active in one while holding the others in a stasis. The unfocused strands sounded like distant song in her thoughts, each a melody, strangely unique but harmonious. Eventually, she released them one by one, touching each and releasing them to fade into a distant purr.

Millie had thought that Bouer would be happy for her success, but instead he felt waxen and wan.

"What is it?" she'd asked.

"We're moving quickly."

"Is that bad?"

"Bad for some things, good for others."

"Bad for me, good for you?"

"You're doing very well, Millie. It means there is a depth to you, a sorrow. I am sorry for that."

The bees sensed empathy, particularly that learned from suffering. Through her work in the library and with other acolytes, she was surprised to learn that the bees did not require true suffering; an imagination could substitute and was often better than real distress, which could permanently damage the psyche. Be it from experience or invention, empathy, sympathy – the ability to imagine another person's plight and inhabit it – was what counted.

"Five bees," he said and then gave her the proud smile she'd expected. "You are coming along very well, Millicent Dagney."

At that moment, she felt something shift in her groo. Though difficult to detect in the usual taciturn Tirgwenin, she sensed him grow pensive and more thoughtful than he usually was. There was a new sadness in his eyes.

Today, a week later, when they mounted the hill together, he faced north while she turned her face to follow the setting sun. She'd done her work, saw the breaking of the moon, and felt the terror of the left-behind.

As she watched the final rays of the light turn to flares of lazy auroras and snow-reflected color, she caught something in Bouer's double-blinking eyes and turned to see what he saw.

It was a caravan approaching the town from the north. Two dozen hests, camlays, and oxcarts, covered carriages and wagons. The camlays swayed on their long legs, their riders two meters above the ground, visible in silhouette against the snow. The hests trotted in smart formation, their riders erect in their saddles. Many held upright lances topped with fluttering banners, dark cloth echoes of the auroras above them. She could tell by Bouer's expression that the caravan was important and expected.

"I should go," Bouer said and stood up.

"What about me?" said Millie.

"Stay here until full dark and then come down."

The sun was below the horizon but still shone on the southern ring. The first third was in shadow. There was an hour left until full dark.

"Why must I wait?" she said. "So you can meet the newcomers without me?"

"I'll see you soon," he said and there was something in his voice that frightened her.

Before she could ask, he disappeared around the crest of the hill.

The bees nestled against her skin and fluttered their wings for heat. Millie shivered from the tickle as much as the cold. Bouer was right, the mind could overcome physical challenges. A year ago she'd have been freezing from so much inactivity in the open, now she was merely uncomfortable. She recalled Mathew and his plight among her people, how he endured so much hardship, cold and starvation – torture – at the hands of the insane Aguirre, and she understood now his power to overcome. He'd tapped into the strength of family. The bees had given him that. He'd died horribly, unnecessarily, at the hands of her people, but he'd died complete and connected. He'd furthered the species in some way. He'd been part of it and he'd died contentedly. It was a strange thing to think of, to die contentedly. These were the thoughts she had there alone on the hill, snow-covered and freezing. She thought of her mother and father and wondered how they'd died, if they'd been content and connected as was Mathew. She felt a tear trickle down her cheek and freeze to her chin.

The light flickered off the rings and died. So strange to have a second sunset, west and south.

She stood and stretched her limbs, working out tension and cramps. The bees were all under her clothes now, burrowed and silent, absorbing her warmth. She was glad to give it.

Her breath blossomed in puffs of steam before her face and obscured for an instant the path she was suddenly afraid to take. She took a deep breath, and sent it out in a long slow exhale that froze her nose beneath her hood. She'd return to the longhouse as if nothing had changed, while knowing, as certainly as if she'd been branded, that things were now different.

A last aurora faded to dark as if Coronam herself had gone to bed. Above Millie, the stars were bright and clear, the same as home but shifted, too high or too low for this time of year, reassuring but wrong at the same time. No moons tonight. Full dark.

It was a bargain, she reminded herself. Whatever happened to her was fine as long as Dillon and the others could continue.

A ripple of fear shook her muscles, pretending to be a chill.

The path was narrow and unlighted, but she knew it well, and in the clear sky of leaking starlight upon the snow, she could see fine. The path was icy in places and she nearly slipped but caught herself. She slowed her already unhurried pace and took her time.

The path joined a more traversed road and she followed that toward the river the locals called the Finger, which flowed between her hill and Beleksha. There was a stillness in the night, a quiet only cold winter air could make. She walked parallel to the river's flow and studied the frigid band of black against the blue-white snow of its banks. The water moved fast, too fast to freeze except in the eddies and edges in crystal planes of glistening ice.

The road turned to meet a low arcing bridge, fifteen meters long, wooden, sturdy and well traveled. It led to the lane, which turned to the boulevard that would take her to the longhouse.

That's where they'd be. That's where they waited for her.

She climbed the bridge, listening to the soft crunch of her boots as she walked.

A crack of ice and a plunging splash made Millie jump.

At the apex of the bridge, she looked upriver for the source of the sound.

A face bobbed up in the river and then disappeared. Up again it came and was gone. A third time – only a few meters away – she saw the terrified face of a man she did not know. In the starlight he was pale, his hair loose and hanging over his eyes. He thrashed weakly against the current and coughed against the water. Speechless and choking, he went under again. Millie could see his cloak spread around him like a wool puddle. The current had it and drew him down and forward at alarming speed.

In a moment he was under the bridge.

She dove upon the cloak.

The cold hit her like a hammer and she screamed. Her cry rose in bubbles and she fought for the surface, her own clothes working against her.

She felt the man's cloak and grabbed it, wrapping her senseless fingers around the hem with all her strength, hoping against the numbness in her fingers that her knuckles would hold.

She crested the surface and filled her lungs. The air made the water feel warm and her cheeks burned with freezing pain.

The man had gone limp, his face below the water, but she held the cloak.

Warmth fled her, replaced by numbing cold, which tightened around her like steel, holding her, thwarting her – stilling her. She knew she had but seconds of movement left before her body would no longer respond to her will.

The man was twice her size, twice her weight. A stranger and a fool who'd fallen in the river, yet she would not let him go.

Kicking toward shore, she pulled the cloak to her face and pushed a corner of it into her mouth. Her teeth clenched and locked on the fabric just as her hands let go, too frozen to further obey.

She was a fair swimmer but her arms felt like bricks and her legs like posts. She tried to remember some of the body control Bouer had taught her, but her mind was as sluggish as her muscles.

All became black and quiet when the current pulled her under.

The river pushed the man against her, then dragged him back away from the shore. Her head spun as the tension on the cloak grew taut and threatened to break her neck. She clenched her teeth harder, kicked, and kept her breath.

Surface.

The shore was near, but her body was clay, freezing to porcelain. Her clothes joined the burden of the drowning man in wanting her at the bottom of the freezing river.

She gasped and drew half water half air into her lungs and went under again. No reason to try to stay on the surface. If she didn't make the shore on this breath, she wouldn't make it at all.

She felt the rocks with her shoulders, a jolt of pain shooting through her entire body that she had to trace to its source. She reached for them, hoping for a handhold, a root, but her fingers were useless, her hands blunt clubs slapping at the mossy stone.

The current tugged her, inviting her back. She felt suddenly warm and thought to let go, to remove her cloak, her shoes, her clothes. To flow with the river.

Madness.

Her mind was freezing too. She had only moments.

She rolled over on her back and kicked. She felt the rocks against her back as a distant thought and then on her bottom as she drew up her knees. She dug her heels into the river bottom and pushed.

They found no purchase.

Her limbs were apparitions, useless appendages she could not control.

Her head snapped around, pulled by the man held in her teeth sliding back into the current.

A parade of faces danced before her – Dillon, Lahgassi, Bouer, her mother and father. Each alive or dead, but all important. She was important too. All were. All were her family.

She wanted to debate her life against the man's, convince herself to let go, sacrifice him for a better chance for herself, but her mind rebelled. The math was simple: one sure to die, or two only probably. She held on.

Her heel caught and she pushed up the bank until her head brushed frozen grass.

Her other foot, a distant relative responding slowly but effective. Another push. Again and again, her jaw straining, her limbs alien ideas, but still moving. Out of the current the man floated beneath his cloak, a pool of half-submerged cloth harboring a dead or dying stranger.

Millie turned on all fours and crawled out of the water. The frozen grass crunched beneath her, the river fronds crackled like breaking blades, stabbing her senseless palms.

She spit out the cloak and immediately regretted it when her teeth chattered so violently they deafened her and threatened to shatter themselves in her mouth.

With some difficulty, she wrapped her hands around the man's cloak and pulled him to the bank. His chest rose and fell, shallow but sure. He was alive. She was alive. For a few more moments at least, they were alive.

Millie fell back and tried to find her breath; it caught shallow and sharp. Pain from the cold. The shaking came and stayed; the cold came and went. Warm flashes and visions of a warm bed bespoke a coming death she must fight.

Climbing up on her knees with the last of her strength and mental reserve, she readied a yell. She might get only one scream, one call for help, before the cold took her mind and body. She had to make it count.

She drew in a long breath, savored it behind her clenched teeth. Then her eyes focused on the group of people watching her from the bank, standing only two meters away. They regarded her with appraising eyes.

Behind her, the man in the water stood and joined them. Millie saw then the thick insulated suit beneath his sodden cloak.

Someone uncovered a lantern and the light was blinding.

Bouer wiped a tear from his cheek and nodded appreciatively. He glanced at a tall woman beside him. "Millie, this is Desarri. She's the primeen, the closest thing we have to a queen on Tirgwenin."

The woman's eyes were soft and caring, proud and warm. "Greetings, Millicent Dagney," she said. "You have come through the ordeal."

Millie let her breath out in a sigh and fell into the snow.

CHAPTER NINETEEN

Selfishness is a primitive emotion: useful in primitive situations but losing efficacy quickly as perspectives increase and wisdom grows. In time it acts directly contrary to evolution. We must try something else.
Lerer Melk, From *The New Day Speech*
7, Eleventh-Month, 513 NE – Apis, Temple

8, Third-Month, 1194 Arrival (939 NE) – Station 2, Mist Ridge, Silangan

Atuow knew he would never return to Tirgwenin. He would die on Silangan and he would die soon. There'd be no retrieval, no rescue. The savages had changed course. They were now sweeping down from the mountains, and though his station was well concealed, he knew it would be found. And once found, it would be ransacked and he would die. He accepted this as a natural fact, a scientific certainty. Unalterable. So, with that problem solved, regardless of his personal distaste for the answer, he could put it out of his mind to focus on things he could affect. His work would continue. He would study and report. He would learn. He would witness.

He surveyed the distant ridge with his binoculars and noted the new black plumes of smoke moving his way, moving fast. They might be here as early as this evening, or as late as the day after tomorrow, depending on what they found to eat in between.

He rolled down the blind and secured the shutter. From a distance the station was now invisible. The structure had been cut into the rock on a steep ledge by a crew of ten men; himself, two from Maaraw, three from Lavland, and the rest from Hyrax. Pirates and partisans, friends of the family. Having made Station One the month before, and using the best Tirgwenin tools, it took them only a week to make this one. Atuow had moved in immediately and the workers left him before his first night. Like the other, this station was hidden behind blinds of textured tapestry and shadow. Ten meters over and three down, the entrance was concealed in a thick growth of thorny vegetation that grew so fast it threatened to seal the door if not cut back every few days. Lately, Atuow had been careful to hide the cut marks and remove the debris, actions he had not bothered with in previous years.

The savages wouldn't find the hatch; it was well concealed and could offer him an escape. Maybe. What would be his undoing was the observation window. They knew what to look for now. They would get close and probe the ridge with torch and spear and they would find it. They would break open the shutters and enter the station. And that would be that.

Looking now in the light of four dim glowglobes, Atuow imagined the pathetic defense he could make here. He had a Hyraxian flamer he didn't know how to even prime, an Enskari rail musket he was afraid to touch, a saber – also Hyraxian – and a Tirgwenian short bow. The last was the only thing he'd ever used and he'd been lucky then to hit the ground after ten minutes of aiming. He was a scientist, not a soldier.

He did not want for food or water or heat. He had secondary air shafts and a sophisticated sewage system. If they were to somehow seal him into the mountain, with a landslide perhaps, he might be able to survive for another two years. His hive and his ward, however, would be lucky to make it to the end of the week.

He called a bee to him – one of his last. It flew out of the hive by the shuttered window and spun over his head in tight rings. His last colony was weak and sickly. He'd come with ten hives, and in three and a half years he'd lost all but this last one. Muqom had three left when his station was burned out.

They'd hoped their hives would grow and swarm and spread across the planet. They'd dropped bees on Silangan before, having pirates place hives in out-of-the-way spots trusting to their natural ability to spread, but all those had failed. The thinking was that they needed a tender for a while, a connected keeper to ease them in. This had proved helpful – their colonies had lived longer than the others, but were still dying.

Atuow had no theory why the bees fared so poorly here. It was one of the most important questions he'd been tasked with. After nearly four years, he had only the evidence of their demise to suggest that the reason there were no bees on Silangan was because bees didn't survive on Silangan. Hardly an award-winning hypothesis.

Feeling the insect strain to keep airborne, Atuow dismissed it. He watched three more enter through a hole in the scrim, bringing nectar to their dying queen. A wave of sorrow washed over him as he imagined the suffering within the hive, the certain death they too were facing, their work continuing until the end because that is what you do. You continue until the end.

A breeze blew through the opening, carrying a scent of smoke and the sound of distant cries.

It was a certainty. They were coming.

He registered this moment with a concentrated thought, placing it with his feelings of fear and obligation in the library, making it, marking it. Joining it.

"Blood! Blood is God. God is blood!"

Atuow spun on the noise, raising his hands as if to parry an attack.

"He runs in our veins. He seeks release. Blood. Blood. Blood!"

With a chuckle of relief, berating his own fear, Atuow lowered his hands and went to Lund in the next room. The Templer had woken up, obviously.

He found the missionary struggling against his restraints. He'd opened up old wounds and his tongue showed he'd made a few more.

"Brother Lund – Rutger," said Atuow, kneeling beside the bed. "You are safe. Be at peace."

The boy looked at Atuow and his face filled with terror as if he'd never seen him before.

"I am a friend, remember? My name is Atuow. I saved you from Serlot. You are safe now. Rest."

Lund's eyes were still wild.

"The prophet sent me." That line usually had an effect and this time it did as well. The Templer relaxed and took his wide eyes off Atuow and searched the room, as he had done every day for three weeks since he got here.

"Drink." Atuow tipped a waterskin for Lund and smiled when he swallowed three good mouthfuls.

"You tongue improves," said Atuow. "Let's look at your hands, brother."

Lund stared, confused. "Are you an angel?" he asked.

The same question.

"A friend."

Lund's hand was bleeding again. The wounds would not close. The stubs of the fingers on his left one had been treated with an ointment that forbade the flesh to properly knit. Atuow had seen the gray smears and smelled the curious unctuous alkali stink but hadn't been able to discover what it was or how to combat it. The best he'd been able to do was wrap the missionary's hands with bandages as tightly as he could and keep him hydrated. He thought of amputating at the wrist, but couldn't see the use of it. Causing this man any more pain or loss was not within him, and there was no call for it. He'd managed to keep him alive this long, a few more hours wouldn't be hard. After that, it wouldn't matter.

Lund's right hand still had its thumb and forefinger. Serlot hadn't gotten to them yet. The stubs of his missing digits on that hand had not been poisoned, and there Atuow had done some good work, sewing the wounds closed and arresting infection. The places where Lund's ears, nose, and penis had been were healing as well as possible. They'd been cauterized by Serlot's torturers to keep him from dying too early.

Atuow felt his jaw quiver in sympathy to his injured charge as he removed the bandages on the poisoned hand. Lund flinched. There was still feeling there. The wounds would not close but neither would he die.

"Am I dead?" Lund asked.

"Nay."

"But I was in hell. I saw hell. I saw God."

"You did not see God, Brother Lund," said Atuow, dabbing antiseptic paste into the oozing sores.

"Then the devil."

"Maybe that."

"I...I can't remember."

"That is a blessing," said Atuow.

Atuow knew his history. He'd learned it not from Lund's lips but from his bubbles in the library. It had not been easy, but he had traced the young man, carefully, diligently, and learned his story. The latter parts were broken and horrific, a cacophony of suffering – betrayal, regret, and sadness. Not a positive emotion in the soup. Atuow traced Lund to his time on Temple, navigating his search by the mad missionary's present psychic tremors. They were disjointed and deranged, suicidal – homicidal – but Atuow's skill allowed him to find the man before the madness, and place him in the library.

"I...I remember...I remember I chose to go. I didn't have to. I volunteered because God wanted me to go."

"Aye," said Atuow.

Atuow himself had volunteered for this fatal assignment. Fresh out of school and entering an apprenticeship to become a groo, he'd petitioned for the then-unlikely ground mission to Silangan. He would not say that God chose him. He did not think in those terms, but there was a fatalistic bent in his life that had led him to Silangan just as the planet collapsed.

His work in socio-evolution was solid but not remarkable. He had a firm understanding of human history and a serviceable knowledge of Coronam Theory, the branch of study investigating the 'miraculous' star system they were now a part of. His grasp of the *viapum*, or the way of the bees, was his strength. Though minimally interested in theory, he was an expert at its practical use. He could effortlessly navigate the psychic threads across worlds and times as easily as falling into a dream on a warm day. He accredited his skill to an early vision from the bees in his youth. At thirteen Atuow mourned the loss of his caos, Barney, a furry animal not unlike a cat but three times the size and loyal to death. Barney had bonded to Atuow before he could speak and its sudden death in a cart accident had shattered Atuow's world beyond what he thought he could bear. Atuow's eyes were blurry with tears and his heart with longing, but the bee showed him a connective light between all things living and dead, past and present.

And he was never the same.

Unfamiliar with the established metaphor, Atuow had imagined the library not as a storehouse of records, but as a four-dimensional space set upon a five-dimensional tapestry, made of sound bubbles linked with breath. It was fanciful, but powerful. He could not describe what a four-dimensional space looked like, let alone a five, or a sound bubble with breath, but the strange talismanic imaginings of the phenomena served him well and ever since. He'd presented his visualization technique at several schools and it had garnered much attention, enough to suggest a new sub-branch of viapum – *semiotic evocation theory*.

Notoriety from this almost kept him out of the running for the Silangan assignment. Some groos argued he had made a breakthrough and he would be more useful at a university. But Atuow petitioned and lobbied, and finally, five years ago, won the assignment with a fellow socio-evolutionist called Moqum. They would be the first Tirgwenin scientists to study Silangan from its surface. A year later, they were on-planet.

It was a dangerous assignment. Silangan was the 'mad planet'. The name had been coined before anything was known of it except that it had no bees. It was the only habitable planet in the system that did not. It was an anomaly and a black hole in geographical research. Early scientists reaching threads to Tirgwenin's nearest neighbor could gather little information but had, unanimously, coined the phrase 'mad planet' to describe it. It was not until that world was populated by the people from the Unsettling that the term became understood as a possible prophetic vision gleaned from the viapum.

"What happened to my hands?" whimpered Lund. "And my…oh my God…my…."

"You have suffered much, but it's over now. Be calm."

"Devil! Yellow devil! What are you?"

"I'm Atuow. A friend from Tirgwenin."

"You were killed. I saw you killed. Serlot's sword crushed your head."

"That was Muqom. He was my friend. He is how I came to rescue you."

"There were others – so many others. My companion, Eyletto. What of him? Is he safe?"

"He perished before I could find you. I am sorry."

He hoped today Lund would not recall the torture of that young man from Maaraw. Lund had witnessed it. Serlot had made him do a terrible thing.

"I killed him!" screamed the missionary. "I murdered Eyletto."

"You had no choice. Do not blame—"

"I am damned! God is blood. God is blood."

"Shhhh…" said Atuow. "Be calm."

Lund thrashed and howled.

Atuow worried the sound could escape his walls, drawing Serlot's soldiers. But he reassured himself that they were still far. They were not stealthful. He'd have heard them if they were so close. It was a strange worry for this moment, and he suddenly recognized that he still held out hope of surviving somehow.

"Hope springs eternal," he muttered.

Lund fell to weeping. Atuow re-bandaged his hands.

Muqom had been tasked with studying the influence of Hyrax upon the planet and the first station was near White Coast, where the mines were. His station was similarly hidden as Atuow's, but when the raid came from inland, from Serlot's crazed zealots, he was set upon while meeting a resupplying shore party. The pirates had fought well, but were overrun. The savages found the station, burned it with coal oil, and left the dead bodies where they'd fallen unburied and partially eaten. The savages were cannibals.

They threw a bag over Muqom's head and dragged him away. The connection with Atuow was lost.

Atuow sent his healthiest bees to look for his companion but Muqom's mind was weak with despair and exhaustion, and it was three days before they found him.

Oh brother, said Muqom. *I am uplifted to see you.*

And me. Look around. Show me where you are, the mountains, remember the path.

Atuow saw the hills and trees through his friend's eyes. One eye was unfocused and filmed.

I'm coming.

You can't save me, said Moqum. *Stay away.*

I have a bearing.

Don't bother. I'm done here. They are blank.

Moqum's despair came from a hidden fear that the peoples of this planet were not people at all. They'd discussed the phenomenon, how neither had been able to penetrate the singular or collective consciousnesses of the Silangians. Atuow could sense people, but could not enter their bubbles. All he received was dissonance when he tried, and it hurt to try.

I overheard them talking, said Moqum. *They followed the bees to me. They found one of my hives. The one I put down the river, I think.*

I remember, said Atuow. *It failed last month, didn't it?*

It did, and now we know why. These people destroyed it.

But why would they do that?

They recognized it for what it was.

How?

I don't know, but somehow they knew what it meant and searched until they found me.

Atuow immediately suspected the Hyraxians. The conquerors were every bit as cruel as the natives. The difference was that the natives were cruel to everyone while the dark-haired off-worlders focused most of their brutality on the locals.

It wasn't the Hyraxians, Atuow.

How do you know?

Don't come after me! I see what you're doing. Take off your boots.

Good. Look here and not there. Atuow sensed the final breath escape a pirate across from where Moqum was tied to a tree. He felt his friend's pain and worry, and rubbed his own wrists, feeling the leather restraints around Moqum's.

Atuow took a horn of bees and stuffed food into a bag – honey, biscuits, wine, and water – and took his camouflage suit over his shoulder on his way out of the hatch tunnel.

The Hyraxians found the one I left in White Coast and wholly ignored it, Muqom said. *They didn't know what it was. No, it was Serlot. The Silangians. They knew what they were and they destroyed them. It was intentional.*

How…? Why would they care?

The mad planet. Muqom's vision blurred with tears and Atuow felt ones rise in his own eyes. There'd been a woman in the group and the savages raped her in a line. The screams echoed across the threads.

Stay away, Atuow, Muqom told him. *Don't risk yourself. Don't risk the work we've done. I am already dead. I'm going home to Davvit. Pax, Atuow.* And with that he closed the connection.

Muqom was older and a widower. He'd lost his husband, Davvit, in a sailing accident and this long assignment was his reaction to that. Solitude and mourning, a way to keep useful and keep going. Like Atuow, he was a serious and quiet man. They communicated once a week through the viapum for a few minutes, giving station updates, weather reports, resupply schedules, and generally making sure they were both still alive. They'd take turns making the weekly contact with Tirgwenin. Neither enjoyed it. Both scientists knew the risks and had accepted them, knowing the work was important enough to justify the dangers.

But the reality was different. Muqom wasn't dead yet. He was captured. He might be rescued or ransomed. There was time for action and Atuow knew he would never forgive himself if he did not at least try to save his partner.

The risk went beyond their lives. The mission itself was in jeopardy. One station was already lost. If Atuow were captured or killed, his would follow suit. Luckily, this scenario had already been considered. Both stations kept journals and notes in a secret safe outside their stations.

Atuow sent a message to Tirgwenin, explaining his plans to rescue Muqom. As he knew they would, the mission committee forbade him to try.

I'm going nonetheless, he said. *I'll leave my work in my research cache. If you don't hear from me, you'll have that.*

We can't have a ship there for months.

I know. He broke off the connection. He had a headache.

Six days later he found the place where Muqom had been when the connection was cut. On a bright but cheerless morning, near the town of Halle, he found the clearing he remembered. In the ashes of a cold fire pit, he found a pair of human skulls, cracked and broken for their meat.

At the sight of those, Atuow forced himself back into the library to trace the fate of his companion. His courage was flagging, but if there was a chance his friend was still alive, he'd go on.

It was a difficult trace. A dozen weakened bees died helping him. It took all of his skill and stamina. This place fought him, the horror distracted him, his fear blinded him. One person's thoughts were always the hardest to find, a single thread in a tapestry as big as the universe. Large swaths of experience, like the Unsettling or the fates of whole nations on Old Earth, were much easier to discover and dissect. It helped that Muqom was a distant relative, a countryman, but still, tracing his fate took several days of total concentration.

He found Muqom's end in Halle through the man's own eyes. He saw the piles of the dead, heard the screams of the tortured and dying, smelled the offal and blood. He saw also the missionaries and the bloodlusted Serlot. When the blow fell onto Muqom's skull, Atuow screamed.

Coming back to his senses, he heard people in the woods moving toward him. He'd been tranced for days and was lucky no one had found him yet. He fled home as fast as he could, hearing his pursuers in his imagination long after he'd left them behind.

He kept off the roads and trails. He was near White Coast, a large mining town. He'd been told to fear the Hyraxians more than the locals. They would recognize him for what he was – an alien who had no business being here. If captured, he was to act the Rowdanae, claim to be a captured slave, and conceal the real sophistication of his planet at all costs. He didn't know much about the political situation that had indentured this philosophy – no more than anyone, that was – but he knew there were others back home who took it very seriously, and so he took it seriously. Back home, there were legions of groos working tirelessly on these political issues night and day. It was the central problem of the high council, the obsession of Desarri the primeen. Muqom was more versed in it than he. That was probably why he'd been tasked with monitoring the invaders closer to the coast, while Atuow's charge had been Silangan itself.

As he marched across country, in riverbeds and over rocks, Atuow cemented his theories of the planet's madness and placed them in the library in case he didn't return.

He didn't like doing this. He had come to no hard conclusions, had no evidence to properly back any of it up, but faced with the real possibility of the sudden end of his mission, he thought it best to save what ideas he had.

When he stopped to rest, he wrote pages and read them, saying them out loud to get multiple levels of resonance. All the past was held in the library, but finding the threads could be hard. Multiple angles of recording – sight, sound, thought, and especially physical manifestations – would make a brighter bubble.

He confirmed there was something about this place that threatened peace. There was something besides the horror of Serlot's raids, beyond the terrors that Hyrax inflicted upon the people, that clung like a disease. Something poisoned the very atmosphere, sent waves of evil like sick birdsong. His hunch, his unprovable theory and idea, was that it was history expressed and recapitulated in the broken psyches of an entire people. The wages of an original sin.

The previous year, he'd traced the threads of the settling of Silangan. He could not approach it from the planet but had to come around from ancient Earth history, to the time of the Unsettling. He'd had to dissect the great event, find a specific and accessible mind connected to the Silangan-bound ship, then realign to the moment's energy and trace it through a group experience to the planet itself.

The work was a major coup, a life's achievement for some, but Atuow's skill managed it in a year. If he ever got back to Tirgwenin, or if he had time here, which was looking less and less likely, he'd record his methods to aid future researchers. As is, he would leave only the work itself, the moments and breakthroughs in his own life, a weak, but not wholly inaccessible, bubble in the library.

What he found was that this planet, like the other lately inhabited ones around Coronam, had been colonized by a powerful family from Old Earth, this by the Proahg family. They were terrible people. Atuow had tried not to put a value judgment here, but there was no way around it. They were the worst of the worst. Even considering the debased condition Old Earth society had devolved into, the inequity and squalor, the Proaghs stood out as devils among monsters. Like the planet they would one day come to rule, they were mad.

Atuow had touched the minds of several of them and been too traumatized to continue. His upbringing could not fathom the level of antipathy, selfishness, and greed he encountered. He'd learned a new word: sociopath, and applied it liberally over the ancestors and descendants of that house.

Unlike the other families from the Unsettling, the Proaghs had not even put up a pretense of hope. They did not lure scientists with the idea of new beginnings, workers with the idea of generational gain. They knew well what they intended: a kingdom of masters and slaves. One group forever serving the other. Laws for one; whim for the other. The Proahg paradise would dispense with even the lip service of justice and create a permanent caste system of brutish labor and cruel, sociopathic masters.

On Old Earth, rumors of insanity had circulated around the Proahg family for centuries, but their wealth made them untouchable and a required partner for the grandest endeavor capitalism ever tried: the Unsettling. Atuow saw a connection and theorized that their insanity, their sociopathy, was the reason for their wealth. Capitalism rewarded cruelty.

They'd filled their holds with slaves. Thousands of despondent weeping people, kidnapped, stolen, and bought. A ship of misery from the beginning. Unable to believe what he was experiencing in the holds of the Proahg ship, Atuow searched Old Earth for a parallel and found it in the North American slave trade. Raids upon villages, one savage group selling their neighbors to foreign invaders. An ancient pattern brought across the stars and relived centuries later on the mad world of Silangan.

The misery did not stop with landfall. The EMP that had crippled all the ships was handled worse here than anywhere. Instead of banding together for the survival of the colony the way the other planets had, the ruling Proahgs had lashed out in fear and savagery. The masters would not allow such an equalizing event as technological regression to stop their plans. They turned on their population and each other. They warred for centuries, regressing even further. On a world peopled with colonists genetically altered to breed, Silangan's population stalled, retreated, and then nearly collapsed as fiefdoms rose and fell, each crueler than the last, until finally all semblance of centralized leadership failed.

Reliving the strife of people big and small left Atuow drained and weak. He finally lost connection with the planet's history, the frequency problem barring clear further access. The last five hundred or so years a mystery. Physical proximity to Proahg descendants had allowed him to get as far as he did. Here too was a mystery, a facet of the viapum with interesting consequences.

It was very difficult to work. The planet, globally speaking, had had the compassion beaten out of it. They were far from the bees. They even lacked that hallmark of civilization, a written language. Along with electronics and computers, gunpowder and nuclear weapons, they'd lost writing and then, at some point, individually and as a society, they lost interest in anything older than their own lives.

This was why it was so difficult to trace the threads. There was no tradition of remembrance here. No records, not even folk tales to plant the universe in good or evil. All was adrift, each alone, rudderless, historyless, and so, futureless. It went far toward explaining the squalor and madness. No lessons could be learned by anyone who transcended their pathetically short and brutal lives. They had lost the ability to farm, and had it not been for Silangan's kind climate and abundant resources, the people would have starved long ago.

When the 'civilized' world of Hyrax arrived, they did nothing but compound the misery here. Temple had tried to bring hope in the form of their archaic conformity, and was making some headway, but like the bees, they were unwelcome.

A strange thought crossed Atuow's mind during the trek home. He wondered if the recent challenges to the chaos of this world had instigated the reaction he was now facing. Was it coincidence that Serlot's sudden and terrible rise matched up with Temple's missionary success and Tirgwenin's arrival with bees? It was an idea that haunted him.

Back home, from a distance, as best he could, Atuow monitored Serlot's sweep across the continent. After the butchery at Halle, as if it had unleashed a nightmare, the savages with no rhyme or reason, no order, no plan – barely a direction, and still with Serlot driving them – plundered White Coast in a month. Then then moved up through Millickus and over to the Jensen mines, destroying a hundred nameless local villages in the wake. His station was now next on the menu on their way to Jatt.

Between Millickus and the Jensen mines, Atuow sensed the Templer Lund. He was still alive, one in a train of prisoners, roped together and dragged along by the healthier ones at the urging of a child with a whip.

The face of the missionary was one of the last things Muqom had seen and Atuow's heart leapt to find him alive. He had to try to save the off-worlder, not just because he was so wretched, forsaken, and tortured – a soul crying out – but for his friend, himself, the family. He'd try to save them all if he could, but doubted his chances at the one, let alone the hundred other doomed prisoners.

It had been a surprisingly easy thing to do. The idea was simple and primitive, and that, Atuow thought, was its strength.

He approached the camp in the dead of night, a dark one, moonless and overcast. His height he could not hide – he was a half meter taller than any of them, save Serlot, who was a half meter over him – but a rag cloak and a hunch could conceal that. Atuow rubbed mud over his skin, thick black bog that stuck like tar and concealed his yellow skin. He used ochre to draw lines down his face as was the fashion, and spattered his own blood over his hands to further the illusion. He took a bundle of supplies and set off.

He walked into the camp boldly, unchallenged, and wove his way between the fires. He walked with purpose, determined and paced, someone going somewhere. He put as much authority and bearing into his stride as he could though his fear threatened to buckle his knees at every encounter. He had kept his hand beneath his cloak, gripping a Silangian dagger of chipped obsidian, his last line of defense.

There were thousands of killers spread over the hillsides. Most of the trees had been felled for fires, their green boughs throwing off thick clouds of smoke in reluctant combustion, the smell of human flesh, sweet and fatty, mingled with the stench of open latrines and the sour stink of disease. He searched for an hour, witnessing horrors and crimes that made him want to retch – rape and murder, butchery and torture. Depravities he could not name.

Finally, he found the cages of the prisoners conveniently located next to a row of butcher tables.

One man in mud-caked furs and a bone necklace that spoke of rank sat near the door and poked at a fire with twisted stick. Two other men dozed nearby with swords and lances.

"I want that one there." Atuow pointed to Lund.

The one with the bones stood up and approached him. The guards opened their eyes but didn't move from where they lay near the fire.

Atuow said, "The white one. Serlot wants him."

"Nay."

"Serlot demands—"

"Who the hell is Serlot?"

Such was the nature of the horde, most did not even know who the leader was. Blood was all they needed.

"Barter?"

"Aye," said the man.

Squatting outside the ring of firelight, Atuow dug into his parcel with trembling fingers. He had pots and beads, knives and ropes, but he went for his most valuable thing first, wanting to be done and gone.

"Here," said Atuow. "One jar for the white one."

The man opened the jar. He wrinkled up his nose.

Atuow mimed for him to dip a finger in and taste it.

The man drew up a long sweet string of honey on his filthy finger and tapped it to his tongue. His eyes went wide.

"What is this?" he asked.

"Loot from the coast."

"Four jars," said the man.

"Nay," said Atuow. "One."

"Three."

"Is there meat on him?" Atuow said, playing his role.

"Stringy, but rare," said the man.

"Two." Atuow raised two fingers and saw the glint of yellow on the back of his hand where the blood had scabbed off. He lowered it slowly into the bag and took his other jar out.

"Done!" said the man and barked behind him to one of the guards. "Bring the whitefish. Now!"

Lund was in terrible shape – no nose or ears, most of his fingers gone – but worse than any of that was the vacancy in his eyes.

"Has he a tongue?" asked Atuow.

"That he does."

Atuow tossed the other jar of honey to the man, who grabbed it out of the air.

A guard wrapped a piece of rawhide around Lund's throat and led him by leash to where Atuow squatted.

"He won't run or fight," said the butcher.

"Because you beat it out of him?" said Atuow.

"Nay. It was never there."

He took the fastest route out of the camp, even though it led in the wrong direction. He had a terrible image of being tracked by animals, or rather Silangian savages, their faces on the ground, their noses picking up his scent and following to the station. It was a false nightmare. He knew the horde spread like an infection, bloodlust the motivation, no personal grudge against him or Lund. Still, the fear was healthy and they made good time.

It was a fortnight before Atuow returned to his station with Lund still at the end of his leash. He'd tried to remove it, to comfort the man, but the Templer reacted badly each time he was let off. Twice he tried to flee into the woods, and once, the last time, he'd attacked Atuow and tried to rip his neck open with his broken teeth. It was only because Lund was so damaged that Atuow could subdue him. Once the collar was back around his neck, Lund calmed immediately. He seemed happiest with it on, with Atuow playing the master.

Two weeks later, Atuow still couldn't trust Lund to be free. He tended the man's physical wounds as best he might, but he was at a loss to find a medicine for his mind. Lund was broken, as mad as the planet. A boy full of optimism and confidence, a true believer who had lost the foundation of his being. God was weak in the face of the blood cult. God had failed him. From the heights of his soaring naive enthusiasm, he'd plummeted double to the depths of a hell he thought himself immune to.

But it would all be over soon.

The sounds of approaching death filtered in the bee hole on the scent of burning villages.

Inevitable.

The strong and bullying always defeated the meek and thoughtful. History was full of examples.

Lund moaned from his bed. "Am I really safe?" he asked.

Atuow turned to see the man's wild eyes, wide and searching, light in the pupils. He was man again, a soul inside the battered shell. Hope.

"Nay," said Atuow. "We need to get out of here. Now."

CHAPTER TWENTY

Sacrifice is the heart of progress. It is not three steps forward, two steps back; but four men forward making steps for the fifth to advance. Nothing good or great is ever gained without such costs. It is the ennobling duty of the expendable classes to sacrifice themselves for the greater success of their masters.

The Earl of Nutorn, interviewed for the *Vildeby Review*
18, Second-Month, 939 NE

4, Fourth-Month, 939 NE – Rodawnoc, Tirgwenin

Smoke.

There was no smoke.

Morgan strained to watch the bouncing horizon out of a porthole of the landing craft. He was buffeted and bounced and already had a cut over his eye from where the low ceiling had clipped him in a trough.

No smoke.

It was early spring, not freezing, but cold. Cold enough for a fire. There should be smoke.

He checked the landmarks, remembered the charts Captain Gillison had used, and confirmed, as well as he could, that the land they were rushing to was in fact Rodawnoc.

The view was something out of his nightmares. How many days and nights had he envisioned this alien sky, its ring, and this coast, searching for his people, his daughter and granddaughter – aching to save them, praying for all he was worth that he would not be too late. Now finally, eighteen months after he first beheld this windblown and wooded coastline, he was back and he saw no sign of them.

He tried to calm himself. There were many reasons for there not to be smoke and not all of them were dreadful. The fires might be small, coals and embers. A cold breakfast today. Maybe it was a fast. Maybe they had learned to endure the cold the way the locals did. Maybe they'd spun wonderful wool and were toasty warm in cloaks. Maybe he was still just too far away to see the smoke.

A wave staggered him and he felt his legs threaten to fail. Blood trickled in his eye and fogged his vision. With a heavy sigh and the unkind weight of real gravity, Morgan sat down with the other men and strapped himself in. The belts felt comforting against his shoulders and waist, a reassuring grasp preventing him from falling to pieces.

He could not help but remember the last time he'd embarked upon this sea in this way. Among his weary colonists, his friends and wards. But also surrounded by enemies – secret and terrible, bent on their failure, their deaths and, God help him, probably succeeding. He'd felt the difference between colonist and crew that day, the first group excited and scared, the second, as he remembered them now, guilty and guileful.

The air in the cabin stank of diesel fumes. A trail of black smoke stretched out behind them, tracing a path of fading soot to the invisible anchor line and buoy twenty kilometers offshore. From there, the shore had been just a suggestion over the curve of the planet. Not the most convenient placement, but safe, as Captain Gillison had told him. "And that's what I'm all about on this damn planet."

Gillison was no coward, but he was the most risk-averse pirate Morgan had ever heard of. He was careful and quick and never overstepped. He walked a precarious line between Hyrax and Enskari, aligned to neither and keeping a low profile to both. His one ship, the *Moonlight*, was a fast raider along the lines of Sommerled's new ones, and it attacked only weak cargo vessels, careful not to single out one side over another. He was a Lavlander, a merchant turned raider, literate, from a family of ruined bankers. He played odds and made lists and hid his money in Temple banks because they were the safest. He was for sale and would do errands and commissions, but never sell out entirely, never align one way or another. He was a businessman, and in that way, he was more reliable than other pirates.

Morgan had sold his soul for this trip and thought it a bargain. What was trust, loyalty, or patriotism to him now? He was betrayed. His family marooned, his fortune spent, his religion in ashes – what matter his name and reputation? Those who had forsaken him should not have expected less. Damn Enskari. If Hyrax would help, the bargain was well met.

The stink of exhaust smoke from the landing craft mirrored this journey's beginning in Nutorn on that fateful day when the deal was made, and God struck down a city. He could not dismiss the thought that somehow his treason had caused the horror. It was chemistry and not theology that had murdered so many, but his conscience weighed it differently. So be it, if it were. He'd gladly be damned for this chance to save his family.

After his meeting with the Hyraxian captain, he'd carried the card in his waistcoat for months, trying to find another way to Tirgwenin. Sommerled would no longer speak to him, his duties were too great, the danger not abated. He'd made a counter-attack upon Hyrax, taking the war to Brandon's skies, and when he'd returned became First Ear of the queen.

The people, the lowborn, were ecstatic and celebrated. The promotion of one of their own to such a rank eclipsed the disaster of the counter-attack. There was a time when Morgan might have joined the throng celebrating his friend's 'triumph', but those days were past. He read the reports in day-old newspapers and did the math with a broken pencil in the margins. Even his limited military understanding showed him the folly of the attack. He also read subtle and sometimes not so subtle derisions cast at the First Ear for being an unqualified upstart. It didn't go beyond letters to the editor, but Morgan sensed the tension in the upper classes as clearly as he saw the jubilation among the lower.

Morgan had dreamed of a paradise beyond political intrigue where virtue would win out. A new start on Jareth's World. What a fool he was. He thought he would be king but he was never more than a pawn in other men's games.

The treason was made at the rail station in Nutorn, a town in northern

Dorothia, about three hundred kilometers from the capital of Vildeby. It was an industrial town. The Armorer of Enskari, it called itself. It turned out weapons, armor, and heavy machines, running nonstop shifts for years. It was located near a coalpit from where it drew its energy. The skyline was a row of tall smokestacks pouring soot out by the ton. The image of a factory, complete with billowing stacks, was on the city crest. The Earl of Nutorn, a powerful man of ancient stock, took pride in the pollution, calling it the smell of progress. He had been at odds with the Minister of Nature because of it.

All this Morgan read in newspapers afterwards. What he knew at the time was that no one should recognize him in Nutorn, so far from the capital. It had a large bustling rail station, and the famous smog allowed one to wear a mask without drawing attention. A good place for a clandestine meeting. It had not been his idea, but he appreciated the care nonetheless. It reflected a professionalism that should have scared him, but didn't.

Morgan arrived punctually on the eight o'clock train, holding a ticket for the nine o'clock return. He had but one bag, a leather satchel with a buckled flap, the kind of thing a lawyer's clerk would carry.

The atmosphere in the station was thick and heavy. It greased the back of his throat. It was a cold morning; his breath burst in puffs in the brown windless air. The station was covered, but open at the ends for trains which filled the rafters with smoke from their stacks to mingle with that coming from the factories outside.

Keeping his eyes low and his collar up, Morgan wandered far into the freight area, a place of harlots and strong grog. There he scanned a dim room and saw no one he knew. The faces were all turned away, no eye contact, as if they themselves were hiding.

Inside was an atmosphere just as thick. Fruity incense, textured tobacco, and grating grease added to the lingering, cloying coal smoke seeping in from under the doors. He took a table far in the back. He was there but a moment when he felt a presence behind him.

"I'll have a grog," Morgan said.

"I didn't think you took strong drink," said Captain Jasso.

"Trying to fit in."

"Aye," said the Hyraxian, taking a seat across the small table. "Safer anyway. Who knows what's in the water here if the air is like this?"

"Are there no places like this on Hyrax?"

Jasso loosened his cravat and adjusted his hat. His dark hair was well concealed beneath it. He seemed comfortable in the seedy surroundings. Morgan wondered how many other traitors he'd met in this den.

"There are," he said. "And I don't drink the water there either."

A barmaid appeared and brought plates of stew, mutton by the smell of it, and two tankards of ale.

"A glass of wine as well, Deary," said Jasso. "For the throat."

"Two," added Morgan.

She left without speaking.

"Wine now?" said Jasso.

"For the throat." Morgan could feel a deep roughness settling in.

"Can't argue with that," said Jasso. "I'll not get ye drunk."

"Obliged."

The maid returned with two glasses of red wine.

"Can't promise they haven't watered these down," said the Hyraxian. "But the potency is palatable and will probably kill anything harmful swimming around in it."

"Grand," said Morgan and took a swallow. It soothed his throat so he took another.

The room was cold but still he sweated. The tall coal fire in the corner did little to bring warmth to his skin, or cheer to his mind.

"I need a ship," Morgan said, wanting this to be over with. "To fly me to Jareth's World."

"And save your people marooned at Rodawnoc. Aye."

"It unnerves me that you know the place."

"I told you," said Jasso, "we have done nothing there. We didn't have to. It was your own people who did this to you and yours."

"I am in hell," Morgan said.

"I speak too frankly?" said the captain.

"In hell…."

"Let me get you out, Minister."

"Are you mocking me?"

Jasso leaned back and regarded him. "I'm trying to be polite. On my planet you're a heretic. Here you're—"

"Also a heretic," supplied Morgan.

Jasso lifted his ale and took a sip. "Aye," he said. "I guess that's true. What shall I call you?"

"Nothing and never again."

"Is our business over?"

"Nay. Nay…let us get to it."

Jasso wiped the foam off his lip and coughed into his sleeve. "I can help. I came prepared to pay top dollar for what I want. Can you supply it?"

"How much?"

"I have sixty thousand dollars," he said, "and contacts that will serve you."

"Enskaran dollars?"

"Of course."

It was the exact amount Gillison had wanted.

"Where is the money?"

"I need to see what I'm buying."

Far off in the distance a siren shrieked. Morgan looked around to see if it raised alarm among the people in the pub. Seeing nothing, he said, "I want a hundred thousand dollars."

"I can do that," said Jasso.

"You have it?"

"I do."

"You know what I have."

"I have an idea. It's the shape of it, you see, that matters. If it is sharp and direct, it is more valuable than something round and hard to fit."

"Riddles?"

"Spycraft," said Jasso. "I thought you'd been educated by Sir Nolan."

"Brett can go…."

"Aye," said Jasso, a grin pulling his lips. "The enemy of my enemy and all that. Show me what you have in your satchel."

Morgan glanced down and then back at the Hyraxian captain. "Could you be arrested now as a spy? You're out of uniform."

"Diplomatic immunity," he said. "I'm well placed."

Another siren wailed, this one closer, but still some distance. Again no distress among the locals, no one looking their way. Morgan reached in his bag, touched the paper there, but hesitated. "What is that sound?" he said.

Jasso cleared his throat. "It's an air warning, telling folks to get inside. A health thing."

"Oh."

"Cost of progress, right?"

"Aye," said Morgan. His hand hovered over the paper, his arm frozen, his fingers resisting his will.

"I have a train to catch," said the captain. "I suspect you want to be on your way as well." A single oil lamp on the table cast uneven shadows across his face. Morgan wanted to see kindness there in his eyes, but saw only the dead face of another pawn.

Morgan took a deep breath and coughed.

"Steady on," said Jasso.

Another deep breath. It tasted like metal – acrid and decayed. "You know of the Bucklers?"

"A splinter sect of the splinter sect which is your queen's new faith," he said. "I can't tell it from another, couldn't argue doctrine or principles, but I know of them."

"You know we are outlawed now?"

Jasso's smile widened. "Aye."

"Not many of us left."

"Nay."

"And you have heard also rumors that Sommerled, Sir Ethan Sommerled, admiral of the realm and hero to the world, lowborn and now First Ear of the queen, was a member?"

There was an absolute twinkle in the Hyraxian's eyes now. "I know he helped arrange for the colony on Jareth's World. I'd heard rumors he was sympathetic but an actual member?"

"He is a founder," said Morgan. "I have our original Articles of Belief. There were only ever three copies. I think this is the last surviving. The signatures are original. His is there."

"Let me see it," said the captain. "I need to know what it's worth."

"I want to see the money. Then you can see it. It's worth a hundred. It is sharp," he said, tears in his eyes. "It is lethal."

Jasso lifted his hand and circled his finger. From out of the kitchen came a man with a small travel trunk.

The man put the trunk on the table after Jasso moved their food aside. "Don't forget to eat the stew," he said. "It's pretty good here."

Morgan wiped a tear from his eye and saw it was black on his finger.

"It's the soot," said Jasso. "Wait until you blow your nose."

"How can you be so calm?"

"This is what I do." Jasso opened the trunk to reveal stacks of Enskari bills and bundles of coins. "I have sixty thousand in coin and the same in bills. See? I came prepared."

"And the ship?"

"I've reserved the *Moonlight* in anticipation," he said. "It's at Vildeby port, leaving in less than four days. It's ready to go, though until you show up, it doesn't know where. I think you've met her captain, Amar Gillison? A Lavlander. Stocky. Has a nasty burn scar on his right arm… just here." Jasso pointed to his elbow.

"I've not seen his arm."

"But you know him?"

"He seemed able."

"He'll do the work. As a favor to me and for the price promised."

Morgan wanted to ask how Jasso had put all this together. He felt the familiar wave of helplessness and realized none of it mattered.

He handed the document across the table.

Jasso unfurled the scroll, twisting it to the bottom. "Beside the signatures, anything else you'd like to draw my attention to?"

"Article six," said Morgan in a raspy voice. "It states an intent, the eventual ascension of our philosophy over all others."

"A call to proselytize?"

"That would be one way to look at it."

"But another might be treason," said Jasso.

Morgan coughed into his fist and nodded. "Aye."

Jasso found the section in the middle and read it by the dim oil lamp. He smiled, drained his wine, and stood up. "Take it all, Minister," he said, sliding the trunk toward him. "Enjoy your lunch. It's paid for. Safe travels." He tipped his hat, turned on his heels, and tucking the document beneath his coat, marched out of the pub. No one but Morgan watched him go.

Another siren joined the others as he finished his wine. It numbed the back of his throat, a blessing for its roughness. Drinking was a sin among the Bucklers. Add that to his list.

He expected to be mugged on the way out, but wasn't. His mind wandered to questions of honor, enemies, and friends. He boarded the train and was glad he'd gone to the expense of a private berth. He felt and smelled toxic.

Sirens grew closer and more abundant. Outside on the platform, looking through his window into the thickening brown haze, Morgan thought he saw people rushing in panic. He thought he might have seen some fall and not get up but he could not be sure. They were all shadow and smudge in the smog.

The station erupted with its own piercing siren and people rushed the cars. The train whistle blew, a pierce over a wail. The train lurched. Morgan glanced at his watch and saw they were leaving ten minutes early.

A face appeared in his window, sooty and terrified. A man with crazy bloodshot eyes pounded on his window. He gestured for Morgan to open it and let him in. He screamed, "Save me!"

Morgan recoiled.

The man tripped and fell below the window, disappearing into the black gas as the train sped out of the station.

There was no sunlight outside, only a diffused ochre glow leaking through thick settling smoke. Ice crystals formed black and spiderlike across the glass, and from under his door that led to the car corridor, Morgan saw tendrils of chestnut smoke seeping into his cabin.

Coughing up gobs of tar, he took off his coat and stuffed it under the door, blocking the air exchange.

He breathed through a handkerchief, watching yellow and black shadows cross his window, grateful to be moving, and suspecting now what the sirens were about.

It took only a few minutes to break through the cloud. It happened all at once as if crossing a frontier; orange light and smudge became landscape and sky. It was not clear like the air on Jareth's World – he'd never known sky like that – but for Enskari, near the industrial areas, they'd broken into a positively gorgeous day.

Morgan opened his window and let the toxic atmosphere rush out. His coat blew out from under the door and smoke was sucked out of the car.

His handkerchief was black.

Soon he breathed clearly and his throat no longer felt like sandpaper. Morgan blew his nose, remembering Jasso's warning in the aftermath.

⋆ ⋆ ⋆

Fours days later, Morgan was aboard the *Moonlight*, speeding for Tirgwenin, and the last newspapers he saw before he left had the death toll above twelve thousand and rising.

Some had thought it a Hyraxian attack or sabotage, but most papers called it what it was: an industrial accident. Weather conditions, cheap coal, and intense burning had combined to create a toxic cloud that settled over Nutorn like a shroud. It lasted two days until a wind blew it away, but by then the damage was done.

The sirens were effective in getting everyone indoors, but this time, the threat had followed them in and stayed too long. Most dead were found in their homes, clutching each other, their faces twisted in grimaces and airless screams.

Ironically, the factories themselves, shielded with semi-filtered air, proved to be some of the safest areas. Workers were kept inside against their will and most survived. Some community members had praised the earl for his quick thinking, while others laid the blame of the whole catastrophe at his feet. As the city died around him, the Earl of Nutorn had kept his factories producing. He took advantage of the imprisoned workers, doubled shifts, produced more smog, and was proud to proclaim afterwards that they'd met an early production goal and earned his family a bonus.

The death toll was expected to rise and none dared guess at what the long-term prospects were for the survivors. It was already a scandal in government and promised to test the new First Ear. There was plenty of blame to go around, but Morgan felt in his heart that it was all his. He'd sacrificed his friend, his loyalty, integrity, planet, and soul for a ride back to Tirgwenin, why not a city as well? The weight was no greater, the choice no different. He'd do it all again because it was the only way to save his family.

He wondered what world he would get back to after this trip to Tirgwenin. There'd be nothing there for him. His life was over, he conceded that. He had only a single task left to do, then, blissfully, he could disappear.

Captain Gillison had been kind and left Morgan to himself, allowing the only civilian on the ship to take his meals away from his board for the first weeks and then welcoming him when Morgan was ready for company.

"Good to have a learned man aboard, Governor," he'd said over dinner.

Morgan allowed the captain to use the outdated honorific but cringed.

"What news of Jareth's World?"

"Bretton is surely established by now," Gillison said. "Two hundred strong and well provisioned. At a place called Placid Bay."

"Where comes the name, Bretton?" asked Morgan, already knowing the answer.

"Sir Nolan Brett, Second Ear of the queen. He and Admiral Aderyn hold the charter for the planet now, at least as far as Enskari thinks. The prophet and Prince Brandon have other ideas."

"Two hundred, you say?"

"That's what they landed. They had four ships and an armed escort. We saw them ourselves a few months back. We kept our distance."

"How long will our journey be?"

"Aye, there, Governor," said Gillison. "We need to speak on that."

"I paid you!" Morgan's voice broke and his eyes filled with tears. His fists were clenched in sudden rage.

"Aye aye aye, calm down," he said. "All's well. I'm a man of my word, but we still need to talk about this."

"What do we need to talk about?"

Gillison absently rubbed his elbow and Morgan remembered that Jasso had said he had a scar there.

"Jareth's World ain't what it used to be," he said. "It's dangerous now."

"It was dangerous before."

"Those ships that landed the Brettons had to fight off Hyraxian frigates."

"Good for them."

"Hyrax has a claim to it. Seems they're doing something about it."

"They'll be glad to see us leave then," said Morgan.

"Landing could be tricky."

Morgan's fists clenched again. Gillison noticed.

"Worry not, we'll do our best. I'd not be getting you or your friends cross with me."

"There may not be many to rescue."

"Truth there," said Gillison. "Word is, the ground is not less deadly than the sky."

"Plague?"

"Was there plague?" Gillison's eyes grew large.

"Not when I was there."

The captain regarded him for a moment, then said, "What I meant was that out of those two hundred souls, half are rumored to be dead already."

"So it could be plague?"

"Or natives."

"I doubt that. I'm sure the queen's spymaster sent enough guns to secure the fences."

"Aye," said Gillison, rubbing the stubble on his chin. "That tracks.

But still, it's a dangerous place for some reason. We'll not be staying there longer than we have to."

"Just long enough to get my people and go."

"Aye, there, about that."

"What?"

"We're sailing the well to get there faster. That should please you."

"And?"

"And, Governor, your chore is the only work we have there."

"What?"

"We're gentlemen of fortune," said Gillison. "Hyrax is in a dither evacuating Silangan. Lots of easy targets there waiting for us to call."

"I know and care nothing about Silangan," Morgan said.

"Be that as it may, you and your folk will be our guests until we're done with our other work."

"Sailing the well, you say?" said Morgan.

"Aye, it's faster."

"And safer?"

"It's away from watching eyes," said Gillison. "Not sure about safer."

"We'll be well treated and fed?"

"As agreed. I'll bring you back to home as soon as we can."

Morgan tried to understand the loyalties of such men as Gillison, on one hand afraid to offend a traitor like him, while at the same time attacking Hyraxian shipping. He could not know the man's sins. Jasso might have contacted him without divulging his race. He probably had. Why else would he tell him that he planned on raiding Hyraxian ships? Lies and obfuscations. A blessing. Just get his people off that horrible planet alive and he'd work out the rest later.

"All's well, Captain. Your hospitality is appreciated."

Gillison seemed to be pleased with that, and toasted the endeavor in the two-thirds gravity of the crew deck.

The *Moonlight* made the trip in under two months, less than a third of the time their last trip had taken – damn Captain Upor to hell and damn his handlers. Damn Brett. Damn Enskari.

And he had.

Morgan found himself unable to pray to his or any god. He felt his soul sapped and bleeding, hoping – for that was all he could muster, and not much of that – hoping that he would be strong enough to finish. It would kill him, he was sure. God had not evolved. He still required sacrifice for favor. So be it. His life was forfeit.

Over Jareth's World, Gillison flew into a low orbit and shot his anchor from there to speed things up. He'd rely on thrusters and a vibrant solar stream to buoy the *Moonlight* to keep the thread taut between rings and atmosphere.

"No signs of smoke," said Captain Gillison, peeking down the hatch from the steerage deck. "Is that good or bad?"

Morgan didn't answer.

Gillison said, "Looks like the shoals are up. Be landing soon. Be quick about it."

The weather was mild and the waves not so rough as Morgan remembered. Perhaps it was the skill of the crew trained in speed and efficiency, there to work and not delay.

He felt the ship slow and then stop, felt it bob in the current.

"Board the dinghies," came the order from Gillison's deck. "Any closer we'll run aground."

Morgan unstrapped himself, feeling the comfort of restraint leave his shoulders like a final embrace. How was it he longed to have fewer choices than more, longed for confinement, for the weight of decision to be removed, responsibility taken away? How could such a simple thing as a seat belt be so philosophical?

He climbed the hatch and outside found the crew had already lowered four little boats.

"This won't be enough," said Morgan. "We were over a hundred."

"We can make several trips," Gillison said, looking out over the abandoned shore. "If there are still that many."

"And a baby," said Morgan.

He'd not known his granddaughter, Diane. He'd barely made her acquaintance before he had abandoned the colony. Perhaps that was why the colonists had chosen him to go: he had an unquestionable vested interest in returning with help. Not only was his entire fortune wrapped up in the endeavor, but his entire future was as well. The future of his family – his legacy – had been left upon that shore in the form of a mewling baby girl.

Each boat could hold a dozen souls but was only manned now with four to keep room for the hoped-for survivors. All the sailors were armed with musket and sword. They rowed forward, casting worried glances over their shoulders at the beach every two or three strokes.

"How far inland was the fort?" asked Gillison, squinting at the shore.

"Not far. A few hundred meters."

"So we should see the walls by now."

Morgan studied the line of windblown trees, tried to recall the paths that led to the palisade but couldn't detect it.

"Captain!" A boatswain from one of the other dinghies waved and pointed back to the landing craft.

"What is it?" asked Morgan

"It's a relayed signal from the buoy," he said. "We have company aloft."

"We're not turning around?" said Morgan. "The shore is right there!" He nearly threw himself out of the boat, pointing to the land.

"Calm yourself there, Governor," said Gillison. "We'll land."

Ten minutes later, Morgan tumbled out of the boat and into the surf.

He searched the tree line and then shrieked when he recognized a path. Here, on this beach, had been Upor's camp, the place they dallied while colonists begged to be taken up the coast to Placid Bay.

"There," said Morgan. "This way." He slogged forward and felt the sand give beneath his feet.

Gillison followed behind along with most of his men, muskets charged and ready. Morgan caught the worry on the captain's face and ran up the trail.

"Don't—" called Gillison. "Ah, whatever." He trotted to catch up.

Morgan burst into the clearing with the fort.

It was abandoned and not recently so. The posts of the stockade had rotted and fallen. The wind had pushed most over, but many were outright gone as if taken. The houses were all crumbled, and strange slithering animals with goatlike eyes scurried out as he looked in.

He saw they'd constructed new buildings, only a few – surprisingly few – and these were collapsing like the rest. The row of stocks was new, centered in the courtyard, stained and worn.

He staggered forward, dragging his legs like they were lead, his feet cold iron, his heart a cracking stone.

He found the cemetery. It was crowded with wooden posts and thorny weeds. Half the grave markers were blown down and broken, the rest eroded and moss-covered. By his quick count, most of the colony was there.

He scanned the names he could read and fumbled through the timbers. Behind him he could hear Gillison giving orders.

"Search the place," he said to his men. "Be quick and thorough. But mostly be quick."

"I can't read these," Morgan cried. "Someone help me read these."

Gillison came over and picked up a plank.

"Weather's got to them pretty bad," he said. "This moss is angry in its attachment to the wood. Eats it right up."

"Look for the names Diane and Daria." Morgan threw himself to the next grave and pulled the marker out of the dirt. He attacked it with his fingers, rubbing away moss and grime, tearing his nails as he did. He revealed some letters but had to wipe his eyes to read them.

"A lot of graves here, Governor," said Gillison.

A long low bellow boomed from the woods. A trumpeting – possibly from an animal, but then cut off and followed by three more short bursts. It was answered from their right by the same pattern.

"Governor, they're dead," said Gillison. "We have to go."

"Nay!"

"Governor—"

"Nay, this isn't all of them, they—"

His eyes fell on a pair of markers still upright, thick-cut and bearing the elements better than most. Poor carving, quick and uneven. He thought of his assistant, Dagney, the carpenter, and knew he had not made them.

He read the names once, twice, three times, making sure he was seeing them and not imagining. Here before him, beneath his weakened body, were the bones of his daughter, Daria, and granddaughter, Diane, the last of his family, sharing a grave. The end of his line. They'd not made it through the first winter. Tragedy and mercy.

He fell onto his back and stared into the impossibly blue sky, tracing the ring like a cut across the heavens.

"Captain, there's a word carved on the gatepost," he heard someone say.

"What?"

"No word I know," he said. "But in the common language. The letters anyway. P-e-m-i-o-c."

"Governor," said Gillison. "Do you know this word, Pemioc?"

Another trumpet farther off made a new signal, two short and two long.

"It's a native village," he said to the alien sky. How different it was from Enskari's. How full of hope it had once been, before he had seen it in real life. He recalled the poison-black of Nutorn's air and had to admit that above him the firmament was beautiful and pure. A single line of bisecting ring, a moon on the horizon;4 otherwise, it was blue and clear and empty.

"Was that village friendly?"

Morgan laughed, remembering the butchery of Hasin's command, the murder of the chief's daughter, the death of his own people at their hands when they first arrived. "Nay," he said. "Anything but."

"Then I guess we know what got them," said Gillison. "I'm sorry."

"Leave me," Morgan said.

"I don't mean to be cruel, Governor, but we have to go. The sooner the better. You must grieve later."

"Nay," said Morgan. "I mean it. Go. Leave me here."

CHAPTER TWENTY-ONE

Progress comes one death at a time.
Old Earth Proverb

1, Fifth-Month, 939 NE – Palace of the Dockmaster, Iquiani, Maaraw

Some said the liberation happened faster than anyone expected. Others, those in Ursula's company, those who'd spent the last half year battling on the fringes of Iquiani, knew it hadn't happened fast enough. Ursula had a list of dead comrades to measure how long it had taken.

After Slaafaw, it seemed like a minor detail to capture the provincial capital, but the invaders had other ideas. Reinforced from orbit by the city's big elevator, they'd fortified for the siege. Maylo had overestimated the desertion rate of Maarawan soldiers, and to the Liberators' dismay, most of the soldiers they faced had been their own people. Ursula didn't care. She killed them just the same.

The battles were fierce, meters purchased with a hundred lives, street-to-street fighting. House to house, rooftop to rooftop. The casualties mounted on both sides, the off-worlders were more than the Liberators, but still it was costly.

The time was well spent, however. While she and the Liberators sieged what had become the capital of the off-world resistance, Iquiani, the rest of the population capitulated without much work as the long-promised slave uprisings finally materialized. The time it took to starve out the city gave the rest of the planet time to be conquered. Rich folks evacuated with all the treasure they could steal. When they were gone, old slave masters found planet pride or were themselves whipped to death by their former property. Maylo had delayed assaults for a week to encourage the off-worlders to leave, but when the power vacuum in the outskirts begged for attention, he'd finally shot a resupplying elevator pod out of the sky. That had brought the city to surrender.

After the garrison in Slaafaw surrendered, Maylo tried to keep Ursula safe in the rear. He tried to claim her age – still four months shy of fifteen – was a reason not to fight. But she'd been fighting already, and besides, there were younger people in the ranks, so that excuse fizzled up fast. He tried to say she was too short, and a female – the last of her family – but each excuse was tossed aside by her and the command staff who didn't like favoritism. Her injuries were minor, the rape quick and nothing she hadn't already experienced. She was fit and fighting before they were out the door of the garrison that day, but she was still sent on medical leave for two months – two months! It would have been longer had she not complained so much and so aggressively that her doctor ordered her back to the front. Maylo kept her close, surely thinking that the end of the war was near. Then, as the weeks wore on and the fighting continued, her skill with a scoped Gauss gun was too valuable an asset to withhold, and Maylo finally let her loose. She was attached to a sniper unit and paired with an Enskaran spotter named Debbie, a sergeant ten years her senior, who'd fled her planet when her family was killed during some religious troubles there.

Their patrols would last between three and twelve days. They moved under cover of night, green-lit auroras showing them new nests from which to 'break the enemy's morale'. They'd averaged five kills a day for the last four and a half months. The defenders in Iquiani dubbed her 'the child of death' and put a fifty-thousand-dollar bounty on her head.

She wondered if the bounty was still in effect after today and who was offering it. She'd ask if she got a chance. Maylo would know who to talk to. She'd see him today, within a few minutes actually, if the surrender ceremony commenced on time.

A fanfare from outside the Palace of the Dockmaster announced the coming of the Liberator contingent. Below her in the rotunda milled the surviving local officials, generals and nobles with retinues and weeping slaves. One of them supposedly was the mayor. His palace was a pool of slag after their plasma cutter had finished with it. No idea how many had died inside, but she had picked off fifteen herself as the hardened structure turned to bubbling death and wept the walls in on them. The Palace of the Dockmaster was nicer anyway, bigger, richer, and overlooking the city, harbor, and elevator from a high hill on the outskirts.

The nobles had dressed in their finest costumes. From the portico above the rotunda, looking down upon the assemblage, Ursula saw uniforms from all the worlds. White from Claremond, an admiral of some kind, she thought. Tan from Lavland – a colonel was all that was left after their early evacuations. There was a general from Enskari in bright burgundy with heavy epaulettes – Debbie had pointed that one out to her. The Hyraxian black and silver were well known but the officers from Temple had shiny gold coats and caps. She'd seen a lot of silver-haired soldiers in the last month and killed most of them. Temple had an army now, apparently; who knew?

"Is that a Temple general?" asked Ursula.

"A field marshal," said Debbie. "Higher than a general. I heard he's a cousin of the prophet himself, a member of the Seventy. He arrived just last week."

"Just in time to surrender."

"Judging by his expression, that wasn't the plan."

Ursula had no reason to doubt Debbie's identification. She was plugged in to the rumor mill. The field marshal's uniform was a cross between a Hyraxian general's and high minister's robes. Ursula didn't think the mash-up worked aesthetically, but it did set him apart from the others, if only for being so strange. She studied him for a while, noticing how he stood the stillest of any of them, practically at parade rest while the others paced nervously about. His silver hair was cut short in monkish fashion and his face was as stoic as his hair. His eyes stared out the doorway with a blank wrath Ursula could sense two stories above.

"I wish those slaves would shut up," Debbie said. "How stupid do you have to be to cry on your emancipation day?"

"I hate them the most," said Ursula. "I can understand those off-worlders, but my people who helped them, who sold us to them – I'd kill them all if I could."

"You better get down there," said Debbie. "Maylo will be here soon."

"Wish you could come. You did as much as I did."

"Hardly." Debbie was five and twenty years old, and though Ursula outranked her, they'd grown to be more like sisters than friends and soldiers.

"Nay, really. You left home to help us. You didn't have to do that."

"I thought I did."

"Why? This wasn't your fight." It was a question she'd skirted around many times but never come out and asked. She'd been half-afraid it would scare her back to her world. Now she asked.

Debbie smiled. "Not in the same way it was yours," she said. "But I couldn't strike in my fight, so I joined yours."

"But it's a different fight."

"Nay. It's the same."

Ursula thought about that for a moment. "My father would have agreed with you."

"But you don't? Now, after all we've been through, you tell me that you don't understand why I'm here?"

Three Liberator guards wrestled down what looked like an elderly butler trying to enter the rotunda. They mashed him hard onto the floor with a crack of breaking teeth. They pulled a hand-flamer out of his coat. The dignitaries waiting to be disgraced by the surrender looked on.

"Think he was coming to kill us or them?" said Ursula.

"You're dodging my question, Captain."

"I guess I understand why you're here. It's about the big picture."

"Aye."

"But big picture means future and I don't think a lot of us can see so far ahead."

"Enough have. You did."

Ursula shook her head. "I'm not sure I can see past today. What's next? Are we going to fight on another world?"

"I don't think this is the end of the fighting here. The off-worlders can't be trusted to leave Maaraw alone. There's no profit in it."

"Then why are they capitulating?"

"Because there's less profit in dying. They'll lick their wounds and come back when they think the time is right. They'll let us fight among ourselves and then restore order."

"Then we should just kill them."

"That would be uncivilized."

"Yep," said Ursula. She'd heard that word bandied around a lot and was frankly sick of it. She didn't even know what it was supposed to mean exactly. "Do you think we'll fall apart like that? Fight among ourselves?"

"Nay."

"Why not?"

"Honestly, Captain?"

"Oh, please lie to me. I'm a big fan."

"The bees," said Debbie.

"What? The bees? That's just a fad. A living piece of jewelry. A political prop to bring the hinterlands under control. How will that make us behave? They're bugs."

Debbie shook her head. "They're more than that."

"I don't believe those stories," said Ursula. The butler was gone and now maids in house livery mopped the blood off the tile floor with rags.

"I believe them," said Debbie. "There was an old woman I knew back home who had one."

"She had a Maarawan bee?"

"Nay, it was from Tirgwenin. We have them too."

Ursula shrugged.

"She was the nicest person I ever knew. She said the bee showed her things. She compared it to a scrapbook. She said she could see her mother's mother's mother's face anytime she wanted."

"How old was she?"

"Not that old," said Debbie with a sneer. "She also said she knew when her granddaughter broke her arm, the second it happened. The bee told her."

"It is a savage who believes in the supernatural," she said, quoting someone. Maybe.

"She also said the people on Jareth's World were experts with them and they talked to her sometimes."

"You're talking about Roy now?"

"She has one."

"So does Maylo."

"Exactly."

Roy was what they called the Tirgwenian who'd joined the command staff. Her real name was Rooiayah, but most found it too hard to pronounce. Their cause had brought partisans from all over the system, but Roy was a complete enigma. She'd come like the others, appearing one day fresh off a ship and seeking to help. Maylo had acted like he knew she was coming and immediately welcomed her into his inner circle. She was one of only three off-worlders he routinely asked for counsel. Like Maylo and those others, she was accompanied by a bee.

"I don't trust Roy."

"Because this isn't her fight?"

Ursula gave Debbie a look but her sergeant didn't flinch.

"Maybe," said Ursula. "But I don't trust those shaman guys who joined us either."

"The ones with bees?"

There'd always been people on their side from the interior, brave men and women, good fighters, who fought alongside them. It made sense. It was their villages the slave raiders attacked. Yet, some of their religious people accompanied them and they had insects. They were simple folk, dirty and wild-looking, and Ursula had assumed the bee was a mark of uncleanliness like lice or ear fungus. She'd never given them much thought, she had her own war to wage, her own demons to exorcise, but after Slaafaw, when Maylo had opened the jar with the bee in it, they'd had a much more prominent place in the army.

"I guess there's a lot I don't understand," Ursula said.

"We'll have time for that now."

The trumpet blared again. They were getting close.

"Sure you don't want to come down with me? I bet no one would say anything."

"Nay, I'm good," said Debbie. "Better view from up here."

"Always is."

Debbie adjusted Ursula's collar. "Keep it buttoned," she said. "At least for the ceremony."

Ursula stuck out her tongue and handed her rifle to the sergeant. "Keep it safe."

She'd been told not to bring the weapon to the ceremony but not having it made her feel incomplete and vulnerable. She'd not been willingly without a weapon since the brick.

Her first real gun had been a Gauss pistol, an expensive thing, but not a great weapon for actual fighting. She had taken it from the master Kaveen whom she had killed with a brick while he slept in his home three days after lighting her schoolhouse on fire.

She had been born into bondage. Her father, Ohginz, was a house slave, an educated man who tutored the Ambridge family's children. When old man Ambridge died, his family moved back to Claremond and gave all their slaves freedom and fifty dollars. Ursula was eight years old then. Six years later, Ohginz had his own two-room schoolhouse and taught the locals for barter and coin. Newly freed slaves could attend for free. Ursula, at fourteen, taught primers, while her father introduced those who could to basic math, map-reading, and his specialty, poetry.

The school ran for half a year before it was burned down, with everyone inside it.

Ohginz had feared it would happen, had predicted it, but still went on. To slow their wrath and assuage their fears, he invited gentry to drop by anytime and promised never to teach slaves to read, which was the law. He didn't. Ursula did. She taught them in their home by candlelight. He always said it was only a matter of time before an educated population, literate freeborn and freed slaves, became a threat to the powerful.

Ursula understood it now. It was the nature of the system to use violence to keep the lower classes ignorant.

The fire killed seventy people, including Ursula's father, mother, and three brothers. She only escaped because she was in the privy addressing her new-woman's time problem when the attackers came.

She saw the horsemen arrive and chain the doors shut before pouring coal oil on the walls. No one inside noticed a thing until flames ran up the clapboard sides like blood ants stirred from a nest. Shouts and calls first. Begging, and prayers. Then the screams.

Windows burst out, from heat and panic. Children were pushed out only to be shot by horsemen. Some tumbled dead to the flames, but most were killed in the opening, their bodies blocking the portal like a gruesome plug. When some managed to climb over and out and ran for their lives to the woods, they were picked off with long rifles – much like Ursula had done to the people fleeing the mayor's mansion earlier this week.

Shaking with rage behind the stinking outhouse, Ursula could do nothing but watch the horror. She never cried. To this day she'd never cried for that. She swallowed her screams and held her tears to keep her eyes clear, to see who was responsible. To witness. To remember. To retaliate.

Kaveen she recognized and he'd been the first.

On her way to his bungalow, she was captured by a middle manager called Seray. He had been part of the raid but hadn't recognized her for who she was when she'd foolishly let herself be seen under the light of the stable door. He raped her in the barn. She didn't scream or fight. Her body went limp, her mind retreated. When he was done, he hit her with a brick and left her for dead in the river. After waking, she washed herself, dressed, and continued her mission.

It was Seray's brick she'd used to kill Kaveen.

Kaveen's master, Turverk, a Lavlandian dandy who owned the land around their school, was next, killed with Kaveen's gun. His wife, child, and three slaves who tried to stop her also died from it. Then it broke. Turverk had a hunting rifle and with that she killed six men from a neighboring plantation who came to check on the family when they missed church. A sheriff from Deatum who came looking for them and two deputies died the next day. A third, however, escaped and Ursula slipped into the hinterlands with the sheriff's musket. She had it still when she heard of the Liberators and rushed to join them outside of the Walsinish plantation.

The Liberators were surprised to hear her story, since she seemed so cheerful, making jokes, smiling, and acting like it was all a picnic. Since then, she'd upgraded her weaponry every chance she got until she had the gun that had made her the child of death – a Claremondian bison rifle. That's what was written on the receipt she found in the box with it. The cattle on Claremond must be fierce creatures indeed if those off-worlders needed a gun like this to kill one from three kilometers away. She wondered if they'd ever even tried to domesticate them.

That rifle was now with Debbie, stashed somewhere on the portico as Ursula went down to meet the Liberator procession. She felt naked without it. Though a ceasefire had been in effect for over a day now, there were still pockets of fighting where crazed third-generation Maarawan slaves resisted their own emancipation. The off-worlders had all capitulated on time, dutifully, but their own people, ignorant and afraid, fought on.

Maylo had encouraged compassion for them, but she couldn't feel sorry for them at all. Stupidity was not an excuse. She had no sympathy for Maarawans who traded their own people's lives. Some their own families. No sympathy from her, no sir. Such parasites were dangerous and culpable – more culpable than their masters – and she did not mourn the massacres when whole communities were erased for being complicit in the system.

Andre Bruin, the mythical figure who'd begun the revolution

before Ursula's time, had made it a custom to allow the slaves to slay their masters after emancipation. Lately, as the war neared its conclusion, Maylo had preached forgiveness and the custom was formally discontinued. Informally, however, it went on as before and Ursula was glad of it. In fact, she'd encouraged it and truly believed that it was the massacre at Bytag last month more than the destruction of the elevator pod that had brought on the capitulation of Iquiani today. After she ordered the soldiers to leave the camp unguarded, the locals swarmed in and claimed their just revenge. Over three hundred dead in four hours, not a soul left standing from a village whose name had been synonymous with child-slavers. Most had been Maarawan conspirators, some 'studs' who raped women to create 'more product', but there'd been eighty notable merchants from off-world waiting to be ransomed. Their deaths had put fear in the hearts of the fighters up here, but the deaths of the Maarawans had put hope in hers.

It was an honor to attend the surrender ceremony. She held the rank of captain, but except for the guards at Bytag and Debbie, she'd never commanded anyone. It was an honorary rank. She was a mascot for the resistance, loved by friends, hated by foes – a symbol – and so had a rank to reflect her importance.

Sobs and moans escaped from behind a closed door as Ursula exited the stairwell on the main floor. She wished she had a gun, a rifle, pistol – a sword even. A brick. A bayonet would suffice. She had the urge to follow the noise, find the servants who mourned their slavery, and deliver them from their new burden of freedom with her bare hands. Instead, she searched for an exit to meet up with the retinue coming up the drive before they entered the hall.

She opened a door, thinking it was to a kitchen, which would have a servants' entrance to the outside. She went in and found herself standing face-to-face with Seray, the man who had raped her back home.

For a long moment she could see nothing but his face echoed in the darkness of that night and glowing in the flames of her father's burning schoolhouse.

"We're almost ready," he said. "We'll be there before they arrive. We still have time."

Ursula came back to herself and took in the rest of the room. There were three other people there besides Seray, two servants dressing him and another officer, sweeping dandruff off his shoulders. They were all Maarawan. Seray wore the rank of colonel, the other man a lieutenant.

"Wait, who are you?" said Seray.

"My God," said the lieutenant. "That's the child of death."

"Who?"

"The sniper," he said. "The war criminal."

Seray studied her face. "Don't I know you? Have we met?"

"They say she shot down a resupply elevator."

"I didn't," she said. "That was a cannon."

"But you are the child of death?" said Seray, squinting at her. "The war criminal?"

"I am a soldier. My name is Ursula."

"That's her," said the lieutenant. "The child war criminal."

The servants stepped back, wide-eyed and worried. The tension in their eyes shifted from her in the doorway to a dresser beside the lieutenant. So that's where she could get a weapon.

"Oh my God," said Seray, shaking his head. "Turverk's place. Last year. You're Ohginz's daughter. I thought you died in the fire."

"I'm surprised you remember me."

"Kaveen. You killed Kaveen. And the others. Was that you?"

She grinned her pleasant smile, the cheerful one everyone liked, but ground her teeth behind it. He had recognized her and not recognized her. Insult to injury? Didn't matter. He was about to die.

She took a casual step toward the dresser but felt a hand drop upon her shoulder behind her.

"Come on, Captain," said General Luft. "We're needed."

"This won't take but a minute."

"That was an order."

She looked in her comrade's eyes and saw an understanding there.

She had no idea how, but she was sure that Luft knew who this man was to her and what she was about to do.

Even so….

"Just a second," she said.

"Nay, come now, Ursula. Today's a day of new beginnings."

"And final endings."

Luft gave her that look she remembered her father giving her. Impatience bordering on disappointment.

Standing behind the general were three soldiers with crossbows and that settled the matter.

Seray seemed to understand what had just happened. He glanced at the dresser where Ursula had been going. "A new day," he said.

"Let's see what tomorrow brings," she said.

"War makes monsters of us all," said Luft. "To go forward, we must look forward."

"And I am really looking forward to meeting you again," Ursula said to Seray.

The look from the general was hard and exasperated, but when Ursula winked at him before skipping out the door, he broke into laughter. "You are a thing to treasure," he said.

"And I have," she heard Seray say as they shut the door.

So he did remember.

She pulled up and was about to wrestle a crossbow away and return, when Luft put his arm around her. "I've never seen you like this," he said.

"I have to kill that man. Please move aside."

"Nay, Ursula. Maylo said not to let you."

"How the hell would he know?"

"He knows."

"And does he know why I have to kill him? Do you?"

"I don't. But I think he does."

"How? The damn bees? Right right right. Bugs are keeping a vile murdering rapist alive."

"I think so."

"Not buying it. Give me gun. A crossbow. That fancy sword you have. I'll be two seconds. I can take them all."

"Us too?"

She looked at the soldiers, tall swarthy inland types with arms as big as church posts bursting the seams of their uniforms. "Probably," she said.

Luft laughed. "I've missed you."

"Please, Luft."

"Nay."

"He deserves it."

"Maylo said not today. Not now. You don't need more heat."

"What does that mean?

A dark shadow crossed his face. "Let's go."

"What aren't you—"

The fanfare made her jump. It was right outside.

Luft gestured for her to lead the way and the soldiers fell in behind her. Outside, they rounded the corner and sprinted up to the procession.

Maylo waited just at the gate, his face sullen and heavy. Behind him were generals and councilors, Roy, of course, and two shaman whose names she really should remember but couldn't.

When Maylo saw her, he dropped his dour expression and beamed with joy. "Ursula! I am so glad we're here together at the end." He glanced at Luft. "All good?"

"All good," he said.

"Okay then. Here we go."

The band struck up a martial and tinny song, something Ursula didn't know. She hoped it hadn't been chosen as the new national anthem.

All around her were Liberator soldiers. Those on guard scanned the grounds while those who weren't on duty passed pipes of strongweed and drank redberry wine, their eyes following the ragtag procession of freed slaves and radicals, imported partisans and fed-up patriots. Ragged or uniformed, decked out in borrowed livery or half-naked like the shaman, they walked up the steps to the palace.

Maylo glanced back at Ursula several times and once his bee lit from his brow and headed for her. It circled around her once, twice, and then returned. Maylo's expression deflated a bit, but she shrugged and smiled and that brightened him again.

It said something about how lucrative the slave trade was that the Palace of the Dockmaster was so fine. They walked up a flight of marble stairs to a wide patio where the ceremony would be. It was big enough to hold a platoon of fifty men. At the top, they passed between two massive fluted columns made of red-streaked stone, quarried from two hundred kilometers down the coast. The brochure she found describing the palace mentioned that two hundred slaves had died in the effort. One for each kilometer. The pamphlet made it sound quaint. The exterior walls were made of carved coral rock, she hadn't noticed from the inside. The house stood eight kilometers from the ocean up the highest and steepest hill over the bay. The blocks were a meter thick and twice as long and had to be cut out of the ocean depths before being dragged up here. No mention of how many slaves that had cost, but it couldn't have been easy. Or cheap. Or quick. The massive bronze doors were engraved with filigree inlaid with precious metals and gems. If this was a dockmaster's house, she couldn't imagine what the palace of Prince Brandon was like on Hyrax. She wondered if she'd ever know.

The contingent stopped at the top of the patio – the bay behind them, the door in front. It had the sense of high parade and formality but it was lost on Ursula, who'd already been inside with the other soldiers securing the place.

The trumpets continued the dumb song and Ursula sidled up beside Maylo as they all waited for the big doors to swing open and the city to be officially handed over.

She didn't want to hear about magic or hunches, or how he knew things he had no business knowing. No time for that. Standing on tiptoes behind him, she whispered in his ear, "Why did you send Luft to stop me?"

"I wanted to see if we could start there," he said.

The music was coming to a rallying crescendo.

"Start the healing process?" she said, sarcasm thick in her voice.

"Aye, exactly," he said. "And I hate the thought of you having more blood on your hands."

"I have no more than you," she said.

"Much less," and there was a sorrow in his voice that came naturally and true.

"Some of these bastards have it coming," she said. "Truly."

"I know. We know."

"So we're just going to let—"

The music cut off and Ursula swallowed her last words.

There was a long prescribed moment of silence. While they waited the interminable twenty seconds, Maylo suddenly turned around and knelt before her.

"You saved me, Ursula. You were my genius. My love of you opened the universe."

"And the universe says forgive and forget?"

"It will eventually."

"Now?"

"We're trying."

The doors swung open.

Maylo stood and straightened to face the approaching off-worlders.

Ursula stepped back. She caught Roy watching her and smiled, which was her defense. The woman from Jareth's World smiled back and nodded knowingly. Ursula felt exposed. If Maylo had known so much with one bee, what about the several hovering around Roy's head?

The yellow woman blinked her double eyelids and Ursula must have made a face because she laughed. "We'll all be like this one day," she whispered. "Double eyelids. Natural evolution from Coronam."

"We'll all be yellow too?"

"Nay. I think your people will be tan."

"But two eyelids?"

"That's what our scientists say."

"You have scientists?"

"Shh," said Luft behind them.

Out came six uniformed soldiers with unloaded and uncharged muskets – they'd made damn sure of that. One each from Lavland, Claremond, Hyrax, Enskari, Temple – which still looked weird – and of course a traitorous Maarawan. The Maarawan was Seray.

Behind them came local nobles and off-world dignitaries. The dockmaster whose palace this was looked fat and frightened. Ursula couldn't place his ancestry, part Lavland and Hyraxian maybe. Not Maarawan for sure.

The Temple field marshal stood back with the civilians, present but separated from the unpleasantness. A wind carried the smell of rich cologne and it cloyed in Ursula's throat as unnatural fragrances always did. No flower smelled like that. It was like an alcoholic rose had puked on a musk otter. The thought made her smile.

The colonel from Lavland stepped up. She noted the pale greenish hue to his skin she'd always associated with greed and cruelty. He'd tanned a bit from being on Maaraw so long and Ursula squirmed in hate. Tan was theirs. Roy had said so.

Maylo stepped up to meet him.

The two men silently regarded each other. The colonel's eyes fell on the bee orbiting Maylo. In the back of the procession, Ursula saw the Templer field marshal's face go red as he too noticed the bee. The rest of the group all stared at Roy, who looked as out of place there among the dignitaries as a rock on a china shelf. Ursula could see the confusion and worry on their faces and liked it.

"You bring a war criminal to this?" said the colonel.

All eyes found Ursula and her grin vanished.

"That child is responsible for the massacre at Bytag. I assume you are surrendering her as a sign of goodwill."

They knew it was her. And if they knew, Maylo knew. Maylo knew everything.

Everything fell into place then. She understood why she hadn't been allowed a gun, what Seray's lieutenant had meant in the dressing room, why Debbie was kept away. She was a sacrifice for the peace. The child of death, whose death would bring on reconciliation. There was no escape. Her survival had to be forfeit for the reckoning.

At that moment, Ursula did something she thought herself incapable of. She cried.

Sobs poured out of her as the ground rushed to meet her, her legs joining the betrayal.

Luft caught her and lowered her into his lap.

Ursula's head spun. She wanted to beg for life, to apologize for all the deaths she had meted out, but could not. She was not sorry. She was not ashamed. She was only overwhelmed then by the death of her family – her father, mother, and brothers, screaming for deliverance against flames that had already killed them. It was the mourning for the lives they might have had, the sorrow for the cost of her own. Potential removed and motion set in place.

"You must have a death wish if you want to open those accounts now," said Maylo.

The colonel sneered.

Maylo regarded him with a stern expression. "I think your side has more blood on it than ours. A few centuries' worth."

The colonel glanced about him, seeing Ursula crying like the child she appeared to be, and the soldiers with loaded guns and accusing eyes watching him.

He snapped his heels and stood at attention. He saluted Maylo with a crisp snap of his wrist and dropped his hand to his sword.

With similar efficiency, he withdrew it and handed it Maylo, handle first.

"The city is yours," he said.

Ursula wiped her eyes and saw him reach out to take the sword.

"I accept—"

His words were cut off while his eyes stared into some middle distance.

Ursula thought that the sword handle had been poisoned but he hadn't touched it yet. She looked for someone to give the order to mow the bastards down, but all she saw was the same blank stare Maylo wore reflected on Roy's face, and the shaman's, and Charlie's, who she saw now also had a bee. The bees were all in flight, not one on a collar or shoulder as often happened, but all in tight orbits.

Maylo turned and looked toward the city.

"Down!" he yelled.

Soldiers they were, so to a man, the Liberators fell flat to the ground just as the first plasma bomb exploded over the city.

A shockwave of heated air rolled over Ursula as she buried her face into the stone, keeping her mouth open for the pressure as she'd been taught. She felt her hair catch fire, smelled the fetor of melting rock and steel, evaporated ocean, and newly dead things.

Another blast followed the first, this one closer. It blew up the hill and shattered the columns of the portico, ripping the roof off the palace and extinguishing her burning head in a rush of killing air.

They stayed down for another minute until Maylo spoke again. She heard him as if from far away, a whisper against the ringing in her ears. "I think that's it," he said. "It's safe to get up."

Roy had a long cut above her ear that bled down her shoulder. Maylo was dusty but all right, as were Luft and Charlie, but many of the soldiers farther from the edge of the hill did not rise.

Ursula saw the city of Iquiani in flames. Water rushed into a vaporized crater that had been the bay. She wondered if the water would roll into town and put out the fires. It would be cool to see.

A purple light flashed in the distance up the coast and then a moment later, another one beyond that. There were towns that way, cities and ports. Liberated communities. Intact and alive until then.

"The bastards are dropping plasma bombs," said Luft.

"Aye," said Maylo, watching the horizon as flash after flash annihilated whole settlements from orbit.

Ursula looked over to where the surrendering contingent had been. They had not heeded Maylo's orders. Many were dead. The Lavlandian colonel didn't have his head. Or his sword. Many others were dead and most were buried beneath the rubble of the ruined house.

Ursula called to a couple of soldiers but they couldn't hear her. She waved and yelled. Then she saw Debbie running toward her. Such a strange day, she thought.

"Captain, are you all right?"

"I am," she yelled over the ringing in her head. "Get some soldiers and police these creeps." She pointed to the dignitaries, who wriggled like worms beneath the dust.

Debbie nodded and ran to get some men.

Ursula stepped over blocks of debris and hot dust, melted marble and coral stone. She saw that the field marshal was missing an arm and most of his scalp but was still alive. She'd seen worse. If somebody cared to help him, he could live.

After a minute of searching, she found Seray pinned beneath some rubble and killed him with a brick.

CHAPTER TWENTY-TWO

From this arises the question whether it is better to be loved rather than feared, or feared rather than loved. It might perhaps be answered that we should wish to be both: but since love and fear can hardly exist together, if we must choose between them, it is far safer to be feared than loved.
Niccolò Machiavelli, *The Prince*
Old Earth, 1513

14, Fifth-Month, 939 NE – Venison Hall, Royal Hunting Lodge near Soria, Hyrax

Tarquin left the apostle in the restroom throwing up Temple wine and Hyraxian gin. D'Angelo's drinking was worse than ever, but no one seemed to care. The real work on Hyrax was done by Minister Rendelle and the planet's closest representative to the celestial throne was at best ceremonial, at worse an embarrassment. This far from the capital, he'd thrown all pretense aside and indulged in Prince Brandon's cellars all night with one of the housemaids.

As a purger this put Tarquin in a situation. His duty was to the church, to the greater moral edification of mankind, but this was about politics. He hated politics. Politics was compromise. Politics was beneath the noble work of the church. Politics was capitulation. There'd been a time, he'd been told, when D'Angelo was as virtuous as any of the apostles. Rendelle had said to pity him, that his fall should serve as example.

Tarquin had met most of the apostles, half at least, and though several were upright and righteous men, most seemed to be more D'Angelo than Eren VIII. It disgusted him, as he knew it did his prophet. The Servant of God Most High had surrounded himself with better men, new advisors and counselors, and he worked God's plan around the rot he'd inherited. Tarquin was sure once the moment was right, and he felt it coming soon, the prophet would turn on these false holy men and make the church right.

In the meantime, Tarquin was stationed on Hyrax.

Not liking the court's decadence, he'd spent his time alone. His thoughts often went to Maaraw and the death of the heretic Bruin, but also he'd find himself remembering the attack on Enskari, standing beside Admiral Clelland, the man who would be damned. He considered they were martyrs: one complete, the other near. He'd not known what to do with these thoughts and didn't like the parallels that intruded into his mind. Bruin was a heretic, Clelland a soldier. There could be no comparison, and yet he kept trying.

He found a book of spiritual thought penned six hundred years earlier by a Hyraxian calling himself Gamley the Monk. It was a treatise on the purpose of man and the place of faith. In it, he proposed a unification of mankind for a single purpose. This he summed up in the simple but compelling motto of 'one faith, one king, one law'. Tarquin could not help but see in this the goal of Brandon's ambition but also the holy motivation of the prophet's own office.

Tarquin left the retching apostle in the privy. Perhaps God was indeed working through the man, he thought. He'd made him this way to ease Tarquin's work. Even as a high purger, he could not work above an engaged apostle, but as he was not engaged, he had only Minister Rendelle to contend with, whom he outranked.

Prince Brandon's hunting lodge was not the opulent pleasure palace of his court in Alameda and most of the retinue had remained there, which suited Tarquin, who liked the chill of an unseasonably cool spring.

Supposedly the court had moved for the hunting season, but even Tarquin knew it was too early for that. Enskari was the real reason. Though an attack had been fought off, there was still danger of another, and the capital city was the prize target. Moving the prince just made sense. Soria, for all its recent history of attempted assassination and retribution, was now one of the best fortified retreats in Brandon's holdings, with a full battalion of personal bodyguards housed in the new barracks on the south lawn.

Brandon requested everyone to join him at dawn. Tarquin had tried to rouse D'Angelo but had only succeeded in chasing off a naked maid and bringing up the prince's wine. He should leave such things to Minister Rendelle, but Brandon's invitation had a certain important ring to it, and still suffering under his oaths of fealty, he'd made the effort for the apostle. Never again.

"High Purger," said Rendelle in the hallway. "Blessed be."

"And to thee, Minister."

Rendelle looked behind Tarquin down the hall. "Have you tried to wake him?"

"Aye."

"I take it he won't be attending the morning event."

"Nay," said Tarquin. "I wouldn't look for him at lunch either."

"For the best," said the minister.

"For the best," agreed Tarquin.

When Tarquin first arrived on Hyrax, he'd felt intimidated by Rendelle. The man moved with a grace and guile that Tarquin could only admire. Here was a man of politics, truly placed in his role. D'Angelo's failings were Rendelle's strengths. It was here that he understood the meaning of 'the power behind the throne'. Tarquin was a blunt instrument compared to Rendelle's scalpel. The apostle's assistant was often compared to the bitch queen's spymaster, Nolan Brett. Tarquin had first thought that an insult, horrified that anyone would compare a man of God to that faithless slut's lapdog, but as he watched the man work, hearing reports from Enskari and home and around the system, seeing a broader battlefield than the narrow spiritual one he knew, Tarquin began to appreciate it. Appreciation turned to admiration to gratitude a few months before, when the prophet needed ships.

"Your prophet asks and so you will obey." Tarquin had stood at the foot of the royal dais in his full regalia. He'd known enough to do that, to wear the weight of his office as he made the demand.

"I think you forget yourself," said Prince Brandon. "You stand before me, Prince of Hyrax in my throne room, in my palace, upon my planet. Obedience is to me."

"Temple, the seat of the father of the church, has called for ships to attack Maaraw. It is a holy demand. I have shown you the writ."

D'Angelo was in the room that day with Rendelle. The apostle was mostly sober and watched the proceedings with horror as Tarquin set God against king.

"I have had greater men than you flayed for raising their voice to me."

"I do not fear death. I serve God."

"You serve the prophet on Temple. This is Hyrax. I rule—"

"At the sufferance of God."

Brandon stared at the purger for a moment, stunned at being interrupted. Tarquin felt the guards in the courtroom tensing up, moving in. He'd gone too far. Though he did not fear death, he feared failing his prophet.

"We are all on the same side," said Rendelle from the sidelines.

"Why is it that a purger speaks for Temple when an apostle is in the room?" asked Brandon.

This was the heart of the issue and the answer was twofold. Brandon answered the first one himself.

"Are you indisposed, Apostle D'Angelo?"

"I am, Your Majesty. I suffer from an intestinal ailment."

"Does the purger speak for Temple?"

Rendelle spoke when the apostle looked flustered. "He does, Prince Brandon. At direct request from Eren VIII."

Brandon cast a look at Tobias, his closest advisor, what would be called on Enskari an 'Ear of the king', but here was 'Minister', to the confusion of churchgoers and bureaucrats alike.

Tobias nodded.

Tarquin understood that to mean that his communication from the prophet had been intercepted. They might be on the same side, but he was not among friends.

Brandon looked at D'Angelo and then back at Tarquin. "All right," he said. "I accept you speak for the prophet, but I must decline."

"It is your sacred duty," said Tarquin.

"We don't think the prophet told you to insult us, or tell us our place." The shift to the formal pronoun carried with it a weight of threat Tarquin had not known he could feel.

"Nay," said Tarquin, bowing. "I seek only to fulfill my master's wishes."

This obsequiousness defused some of the tension.

"You are zealous, High Purger Tarquin," said Brandon. "You are a hero of the Enskaran campaign, trusted envoy of the prophet, friend of this throne. We forgive you your eagerness."

"You are kind," said Tarquin.

Brandon said, "We haven't the men or ships or arms for His Holiness's new crusade. Please remind Eren VIII of recent events."

"We lost an elevator to the Enskaran—"

"We lost three," said the prince. "Temple can and must defend herself with the weapons she has. You are in little danger. The war is fought here."

"We seek not defense ships, but attackers," said Tarquin, raising his voice. This point was made clear in the earlier briefing with Minister Tobias. Tarquin's frustration might be justified, but not his etiquette. Theoretically, purgers had power over all the Saved, but he knew enough politics to know Brandon was beyond his reach. He could get a peasant killed or a merchant flogged on the spot for disobeying, but rank had its privileges and here his high purger sash was no weapon of authority; it was a thin shield at best.

"My lords," said Rendelle. "May I approach?"

"Aye," said Brandon, glaring at Tarquin. "Your counsel would be welcome."

Rendelle knelt quickly before the throne and whispered in Tarquin's ear. "I don't know what this is about, but I believe it is important. Is that true?"

"Aye."

"Can you share with me the urgency?"

"Not without the prophet's consent."

"Will he give it?"

"Nay."

"Do you understand it? Is it truly this serious or are you merely a zealot following orders?"

"I do as my prophet asks." Tarquin's retort was louder than a whisper and he flushed to realize it too late.

"I'm a practical man, High Purger. My question was not an insult."

Tarquin closed his eyes and calmed himself. "Minister Rendelle," he said slowly, "I have personal experience with this threat and it goes far beyond the squabbles of courts and countries. The prophet speaks for all civilization when he asks for this."

"Blessed be," said Rendelle.

"And to thee."

"Prince Brandon of Hyrax," began Rendelle, "the prophet would have your assistance for a holy crusade."

"And I said, Hyrax is not now in a position to help."

"Perhaps if Temple could allay the costs?" Economics, the blood of politics. The minister was shrewd.

"Allay the costs?"

"We understand the men cannot be spared. The ranks need refreshing, and that will take time. Temple is raising her own army."

"We've heard," said Brandon.

Tobias looked on.

"We lack warships," said Rendelle, glancing back at Tarquin for confirmation.

He nodded assent.

Rendelle was quick to understand. "Might the holy planet borrow a few to see the work begun?"

"And allay the costs?"

"And then some," said Tarquin, sure he could get any amount.

"Ship and crew?" said Brandon.

"Hyraxian ships and captains," said Rendelle. "Only the best will do in service of God and the prophet."

"Just to subdue Maaraw?" said Brandon, showing that he had indeed been briefed.

Rendelle looked at Tarquin, who begrudgingly nodded.

The order had come to Tarquin in a letter in a diplomatic pouch delivered to him by a Lavlandian acolyte with eager eyes. When Tarquin opened the missive, he felt the same awe that the acolyte must have felt. It was a handwritten letter from the Prophet Eren VIII himself – his writing, his hand, pen on holy paper – speaking directly to him from his throne atop all men. He read it and reread, held it, admired it, memorizing the great man's handwriting, clear and sharp. He could not keep the letter, of course, he was to destroy it immediately, lest it fall into the wrong hands. Though Hyrax and Temple were as aligned as any two worlds had ever been, the prophet knew politics and trusted prudently. He trusted Tarquin to be his agent in this. The task was to get attack ships first and foremost. Troops if available, war supplies if possible.

The real enemy is the real secret, the prophet had written. *We must not let this be known, panic would follow. The evil one has sown this seed on all the worlds and many have already fallen to its influence. We must not let it be known that we have seen through the veil to the real danger. Tell no one.*

He'd asked for an immediate audience and was summoned to brief Tobias, where Tarquin carefully walked around the threat. It wasn't easy. He told him only that Maaraw was the target, nothing about the eldritch bees.

"Let me guess," Tobias had said. "Temple traders demand action against the Maarawan savages since the other civilized worlds are distracted fighting among ourselves?"

Tarquin nodded at his assumption. "I know little of commerce, Minister Tobias."

Now, Rendelle said to Brandon, "Maaraw must be pacified. Lend us a few of your mighty ships and Temple will bear the cost."

Brandon rubbed his neck and rolled his head to free the tension, then glanced back at a minister, a man in official robes, not a uniform. The man gave the prince a little nod and Tarquin figured him to be a treasurer.

"I think we could spare a few ships, for a time," said Brandon. "We'll find a couple and fix a fee."

"You are gracious and wise," said Rendelle.

"Blessed be Prince Brandon!" said Tarquin, raising his arms in divine supplication and summoning the power of his office.

And just like that, for gold and not for God, the prophet got his warships.

Politics.

★ ★ ★

"I'll just make sure the apostle is comfortable," said Rendelle. "I'll meet you outside."

"Blessed be, Minister Rendelle."

"And to thee, High Purger."

Tarquin avoided Prince Brandon after that, letting time heal the insults he had levied. No one missed him and he did not miss the petty intrigues of the court, which were the day-to-day burden of the institution. How the prophet in his infallible wisdom could tolerate anything like this was beyond him. The time would come when it would be righted, he told himself, the time would come.

For his part in procuring the ships, Tarquin was left on Hyrax. He'd tried to explain that it had been Rendelle, but it didn't matter. In a second letter the prophet thanked him and told him that he alone on that world knew the danger the church faced. He needed him to be there. More would follow.

And so he remained and tried to learn what he could to be useful. He read and reread Gamley's book and thought to improve his politics. There wasn't much of spirit to learn in the halls of Brandon's castles so he shadowed Rendelle, a man of the world in the cloth of heaven. His sins were great – dishonesty, pride, collusion – but they served a higher purpose. In his firelit meditations, Tarquin came to understand that God had given Rendelle these traits and put him here to help this holy cause. God was great; his power manifest.

There were few men in Brandon's court who Tarquin put in the same league as Rendelle. There was the prince himself, of course, and Tobias seemed shrewd. They were wary and quick. Seeing Lady Vanessa Possad in the doorway, he had to include her among the perspicacious.

"High Purger Tarquin," she said and curtsied low. "Good morning, and blessed be."

"And to thee," he said. "I see you have cut your hair. Keeping it short?"

"It is a rare man who notices a woman's hair," she said. "But aye, I think the prince may have use of me again off-world. Long hair may be the fashion in court, but it is a nightmare in space."

"You are different from the others," he said. "A credit to your sex."

"You are kind."

They passed out into the morning air, moving across the front courtyard to where people were assembling farther out and some tents had been erected. They fell at discreet distance among others, pockets of nobles and courtiers summoned to attend. Some of these had not been to bed yet from the night before. Others looked haggard and sleep-deprived, their clothes half-fastened in haste.

Lady Vanessa paused and regarded Sir Tom Kolbert, Prince Brandon's raucous friend. He looked terrible. He'd been crying, his face was pale. He skulked behind a bush, tipping a bottle and swallowing deep. Tarquin knew the signs of regret but never thought to see them on Kolbert.

"I was sorry to hear about the attack on Temple," said Lady Vanessa. She had an excited gleam in her eye, or maybe it was just reflected dawn light.

"Terrible thing. The heretics know no shame," Tarquin said.

"The presidency came through it all right?"

"Aye, no danger to the ground. Just a cowardly attack on defenseless civilians from orbit."

Lady Vanessa nodded in a way that made Tarquin wonder if he'd said something wrong.

"Any news from Maaraw?" she asked.

"The planet is embargoed. We'll starve them to submission."

"Back into submission," she said.

"Aye."

"I have heard rumors," she said. "Plasma bombs lowered from orbit. Six cities destroyed with seven bombs. Two on Iquiani to destroy the rebel leadership."

"That is the rumor."

"The same thing that Clelland would have done on Enskari."

Tarquin felt uneasy with that. If Clelland had succeeded, the act would have been one of the most murderous deeds ever committed. He and Hyrax would be infamous – remembered and hated for centuries because of it. It had not come to pass, but if the rumors of Maaraw were to be believed, Temple and the prophet Eren VIII now stood in that place.

Lady Venessa shook her head in pity. "Great loss of life. I even heard there was a recently arrived brigade from Temple in Iquiani."

"There are always rumors. Don't believe anything told in rumors."

"It does seem that the news arrived rather too quickly."

"I hadn't thought of that," said Tarquin.

He stopped his step and did the calculations. He knew when the ships left Hyrax and knew generally the travel time. The soonest they could arrive at Maaraw was the first of the month. And yet he'd heard rumors of the attack only last week, on the fifth or sixth. "It's not possible for anyone here to yet know what's happened there."

"Nay."

Tarquin shook his head, ashamed he hadn't thought of it before. Lies. It could be nothing else. Rumors and lies that had sounded plausible but could in no way be true. The fastest ship ever built could not have brought the news to Hyrax from Maaraw so quick. Sailing the well or not. It was impossible. Nevertheless, stories were floating about – terrible, demoralizing lies spread by enemies of the faith to weaken the cause. He could give them no credence and was now more ashamed than ever at apostle D'Angelo, who'd drunk himself sick on the rumors, lamenting the loss of a relative in one of the fabricated fireballs.

"Is this how civilized people make war?" he'd railed the night before. "Incinerating her own children to spite the enemy? My God, we are lost."

If only he'd considered the timing of the rumors, he might have calmed the man then. He might have helped. Instead, he'd been disgusted. Whether the stories were true or not, one did not react that way, not while in the service of God. One did not drink and one did not bemoan.

Politics.

Ahead of them, a caged cart pulled up before a row of the tents. Tarquin thought he saw an Enskaran among the prisoners in the back of it.

"I understand you were upon Enskari for a while, Lady Vanessa," said Tarquin.

"Before the war."

She walked on the gravel path with a practiced muted step that made Tarquin's own tread sound like an ox.

"You were set upon?" he said.

"Aye. A narrow escape."

The prisoners were marched behind a tent.

"Enskari is twice damned," Tarquin said.

"Why twice damned? For assaulting me?"

"For heresy, which is unbounded with the bitch queen in charge, but now also for the inexcusable attack on the holy planet. Many innocents were killed in the skies over Temple."

"Have you visited the House of the Purgers in Almuda?"

"What? Uhm, aye. I have visited."

"The prophet assigned you to the court specifically?"

"Aye, specifically," he said and then realized that might not be something he should voluntarily disclose. A more policed man would have said, *"I go where I'm useful,"* something noncommittal but polite. But she was only a woman, he reminded himself. "Why do you ask about the House of the Purgers?" he said.

"Just curious why we are so lucky to have you so near. You faced the front of the war beside the admiral. You are a hero. It is good to have you here."

"Thank you, lady." He tried to remember if there was anything different about the House of the Purgers there compared to any of the others he'd visited, but couldn't think of a thing. It was a place dedicated to the work of his order, a place to inquire about faith and fidelity. A place to seek the truth. Extract it. To punish and retire the unworthy. The same on all the civilized worlds.

As sun peeked over the horizon, horses galloped up from the far forest.

"I think this may be about the interior minister's new report," said Lady Vanessa.

"And what is that?" said Tarquin.

"Hyrax is running out of wood," she said.

Tarquin looked at her in disbelief.

"It's all the court is talking about. Well that, and those rumors," she said. "Hyrax is running out of forests."

"I don't understand."

"It's being used up at an alarming rate. Coal and oil are running out too."

"What is to be done?"

"Prince Brandon has added trees to the poaching provisions."

"I see."

"All planets will have to do something to protect their forests soon," she said.

At the tents, breakfast was being served buffet-style by Maarawan slaves. They poured hot coffee into dainty china cups, arranged and served pastry and breakfast meats. The prince and his entourage leapt off their horses and joined the party.

"The prophet gave Prince Brandon Jareth's World, though. Lots of trees there," said Lady Vanessa. "He will soon have all the wood he needs. Our forces should arrive there by the end of the month and take it from those Enskari squatters."

"Plenty of resources there," agreed Tarquin.

"And Prince Brandon needs a victory, for his reputation."

"His reputation?"

"It's one thing to be cruel and successful, it's another to be cruel and fail," she said.

Servants escorted them to the food, holding their plates and dishing up what they wanted. Buffet was one thing, self-service another.

Tarquin thought Lady Vanessa would leave him and join the other females, but she did not. Instead, she remained as if he were her escort. There were upwards of a hundred people, not including that many servants and soldiers – most of the household to be sure. The only notable absence was D'Angelo. Rendelle arrived a few minutes later.

They ate with rest, slowly, deliberately tasting confection and treat. Past the shadow of the house, they were bathed in warm sunlight. The summer chill quickly evaporated, and the men removed their heavy coats while women's shawls fell from their shoulders to around their arms.

"I still don't know why we're here," said Tarquin, turning to Lady Vanessa. "Is this some kind of game?"

She was watching the prince across the crowd, and for an instant he thought he saw something dark in her expression. It was gone before it could fully register. She turned to him, wiping her lips with a blue linen napkin.

"I suspect it will be some macho thing," she said. "He's been riding. That always brings out masculine energy in him."

He wondered if she'd insulted her king.

She seemed to understand. "The prince has lady friends," she said. "They gossip."

"What do they gossip?"

"About his 'masculine energy'."

"Oh," said Tarquin.

She turned back to watch Brandon and again Tarquin thought he sensed something there, but it could have just been the clouds and the light.

"Nobles and friends," Brandon said, raising a glass above his head to draw everyone's attention. "Thank you for rising so early."

He swallowed a deep gulp and threw his glass on the ground, where it shattered.

Everyone stared. The violence had startled and scared them.

"I want you all to witness this," he said. "Noble and commoner, minister and whore, come see."

And with that he turned and walked behind the tents.

Tarquin and Lady Vanessa exchanged looks. They handed their cups to a servant and followed the throng around.

"Still think this is about the forests?" said Tarquin.

"Actually, I do," she said.

Five posts were set up in a line across the lawn. Tied to four of them were bound and hooded figures. Between the posts and the audience was a table where five muskets lay charged and waiting.

Realizing what they were about to see, and staring in terror at the fifth and empty post, the people hesitated and had to be pushed forward by those who had yet to behold the threat.

Silently, with soldiers acting as ushers, they were arranged in a rough semicircle behind the table. The women were allowed to hold back, but Lady Vanessa stayed with Tarquin as if he offered her protection. He liked that.

Brandon waited by the table, leaning against it, casually drinking from a new stemmed wineglass.

When they were all settled and watching, Brandon drained his drink and carefully handed it to a servant.

He allowed a moment of silence as the servant disappeared. His eyes panned across the nobles' faces while theirs shifted from him to the posts.

"There is law," said Brandon. "It is law that makes us what we are – a civilized society, the height of humanity, the pillar of the universe."

He ran his fingers though his hair, casually pacing.

"Laws are what separate us from the savages. They are our guide and goal. Laws are the wisdom of the wise controlling the acts of the foolish for the safety of society. Without laws, we are nothing. We cannot turn a blind eye to crime. We cannot abdicate our responsibility by letting others abdicate theirs."

He turned dramatically and raised his hand. It had a theatrical flair to it that brought a *hmph* from Lady Vanessa.

At his signal a soldier walked up the first post and removed the hood from the bound man.

"Here is a poacher," said Prince Brandon. "He was caught with two rootbadgers, cut and dressed, and a cord of our noble forest."

The man was Hyraxian, thin as a rail, eyes wild and searching. He had a gag in his mouth and blood dripped from its corners.

"The penalty for these crimes, per law, is death," said Brandon. "He is poor and needy. The wood was ground fall, the animals pests. But this does not excuse him from the law."

He picked up the first musket, aimed, and fired.

The noise made Tarquin jump; the shot made the man's chest explode. There were gasps and cries, small and shortened. A woman in the back might have fainted. Lady Vanessa turned her face away as the lifeless body slumped, hanging dead by the wrists bound to the post behind him.

Brandon put the musket down and drew up the second gun. He gestured again and the soldiers removed the hood from the next man.

It was the Enskaran that he'd seen dragged out of the cart. His red hair and strawberry-hued skin shone clear in the morning sun. His eyes were swollen, his left leg hung at his hip. Tarquin recognized the signs of torture and also the look of defiance. A martyr at his stake.

"A spy," said Brandon. "Motivated no doubt by allegiance to his master. He has been misled, but that does not excuse him from the law."

Brandon fired and the shot went through the man's torso and caught the post behind him. When his one good leg went out from under him, he took the splintered pole with him to the ground.

Brandon put that musket down and stared out at the people.

Tarquin met the prince's gaze, but Lady Vanessa hid behind a handkerchief, wiping tears from her eyes.

"I am the law," said Brandon. "Maker and enforcer."

He waved his hand again and another hood came off.

Tarquin's heart skipped a beat as he saw there, tied to the post to be executed, a man of the cloth. His tonsure was grown out but unmistakable, a ring of hair adopted by some orders. The robe too was a holy raiment. He'd not recognized it before for its filth. The man was a monk, one Tarquin did not personally know.

"This is a rapist," said Brandon, his stare finding Tarquin and Rendelle in turn. "He raped a peasant girl. No one of worth. No one of title. Just a girl. A child of a farmer."

He picked up the next musket.

Tarquin heard women's sobs behind him, and nearer, the hitched breaths of men. Lady Vanessa shook with terror and pity. He thought he should speak, demand the cleric be taken to the House of the Purgers – his innocence or guilt investigated by the holy church. It was their custom. It was the way. It was the law.

"This man raped a child," said Brandon. "He is a man, a man of the cloth, but a man. This anointed minister has broken his vows. He drinks and fornicates." Here Brandon looked right at Rendelle. "But those oaths were not made to us, his crime today is not there but here. He is a rapist, and minister or no, he is not above our law. And the law says he must die."

He turned and leveled the gun. Tarquin saw Rendelle step forward, or try to, before two men had their hands on his shoulders. Glancing behind him, Tarquin saw two more like them behind him.

Brandon fired and the minister was killed.

"We have too long allowed for compromise in the law," Brandon said, putting down the gun. "There is a time for mercy, there is a place for forgiveness. And there are times where there can be none."

He waved his hand and the crowd gasped in unison.

Tarquin squinted to see what they had all seen, to understand the importance of the next unhooded man. He was well dressed, a noble or rich merchant perhaps. He was Hyraxian. He had not been tortured but like the peasant he had a gag in his mouth and crazed eyes.

Lady Vanessa stared at the man on the post, her eyes large and excited.

"Who is that man?" Tarquin asked.

Brandon raised the fourth musket above his head. "The crime is treason. The proof undeniable. The law is clear."

"Nay, nay!" cried someone in back. "You cannot."

Brandon noted who had spoken but Tarquin could not see.

The prince said, "There is a fifth post, my lords and ladies, my servants and slaves. Let it be there for you. Let it be there to remind you of the law."

Lady Vanessa lowered her handkerchief and stared at the man tied to the post – the scared and whimpering man. The sun caught her eyes and they appeared to twinkle in the light. Stoic and strong, she stared as Brandon aimed the fourth musket.

"That is Eric," she whispered to Tarquin. "Eric Drust. A direct descendant of Andreas Drust the Prime. He is the prince's only brother and last living relative."

CHAPTER TWENTY-THREE

The Great Man Theory was coined on Old Earth in its nineteenth century as a way to understand the currents of society. In this thinking, history can be seen as a series of events done by extraordinary people with extraordinary gifts doing extraordinary things. This idea eventually fell into disfavor and was seen as short-sighted and an aristocratic apology. More sophisticated reasoning proposed that regardless of who did it, eventually certain mileposts would be reached – sooner or later. Thus, we might remember Jareth leading the first human migration to another planet, but if it hadn't been him, it would have been someone else. The tide of human progress dictated that it would happen eventually. We may remember him fondly, but he was a manifestation, not the creator of events.

This is not to say that individuals cannot affect history or leave a personal mark. They can – for good or ill, be hero or villain. But in the tides of evolution, provided we survive, the most anyone can do is slow or speed the process.

Class Lecture by Groo Moreka
Jutap Academy of Human Development
Jutap, Tirgwenin, 107 Arrival (148 NE, 2502 Old Earth Calendar)

11:40, 30, Fifth-Month, 939 NE – Aboard Brandon's Blade *over Tirgwenin*

Intelligence said to expect a colony of civilians on the ground, two hundred farmers in a place called Placid Bay. Some women and slaves. In space they might encounter a supply ship but it would surrender or run at first sight of the man-o-war, being spent from the long passage along the western trade route to the savage planet Tirgwenin.

A single ship was all that was needed to mop up the whole affair, but Admiral Clelland had had a hunch and asked for no fewer than five warships. He'd set out with six only days before the Enskaran attack on Hyrax and had returned in time to help decimate the retreating fleet. From his battle bridge he watched them flee under the sun, knowing that Coronam would take another one in five before they made it home.

Militarily speaking, Hyrax could claim complete victory from Sommerled's attack. The enemy losses were staggering; theirs trivial and less than anyone predicted. Nevertheless, the attack had scared the population.

He didn't understand why the prophet had changed his mind about Enskari and the queen in the first place, but after the Enskaran attack on Temple, he was utterly bewildered by it. The prophet remained adamant that the war cease. It was one thing to buy time to rearm, but this was something else. There were even rumors that Zabel would be accepted back into the faith, recognized as planetary ruler without a king, if she would return to the civilized path of the prophet's leadership.

While diplomats and strategists debated behind closed doors, Clelland continued with the conquest of Jareth's World. There were resources there, silver and gold to replenish Brandon's coffers, lead, iron, and heavy metals to rebuild the fleet, and people, tall and strong, who could fill out his ranks. They had a reputation for being difficult to control, but after a generation or two to breed out the stubbornness, they'd comply. The civilized worlds knew how to dominate the savage ones. Hyrax just had to subdue that planet and everything would be right again. Here the prophet of the Saved could not have been more in agreement.

When Clelland finally departed, he was only allowed two ships: the *Galga*, an armored transport, and the *Modest,* a capable but vulnerable frigate. This was thought to be more than enough since all they had to do was land a few marines and stay in orbit awhile. He got a frigate and an armored transport. Clelland was not pleased with this – too far from home, too many variables not to arrive with overwhelming force. He petitioned his prince, who understood and gave him the planet's flagship man-o-war, *Brandon's Blade*. "A comfortable ship for a long journey," he had said.

And good he had, because no sooner had the armored transport *Galga* dropped the commandos twenty kilometers north of Placid Bay and received confirmation of safe descent, than they had company in the sky. The *Galga* severed its thread and rushed back to the formation.

The sky over Tirgwenin was bare compared to the battlefields he'd fought over recently. There were no station ships or orbiting platforms to identify and delay. No civilians here. Friend and foe were clear. There were six objects over the backward planet: three of his and three of theirs.

The Enskarans appeared over the horizon but under the planet's ring. They'd been hiding in low orbit. They might have been doing a drop but it looked like a planned ambush. They were already in formation, their sails pulled to battle trim.

"Two frigates and a destroyer," said the watch.

"A full destroyer?" said Clelland. "Lovely."

His hunch had been right and his prince wise in heeding it. If he had arrived with only the two, he'd be outmatched beyond hope right now. They'd be fleeing for home to save their tonnage, their men abandoned to their fate on the planet below – without rescue, support, or resupply. A destroyer and two frigates would have been checkmate. Now however, listening to his man-o-war come to battle stations, he knew the fight was fair, if not tilted in his favor.

"Enskaran for sure," said the watchman. "And the destroyer is the *Dragon*."

Clelland felt the hair on his neck rise in excitement. "Aderyn's ship? Could it be? Could Aderyn be here?"

"I thought he retired," said the first officer, Mr. Korbo.

"It is definitely the *Dragon*."

In his briefings before the mission, there had been mention that Admiral Aderyn, the first man to circumnavigate the system, might have a financial interest in the new Enskaran colony. Aderyn was a legendary pilot, a hero of Clelland's and of every spacefarer everywhere.

"The last I heard, Aderyn was still commanding the *Dragon*," said the first officer, consulting a ship's registry. "Aye, here it is."

"He'd be an old man by now," said Clelland.

A quiet spread over the command staff as each man realized they were facing off with a legend.

"Guess what they're signaling to us, sir," said the watchmen.

"The *Pempkin*?"

"Aye. They say, 'Remember the *Pempkin*.'"

"Signal them back," said Clelland, sinking himself into his command chair. "Tell them we do remember, because we were there."

"Aye aye, sir."

The signalman tapped his keys; the ship shifted as sail pulleys turned and tightened.

"Bring the *Modesty* and *Galga* alongside," said Clelland. "Have the *Galga* on defensives phalanx and invite *Modesty* to join us in targeting the destroyer."

"They'll have the first shot," said the weapons master. "They knew we were coming."

"Loose lips…" said Clelland.

"Frigate firing," called the watchman.

"Not the destroyer?"

"Nay, they're slowing," said Mr. Korbo.

"Hesitating?" Clelland said. "Aderyn's no coward."

"Neither is he a fool," said Korbo. "We are a big fish with big teeth."

"*Modesty* taking evasion. The shot will miss. Second salvo incoming."

"Get them back," said Clelland. "Line us up."

"Incoming."

"Keep faced and weather. I want a solution on the *Dragon*."

"Eighty seconds," called the weapons officer. "*Galga* intercepting."

Clelland watched through his scope as little bursts of light flashed in front of his fleet where the *Galga*'s phalanx slugs met the frigates' incoming railshot.

"Bring all defense online, I don't want the paint scratched."

The *Modesty*'s pod batteries joined the *Galga*'s and then those from the man-o-war. Tons of metal were diverted or vaporized before they hit. The remaining metal shards plinked against their thin metal armor like coins scattered on a floor.

"The destroyer's running," said Mr. Korbo. "Looks like the frigates are trying to buy it time."

"Recalculating firing solution," said the weapons master.

"Admiral," said Mr. Korbo, "if it is Aderyn, should we not let him go? The day is ours, he…he is Aderyn."

"Aye," confirmed the watch. "The frigates are turning too."

"I have a firing solution, sir. *Modesty* confirms the same."

Clelland looked out his scope and saw the enemy ships running for the fastest retreat. There was the *Dragon* and in it, a commander of legend – a hero of all humanity – now bested and done. He was an old man far from his native home looking for adventure in retirement on this last frontier. Decades separated their best years but Clelland had always wanted to meet Aderyn. He never thought he would. Yet here on the fringes of Coronam's heat, far from the niceties and hypocrisies of court and politics, religion and creed, in the true darkness, where warriors like them were asked to fight and die, they met.

It was a short battle to be sure. A skirmish at best, the first – an overture of what would doubtless be an ongoing struggle to dominate this world – but small victories early have far-reaching consequences. Six ships here, a few hundred Saved below: a world in the balance.

And Clelland had won.

Jareth's World would be Brandon's, and Clelland would be remembered as the man who'd won it for him. Redemption was at hand. In time, the failure of the armada would be forgotten. His name would not be associated with the *Pempkin* and his execution of guilty radical pirates by spacing, but for this battle, against this adversary, for this prize.

"What better way for a spacefarer to die than in space?" he said out loud.

The cabin went silent.

"There'd have been no mercy the other way," Clelland said. "They were here in ambush. Make no mistake. There'd have been no mercy."

"Bringing the ship to fire," called the weapons master.

"Close in, Mr. Korbo. We'll want the frigates too."

Clelland nodded. He would be remembered for many things. Including this. "Fire when ready," he said.

Momentum carrying it nearer, the ship turned to face its side to the enemy, opening a firing arc for the gun platforms protected behind the ship bell. Clelland watched the maneuver through his scope, keeping his sight on the fleeing ships. A sputter, a jolt, and a whir repeated four times, indicating the firing of the four full-ton railguns.

"The day is mine," said Clelland.

Across the battle bridge, behind the admiral's station, the aft lookout raised his voice in sudden alarm. "Sir, you should look at this!"

CHAPTER TWENTY-FOUR

Ten cent a day and twenty for a fight
Kill a stranger,
Serve the cause,
We all know we are right

Lash me if I stumble, hang me if I fear.
Take their money,
Spend it fast
On whores and weakened beer

March into the fire, step onto the gore,
They are the same
As us we know,
Here and then no more.

A Soldier's Song, Traditional

12:15, 30, Fifth-Month, 939 NE – near Bretton on Placid Bay, Tirgwenin

"The Hyraxian bastards are just over this hill," whispered Captain Felps. "Everyone ready."

Morgan held the crossbow as he'd been shown. It felt heavy. He was weak with hunger like the other colonists, but unlike them he was not afraid. Looking into the eyes of the new Enskarans upon Tirgwenin, the denizens of Nolan Brett's new colony, Bretton upon Placid Bay, he could see terror in their faces. His people had known terror too, worse terror, the terror of abandonment and betrayal. These men were supplied, reinforced – ready, but still facing the unknown, they feared.

Morgan had known nothing but fear for so long that not having it now made him nostalgic. He'd been granted suicidal exile at Rodawnoc, wanting to die on the grave of his daughter and granddaughter, a last set of bones to mark the failed dream. There was nothing for him on Enskari, nothing for him anywhere. He had only to die. Gillison would bring news of his death back to Vildeby whenever he ported there again, and if Sommerled were alive to curse him for his betrayal, he would have his chance then.

But he wandered. A day and a night, two on the grave. Then to the collapsed fort, not lighting a fire, letting hunger come, watching the sky as if God would reach down and strike him.

His body fought his soul and he could not maintain his fast. He ate the sparse provisions left behind for him and then wandered the woods looking for more. Something cruel drove him north toward Bretton. He wanted to see Placid Bay, the place where his colony should have been, the place it would have succeeded. It was a perverse last wish, but it gave him reason to move, hoping a vengeful native would kill him on the way.

But there was no one. He saw not a soul of Saved or savage for the entire trip, heard no sign of any animal larger than a squirrel. The fish even seemed to be gone. It was like the whole countryside had been evacuated.

When he staggered to the walls of Bretton, a triangular fort with three-meter ramparts, no one was there to greet him. The height and construction bespoke an impending danger, but the lack of sentries told another story. He rapped at the gate for someone to let him in, weak and frail, his clothes falling off him from thorns.

The settlement stood between the bay and the forest. Trees had been felled to create a perimeter but nothing had been done to the ground. It had not been prepared for seed. A ways up he saw fields made in the savage way – one wild place, one fallow, one under cultivation – but they all were unattended now. Months of neglect. Beyond them was what could have been a village but was now humps and heaps of green where the forest returned.

"Who are you?" came a voice.

"I am marooned." Morgan saw two men looking down at him from the wall.

"I think we got another one," one said. "Do him now?"

"Nay. He'll be another gun."

"Fine. Let him in."

A gate opened heavily and Morgan staggered inside. Outside the walls was no one, but inside was a cramped and crowded town. There were hundreds of people – soldiers mostly, or at least they were the most active. Civilians were there too, but they had not the animation of the soldiers. Nor the body fat. Hunger was already here, at least among some.

"What is all this?" said Morgan.

"I'm Governor Graves." A man dressed too well for any wild place offered him his hand. He looked like a rich merchant – silk hose and buckled shoes, neither of which would last a moment plowing a field. But of course, no one had plowed.

"I'm Morgan."

"Morgan? Alpin Morgan?"

"Aye."

"What…why?"

"I came to rescue my people," he said. "There are none left."

Graves shared a look with the two men who'd let him in. "So you stayed?"

"I have nowhere else to go."

A captain in sharp uniform, flanked by two soldiers in slovenly ones, marched forward.

"Captain Felps, this is Alpin Morgan, the governor of the lost colony, freshly arrived."

"Good you have those locks of red hair," said the captain. "Our lookouts would have shot you dead otherwise."

Morgan knew the captain was lying. No one had watched him come. "Why so many soldiers?" he asked.

"Defending the colony from Hyrax," said Graves.

Morgan heard the news with interest but nothing more.

"Feed him," said Felps. "Arm him and bring him along. We leave in the morning."

"Where are we going?"

"To battle."

They gave Morgan hot water and warm porridge, cool clothes compliments of Governor Graves. He slept in a real bed, with posts and sheets, and marveled that it was here. There were many luxuries in Bretton that bespoke of either confidence or foolishness, buckles and beds being but two.

He'd been given a servant to see to his needs, a commoner called Beedle. He was one of the few colonists with any industry or energy at all.

"Did you not arrive in time to plant?" asked Morgan.

"We have no plans to plant," Beedle told him.

"What? How? Are you supplied so well?"

The man hesitated, a beeswax candle casting shadows over his face. "Nay. We've been on quarter rations since we got here."

"Enough food for a year?"

He shook his head.

"How did you expect to survive?"

Beedle scratched a bare spot on his scalp. "We came with lots of weapons," he said. "I think they figured we'd just take it from the natives."

"And?"

"And damn it all, we haven't seen a one yet."

Now Morgan shook his head.

Beedle went on, "Neither a boar or a deer, or a musk-elk even. Nothing. Not another living thing we could eat save the Hyraxians tomorrow."

Morgan was woken before dawn, given a crossbow and five minutes of instruction before the entire fort marched for a place ten kilometers north. There were a hundred civilians and twice that many soldiers, recently arrived, sent by Aderyn himself. Morgan hadn't seen a single female in the camp. The menial work was done by Maarawan slaves who, by the blood on their shirt backs, were becoming difficult to control.

The armed party arrived at a narrow river ravine and were told to take up positions below the edge of the berm, to hide themselves and wait.

Beedle stayed with Morgan. "Three days ago, we heard the Hyraxian anchor line land," he said. "We'd been waiting for it for weeks. I was beginning to think they'd never come. That would have been bad."

"Why would that have been bad?"

"We figure they'll have supplies," said Beedle.

A cracking boom rumbled over the sky, the kind of sudden startling noise that drove birds to flight and animals to run, but there were only Enskarans there to wince.

"Another anchor?"

Beedle shook his head. "A broken one, I think."

"Mouths shut and eyes sharp!" Felps commanded.

Beedle swallowed, the sound loud enough to draw Felps's attention.

Morgan slumped against a rock and stared into the brilliant godless sky until the captain whispered that the Hyraxian bastards were just over the hill.

"Remember how to use that?" Beedle asked Morgan.

"I've never shot before."

"Should be nothing to it. Just point and squeeze the lever. Back the string and reload. They'll be thick and hard to miss."

Morgan was about to say that he'd never killed anyone before, but hesitated at the lie, his daughter's face etched in his eyelids.

"It's them or us," said Beedle. "Right?"

Morgan regarded the soldiers around them, the cliques of killers. Though better fed than the colonists, they were similarly undisciplined. They complained constantly and were slow to follow orders. Morgan realized they were mercenaries and not the queen's men, not regular soldiers. They wore cast-off Enskaran uniforms, some with tears where insignia should be, and some were not even Enskaran. It was a motley group, doubtlessly recruited out of the pirate havens and dead-world backwater hives.

"You know when you came up to the gate?" said Beedle. His breathing was heavy in fear.

"Aye," said Morgan.

Beedle looked around him to see if anyone were listening. "You know how Dowman said, 'We got another one? Should we do him now?'"

"I don't know the man's name, but aye, I remember that."

"Want to know what it means?"

"Sure," said Morgan. God, the sky was bright and beautiful, the ring like a promise cutting a line across it, connecting horizons.

"We've had other folk come to the fort. Folks from your group."

His eyes came back to earth and he stared into Beedle's. "And?"

"And we have orders not to help them except...."

"Except what?"

"Except to put them out of their misery."

"Why?" Morgan felt sick.

"We hear that if any of yours are found alive, they could challenge our rights. I wanted you to know before things got started, in case I couldn't tell you after."

"How many?"

"Five so far. All crazy mad, they were. Looked much worse than you. They didn't come together. One by one since we got here. Some screaming they were selected by God and demanding our obedience."

"You sent them off?"

"Starving, they were. Starving is bad."

"You killed them."

"All five. Then this bunch of soldiers got here. Maybe after all this is done you should find another direction to go instead of back to the fort."

"But Governor Graves?" He'd remembered the bed and the food he'd given him.

"He'll be the one ordering the execution," said Beedle.

Morgan laughed, laughed loud.

"Damn you, man! Shut up," said Felps. "The battle's afoot!"

Beedle put his hand over Morgan's mouth to quiet him as one of the mercenaries approached with a drawn dagger. Morgan quieted and the soldier returned to his post.

Felps had said there'd be a battle, but it was no battle. It was a massacre. The place had been prepared in advance for this dirty day. Concealed among the sides of the narrow gulch were gun emplacements armed with massive flame shooters and cannon. The troops along the top were for cleanup.

The uniformed Hyraxians marched in loose step into the ravine, entering the water when the trail along the side slid into it. When the head of the column approached the final emplacement, the order went up and the shots went out.

Morgan hid behind the ridge as the horror of heat erupted below. Two hundred men were disintegrated by grapeshot, cooked in the napalm, and steamed by the flash-boiled river.

When the cloud of fatty smoke had risen to stain the otherwise perfect sky, there was little work left to be done below. Air had been pulled from their lungs by the flames, the cannon making new holes for it to happen faster. The dead lay as they'd marched, in loose order, their guns still on their shoulders. A few mercenaries fired their muskets into the twitching bodies, a colonist or two let go a crossbow bolt, but that was all.

Captain Felps stood triumphantly. He raised a sword in victorious salute. "Have at them, men!" he yelled.

The mercenaries poured over the sides of the ridge into the ravine. They dove onto the bodies not with sword or dagger, but with digging fingers, ripping into pockets and robbing the dead while they lay dying.

The men tore open burning shirts for necklaces, cut fingers off for rings. Almost immediately came the complaints of poor spoils, curses and backward glances aimed at Felps.

"It's how they're paid, I guess," said Beedle.

Morgan watched the carnage and bloodlust, the looting and mayhem, and couldn't turn away.

Beedle stood and slapped dust from his pants. "I hope there's a supply train just over yonder," he said. "We should probably…."

"Probably what?" said Morgan in a cracking whisper.

"Captain, Captain Felps!" said Beedle, pointing. "You should look at this!"

CHAPTER TWENTY-FIVE

Think of what we can buy with the money we're wasting now on wars. What culture could we have if we stopped fighting among ourselves?
Address before the Assembly of Peers
By the Marquis Rossin of Kafford
Galisium, Claremond, 646 NE

13:00, 30, Fifth-Month, 939 NE – Aboard a boarding shuttle attached to the Lady's Rage *over Tirgwenin*

Dedikodu watched the *Dragon* explode in a fireball of burning-air-orange and purged-plasma-purple. The great Enskaran destroyer captained by the great Admiral Aderyn was gone. With him went hundreds of sailors, indentured and bound, some freemen, some officers. A cross section of struggling society evaporated in molten vacuum. He felt it as a personal loss and it shook him. He was a sailor and even without his training, his connection and bee, he'd mourn the loss of men to the dark. Now, he could almost hear them take their last breaths and he wanted to scream with them.

He took a deep breath and smelled the charcoal filter of his spacesuit. He calmed himself with a lullaby of honey, and touched the bee beneath his right ear with a thought, and it scurried and hummed it back to him. He glanced over his shoulder to the rows of men – nay – men and women – who he would deliver them to *Brandon's Blade* for the boarding action. He had a hundred, two and twenty souls to spend to take the man-o-war.

They'd finally been seen. He could tell by the maneuvers the fleet took. The Enskarans were a little behind and had yet to notice the pirate fleet sailing out of the sun. Then again, maybe they had but were enraged at the *Dragon*'s destruction. In any event, the frigate angled for shots against the Hyraxians, and in short order unleashed a timed barrage against them.

"Think there'll be anything left?" asked Poliop, his copilot on this run. He was a Silangian by birth but raised by pirates in space. He'd told Dedikodu that he'd had less than a month of real gravity on his bones his entire life. Dedikodu believed it.

"Because the ships aren't turning to defend?"

"Aye."

"We'll know soon enough."

Though Dedikodu was a junior member of the crew, he was given command of this boarding shuttle over Poliop because he had a bee. Poliop seemed okay with it. Dedikodu hoped he was.

"They'll run," said Poliop, "when they see us all."

"They got nowhere to go."

"Then they'll scuttle her for sure."

"Aye," said Dedikodu. "They will try."

Dedikodu steered the craft below the plane of conflict hoping to avoid flak from the Hyraxians and shot from the Enskarans. Behind him came the fleet led by Sadya of Jont, captain of the *Lady's Rage*, his captain. His savior. With her came a pirate fleet, so named for now, but not for long. She led eighteen warships, half-crewed but fighting-ready. Left behind, hidden in the well, were again that many plus twice that in support vessels of every stripe and origin. They'd been collected over the years in raids and battles, found drifting and salvaged, purchased from yards or traded for honey, then all hidden in the well, waiting until needed. Now they were needed.

Boarding craft were scary. They were short-range shuttles outfitted with anchor spinners and grapplers. Against an unarmed ship, a squadron of them was a terror in the sky. Against an armed one, it was the squadron that quaked in fear. They had no armor. They could be shot out of the sky by phalanx or point-blank plasma. Only pirates dared to use them in true battle, the greater powers not bothering with them, instead coming alongside and stringing tethers to carry their men over. Dedikodu had wondered why, with such a fleet as they had now, they didn't go that route. He'd finally asked at the dinner the night before as the fleet was speeding to battle.

"We want her," Sadya of Jont had told him. "The only chance we have of that is stealth."

"Begging your pardon, lady, but the empires don't man boarding craft for battle, for fear of mutiny. It makes external hull gun batteries seem like a retirement plan."

Sadya had laughed at that. "Aye, aye," she said. "True that. It's all volunteer. If we get no one, we'll just burn her down."

"Captain, you already know I've had to turn down a hundred souls already."

She nodded and poured him another mead. Mead was the drink of the fleet, a sweet concoction of fermented honey he had come to love.

"They won't expect you," she said. "You'll have one ship. You might even get there before they see us."

"They haven't seen us yet," said Warner.

Dedikodu didn't need to ask how he knew this. Warner was a groo, a Tirgwenin ambassador and liaison. He was also Dedikodu's teacher and had nurtured him back to sanity and strength after Sadya rescued him from Dajjal.

"They aren't looking this way," said Dedikodu.

"That is true," said Sadya. She too had a bee but not the insight of Warner, who by his own confession was 'good at that'.

Sadya said, "If our calculations are correct," and here Warner nodded then shrugged – 'there are no exact sciences' was one of his favorite phrases – "we'll arrive just as the battle begins out of the radiance of the sun. Our plan is to have them distracted and then overwhelm them by numbers. We aim to capture, but we cannot have a single one escape, from either side."

"They won't like being captured," said Dedikodu.

"We hope they like that better than being dead."

"There'll be a lot of dying tomorrow," said Warner.

"The future?" said Dedikodu.

"The odds."

"Not on our side," said Sadya.

"Aye."

For a fleet raised and designed for the interests of Tirgwenin, there were surprisingly few Tirgwenians aboard. That would be changing, Dedikodu was told, as more of their people had access to ships and training. Already whole academies were teaching sailors on Jareth's World. It was simulation and theoretical only at the moment, but not for long.

Warner had explained it in one of their many sessions. "The problem is that we don't have our own ships. We don't have the manufacturing plants, or even an elevator. Our access to space has been unneeded for most of our history. We've had rockets and probes, but no ships. We've had to make do with what the other planets have given us."

"Giving is a pretty loose term," said Dedikodu.

"Lately, we have been borrowing a few, but not at first. We've had spacefaring friends for a long time."

"Before Aderyn's historical visit?"

"Aye. He was hardly the first."

Dedikodu struggled to learn to open his mind and heart. He was fundamentally ashamed of his part in the deaths of the Enskaran colonists but also, and worse, his role in the massacre of Pemioc years before.

Warner had entered his mind with a connection that felt like a warm towel around his head. He saw the horror, felt the pain, suffered the guilt with him, then he researched the library for other accounts.

"You wept for the dead," said Warner. "And were enlightened for it. Be forgiven, Dedikodu. We sense who you are now."

"Not so easy."

"Then do as Sadya would have you. Serve and make amends."

"I owe her my life."

"There are many debts you can repay here."

"Pemioc? The planters?"

"And your ancestors, Dedikodu. How big is your family?"

There was much to the philosophy he did not understand and his access to the library was limited at best, but the bees stayed with him, hummed, and loved him as he worked to turn his sin into energy for action. He felt the greater cause and that was enough. He could also communicate through the bees with Warner and Sadya and a young boy named Houyum on Tirgwenin, who was ten at a school in a rural agricultural district and who'd found him after his parents were killed in a flood. They'd made it part of his training in viapum to pen-pal with him. Warner had arranged it.

The Hyraxian transport *Galga* was rent in two when the Enskaran fire reached it. There was a puff of escaping atmosphere and then half the bell tumbled away to ricochet off the atmosphere while the other half, trailing the five-kilometer mast and lifeless sails, hung in the sky as if transfixed.

Dedikodu plotted his course beneath *Brandon's Blade* along its massive mast, between bell and sail.

The man-o-war pivoted to fire on the incoming fleet. The other Hyraxian ship, the frigate *Modesty*, angled to do the same.

The Enskarans went to full burn, running for the upper well.

"Nay," said Poliop. "Nay, don't do it."

"You talking to them or Sadya?"

"I don't know."

The *Lady's Rage* steered toward the Enskarans with eight other ships.

Dedikodu activated his thrusters and aimed the forward hatch at the spinning service deck behind the great bell.

Poliop said, "They're too far. They have the planet's gravity. They might get away."

"We'll get there."

"Nay, I mean those two frigates."

"Buckle up!" Dedikodu yelled to his landing team. "Lock and load."

Helmets clicked tight; suits sealed with a hiss. Weapons primed; flamers lit. Battle-ready.

"Poliop, foul the rigging."

The copilot turned in his chair and fired grappling threads into the cabling and flak shot into the silks. "They'll know we're here now."

"Now they have something else to look at."

The *Lady's Rage* had fired one of her three torpedoes. War would never be the same after this. Never again would a ship need to align itself to fight. The Tirgwenians had devised a weapon that could steer and home and turn like an unmanned ship. He saw it fly out like a streak of light, burning with plasma rockets – another technology that would change everything. It went for the far fleeing frigate. It pulsed corrective jets, maneuvered, and realigned. It aimed itself at the weak aft hull, paused for a heartbeat, and then, point-blank, fired its quarter-ton railshot into the bell. That ended the ship in a moment. The recoil engines sputtered and stopped and the empty hull of the spent torpedo hovered like a circling vulture over the ship it had killed.

"Impact!"

Dedikodu's shuttle rammed the service hatch and deployed hydraulic hooks to hold it.

"Go!"

Above him on the raiding deck a hatch swung in and engineers went to work on the door to the man-o-war. Dedikodu felt some atmosphere escape but not so much. It was a good raiding seal; it would suck the atmosphere from the enemy ship without decompression bursts, provided they moved fast. They'd putty it up later. If there was a later. Either they took the Hyraxian flagship this hour, or they'd die in it.

The ship emptied of troops while Dedikodu and Poliop unstrapped and armed themselves, before climbing up to join them.

We've boarded the ship, Sadya, Dedikodu reported. *Wish us luck.*

He didn't get a verbal response, only a wave of thanks and concern that warmed him.

Their main force drove for the battle bridge, sweeping aside defenders with trained and murderous precision, while Dedikodu and Poliop led a group of ten to the upper decks. From the library, with Warner's help, he knew the design of this massive man-o-war. He had studied its plans, saw its building from the perspective of six different workers, and knew the official sequence for scuttling as outlined in the ship's procedure manual. It had a self-destruct mechanism built in, a thing unheard of in spacefaring. If the crew knew such a thing even existed, there would be mutiny; one lever would flood plasma fuel from the thruster carriage to the bell, slagging everyone and everything not harder than diamond.

There'd be no stopping it. Taking the engineering decks wouldn't help. Turning the crew on the captain would be no good. However, there was a certain access panel on the eighth gravity deck where the cabling could be accessed near the pulley.

They'd chosen the most experienced fighters to find the cable, cutthroat pirates, now with a cause, but still with all their venom. They melted through the resistance with flamer and grenades, crossbow and cutlass, opening hatches behind them to sap the atmosphere and keep the smarter crew members locked in rooms with air. Without atmosphere they had to communicate with gestures, but to be honest, Dedikodu knew the battle force would do better without his input.

The panel was just where it should be. Dedikodu marched up to it as if he'd installed it, with a memory of having done just that. It was borrowed and false, but still in his head, thanks to the library.

Dedikodu pried it open with a crowbar and shone a focused glowstick inside.

Poliop passed him a pair of long-handled steel bolt shearers, rusted but sharp.

A crossbow bolt flew past him and lodged in the wall by his head. Spacesuited Hyraxian defenders ran up the corridor. Dedikodu left them to the others and aimed the cutters at the cable, recognizing it was the third one – as unassuming as a guide wire – that had to go.

Poliop shone the glowstick for him while behind them in the silence of vacuum, sailors fought and died.

It was an awkward stretch, just at the very edge of what he could reach. He grabbed it once and had it slip off and nearly lost the cutters down the shaft. Another stab and it slipped after a pinch. Then at the third, half inside the shaft, blocking most the light, Dedikodu caught it and cut it. The wire went slack.

He pulled himself back into the hall and regarded the dead behind him. They'd lost two people. The Hyraxians a dozen. The fighting here was over.

Dedikodu signaled to seal the corridor for atmosphere. When it was done, he opened his ventilator and tasted ship's air.

Poliop did the same. "Well, that was—"

Inside the shaft they saw the third cable draw taut and pull away, its severed end disappearing down the shaft like a fleeing snake.

"Does that mean they tried to do it?" said Poliop.

"Aye, I suspect we've taken the ship."

"What now?"

"I think we get a sword," said Dedikodu.

"What?"

"It's an old custom."

"Oh."

"Let's get this done," he said.

They met up with the main force at the barricaded battle bridge.

Dedikodu knocked on the hatch politely with the pommel end of his sword and waited. His people readied cutting torches and grenades, took positions in the zero-gravity corridor, flamer and pistol, crossbow and sword at the ready. He saw blood splattered over their suits, seeping rents sealed with the tape.

"Steady on," he said and knocked again.

The hatch swung open and Dedikodu thought how far he'd come, how guilt and love – and family – had brought him here.

"I am Admiral Clelland," said the man before him. "I assume we're to be held for ransom."

The pirates quickly swept in and secured the room. The faces of the surrendering officers showed fear but also relief.

Dedikodu's eyes fell on the self-destruction lever at the captain's station. The entire console had been pulled up.

"Technical difficulty?" asked Dedikodu.

Clelland just stared.

Sadya, we have the ship. We have Admiral Clelland.

Excellent.

We lost a lot.

I am sorry.

How goes the rest?

No casualties here. The last Enskaran frigate surrendered. We had to destroy the other Hyraxian ship. It had turned to fire on you.

"You are a true believer, sir," said Dedikodu to Clelland. "I am sorry for the disgrace you will suffer for this, but it seems to be your lot."

"Damn you."

Dedikodu, said Sadya. *Take command of the man-o-war. She's yours. Get her flying again. We'll need it when they come looking for her.*

CHAPTER TWENTY-SIX

Just because we choose not to make war shouldn't mean that we won't know how.
Chancellor Arden, *Designing a New Civilization*
Landing Plain, Tirgwenin
3 Arrival (2398 Old Earth Calendar, 252 NE)

13:35, 30, Fifth-Month, 939 NE – near Bretton on Placid Bay, Tirgwenin

They'd watched. They'd witnessed. They'd let it happen.

Here then was the proof the council wanted to make the hard decision. Here was the example that would harden a heart. The 'civilized' had chosen conflict over co-operation, murder over mercy.

There could be some argument as to whether the sides knew they were abandoned, arguments about power of an evil few over the good many, but it was irrelevant if the results were the same.

Bouer had come a long way to witness this himself, to record it, absorb it, and learn it all for Millie. They needed her to be sure. She was the link that could bring the change.

Knowing a thing was not the same as being it. Theoretical knowledge – even immersion into the library and the viapum – was no substitute for personal experience. The Tirgwenians who had learned to operate spaceships could come aboard with encyclopedic knowledge of the systems and controls, but until they'd spent time in space, felt the false gravities, sensed the steel, breathed the recycled air, they were poor shadows of the real spacefarers. The same was true of soldiers and diplomats. The bees had given them knowledge, technology, and wisdom, but at a distance. A threshold of sympathy opened a galaxy of thought, history, and knowledge, but applying these wisdoms required doing, and there was not always time for that. Thus, an off-worlder who'd been accepted by the bees offered a special connection to their society and vocation that no studied Tirgwenin, however disciplined, could match. Thus, Sadya of Jont commanded their fleet and young Millicent Dagney would lead the assimilation, provided she could be made to see.

Bouer had watched the massacre from a hill with General Gan. They sat upon their hests, large fast animals with prehensile feet, short snouts, and thick button-sized scales. Intelligent creatures, strong and loyal. They shied at the sound of the cannon and snorted when the smoke reached them.

Gan shook his head, watching the attack. "Not very sporting," he said.

"Is this not how war is made?" asked Bouer.

"It is."

"It's horrible."

"Aye, it is."

"Could they have captured them?"

"I'd think so," said General Gan.

"Then why didn't they?"

"Probably provisions. Killing the enemy means not having to feed prisoners, and of course letting them go was never an option, they'd be clear and constant danger." He raised an eyebrow for emphasis, having used the phrase so bandied about in the council briefing before this mission. "But I really can't answer the question, Groo Bouer. I'm not wholly sure what they're fighting over. Is it provisions? Or honor? Class? The pride of their planets?"

"Us," said Bouer. "They're fighting for control of our planet."

"Nay. Not with that little force."

"I've seen it myself."

"Don't they think we'll have a say in that?"

"We don't look dangerous to them."

"Well, let us fix that today."

"Eradicate the infestation."

"I don't like that phrase," said Gan. "It dehumanizes them."

"Dehumanizes them?" Bouer laughed. "Having just seen that, you believe so?"

The general shifted in his saddle, tightening his belts. "I'm trying to remember this is war and terrible things happen in war, but you made your point."

Gan urged his hest down the slope with a word and a touch of his heel. It sprang into a smooth canter. The general didn't even look where he went, confident his hest understood and would perform. He instead drew up a war bow and collected a handful of arrows.

Bouer was still learning to ride the animal, but it understood what to do. He held on to the saddle horn and tried not to pull the reins too far either way. Hests could turn their heads all the way around, and more than once on the ride down, his had turned to look at him as if wondering what he wanted when he'd mistreated the reins. The last time, the big star-pupiled eyes were so sad and frustrated by his confused inputs that it had made Bouer laugh out loud, which had made his hest laugh out loud, which then spread to other steeds nearby and stopped the whole column for a while.

Returning to the army, they passed scouts up in trees, their hests having carried them to the highest branches, thirty meters up or more. Bouer sensed them more than saw them, feeling through their bees.

Bouer was surprised at how well his people had made an army. This was but a fraction of what was ready, of what was being made, but after only a decade of effort, from nothing to this, it made him think they had a chance. It was a guarded optimism. Having seen what the enemy was capable of, he wondered if his peaceful people could really match that. He was not alone in thinking this. Thus, they needed help from off-worlders, like frightened Millie.

The general raised his bow and the army readied to march. Five hundred bowmen on five hundred fleet hests, all armored in composite ceramic plate, gilded and bright. It was a sight to behold. War bows of amberwood, venom-tipped arrows, and curved swords made by the men themselves. An army of individuals, an army of artists, men and women golden-skinned and plum-purple-tattooed, feathered helms and war paint.

Bauer rode near the general and kept his senses keen, acting as recorder, a witness to the day.

They rode out of the forest just as the first Enskarans returned up the ravine with their looted treasure, gore-soaked hardtack in smoldering pouches, charred muskets, shot and boots. Their hands red in blood. Bouer saw it all.

A colonist saw them and raised an alarm.

Gan's army maneuvered into place.

The Enskarans, amid roar and panic, regrouped and made ready to fight. The army watched them.

"Are you being too sporting, General?" asked Bouer.

"I want them all to see they're outnumbered," he said.

"What if they get the cannon up the ridge?"

"The battle will happen or it won't. Be at peace. You might want to return to the rear."

Bouer stayed where he was, and realized he was distracting the general. He directed himself to his own job. He organized and concentrated his impressions, pouring them into the library as complete sentences. Formed thoughts, crystalized in words, made for much easier discovery. He only wished he could write it down, or sing it – logic and emotion – to do even better. Such tracings of moment and time lingered best in the library.

They waited for what seemed like forever, but Bouer knew the elasticity of human time. It was one of the wonders of viapum and whole schools of scientists had studied it since before the landing. History, time, and man's place in it was at the heart of his civilization.

General Gan glanced back at the tree line and Bouer inferred that the scouts had told him something. He signaled to advance, and the whole army moved forward fifty meters and then stopped.

From this distance he could see the sun reflecting off the muskets, see the full faces of the fearful men.

In clear common language, though with an accent, Gan addressed the enemy line. "Off-worlders, lay down your weapons and come forward. No more need die."

Murmurs and orders echoed back. Bouer could sense the lack of discipline on the other side and the clear presence of the same on his.

"I am General Gan. I represent the ruling council of this world. I speak for the Primeen Desarri when I command you to surrender."

Bouer caught wisps of oaths and foreign sounds. Curses and orders. The smell of death. Then a cannon topped the ridge at the end of ropes pulled by bloodied men.

A man rose up from behind a boulder. "I am Captain Felps. I give you yellow bastards one minute to go back to your mud huts 'fore I let loose hell upon you."

The cannon was hastily aimed and charged and a minute came and went.

A passing cloud threw a migrating shadow across the meadow between forest and ravine, wafting with it the clean briny smell of nearby ocean.

When the cloud was passed a new angle of light brought doom upon them.

Gold.

Their armor was gilded in places – gold, silver, copper green, and bronze amber. Gemstones and agates, whatever was beautiful and loved, the soldiers had used to make their armor their own, but it was the gold that drew the attack.

Bouer saw the yellow reflection of a golden breastplate flash onto the captain's face and pan across his soldier's eyes.

Greed.

It was who they were.

And the Enskaran captain commanded, "Fire!"

The first volley filled the air with din of Gauss rifle fire and cannon grapeshot.

To Bouer's right, a dozen soldiers went down to the cannon, their steeds killed beneath them, their armor pierced by its power. Several soldiers were pushed over, alive in scarred armor – their lives saved, their technology the advantage.

On the left and center, crossbow bolts bounced off breastplate and hardened hest scales. Few casualties there, wounds in arms and legs. A lucky shot in a hest's eye. Six or seven wounded, the rest incensed.

Having given them the first volley, Gan spurred his hest to charge and unleashed arrow after arrow into the invaders' lines. A step behind him came the rest and more from the opposite ridge.

Bouer's own hest whinnied to join the charge and he allowed it, putting himself in the bloody business he would witness.

The steeds were faster than the horses the Enskarans knew and he could see the surprise on the faces. Worse, in the slowest hands, their bows could fire four times to their muskets' once; in the best, six or seven. And their aim was better.

Arrows flew into them like swarming bees. Men found themselves pierced by five before the first had settled.

The cannon never got another shot, its minders a forest of poisoned shafts.

Their captain took two of the general's own, one arrow in the heart for kindness, the other between the eyes for rage.

Still, the invaders fought on, raising sword to swipe the circling hests only to be cut down from a distance. It was as if they couldn't believe they were losing the fight, had already lost it. Pride kept them fighting. Their officers were dead.

One man raised his musket, fired, and then threw up his arms to surrender in one motion. He had six arrows in him before Bouer was aware the man had shot him.

His steed smelled the blood and balked. It was afraid and stumbled in the gallop. Then it turned and ran retreat. Whether it did this for his or its own sake, he wasn't sure, but was grateful nonetheless. Hests were smart creatures. What ancient deal had the hest herders made with them to enable such wonder?

He felt his own warm blood pouring from his side down his leg and into this boot. It did not hurt. It was curious was all. A new sensation, a new experience he'd never had. An adventure awaited. Perhaps the greatest one.

He knew he was in shock and went with it. He did not struggle.

He summoned the peace of meditation and witnessed. He was glad to be away. The slaughter would continue for a while, half an hour, ten minutes, five. A lifetime. There'd be no mercy. The infestation would be eradicated. For the good of the family.

His hest ran straight to a hospital cart and stopped.

Bouer unbuckled his saddle belt as his hest kneeled forward.

He slid off into a heap but was caught by the hest's neck and two medics in clean white robes.

CHAPTER TWENTY-SEVEN

Say first, for Heav'n hides nothing from thy view
Nor the deep Tract of Hell, say first what cause
Mov'd our Grand Parents in that happy State,
Favour'd of Heav'n so highly, to fall off

John Milton, *Paradise Lost*
1667 – Old Earth

2, Sixth-Month, 939 NE – Government House, Vildeby, Enskari

Sir Nolan Brett watched the proceedings from his secret balcony closet high above the floor of Government House. The players were present: Archbishop Connor for the prosecution, Sir Edward Kesey, former First Ear, for the defense. Kesey was Brett's man and they'd worked the moves out together. Kesey understood his role, their goal, and was happy to serve again. He was noble in the best sense of the word.

It would be a hard day. A necessary thing in the wide scope of ruling, in the survival of his queen's reign, and his planet's stability. But up close, it was a cruel tragedy.

Contrary to his reputation, Brett was not in control of all political machinery. He seldom was. Mostly, he could react well, sooner and better. That was really what he did – react as well and as soon as possible. A master of countermoves, he took the tides of fate as he found them, seeing dominos fall and trying to steer them in a direction that would do the least harm.

Second Ear, spymaster, the listener at doors. The cloak of fear was useful, information was power, and power allowed him to steer events as he might, for his queen, his planet, his people.

His was often an act of triage, determining which movement, idea, or person could be saved and which had to be sacrificed for the greater good. Who stood in the way? Who could be moved? Who could be used? Progress was done in baby steps, medicine administered in tiny spoonfuls, slowly, steadily, carefully, or else it would all come up again, a vomitous reaction that would undo everything.

The War of Ascension, that bloody struggle to put a woman on the throne, was never far from Brett's mind. The nobles threw people at each other in phalanxes and waves until the streets scabbed hard with brittle blood, bodies unburied for months.

It was hard but necessary, but by God the price had been high. Society upturned. The loss of great houses, the loss of the church. But it had to be. Brett knew that the civilized worlds had reached a point where the old ways were untenable. The old houses were weak and decayed, and the ascending middle class was rising fast. Society was destined to have a new form, and the sooner it got started, the easier it would be. You could sit back and watch the pressure build and then hope there'd be pieces left over to rebuild after it blew, or you could find ways to seep it off in little bursts or long hisses. The War of Ascension, for all the upheaval. was still a bleeding off of pressure. Zabel's reign a compromise between tradition and progress, though few nobles understood that. Had Zabel not taken the throne, Brett had little doubt that the masses would have risen up and completely overturned the systems of society. They'd have demanded rights beyond their birth, potential beyond their castes, resources beyond their inheritances.

But Zabel had been enough. For now. She had given souls to half the population who had been denied them before. It was a small thing, symbolic, but spoke to the idea that progress is possible, that folk could rise above their station, be it female or slave, to become something more.

Brett had seen this current and nursed it and controlled it as best he could. The nobility hated the lower classes, but if they had a sense of what *they* thought of the aristocracy, they'd have firebombed the entire planet and moved to Dajjal.

Hyrax was terrifying, but the real danger to civilization was not off-world but among them. A thousand years of stunted progress had finally reached the breaking point and peasants were waking up. Brett foresaw a wave of retaliation against the upper classes. He foresaw heads in baskets, great houses burning, slaves running wild. This was what he fought against. Nay, not against so much, but endeavored to control, to seep off the pressure and avoid the explosion that would threaten all civilization. He understood and even sympathized with the downtrodden, feeling they had every right to vengeance, but he knew that they were not ready to rule. They frankly did not know how. It was a question of education and experience, which had been denied them, purposefully. Unable to go forward, should they rise, they would only be able to mimic the institutions they'd pulled down.

That was not progress. That was a vicious cycle.

Brett struggled daily, keeping the lower classes controlled for this reason. But they were not the only forces here. The other side, the nobles, also had their hatreds, fears, and jealousies, and they had as much power as the masses to overturn society. The difference was that they knew it, and the masses had yet to figure it out.

Today's task was appeasement to them. Three steps forward, two steps back. Reacting to events in the calm before they burst in the storm. He'd seen it coming as a force, but like most things, the details were a surprise.

"I've got it all set up, Sir Nolan." It was his assistant, Jim Vandusen, slipping into the narrow room to whisper in his ear.

"Thanks, Jim."

Vandusen surveyed the nobles below. "He'll never take it," he said. "He'd sooner die."

"You may be right," said Brett. "Now get down there. It won't be long now."

"Aye."

It was all reactionary, a way to keep peace and serve his queen. It was a simple plan and should work but Brett had found Sommerled difficult to predict.

Archbishop Connor, dressed in his purger-esque uniform, paced the floor below. He pointed to Sir Ethan in the dock with a theatrical gesture. "What say you to this, Sommerled?"

The noble court was full of well-dressed, well-placed witnesses to the man's destruction. Commoners, of course, were not allowed in. This would be settled among the peers – not that Brett thought there was a man among them who could hold a candle to Sommerled.

Sir Ethan kept his chin up and said, "As Admiral of Her Majesty's Fleet, leader of the attack force, I dealt with Captain Gravny as his offense merited."

"You killed a noble."

"I disciplined an officer."

"You murdered a duke."

"I removed a threat to the fleet."

"Murderer!" The call had come from the audience. Brett wondered if Connor hadn't planted someone to do that at certain times or if it was genuinely spontaneous. Both were possible. Connor was devious but the nobility were truly enraged.

"He was your better."

"He was a captain. I am an admiral," said Sommerled. "Perhaps you should study up on the ranks of the navy, Minister." Brett had to smile at the gall, but the gallery exploded in hisses and catcalls. It was over before it began.

"To destroy so great a man, to hobble so great a house, is an atrocity to civilization!" roared Connor to the crowd's affirmation. "It is the kind of thing one would expect from an enemy of the state."

"I am First Ear of the queen," said Sir Ethan, glancing back at the empty throne.

Brett's heart slipped as he imagined Sommerled's pain at facing this without her.

She had wanted to come, but Brett outlined specifically what Connor had to present. She knew already the court's feelings, and against her heart and hopes, she saw the inevitable outcome as clearly as did Brett.

"You must not be there," he told her. "The nobles would not forgive you for helping his defense, and the commoner will hate you for not succeeding."

"Must I give up?"

"I can only advise," said Brett. "Tell me how to proceed and I will try."

He'd known her her entire life. He'd seen her sad and scared, strong and wise. He'd seen her grow into the greatest statesman the planet had ever seen, but until that moment, he'd never seen her heartbroken. As she swallowed her tears and folded her hands, Brett's own eyes began to water, for he knew what she would do. She would give up her own happiness, what little she'd been allowed, for the health and wellbeing of an ungrateful people.

"Try to keep him alive," she said and then softly, resignedly, "if you can."

"It's what we get for letting a commoner have so much power!" The cry was from the same voice as before, and Brett was leaning toward scripted Connor shill over spontaneous outburst.

One rides as far, and as fast, as one can, always remembering the ride cannot last.

"Here is the proof, my noble brethren," said Connor, raising the document above his head.

On cue, pages ran up the aisles handing out copies of the damning document to nobles who stood as judge and jury over Sir Ethan Sommerled.

Brett knew the document. He'd read it years before. He owned one of the original copies. It was in his safe. How Connor got ahold of one of the others was a mystery, but one that Brett could guess. He wondered if Sommerled would make the same connection.

Connor held the document high and roared, "Behold, the Bucklers' Articles of Belief, that heretical sect of separatists and reformers. We have sought to eradicate them and had nearly done so, while all the time we've had one slithering beside our queen!"

Careful, Connor, thought Brett. Do not aim too high.

"See here the very words – the very promise to convert, subvert, and crush our society. *The eventual ascension of our philosophy.* It is a declaration of war against our state and system. Against our very queen."

The gallery exploded. One would think all that breeding would show, but except for the nice clothes, Brett would be hard-pressed to tell the rabble below from a bawdy house revelry. Or a lynch mob.

"Sir Ethan," said Kesey, "what say you to this? Tell these good people that this is not your signature, that you are not a member and never have been a member of this outlawed sect."

Sommerled looked around the courtroom, at the gallery, Connor, the empty throne.

Sir Edward raised his hands for silence.

"I do not deny it," said Sommerled.

Brett had expected nothing less.

"But cannot a man change? Cannot a man learn? Cannot a man love and be made better?"

"Don't go there, Ethan," murmured Brett to himself.

Kesey stepped in. "Your love of queen and country is as great as any subject to their sovereign," he said, glaring at Sommerled. "Your service to the realm has been incalculable."

"In the service of a hidden agenda," said Connor, and again the gallery exploded.

Brett tried to see Sommerled the way they saw him, as an inferior, as a threat, but he could not. Ethan Sommerled was a great man and every inch the reality of the image he himself had cultivated: a self-made man, honest, and caring, who rose to heights for his virtue and not his birth. That of course was the threat he posed, the snub he'd always been and would always be to the entitled ranks who damned the very man who'd allowed them to remain free enough to do it.

"I denounce the document, and the bastard who betrayed me!" Sommerled said.

So he'd made the connection. A rare but momentary wave of guilt swept over the Second Ear as he recognized his part in Sommerled's fate – the colony, the Bucklers. Alpin Morgan.

"I am a different man," said Sommerled. "I am one of you—"

Booo! Hiss!

It could go no other way.

The threat was passed. They had no need for him anymore. Brett had seen it coming, knew there was no stopping it. It had been set in motion the moment the rabble had chanted his name. He'd warned him, but there was nothing he could do – nothing any of them could do – to stop it. The best they could hope for was to minimize the damage.

"Shall we discuss again the devastating attack on Hyrax? How many ships did we lose for nothing? How many true Enskaran patriots perished, weakening our domestic defense?"

Connor was on a roll, but to be fair, a ham sandwich could try this case and win it.

"Call the question!"

"Call the punishment!"

"I would remind my noble brethren," said Kesey, preparing the way, "that an Ear is not subject to the judgment of this assembly."

Connor smiled, ready for the obvious move. It made Brett lose respect for the man that he thought he'd outsmarted them. "I call for a vote to remove Sir Ethan Sommerled from the office of Ear of the queen. By her consent."

Sommerled reeled as if he'd been physically smacked.

"Second!"

"Vote!"

"All those in favor?"

Unanimous and uproarious.

"Those opposed?"

Kesey's hand went up.

Sommerled slouched back and fixed his eyes on Zabel's empty chair.

"Confirmed. You are no longer protected by office."

Of course, had Zabel been there, she could have overruled the vote and the entire proceedings, but it would have just delayed and made things worse later.

"The man before you, my kind and noble friends," said Connor, "is accused of sedition, willful murder, treason, treachery, and blasphemy. What say you?"

"Guilty!"

"Guilty!"

"Guilty!"

Three times for the seal.

"Any opposed?"

Again Kesey raised his hand and Brett knew he did so not as part of the plan but because like him, he knew Sommerled to be good and repentant – none could say he was not guilty. Never sign anything.

"Call the punishment."

"Death!"

"Hang him!"

"Draw and quarter the bastard!"

"Space him!"

And here was where Brett was set to steer the moment. He feared he might fail, however. The furor was greater than he expected and he wondered if Kesey was up to it.

"My noble brethren," said Kesey. "Let us not be insensible to the services this man has delivered."

That got nothing but more hisses from the crowd. Their bloodlust was high.

Connor thumbed through legal books, considering his options. Stripping him of his office was one thing, but doing more would be tricky without involving the queen. Connor no longer had the free rein given him by the Defense of the Realm Directive and that surely vexed him. Brett sometimes thought it had been written with Sommerled specifically in mind.

"Let us also not be insensible to the queen's affections," said Kesey.

Better. They quieted down.

"Let us also be not unaware of the rank of the man in the dock. He is noble. He is a veteran. He is a hero of the masses." Kesey put a deliberate weight upon the word *masses* to stress the import – the real threat of uprising.

Brett was pleased.

Connor dug into his papers.

"This body cannot execute a noble," said Kesey. "We may remove him from office, but we cannot strip him of his title, and so cannot execute him. Only the queen may do that."

"Bring us the queen!"

"Where is Zabel?"

Brett gritted his teeth.

Kesey went over to talk with Connor. Sommerled stared blank-faced into some middle distance where his life had been. There was the picture of a broken man. Brett wondered if he was doing him a kindness trying to keep his promise to the queen.

After a moment, Connor and Kesey separated.

"This is an ugly business," said Connor. "Let it not besmirch the holy royal throne."

"Summon the Second Ear," said Kesey, waving to Jim Vandusen in the back. His assistant left the room. Brett straightened his robes and went to meet him.

"Lead on, Jim," said Brett, meeting him in the hall. "It's not very often a tiered justice system pays off."

Brett burst into the room and all eyes fell on him.

"What is the noble Ear doing in the dock?" he demanded.

Some of the gallery retreated into their collars as he passed by them.

"You went ahead with this prosecution, Archbishop?"

"I did."

"And what have the nobles decided?"

"Guilty, my lord."

Brett panned over them again and noted who if any met his eyes. He looked then at Kesey beside the dock, his shining hair more gray than red, his eyes sad and sorrowful.

Brett said, "What say you, Sir Ethan?"

"You are out of order," said Connor.

Brett gave him a look and the archbishop sat down and went back to his papers.

Ethan Sommerled looked about him as if dazed, searching for the source of the voice. He saw then Brett in his black cloak and shook his head. "I would only serve the queen," he said.

"Sir Edward?" said Brett.

"My lord Second Ear," Kesey began, "Sir Ethan has been found guilty of capital crimes. The archbishop, on behalf of the people, will allow extraplanetary exile in lieu of execution."

"To save the queen from the decision," added Connor, as if he'd thought of it.

"What planet would have him?"

"Do you not have a ship leaving this very week for Jareth's World? A ship of settlers?"

"Impressed convicts," said Brett.

"So much the better!" from the gallery.

"He may choose death," said the archbishop.

Brett had wondered if he would find that loophole.

"He may choose it voluntarily, nobly," said Connor. "It would save the queen from sentencing, and himself from the hell of exile. He may choose death himself."

"I have failed her," murmured Sommerled. "What is there to live for?"

Brett stepped forward to the dock.

"Sir Ethan, take the exile."

He shook his head.

"You would not be hanged," said Connor. "You have the right to death by steel. It'll be quick. And justice will be served."

And the queen would mourn.

And the people would rise.

And much would be lost. Perhaps all.

"Dammit, Ethan." Brett grabbed him by his collar and locked his eyes. Holding his gaze, he bent in close and whispered, "Take the exile. She wants you to. She begs you to. For all of us, take the exile."

There is a narrow line between stupidity and nobility, stubbornness and righteousness. Sir Ethan Sommerled, captain, admiral, First Ear and savior of the planet, teetered upon that line. Brett knew it was fifty-fifty. Broken-hearted and already dead, he was as unpredictable as a cornered beast.

"There are some things worth dying for, my friend," said Brett. "And there are greater things worth living for."

Sommerled stared back into his eyes. Brett had meant it when he'd called him friend. Could the queen's lover see it now? See what he offered, horrible and tragic as it was, was in fact an act of love, for him and—

"For her," Sommerled said looking at Brett, through him and beyond.

"Aye," agreed Brett.

Connor raised his voice so all might hear the demand. "So he'll accept the exile?"

"He will," said Brett.

CHAPTER TWENTY-EIGHT

If we do not think there is more than this – more potential, greater achievement, a higher place in the universe for mankind – then all of this is for nothing. We might as well burn the houses down around us, kill, rape, and steal from each other. Eat the seed corn. Build walls and hoard.

If, however, we believe in a greater future, then we must seek it together. We must have faith it is there, have the power to look for it in places unseen, and the strength of courage to go there when it is found. And then, once achieved, we must do it again. It is a choice. It is The Choice.

Lerer Melk

26, Third-Month, 514 – Apis, Temple

4, Sixth-Month, 939 NE – Pemioc, Tirgwenin

It flew. The carriage that brought them from Beleksha to Pemioc flew. Primeen Desarri explained.

"We have about twenty of these."

"How?"

"It's just technology."

"From the viapum?"

"Nay. It's from Old Earth."

"Recovered knowledge?"

"We never lost it."

"But the Unsettling? Didn't you suffer the bursts that burned the memories?"

"Elegant way of putting it," said the primeen. "We had our computers hardened, but also, and mostly, we had scholars. We took a step back, true, but we had books. Seventeen thousand tons of paper arrived here from Old Earth."

Millie watched the ground speed beneath her, seeing it as a metaphor of her own life. After she'd passed the initiation, Bouer had given her over to Desarri. The primeen was something like the ruler of the planet, or perhaps a council leader – something like that. There was nobody higher, but she wasn't all-powerful. In any event, she'd chosen Millie to apprentice beside her, and Millie took her instruction from her much the same as she had with Bouer, the difference being Bouer had dedicated himself wholly to her education, every moment of every day, while Desarri had other duties and often left Millie alone to traverse the library, work the viapum, or just walk the paths of Beleksha, mingle with the people alone. During her formal lessons, however, Desarri had echoed Bouer's emphasis on history but lately had steered away from Old Earth – 'the foundational lessons and trials of our ancestors' – to concentrate on the differences between Tirgwenin and the civilized worlds. The lessons were fast, and often details – sometimes large ones, like flying machines – slipped through the cracks.

"Why do we only have twenty of these?" Millie asked.

She saw the primeen smile and realized she'd said 'we'.

"There is seldom such a hurry we need one," she said. "We chose a simple life."

"The choice."

"Aye."

"And now?"

"It's getting complicated."

"Do you know the story of the Garden of Eden?"

A wide smile spread over Desarri's face, friendly but amused. She blinked her double eyelids and nodded. "Of course."

"Is that happening here?"

"Nay. We guard the garden."

"We?"

"Aye, Millie. But there is a cost."

"Bouer?"

She'd lost connection with him two days before. He'd said he'd been wounded. He would not explain or give details. The last thing he'd said to her was, "Ask the primeen if you can journey the light with me and come if you can."

She did not know what it meant, but sensed an urgency that frightened her.

Desarri came to her and told her to prepare for travel before she could even ask.

The closest inhabited place to the developed regions of Tirgwenin, to the battlefield, was Pemioc.

"We evacuated the Rowdanae," Desarri explained. "Also the game, what we could."

"Game?"

Here Millie saw the primeen grimace. It was an area she was not comfortable in talking about. "We warned them. Most left."

"So they were set up to starve?" said Mille, recalling the horrible year of hunger she and the other colonists had endured.

"Had people been left there, they'd have been...taken advantage of."

"And the animals?"

"Would not have saved them. The Brettons would have only eradicated their herds," Desarri said. "Millie, there is a covenant we hold with this world, with all worlds. We defend it together."

The dark martial tone in the primeen's voice spoke of a question unasked but which was coming. Millie felt it. Bouer had hinted at it, the primeen held it, waiting, but was growing impatient to ask.

She watched out the window as the hills flew by. She'd seen a world from up high before, in an elevator over Vildeby and hanging on the anchor thread from the *Hopewell*. She'd ridden a train and knew their speeds, the blur of passing scenery. This was something like that, but quiet and serene. There was no sound of motor or strain of cables. She could hear the wind beneath the outstretched wings, their shining surfaces converting light to an occasional hiss of propulsion. Dillon would love this.

"I miss my brother," Millie said.

"You'll see him soon. He does well in Pemioc. As do all your people there. None have been outright refused by the bees."

"Everything is bees."

"If one does not have sympathy, one is beneath."

"There is a hierarchy here too, you know? An *–ocracy* like the civilized worlds you're afraid of."

Desarri didn't react.

"I'll tell you," said Millie, thinking of starving people, "it's one capricious system over another."

"Is it?"

"Here though instead of heredity, you elevate the injured," she said.

The primeen smiled again. "There is something to that."

"Could these bees not be manipulating us?"

"They might be."

"And we're supposed to align with an alien bug over humans?"

"You know it's not that, Millie," said Desarri. "You've seen the question that's coming." It was not a question.

Millie looked out the window again. The land was changing; they were getting close. "The library is full of information," she said.

"I'll ask you when you're ready."

"What if I—"

"The question has not been asked yet, kind Millie," said the primeen. "Today is not for that. Today has a different purpose."

"I still think the bees might have an agenda."

"I'm sure they do."

"But they're steering—"

"They only witness," said Desarri. "We interpret."

Witness. A continuing theme. If there was a single word to describe the viapum, it was witness.

Millie knew she was being childish attacking the bees, suspecting aliens and motives. She knew the request was coming. She knew what it was about, knew why she'd be asked, and she was afraid.

"Fear was an enemy, an ancient foe, one that we can grow out of," so Bouer had said.

"Fear can be memory of a real thing," she'd countered. "A hunger pain in the stomach, the loss of a father, a mother, a friend. Fear can come from experience. It is warning and training."

"That is true. But it is knowledge, and knowing how to use knowledge is the strength of the species. Knowledge should never in itself destroy us. Fear, in its basest form, can do that."

Below was Pemioc. It was much as she remembered it. She traced the walls around the city, saw the familiar roads leading in and out, saw her hut and the fountains. Today, however, it was crowded and bustling with activity. Tents and stables surrounded the city littering the fields with people – soldiers she saw. Hests stood on their hind legs to watch them as they circled and then lightly fell to the ground in an open space beyond the river.

The primeen exited the craft first, followed by her entourage, two men and a woman who had halos of bees. Mille had two of her own, but still, seeing so many around anyone always made her skin crawl a little. It was a sign of high office, enlightenment, but to her Enskari-born eyes, there was still a creepy-crawly factor about it.

"Millie!" Dillon ran up to her and threw his arms around her.

She hugged her brother for a long time, closing her eyes and being in the moment. He'd grown half a meter since she'd last seen him. He had their father's face, their mother's eyes, a new haircut, and – was that a tattoo under his ear?

"Dillon?"

"Don't be mad," he said.

"Lahgassi," said Desarri, bowing to the city elder.

"Bost!" said Millie, seeing the Rowdanae boy in the back. He waved.

"And there's someone else," Dillon said. "Come on."

He pulled her by the hand and led her toward the visitors' hut. Desarri nodded that she might go, but Millie sensed she should not be long.

There inside the hut were many of the Enskarans she had left. They all beamed when they saw her. All were dressed as Tirgwenians now, their old clothes finally fallen to rags. Several had new tattoos like Dillon. Some of the women too. They were settling in nicely.

There on a bunk was the surprise that Dillon had brought her for. Looking like a man who was not sure if he were dreaming or awake lay Governor Morgan.

"Millie? Millicent Dagney?" he said, shaking his head in disbelief. "So many miracles. So many. This must be heaven." He threw his arms up and then fell to weeping in his hands.

"He's been doing that a lot," said Dillon. "Hard to talk to, really."

"Have we told him what happened?"

"Nay," said Richard Tomkins. "Not yet."

"For the best," said Millie. "Are you behaving yourselves?"

"You mean am I?" said Tomkins.

"Aye."

"I am, Groo Dagney," he said.

"Groo Dagney?" she said. "What have you heard?"

"Lahgassi said you were being trained to be a groo," said Dillon. "She spent like a week explaining what groos are. I'm still not sure I understand."

Morgan wailed some joyous but painful cry.

Lahgassi was at the door.

"Millie," she said in common language, her accent thick. "Come now. Little time."

Leaving the house, she saw an Enskaran in armor.

"Emme Mirrioth?" she said.

"Hi, Millie."

"You are a soldier?"

"I help where I can."

"Did I not hear you were engaged?"

"I am. To good man. A potter. Guqinu."

"I know him. He is very talented. He could trade his work in the developed lands."

Emme looked confused.

"I like him," said Millie.

"You approve the match?"

"I do."

Emme smiled and stood a little taller, her lance straight at her side, soldier-fashion and bright.

Lahgassi signaled her to the chief's hut and Millie followed. Inside she found Desarri and several soldiers. One was a general. Bouer lay on a cot, pale and dying.

Before introductions could be made Bouer signaled Millie to come.

The others bowed and retreated out of the hut.

He met her eyes and blinked. A sad smile spread over his cheeks, like ice melting at light.

"Millie," he said. "I'm dying."

"Nay. Nay. There is technology here."

"And it has done all it can to save me until this moment. It is time to go."

Tears she'd held back, hoping and wanting, came flooding now down her cheeks as her worst fear unfolded in front of her. She knew this man and loved him. They'd shared the most intimate thoughts. Millie had never known physical love, but she could not imagine it compared to the connections the viapum allowed them. She was at home in his thoughts as in her own.

"Nay. Nay. My groo. My groo. Don't leave me."

"That's why you're here, dear Millie."

"To say goodbye?"

"To know what goodbye means," he said.

"If there's one thing my wretched life has taught me," she said, "it's what goodbye means."

Bouer smiled a wan grin and shook his head.

"I came to the war to show you the means," he said. "It can look the same – violence and pressure. But the end makes all the difference."

"Death."

"Nay. A vision," he said.

Millie wiped tears away. "I don't want to see you die, Bouer. This is cruel."

"Will you come with me?"

"What?"

"As far as you can. Will you come with me?"

"Okay, okay. I am here."

"More than that, Millie," he said.

"More?"

"Come."

He reached into her mind, a gentle caress, a viapum connection, intimate and warm. He drew her deep inside him, past logic and memory, to the core of his light, the deepest parts of him.

Dizzy and disoriented, Millie tumbled onto his lap.

She felt a hand stroke her hair and then the way was dark.

She had a sense of a tunnel curving and rising, falling to rise again. Darkness around her, but she was not alone. Beside her walked Bouer.

He was excited but also afraid.

Millie was confused and overwhelmed with the intimacy, but strengthened and grateful to be there with her groo.

The tunnel turned and there, as legend foretold, was a light.

Come.

Bouer moved inexorably toward it. Millie hesitated.

As far as you can.

A step, a movement, a flight and flurry and she was in a room of light.

Blindingly bright and yet visible all around her. She could see all directions, forward and behind, above and below.

The room was filled with people. She did not know them, but they welcomed Bouer and she felt him dissolve into them like sugar in water.

It was all light. And then it was moving, settling. Growing.

She stumbled to follow.

As far as she could.

Airborne and weightless, bathed in radiance. Like a warm breeze. All metaphor and reflection but truer than stone and steel, blood and bone.

Light extending. Joining. Progressing. A universe of yearning, a galaxy of souls reaching for a farther light beyond brilliance, beyond realm or reality.

Behind her, centuries of growth; ahead of her, coming fast, a promise and a return.

Bouer flowed into the encompassing light, joining a chorus of angel song, a piece of a tapestry, the library entire, reaching from spark to glory. The family complete, infinite and whole. A part of it all. Intricate and necessary.

The movement on.

The dance continuing.

The destination, the goal.

She could move no farther.

As if held back by a chain, she came up short and watched as Bouer joined the infinite and rejoiced.

In the last moment before she snapped back to her body, Millie felt her place, temporal and infinite, in a universe beyond her senses, and knew there were greater things.

She rolled off Bouer's lifeless body into a pool of her own tears on the clean warm floor.

Raising her arms as Morgan had done, joyful and sad, unsure if she were dead or alive, in heaven or earth, she proclaimed the one meaningful word she knew: "Life!"

Desarri rushed in with the others. The marks on Lahgassi's severed arm caught the light, the stump a web-fractalled scar and purple ink – lined facets of a polished gem. A wound made beautiful, celebrated and possessed.

"I'll do it," said Millie in a choked and quavering voice. "I'll bridge the worlds."

ACKNOWLEDGMENTS

To the readers first, I am grateful. Your energy, imagination and partnership bring to life the lonely scribblings of any author. From my poor scratches to your magnificent minds are manifested the images of a tale, are rooted the seeds of a theme, are grown the crops of perceptions, where come the fruits of hope. To you intrepid people, who value candles in the age of the LED, who open yourselves to live other lives: I give first thanks and welcome for the trust you have shown in spending your time around Coronam.

Mechanically, my angels have been Don D'Auria, Imogen Howson and Josie Karani, who plastered the cracks and righted the ship in kind and magnificent edits.

Thanks to Jonathan Maberry, the classiest writer I know, one of the good guys through and through. His aid in my career has been pivotal. Thanks to Lee Murray also, another kind and giving author who reminds us that giving back is the way forward. Thanks to Dan Yocom for his undying support, Michael R. Collings, a grand master ghost in the machine, distant friend, colleague and teacher; to Blake Casselman for his friendship – another soldier in the war, and Sean Ricks for being there when a brush saved the pen.

Friends and family, caffeine and Buddha, schools, computers and a cat named Roy, all deserve thanks, as do countless others whom I love but haven't the space to mention here.

All, blessed be.

ABOUT THE AUTHOR

Johnny Worthen is an award-winning, multiple-genre, tie-dye-wearing author, voyager, and damn fine human being! Trained in literary criticism and cultural studies, he writes upmarket fiction, long and short, mentors others where he can and teaches at the University of Utah. Find out more on his website: johnnyworthen.com.

FLAME TREE PRESS
FICTION WITHOUT FRONTIERS
Award-Winning Authors & Original Voices

Flame Tree Press is the trade fiction imprint of Flame Tree Publishing, focusing on excellent writing in horror and the supernatural, crime and mystery, science fiction and fantasy. Our aim is to explore beyond the boundaries of the everyday, with tales from both award-winning authors and original voices.

•

Book 1 in the *Coronam* series by Johnny Worthen:
Of Kings, Queens and Colonies

You may also enjoy:
The Sentient by Nadia Afifi
The Emergent by Nadia Afifi
The Transcendent by Nadia Afifi
Junction by Daniel M. Bensen
Interchange by Daniel M. Bensen
Second Lives by P.D. Cacek
Second Chances by P.D. Cacek
Sebastian by P.D. Cacek
The Widening Gyre by Michael R. Johnston
The Blood-Dimmed Tide by Michael R. Johnston
What Rough Beast by Michael R. Johnston
Those Who Came Before by J.H. Moncrieff
The Sky Woman by J.D. Moyer
The Guardian by J.D. Moyer
The Last Crucible by J.D. Moyer
The Goblets Immortal by Beth Overmyer
Holes in the Veil by Beth Overmyer
Death's Key by Beth Overmyer
A Killing Fire by Faye Snowden
A Killing Rain by Faye Snowden
Fearless by Allen Stroud
Resilient by Allen Stroud
Screams from the Void by Anne Tibbets

•

Join our mailing list for free short stories, new release details, news about our authors and special promotions:

flametreepress.com